Prais

Sizzling and sensual, *Nobody's* .... story with a battle-scarred Dom who will simply steal your heart away.

~ **Cherise Sinclair, Author**

~ ~ ~

I didn't want it to end. With each new book Ms. Masters is weaving great stories for her Masters and making me fall in love with each couple. Karla and Adam are definitely my favorite, especially after this ending, but it definitely makes me want to read about Damián and Savi.

~ **Amanda, Guilty Pleasures Book Reviews**

~ ~ ~

This story made me laugh and brought tears to my eyes as Karla and Adam struggle through issues that most of us have. I love that these characters are portrayed as average humans and not perfect fantasy beings. Adam has his flaws as I think any Master does. What's important is how he overcomes and adjusts to those as he learns what they are as well as how they affect Karla.

~ **Star, BDSM Book Reviews**

~ ~ ~

You show a higher level of respect for military details than any romance author I have read. As a retired Navy spouse, I really admire and respect you for the extra care you take with your writing.

~ **Kathy Holtsclaw, Reader**

~ ~ ~

I loved this book. I laughed, I cried, I wanted to slap Adam upside the head a few…several times. It's such a sweet story. But it's also hot and steamy. (I think Ms. Masters made Santa's naughty list.) The characters are awesome and well rounded. Some of the fantasies were very very um…yeah…there's a reason that they are fantasies.

~ **Riane Holt, Kinky Book Reviews**

Rescue Me Saga
Reading Order

Not stand-alone novels
(These love stories can't be contained within one book! In a saga, of course, characters recur to continue working on real-life problems in later books.)

These four titles are available in e-book and print formats, and will be coming in 2014 in audiobook form (digital only), narrated by the award-winning team of Phil Gigante and Natalie Ross.

Masters at Arms & Nobody's Angel (Combined Volume)
Nobody's Hero
Nobody's Perfect
Somebody's Angel

Next expected title in series:

Nobody's Dream

Also available in Spanish editions:

Sargentos Marines (*Masters at Arms* in English)
El Ángel de Nadie (*Nobody's Angel* in English)
El Héroe de Nadie (*Nobody's Hero* in English)

Additional titles are being translated into Spanish as quickly as feasible, but it takes time to do a good translation!

Nobody's Hero

(Second in the Rescue Me Saga)

Kallypso Masters

Nobody's Hero
Second in the Rescue Me Saga
by
Kallypso Masters

Copyright © 2011-2014 Kallypso Masters LLC
Print ISBN: 978-1481152716
Revised April 4, 2014

ALL RIGHTS RESERVED
Edited by Jeri Smith, www.booksmithediting.com
Line edited by Jacy Mackin, Rosie Moewe, Meredith Bowery, Fiona Campbell, and Annie Van Camp
Cover art by Linda Lynn
Formatted by BB eBooks
Cover image licensed through Hot Damn Stock and graphically altered by Linda Lynn

This book is a work of fiction and any resemblance to persons—living or dead—or places, events, or locales is purely accidental. The characters are reproductions of the author's imagination and used fictitiously. This book contains content that is not suitable for readers 17 and under.

All rights reserved. Please be aware that this e-book is licensed for *your* personal enjoyment only. It may not be reproduced, uploaded to share on Web sites, e-mailed, or used in whole or in part by any means existing without written permission from the author, Kallypso Masters, at kallypsomasters@gmail.com, or within the sharing guidelines at a legitimate library or bookseller.

WARNING: The unauthorized reproduction, sharing, or distribution of this copyrighted work is illegal. Criminal copyright infringement, including infringement without monetary gain, is investigated by the FBI and is punishable by up to five years in federal prison and a fine of $250,000.

Special Permission obtained to quote the poem "Touch Me" (c) 2012 by Kellie Kamryn
Published in *Secrets and Desires of the Heart*, by Kellie Kamryn
Reprinted with the permission of Romance Divine LLC

To discover more about the books in this series, see the *Rescue Me* Saga at the end of this book. For more about Kallypso Masters, please go to the About the Author section.

Dedication

To the people who volunteer to help me with edits, beta reading, subject expertise, and research, you help me achieve the attention to detail that makes these characters so strong in everyone's minds. I appreciate your time and dedication (even when I am always weeks behind and rushing you!)

To my husband—thanks for nurturing me during my writing marathons.

To Master Adam—Thank you, Sir, for not pulling a "Master Marc stunt" three weeks before publication.

Acknowledgements

As always, there are so many people to thank, and my apologies to any I leave out.

First, I'd like to thank Jeri Smith, of Booksmith Editing. My writing continues to improve and I grow as a writer with your explanations, suggestions, and corrections. Most of all, your unflappable belief in my abilities and potential.

To my first-version line editors, Jacy Mackin and Rosie Moewe, thanks for pulling those all-nighters with me and for the attention to detail you bring to the table. Rosie, you're the queen of time lines and Jacy of grammar and punctuation. I'm learning from you two, too! Meredith Bowery and Susan Wasek, you also saved me from great embarrassment for some errors and inconsistencies as we edited the book for the print version. Fiona Campbell, while you were called a beta reader for my first three books, you did provide some awesome editing insights and I'm glad to have you on my editorial team!

Linda Lynn, the cover artist for all of my books, for your patience (because I know this isn't something you ever imagined yourself illustrating!) and for your knowledge about the visual world I don't see quite as well.

Thanks to "Toymaker" and his beloved submissive "Eirocawakening" from FetLife for the many, many hours of reading my e-mails and scenes and offering suggestions and ideas to make the book more realistic. (All errors are mine, of course.) You've helped this BDSM neophyte learn, always with patience and enthusiasm. Toymaker, I do believe you will keep me torturing poor Karla and some of my other submissives for years to come with your innovative and diabolical ideas.

To Kathy Holtsclaw, for going through the original "advanced reading copy" of *Nobody's Hero* so meticulously and sharing your great insights. Welcome aboard the good ship USS *Masters at Arms!*

To my incredible crew of beta readers: Ashlee Davidson, Kathy Holtsclaw, Kris Harris, Kellie Hunter, Kelly Mueller, and Kathy Treadway. I'm always amazed at how each of you finds something monumentally wrong—but it's never the same thing. You also help me add additional layers to make the story even more complex in its character and plot development.

To the Kentucky Indie Writers, especially Sondra Allen Carr and Donna MacDonald, for all of your advice and support as we try to revolutionize the publishing industry one indie book at a time.

Thanks to my fans and readers, affectionately known as the Masters Brats, for falling in love (as I have) with Masters Adam, Marc, and Damián, and for encouraging them (with your bratty behavior) to make regular visits on Facebook to keep you in line. (Master Adam's fond of deprivation when you get too bratty, though, so behave or he won't come to visit.) Oh, and let's not forget Baby Dom Luke who is receiving great training at the hands of the Masters at Arms club owners.

I discovered while writing this book that my Facebook friends and fans restore my energy levels, which may be why I spend more time there than most writers do on deadline. You build up my adrenaline and help me find answers to a character's or my most puzzling questions.

Many of my Facebook friends also have added in big and small ways to the plot and character development in this ongoing saga. To mention a few: Jennifer P. for providing the perfect setting for the final scene; Patricia Wheeler, Top Griz, and Susan Wasek for help with information about the Marines; Lindsay Klug for the self-defense moves; Rosie Moewe and Joanne MacGregor for research videos on self-defense and rope bondage, respectively; Sherri Hayes for your brainstorming help, because you always seem to know what Master Adam would do or think; Kelly Timm for help with facts about my fictionalized settings of Eden Gardens in Solana Beach (apologies to anyone you know there, but my fictional version is a little rougher than the real place!); Fiona Campbell, Maria Nespolo, Stacey Price, and everyone who helped me fill "the box" of special memories in this story; and for all who gave me suggestions for public and private BDSM collars (Susan F., Crystal H., Evita's Reads, Gail M., Joanne M., Tamara M., Suzanne O., D.F. Starr, and Beth W.). All are appreciated, even if not named here.

Thanks to Fiona Campbell also for her medical expertise and for keeping 50-year-old Master Adam (with his fondness for rough sex) from going at Karla like a teenager, well at least not until he was fully healed from his wounds.

Thank you to my supportive, innovative, and kinky "Playroom" friends, for lifting me up, making me laugh, giving me delightful and informative inspiration into the BDSM lifestyle, and for providing me with an awesome social-networking fix! You're the best!

Special thanks to everyone who came to my aid whenever I put out the call for help, including when I needed encouragement and support both for writing and for the situation with my sister and her battle with cancer. To those who took the time to post a review (size does NOT matter—I love them all!) or rated my book at e-book sales sites, you cannot know how this helps getting a book to move up the bestseller lists.

And thanks to those who sent me e-mails or private message saying how much you love the characters in my world, which just fed the flames and kept me going!

Author's Note

If this is the first of my books you've ever picked up, you need to know that I do not write stand-alone novels, not with this saga, at least. We'll both be very frustrated if you don't go back and read the combined volume *Masters at Arms & Nobody's Angel*—*Masters at Arms*, an introduction to the saga with nine important years in the development of this couple's romance, and *Nobody's Angel*, which included the dramatic scenes with this couple leading up to the opening in this book).

The lives of the three men in the first books of the saga are very intertwined and these characters will have recurring roles throughout the stories to come. And let's not forget Luke who was introduced in *Nobody's Angel*. His story will continue in the books to come.

I strive to write emotional stories filled with both dramatic and humorous scenes for characters who are or eventually may become involved in the kinky world of safe, sane, and consensual BDSM (bondage, discipline, domination, submission, sadism, masochism, Master, slave, and possibly even other dynamics I'm not aware of yet). But this is NOT a BDSM-genre series. I write romance stories first and foremost. As one reader wrote to me recently, "I loved that the story was about the *story* and the characters first, and they happened to be into the lifestyle."

In this book, probably one with more BDSM than any of the others in the saga, you'll find scenes with Shibari rope bondage, breast bondage and torture, anal play, orgasm torture (multiple forced orgasms), subdrop, and other aspects of this lifestyle that are more advanced than those in *Nobody's Angel*.

I also strive to write stories about realistic people and scenes, not fantasy Doms or the more "dark" or hardcore BDSM erotica or erotic romance with dubious consent or non-consensual scenes. (But I do write very explicit, sensual, hot sex scenes that also advance the story and romance in some way. So, if you think you can just skip over the sex scenes, this saga might be a frustrating read for you to follow.)

Those who want to try any of the play scenes from this book at home, please find mentors in the lifestyle (real life, online, at fetish conventions, or in the enormous online BDSM community at fetlife.com) and do your homework.

Master Adam has been in the lifestyle for thirty years. He would be very upset if anyone attempted to do a Shibari rope bondage scene, much less a rope suspension like the one he does here, without first receiving training from a master or expert in the art of Shibari. My subject expert, "Toymaker" from the FetLife community, says these are not skills you can learn from watching videos. They require hands-on training, as you'll see Master Adam doing with other Doms throughout the saga. Improper use of the methods can be dangerous if done incorrectly, resulting in a sub's having nerve damage, broken bones, and even being killed.

And if you or a loved one suffers from Post-Traumatic Stress Disorder (PTSD), please reach out to people who have been there and can provide support and advice. For military-related PTSD, contact the Hope for the Warriors (http://www.hopeforthewarriors.org/) and other non-government organizations, as well as the Veterans Administration (http://www.ptsd.va.gov/).

For non-combat PTSD issues like Savannah's, you can start with one of these sites:

Crisis Services:
http://crisisservices.org/content/index.php/information-resources/

Rape Abuse and Incest National Network:
http://rainn.org/

To Write Love on Her Arms:
http://www.twloha.com/

And now I turn *Nobody's Hero* over to you and hope you will enjoy this continuation of Adam and Karla's story.

Cast of Characters for
Nobody's Hero

Staff Sergeant Anderson—The man saved by Gino D'Alessio during a mortar attack in Afghanistan

Marisol "Mari" Baker—Savi Baker's daughter

Savi Baker (was **Savannah Gentry**)—she met Damián Orlando as Savannah Gentry in *Masters at Arms* but changed her name to Savi Baker when she escaped her father's house

Gino D'Alessio—Marc's older brother; killed in action in Afghanistan; involved with Melissa Russo

Marc "Doc" D'Alessio—Navy corpsman ("Doc"); co-owner of the Masters at Arms Club and owner of a Denver outfitter store. Dating **Angelina Giardano**.

Luke Denton—Marc's search and rescue (SAR) partner, an artisan who makes furniture, including pieces for the kink community, and does cabinetry

José Espinosa—Damián's young nephew

Julio Espinosa—Rosa's abusive ex-husband and Damián's brother-in-law

Rosa Espinosa—Damián's older sister

Teresa Espinosa—Damián's teenage niece

Megan Gallagher—daughter of Mrs. Gallagher

Mrs. Gallagher—mother to Patrick and Megan

Patrick Gallagher—son of Mrs. Gallagher

Ryan Gallagher—second husband of Mrs. Gallagher

Thomas Garcia—one of Adam's recon Marines killed in Afghanistan

Angelina Giardano—Marc's girlfriend and submissive; nicknamed Angie by Karla and Angel by Luke

Gramps—Marc's grandfather, a US Marine who served during World War II in northern Italy

V. Grant (Mistress Grant)—a Lance Corporal communications specialist on special assignment with Adam's recon unit in Fallujah and later in Black Ops. Now a Domme at the Masters at Arms Club and remains shrouded in mystery.

Virgil Griffin—a Marine who served in Vietnam at the rank of Staff Sergeant; first husband of Mrs. Gallagher

Pamela Jeffrey—Marc's most recent girlfriend before Angelina

Cassie Lôpez—Karla's Peruvian friend from college who now lives in Colorado, an artist

Allen Martin—Angelina's former boyfriend who abused her in the club leading to Marc's rescuing her (in *Nobody's Angel*); also known as Sir Asshole, a poser Dom

Father Martine—The parish priest at Savannah's church in Eden Gardens, the same church Damián attended in his youth

Sergeant Thomas Miller—Recon Marine killed on the rooftop in Fallujah during the firefight in *Masters at Arms*

Adam Montague (pronounced MON-tag)—retired after 25 years in the Marine Corps as a master sergeant; patriarch of the Masters at Arms Club "family"; surrogate father to Damián

Johnny Montague—Adam's great-great-grandfather; a Marine who served during the Civil War. His mother was Lakota and his father a French trapper

Joni Montague—Adam's first wife who died from cancer

Kate Montague—Adam's great-great-grandmother; much younger than her husband Johnny. She emigrated from Ireland to the Black Hills of South Dakota

Damián ("Damo") Orlando—served with Adam and Marc in Iraq; rides a Harley; Patriot Guard Rider; in love with Savannah Gentry

Carl Paxton—Karla's father, an executive with an airline at O'Hare

Ian Paxton—Karla's brother who has joined the Army National Guard when she was sixteen; killed in a motorcycle accident in *Masters at Arms*

Jenny Paxton—Karla's mother, a nurse

Karla Paxton—a 25-year-old Goth singer who carries a torch for Adam Montague; works as a singer in the Masters at Arms Club; nicknamed Kitty by Cassie and Kitten by Adam

Vivian Paxton—Karla's grandmother

Captain Reed—a Navy chaplain

Master Gunnery Sergeant Kevin Richardson—a recon Marine who served with Adam in the First Gulf War and remained friends over the years

Melissa Russo—a woman Marc almost married before he joined the Navy; she cheated on him with his brother, **Gino D'Alessio**, becoming Gino's fiancée

Marge Winther—Joni's mother

Playlist for the Rescue Me Saga

Here are some of the songs that inspired Kally as she wrote the books to date in the series. Because each book isn't only about one couple's journey, she has grouped the music by couple, except for the first one.

Spanning Multiple Rescue Me Saga Characters

Darryl Worley – *Just Got Home From a War*
Angie Johnson – *Sing for You*
Evanescence – *Bring Me To Life*
Dan Hill – *Sometimes When We Touch*

Adam and Joni
(backstory in *Masters at Arms* & *Nobody's Angel* and *Nobody's Hero*):

Sarah McLachlan – *Wintersong*
Rascal Flatts – *Here Comes Goodbye*
Aerosmith – *I Don't Wanna Miss A Thing*

Marc and Angelina
(*Masters at Arms* & *Nobody's Angel* and *Somebody's Angel*):

Andrea Bocelli – *Por Amor* (and others on *Romanza* CD)
Sarah Jane Morris – *Arms Of An Angel*
Fleetwood Mac – *Landslide*
Mary Chapin Carpenter – *The King of Love*
Air Supply – *The One That You Love*
Air Supply – *Goodbye*
Lacuna Coil – *Spellbound*
Air Supply – *Making Love Out of Nothing at All*
Styx – *Man In The Wilderness*
Keith Urban – *Tonight I Wanna Cry*
Michael Bublé – *Home*
Leighton Meester – *Words I Couldn't Say*
Halestorm – *Private Parts*
And a "medley" of heavy-metal music cited in the acknowledgements of *Somebody's Angel*

Adam and Karla
(*Masters at Arms* & *Nobody's Angel*, *Nobody's Hero*, and *Somebody's Angel*):

Tarja Turunen – *I Walk Alone*
Madonna – *Justify My Love*

Sinead O'Connor – *Song to the Siren*
Paul Brandt – *My Heart Has a History*
Rascal Flatts – *What Hurts The Most*
Marc Anthony – *I Sang to You*
Simon & Garfunkel – *I Am A Rock*
Alison Krauss & Union Station – *I'm Gone*
The Rolling Stones – *Wild Horses*
Pat Benatar – *Love Is A Battlefield*
The Rolling Stones – *Under My Thumb*
Lifehouse – *Hanging By A Moment*
Leighton Meester – *Words I Couldn't Say*
Air Supply – *Lonely Is The Night*
Beyoncé – *Poison*
Randy Vanwarmer – *Just When I Needed You Most*
The Red Jumpsuit Apparatus – *Your Guardian Angel*
Oum Kalthoum – *Enta Omri* (Egyptian belly dance music)
Harem – *La Pasion Turca* (Turkish belly dance music)
Barry Manilow – *Ready To Take A Chance Again*
Paul Dinletir – *Transcendance*

Damián and Savannah
(*Masters at Arms* & *Nobody's Angel*, *Nobody's Perfect*, and *Somebody's Angel*):

Sarah McLachlan – *Fumbling Towards Ecstasy* (entire CD of same title)
Johnny Cash – *The Beast In Me*
John Mayer – *The Heart Of Life*
Marc Anthony – *When I Dream At Night*
Ingrid Michaelson – *Masochist*
Three Days Grace – *Never Too Late*
Three Days Grace – *Pain*
Drowning Pool – *Let The Bodies Hit the Floor!*
Goo Goo Dolls – *Iris*
John Mayer – *Heartbreak Warfare*
Three Days Grace – *Animal I Have Become*
The Avett Brothers – *If It's the Beaches*
Leonard Cohen – *I'm Your Man*
A Perfect Circle – *Pet*
Pink – *Fuckin' Perfect*
Edwin McCain – *I'll Be*

Chapter One

"What the fuck are you doing in my bed?"

Karla Paxton smiled. Adam Montague had always been so careful not to drop the f-bomb around her before—although she'd certainly heard him say it enough times to everyone else, when he didn't think she could hear. Were his walls coming down enough for him to see her as an adult for the first time since they'd met?

"I needed to be close to you. Do you remember what happened?"

As if just coming to his senses, he glanced up at the IV pole and took in his surroundings. "Where am I?"

"At the medical center in Denver. You were attacked by a cougar."

Realization dawned and he cupped her cheek, searching her face. "Are you okay? It didn't hurt you? You've got circles under your eyes. God, you've lost so much weight."

Adam, Adam, Adam. Always thinking about everyone else.

She didn't want to think how awful she must look. If she'd known he would wake up today, she'd have at least put on a little makeup and brushed her hair. She needed to reassure him before he became any more agitated. "I'm fine, Adam. You got the cougar to chase after you and..." Her throat constricted as she pictured Adam lying on the ground with the large cat ripping at his neck and back. She closed her eyes and laid her forehead on his chest, but the image was seared into her memory. "I was so scared, Adam," she whispered.

He stroked the back of her head and she wished they could stay like this forever. Intimate. Sharing. Close. But the walls wouldn't stay down forever. She pressed her face against him, comforted by his heart beating against her cheek and the rising and falling of his chest.

His hand brushed a tendril of hair away from her face. "Thank God you weren't hurt, Karla."

"You saved my life. Again." She stroked his neck, her head nestled in the crook of his shoulder, feeling as if she'd come home at last. Her hand traced a path down one of his pecs, which she'd ached to touch for so many years. She let her fingertip circle the hard nip.

Adam's hand caught and stilled hers, his body tensing.

He pushed her away.

"You need to get out of this bed, Karla. Now."

* * *

What the fuck was he doing touching Karla like that? When her body had stretched out against him, before the cobwebs had cleared, he'd thought perhaps he'd done something unforgivable—like taken advantage of an innocent girl. But wouldn't he remember doing something like that?

His head pounded. Okay, one head pounded—the other throbbed, just as it had been doing whenever he was around Karla since the July day in his office when she'd come back into his life after almost nine years. Only now she was all grown up. If she didn't get out of this bed soon, he was going to do something they'd both regret. His resistance had been lowered, but damn it, she felt so good lying against him.

"Adam."

"Yes?"

"I have to tell you something."

Oh, fuck. The last time she'd said that, she was sixteen and had declared her love to his forty-one year old self. Not ready for another such declaration, Adam tried to move her off his chest, but she wouldn't budge and he didn't have the strength to lift her. He hated being physically compromised. "Look, Karla..."

She giggled. His dick grew stiff. What was it about a woman's giggle that turned him on?

"Don't worry. It's nothing like what I said on my parents' front porch."

He relaxed and she grinned.

"What is it, hon?" *Don't call her "hon."* She may get the wrong idea—again. Why didn't she do as he'd told her and get out of this tiny fucking bed? *Don't mention fucking and bed while you're holding Karla in your arms.*

Her hand stroked his chest almost absently, although she certainly had his undivided attention. Her touch was tentative, gentle. He hadn't let a woman get this close since Joni. Even with Grant, his friend-with-benefits partner at the

Masters at Arms Club he co-owned, sex had been rough, hard, and sometimes even brutal. A physical release for them both, nothing more. Neither had ever wanted anything more.

But Karla was more fragile both physically and emotionally. She'd just lost her brother, who had meant the world to her. That grief was what had brought her to his club in the first place. Adam had cared about her since he'd rescued her nine years earlier in the Chicago bus station, not that he'd shown her much support these past few months. Hell, no. He'd been too busy running in the opposite direction. Adam didn't know what it was that scared him the most—their age difference of twenty-five years, the thought of his corrupting her any more than he'd already done by bringing her onto the payroll at his kink club last July, or that she might get under his skin and expect more from him than he could give.

Hell, he'd lay odds she was still a virgin, or damned close to being one. She didn't have any interest in BDSM and had no place in a club where she had to witness so many things that obviously freaked her out. He'd seen her cringe as she watched Damián Orlando, one of the club's co-owners, wield the whip or heard one of Grant's subs screaming at the center post as the female Marine delivered a public and painful punishment.

"When I saw you lying there on the ground…" Karla cleared her throat. "The cougar was so big. You were bleeding. So much blood. I thought you'd been killed."

He pulled her close to him. *Just this once.* He needed to reassure her that he was going to be fine. "I'm pretty ornery. No cat is going to get the best of me."

"Well, I'll give you ornery."

He chuckled. "Ah, glad my secret's out. Keeping up appearances can be exhausting." She felt so good lying in his arms, even though he was too weak to keep his arms around her much longer. His biceps were feeling the strain. Damn, he was getting old.

"Worst-kept secret around. You've been *very* ornery lately." She paused, stroking his chest. He wished she'd get the fuck out of this bed. His dick was throbbing to the point of pain. Having her in his arms was totally wrong.

"I'm sorry about whatever I did to upset you…" Her voice broke, along with his resolve.

Oh, shit. He'd made her cry. "Hon, you didn't do anything." *Except look so fucking sexy you drive me insane.* "I just have some shit going on in my head. I never meant to make you feel bad." *So why are you about to make her feel worse?*

"But I think it might be good for you to think about moving back to Chicago. You don't belong in a kink club."

She pushed herself up and looked him in the face, her blue eyes steely as she glared at him.

"Adam, you will not send me away—not until you're better, at least. I know you're too stubborn to see it, but you need me. I'm going to take care of you, just like you took care of me when I first got here. This is all my fault. If you hadn't distracted that cougar…"

He pressed a finger over her lips and then pulled back. He didn't need to be thinking about touching her sexy pink lips at the moment. The dark circles under her eyes and her thin, pale face worried him. But if she'd been attacked…

"If I hadn't distracted that cougar, you'd be the one hooked to the IV. Or worse." He stroked her cheek, unable to help himself. The thought of that dangerous cat marring any part of her beautiful body tore at his gut worse than the animal's claws had torn up his back. She wouldn't have survived. He shuddered. "I did what anyone would do. Besides, my hide's tougher than yours. Damned cat didn't stand a chance." He grinned. When she reciprocated, he stared at her lips for the longest time, wondering what it would be like to kiss them.

Fuck. Fuck. Fuck.

"Get out of this bed, Karla. Now."

* * *

Eleven days later, Karla waited in the hallway outside Adam's bedroom, pacing. When she heard the door, she turned and watched Marc D'Alessio come out, carrying his first-aid bag. Adam had been home nine days and seemed to be healing, but he was still recovering, first from the infection and then the deep injuries to his muscles. She hated watching him suffer in pain every day. He'd always been such a vital force.

Adam would take the antibiotics from her, but sometimes refused his pain pills and absolutely refused to let her see his back. Marc had stopped by twice a day since Adam had come home to change the dressings and apply analgesics to try to keep Adam comfortable. Karla was secretly glad Marc didn't mind redressing his wounds, because he—having served as a corpsman with Adam's Marine unit in Iraq—certainly had more expertise in the area than she did.

She didn't want to fail Adam now.

"Whatever you're doing, Karla, keep it up. I can see a huge improvement from one day to the next. Now he's getting cantankerous, too. Should be back to his old self again in no time."

Some of the tension left her body. "Thank you." The words were barely spoken above a whisper. Exhausted, she wondered how she managed to remain upright anymore. Word that Adam was doing better overloaded her with emotion and her upper lip began to quiver. Marc held his arms out and she walked into his embrace. Really needing a hug right now, she let him bear her weight for a moment. If only it were Adam holding her.

"Where the stitches were removed, there's no sign of re-injury. We just need to try and keep him from overdoing it when he gets up and about more. He's chomping at the bit to get out of bed. I gave him one of the pain pills, though, after I treated the wounds and bandaged him up again. He'll sleep for a while. Come down and have lunch. Angelina's cooking up something good, I'm sure. Cassie's downstairs, too."

"No, I…"

He placed his hands on her upper arms and pushed her away from him, waiting until she looked up into his eyes. "Apparently, you misunderstood me, Karla. You *are* coming downstairs to have lunch with us. Now." Without waiting for her to respond, he took her elbow in his firm grip and steered her toward the stairs. "You know you aren't going to do him any good if you don't take care of yourself. You need to remember to eat and sleep, too."

He was right, but the guilt that plagued her every waking moment wouldn't release its hold. Adam had been injured trying to save her when the cougar threatened her, and he had suffered terribly in her place.

They reached the bottom of the stairs and he motioned for her to precede him down the narrow hallway and into the kitchen. Cassie sat at the table with her sketchpad, lost in her drawing.

Angie turned around, left the stove, and came toward her. "Oh, sweetie, you look exhausted. Didn't get any sleep last night either?"

"Not much. It's hard to sleep in a chair." *And I don't want to miss it if Adam needs me during the night.*

Angie wrapped her arms around her and Karla's already shaky rein on her emotions evaporated. She held on for dear life, too exhausted to fight the tears off anymore. God, she despised being so powerless. She imagined Adam must feel equally frustrated, though, and shouldn't complain.

"I hate seeing him lying there. He's always been so strong. Invincible. I know he's getting stronger, but he still has so far to go…"

Angie stroked her hair. "He'll get there, thanks to how well you're taking care of him. You just let me know what you need. I'm here for you, day or night."

Karla was so glad she'd met this woman, despite the circumstances. When the man who had brought Angie to the Masters at Arms Club in late August had become abusive toward her in one of the club's theme rooms, Marc rescued her. When he'd had to go back to his duties at the club, Adam gave Karla the rest of the night off from singing so she could watch over Angie.

Karla had dropped her off at her home about three hours away the next morning, battered and disheartened. Karla had never expected to see her anywhere near the club again. But Angie and Marc had somehow reconnected in her hometown a month later. Out of the blue, Karla had gotten a call from Angie saying she was on her way back to the club with Marc and his SAR partner, Luke. There were some tense moments, but thank goodness Marc and Angie worked things out. They'd been together since the night before Adam had been attacked on the mountain.

Since Angie returned to Denver, she and Karla had become good friends in a short time, removing some of the loneliness Karla had experienced since arriving at the club in July reeling from Ian's death.

Karla glanced over at the table. Cassie López, whom she'd known since college, looked up from her sketch and smiled sadly.

"Kitty, let me sit with him tonight so you can get some sleep. I feel like a fifth wheel around here."

Karla had rarely left Adam's side since he was in the hospital. After he'd come home, Cassie stayed on to support her friend, helping with meals, laundry, and watching over Adam while Karla showered or napped.

"Just having you here has helped me so much, Cassie."

Cassie stood and came across the room. Her exotic Peruvian heritage, with her lustrous long dark hair and beautiful olive complexion, was something fair-skinned Karla envied. Her best friend wrapped her in a big hug, the scent of freesia surrounding her. Karla wished her friend hadn't gotten caught up in all this drama. She avoided drama almost as much as she avoided men.

She remembered how they'd all come to be together that fateful night that had almost taken Adam away from her. Karla picked Cassie up at her remote mountain cabin home during the first week of October to go on the annual overnight camping trip she and Cassie had been taking since Cassie moved out here. The campout always included some kind of cathartic ritual ceremony and Karla needed that more than ever this year. They'd invited Angie to join them, because she needed to release some painful shit, too.

But soon after they'd arrived at their camping spot, all hell broke loose. Karla shuddered. She didn't want to think about how close Angie had come to being hurt even worse by her abusive ex-boyfriend. Because of that bastard, Adam, Marc, Luke, and Damián had wound up on the mountain that night. Tears pricked her eyes. When Karla had been threatened by a cougar, Adam enticed the big cat away from her only to be attacked by it himself. Karla cringed, forcing herself to block out the image of the animal clawing and biting Adam.

Since the cougar attack, Cassie had stayed here with Karla until she could get a ride home. Angie was staying at Marc's house—well, when they weren't here, too, helping out. Marc was one of the co-owners of the club, along with Damián. They both were like family to Adam.

The kitchen door opened and in walked Marc's partner, Luke. "Something smelled good all the way out on the porch." He walked over to Angie, placed a hand on her back, and started to kiss her on the cheek, then halted and turned to Marc. "Permission to kiss the cook." Marc's gaze homed in on Luke's hand on Angie and the newest Dom at the club removed his hand as if burned.

"Granted—but only on the cheek."

The two Doms exchanged an amicable grin and Karla relaxed. She had to wonder if there hadn't been something between Luke and Angie at some point. These days, however, the woman clearly had no interest in anyone but Marc. "I think I might need to do a better job of explaining some protocols to you, Baby Dom—like teaching you to ask before you touch—not just before you kiss—another Dom's sub."

"Oh, behave, you two," Angie said, walking over to the refrigerator. "Too much testosterone in here. Besides, we're not in the club right now, so protocols don't apply."

Angie had told Karla she and Marc were strictly Dom/sub in the bedroom and while playing at the club. Since Karla had gotten the job singing at the club, Karla had been surprised to learn about the range of commitment available to people in the BDSM lifestyle—everything from a single night to a lifetime commitment.

There was still so much she didn't understand about this stuff.

Marc watched as Angie placed the salad dressing on the counter. "Some protocols *always* apply, *cara*, such as respecting another Dom's property. Maybe we need to renegotiate our agreement."

"But you promised…" Karla saw a flash of uncertainty cross Angie's eyes and Marc chuckled.

"I'm not saying I want less Dom/sub time, *cara*, but maybe more." When he held his arms open, she smiled and walked into his embrace.

Karla looked away, tears stinging her eyes again. She was happy for them, but wished she and Adam could have a relationship like theirs. Hell, she'd be happy to have *any* kind of relationship with Adam. Period.

Luke turned his attention to her. "Karla, how are you doing, darlin'?"

She shrugged. "Hanging in there."

"Hope you don't mind my dropping by." Adam and his friends pretty much had run of the building, which included the club and now even Adam's private living quarters. She'd become used to people dropping by whenever they wanted.

"Marc promised food." Luke placed his hand against his stomach. "I can't cook worth shit."

"Join the club. Angie's tried to teach me, but…well…"

"Don't worry, Karla," Angie chimed in. "We'll get back to lessons when things settle down again. You were coming along great."

Karla couldn't believe a local restaurant hadn't snatched up Angie with her amazing culinary skills. Angie wanted her financial independence, which Karla understood. Singing at the club part-time didn't pay a lot, but Karla hadn't been sure she'd be staying here, so she hadn't looked for anything to supplement her income. Adam provided for so many of her personal needs—room, board, clothing. It made her feel guilty. She'd been independent while working at the Goth club in New York City for a couple of years, until she'd gotten fired a couple months after Ian had been killed.

And, while she'd never admit this to her liberated mother or friends, she liked the way Adam took care of those physical needs at least. If that was the only role Adam wanted to play in her life, then she'd be content.

Or try to be, at least.

When Luke's attention homed in on Cassie, focused on her sketchpad again, Karla wished her friend would at least give him a chance. His shy, self-deprecating grin and that Texan drawl were endearing. In the hospital waiting room almost two weeks ago, Karla had first realized there might be some cosmic connection between Cassie and Luke. Something definitely had brought them together, based on the sketch Cassie made of Luke's dead wife and baby. Needless to say, Luke had been understandably moved by the haunting image, but Cassie retreated into her internal world again.

Karla would like to help her friend find love and happiness, even if those emotions weren't possible for Karla—at least not with the man she wanted to enjoy them with.

Karla walked closer to the table. "Cassie, I know you probably need to get back home soon. There must be any number of artist commissions you need to be working on."

Right on cue, Luke offered, "If you need a ride, Cassie, I'd be happy to run you home."

Cassie's pencil stilled and her hand hovered over the sketchpad. Okay, it was too soon for that. Karla went over and stroked her friend's back. With her history, of course Cassie wouldn't be comfortable alone with him, even if he didn't pose an actual threat to her, by Karla's estimation.

Luckily, Angie came to her rescue. "Cassie, I need to go back to my house in a few days and pack up some more things. I could take you home then." Cassie was only about thirty minutes from Aspen Corners.

Cassie's face relaxed. Gentle Luke wouldn't hurt a soul, though, nor would any of the Doms at the Masters at Arms. She wished her friend wasn't afraid of all men, but certainly understood why. Perhaps if Cassie wasn't alone so much, she could become more comfortable around men.

"Thanks, Angie. I'd like that, but only when Kitty's ready to kick me out."

Thinking about anything other than Adam right now was more than Karla could manage, but knowing Cassie had a way back to her cabin was a relief for her, if his recovery stretched out too long. There were plenty of people around to help, even though she'd miss Cassie.

Marc came over and stroked Karla's arm. "You're going to take a nap after lunch while one of us sits with Adam."

Karla pulled away and wiped her suddenly damp eyes with the sleeves of her black T-shirt. Time to change the subject before she started sobbing and embarrassed herself—again.

Looking at the stove, Karla asked, "What smells so good?"

"I've got penne pasta with roasted red peppers and garlic in the oven."

"God, Angie, you make cooking seem so simple. Will I ever…" Oh, what was the use learning how to cook for Adam now? Karla wouldn't be here long enough to make anything for him. Once he was stronger, he'd be sending her home to Chicago. Her eyes burned again and she blinked rapidly. "What can I do to help?"

"Nothing," Marc said, taking her elbow and steering her to a chair. "Table's all set. Come, sit down."

He pulled out Adam's chair at the head of the table. Seeing it empty reminded her that Adam wasn't able to join them. A lump lodged in Karla's throat, and she took the one beside it instead. Angie carried a baking dish to the table and Marc went over to the counter to retrieve the bread, wine, and salad dressing. Seeing them so in sync together just made her feel even sadder, which, in turn, made her feel more guilt. Why begrudge them happiness, just because she could never have it herself?

Luke sat beside Karla, with Cassie on his other side at the end of the table. Oh, dear. She probably should have sat closer to her friend. Marc and Angelina sat close to each other across from Karla and Luke. The meal began in silence with them eating their salads, and then Angie dished out the main course and passed a plate to each of them.

Karla's eyes were drawn to her as Angie reached out and touched Marc's hand. Even a simple gesture like that was more than she could have with Adam, more than Adam would *let* her have, anyway.

Angie held onto his hand and squeezed. "Marc, the sheriff's office called. Allen's bail request was denied. Looks like we won't have to worry about him getting out for a while. Apparently, they take kidnapping a whole lot more seriously than battery."

A look of pain flickered in Marc's eyes. Angie had suffered at the hands of her ex-boyfriend, Allen Martin. Karla had seen the fear on Marc's face that evening on Mount Evans when they'd gone to rescue Angie, no doubt thinking the worst had happened. He cared a lot about Angie.

Karla's hand began to tremble and she rested it on the table so no one else would see the fork shaking in her fingers. Too late. Luke reached out and squeezed her hand until the shaking stopped. When she looked over at him, he smiled.

"Adam would want you to eat more than that."

"I know. I just..."

He picked up the fork and stabbed some pasta holding it up to her mouth until she parted her lips and accepted the offering. Everyone was taking such good care of her, so she could take care of their friend, Adam. This rag-tag family Adam had brought together would be lost without him.

Visions of the blood pooling beside Adam's neck as he lay motionless curdled her stomach. Karla couldn't block the horrific images from her mind. Everything had happened so quickly. Adam running toward her to try and calm her fears. His distracting the cougar, which chased and attacked him. She'd tried to wrestle the cat off him, until Marc had pulled her away so Damián could shoot the beast.

The graphic memories led to a roiling stomach and, after a couple more forkfuls, Karla took the utensil from Luke, fearing she'd get sick if she ate another bite. But she smiled at him, appreciating his support.

"Just remember, *cara*, he's still strong or he wouldn't be here," Marc said, using one of his native Italian endearments. "You just wait. He'll be back to his old self again, ordering everyone around and running his tight ship, same as always."

Yes, but without me.

Karla was pleased when Luke took advantage of the lull in the table talk and struck up a conversation with Cassie, trying to draw her out of her silence. His knowledge on the subject of fine art surprised Karla. He worked as a carpenter and woodworker. Of course, he'd shown a knack for designing some of the unique pieces of equipment used in the club.

Cassie seemed equally surprised. "How do you know so much about art?"

"Art major in college." When Cassie's eyes opened wider, he explained. "The University of Texas, where I went on a football scholarship, didn't have the industrial arts major I wanted. But I'm really glad I chose studio art instead. It's helped me a lot with my work."

Cassie gave him a hesitant smile, then her brow furrowed and she retreated again, focusing on her food. Well, it was a start. At least the two of them had found common ground to build on.

Karla's eyelids burned. She wished she and Adam could find common ground. Karla laid her fork on the table, no longer able to eat for the anxious churning in her stomach.

Chapter Two

That night, Karla's neck ached from sleeping curled up in the chair beside Adam's bed yet again. After two weeks of bedside vigils—first in the hospital and then at home—it was a wonder she could move her neck. She glanced at him, all stretched out on the other side of his king-sized bed. His chest rose and fell in rhythmic breathing. As usual, he slept without a shirt; the sheet and blanket pulled down to his waist. His pecs were ripped, those delicious nips begging to be sucked to granite-hard peaks, just the way she'd always fantasized. His body looked as firm and tight as she'd imagined it all those years ago. She smiled when she remembered wanting to try to bounce a quarter off his chest and licking his pecs the first time she'd seen him without his shirt.

Oh, don't go there, Kitty.

She hadn't reverted to her high-school nickname in a while. Must be because Cassie was here and still called her that. Karla looked longingly at the large bed. Surely Adam wouldn't mind if she lay down on this side. There easily was room for three people in the bed. She was exhausted and hadn't been able to sleep more than in small snatches since the attack.

Karla lifted the sheet and blanket and crawled between the sheets. Heaven. Funny how a bed could make such a difference in the ability to relax. Knowing Adam slept peacefully beside her and was on the mend, reminded her that her time here was limited. She would take what she could get. If this would be the only time she "slept" with Adam, then so be it.

The thought that he didn't want her in his house or club anymore, and had said as much at the hospital, caused an ache in her chest. He hadn't mentioned it again since they'd brought him home—and she certainly didn't bring it up—but she wouldn't continue to live with him as she had been. Wanting, needing, but having him ignore her. The pain of having him so near and not being able to touch him, to love him, was more than she could bear.

Except for tonight. Even though he slept beside her, she still couldn't embrace him. But she could pretend. They looked like any married couple sleeping side by side after many years together. Not touching, but still irrevocably connected. Tonight, she felt closer to Adam than ever before.

At last, the sleep that had eluded her since Adam was injured beckoned. She surrendered...

Adam's hard body nestled against her backside, and his arm curled around her waist with his firm hand cupping her breast. She'd had erotic dreams of Adam before and gave in to this one, snuggling against him. His erection—larger than she'd dreamed it in the past—pressed against her ass. The hand on her breast stirred and his finger and thumb rolled her nipple, causing her hips to jerk back against his hard penis.

Karla gasped. Too real. Her eyes flew open to find her in near darkness, but she came fully awake in an instant. This was no dream.

More like a dream come true.

Adam!

He continued to play with her nipple, teasing it to the point of pain, sending jolts of electricity to her girly bits. She held her breath, not wanting to wake him. Not wanting to stop him.

Touch me.

His hand left her breast and roamed across her abdomen. Oh, dear Lord, had he heard her silent plea? Or had she spoken the plaintive words aloud? She raised her leg, tenting the covers, giving him easier access. Usually she slept in the nude, but the thigh-length T-shirt had been her concession to decency while watching over Adam. She wore no panties and was seconds away from having Adam's fingers on her...

Touch me there, Adam.

His hand continued to glide down her body, over her hips, onto her bare thigh, and then he stopped. *No! Not yet!* He stroked her inner thigh and pulled her legs even more open, and his hand moved upward. Her heart pounded in her ears.

Oh, yes, love. There.

If he put an end to this now, she'd surely die. She licked her lips, which had gone dry. When had she started panting like a dog in heat? *Oh, dear Lord.* She should wake him. This wasn't right. He didn't even know he was with her. He could be dreaming of Joni.

No. She wouldn't think about his dead wife now. Joni was gone. Joni couldn't give Adam what he needed anymore.

But could Karla stop him, even if she wanted to? She needed his hands on her so badly. Had craved this moment for so many years. When his finger slid over her clit, she gasped. So sensitive. The little nubbin went into spasms. She'd touched herself there before with her fingers and her vibrator, but no one else had ever done so. What a difference—not knowing how he would caress her, where, when, how much pressure.

His finger delved between her curly folds and pressed against her pussy's very wet opening. He entered her, filling her tight hole, but didn't go far before he pulled out again and returned to touching her clit. She'd dreamed of having Adam touch her like this for so long. Now he was doing just what she wanted. She'd always hoped one day he would make love to her.

But not like this.

She had to wake him. Whether he was in a deep sleep or under the influence of the painkillers, it was wrong to take advantage of him like this. She scooted onto her back to face him and he nuzzled her neck, his whiskers scratching against the tender skin there. Her clit throbbed against his finger.

"Oh, God, Karla. Now you've invaded my fucking dreams."

Karla? He'd said her name! Adam was dreaming about *her*. Not Joni. A delicious euphoria spread through her, like when she hit a particularly high note with perfect pitch. She relaxed and smiled, wrapping her arms around his neck, then easing away again when she remembered his injuries. His finger continued to stroke her clit, and she rocked against his hand, moaning.

Don't stop, Adam.

Her heartbeat sent an insistent throbbing to her clit. *More.* Oh, dear Lord, she wanted so much more of him. As if he heard her, he raised his body, groaning in pain. Marc had said he should avoid strenuous activity. Oh, God. How strenuous was too strenuous?

All lucid thought vanished as his body hovered over hers, his finger inside her. Soon she worried about whether she should stroke him; how she should move. With tentative fingers, she stroked his bulging, corded biceps, shivering at the raw power there, despite his having been weakened from the cougar attack.

"So wet," his voice rasped.

His finger entered her again. Then another finger. *Oh, God, yes.* She bucked her hips up against him.

"I can't wait, Kitten. I promise I'll go slower next time."

Kitten. The endearment melted her into a pool of Jell-O.

He pushed his sweatpants off his hips, releasing his penis. His very hot, hard penis which now pressed against her pussy. He rubbed the tip against her cleft, from her vagina to her clit, again and again. *Oh, yes.* At last, he pressed against her pussy, pushing himself inside, slowly filling her. Her hips bucked up toward him, taking him deeper.

"So fucking tight."

His finger stroked her clit and she moaned as waves of sensation spread through her. She could have flown off the bed.

"Yes, Adam. Don't stop." His finger moved faster. "Oh, God!" She moved her hands up to stroke Adam's chest. His pecs were like steel. "Oh, please, don't stop!" Her hips began to buck even harder, against his finger, his penis.

"Come for me, Kitten."

His finger against her clit stroked faster, sending waves of electricity throughout her pelvis. "Yes. Oh, Adam, yesss!" She found herself just on the edge of a precipice, hovering above the unknown, and held her breath. *Step off. Fly.* "Oh, oh, ohhhh!" So close. She wrapped her arms tighter around his neck, pulling him down to kiss her. With a groan, he rammed his penis fully inside her.

Her scream of pain filled his mouth and brought his body to a halt. The unanticipated pain registered in her mind a half-second later. Tears stung her eyes. She'd read about the breaking of a woman's hymen and how much it was supposed to hurt, but she'd had no idea. Luckily, just as quickly as the pain had come, it receded.

"No fucking way."

She opened her eyes to look up at him and found Adam staring down at her in disbelief as realization dawned.

She whimpered. She wanted. She needed.

"Adam, I saved myself for you. I wanted only you. Please don't pull away from me now."

The look of torture and remorse on his face hurt exponentially more than the physical pain she'd experienced a moment ago. "What have I done, Karla?"

"Nothing I didn't want you to do." She reached up and stroked the planes of his beautiful face. "I wanted you to make love to me more than anything, Adam."

But not as much as I want you to love me.

"I've never wanted anything more in my entire life." She tilted her hips, wincing at the residual tenderness, but she wanted Adam to finish what he'd started, damn it. "Please, don't leave me like this."

Please don't leave me—ever.

With a groan, he lowered his forehead to hers, gasping for air from his earlier exertions. Then his hips began to move as he pulled out of her. *No, Adam!* She clenched her vagina around his penis, not wanting to let him go. When he thrust back inside her, it caused some discomfort, but she controlled her facial expression, not wanting to reveal any negative emotion for fear he would stop. Oh, she didn't want him to stop. She smiled, then gasped and held on when his finger stroked the nubbin that had become even more sensitive than before. She tried to evade his finger.

"Stop. It'll be better for you this way."

Trusting him, she spread her legs open wider and wrapped them around his waist, resting her heels at the small of his back, hoping she'd avoided the places where he'd been mauled by the cougar. He pulled out and rammed himself inside her even deeper, forcing the air from her lungs. So full.

"Oh, yes!"

At her cry, his movements increased. The feeling of oneness with him was unexpected. Her Adam, at last making love to her. She raised her hips to meet him, stroke for stroke. His finger slid along the side of her clit, not quite touching it directly now, matching the movements of his hips. Pressure built up inside her again, even more intense than the last time. As he continued to thrust in and out, his finger touched her clit and she climbed toward the precipice again.

"Oh, Adam! Please don't stop!"

"As if I could." His voice was raspy with sleep, or perhaps the drugs. But he knew it was Karla he was making love with. She smiled.

His strokes increased again. Hips. Finger. Penis.

"Come with me."

His finger applied direct, rapid pressure against her clit. The sparks of electricity ricocheted throughout her body. "Yes! Oh, Adam! Yesssss! Oh, God, yesss!" She hurtled over the precipice as her insides exploded. Her hips convulsed against him and her pussy clamped onto his throbbing penis as he spurted inside her. She screamed her final release.

Adam grunted as he pumped his seed inside her. "God, yes, Karla!" Then he stopped abruptly, his breathing labored as he recovered from the exertion, the first real exercise he'd had since before the attack. "Aw, fuck."

Aw, yes, Adam. A great fuck.

"Tell me you're on birth control."

What? Her mind was still floating back to earth from the experience and he wanted to talk about contraception? "Birth control?"

He looked down at her, worry and regret in his eyes. She didn't want him to regret anything about this beautiful moment. But she had to be honest. "I'm sorry…No, I'm not." *Not sorry in the least.* If a baby came as a result of what they'd just done, then it would be the most precious gift anyone had ever given her. Even if Adam didn't want it—or her—she would love his baby for the rest of her life.

He rolled off her, the friction of his penis pulling out of her causing her to wince again. When he covered his eyes with the crook of his elbow, a tear slid from the corner of her eye and she brushed it away before he could see it. He already regretted what they'd done together. She needed to get away from him before she started crying—or decked him. Karla swung her legs over the side of the bed.

"I'm sorry, Karla. I never wanted that to happen."

He doesn't want me. Reeling from his rejection, she stood and ran to her bedroom, feeling a sticky wetness between her thighs. First, a shower. But she wouldn't be able to wash away the feeling of dirtiness his callousness had made her feel.

No!

No way would she let Adam's feelings of regret, guilt, and remorse taint the beauty of what they'd just experienced. His lovemaking had been the most wonderful thing to happen in her life. Even better than anything she'd fantasized about all these years. She would hold onto the memory of this night forever.

* * *

Jesus Fucking Christ, what had he done? A virgin. He'd had an inkling she was one, because she'd never spoken or written about any men in her life. He'd avoided her for months, because he sure as hell had had no intention of finding out. Not with his goddamned dick, anyway.

Not like this.

She was young enough to be his daughter. Shit, she'd come to him for comfort and now he'd taken advantage of her. What the fuck was he going to do if she got pregnant? He wasn't worried about STDs. He was always so damned careful—well, until tonight—and she'd obviously never had sex with a man before. *Goddamn it.* What *if* she got pregnant? No matter what she would choose to do about a baby, it would change her life forever.

Not to mention his.

Goddamn it. What had just happened in here? He'd finally started to regain some strength, most likely from the crunches he'd been doing when Marc and Karla weren't around scolding him like a child. But he'd overdone it yesterday and had to take another of those damned pain pills before going to sleep. Clearly, he'd been out of it—well, until he was into it. *Into her.* He'd regained his faculties quickly, but it was already too late.

Why the fuck hadn't he trusted his gut last July and defied Damián when he'd insisted on hiring her after her audition? He should have sent her home to Chicago immediately. No, instead, he'd let Damián hire her to sing at their BDSM/kink club. Hell, he'd even done a rope bondage demonstration on her at Marc's house a couple of days before the cougar attack.

Now he'd fucked her. A goddamned virgin.

Jesus Christ.

One more thing to add to his life's long list of sins for which there wasn't enough contrition to absolve him.

Adam reached over and turned on the light. Glancing down at the sheet, he noticed the bloodstain and closed his eyes again. He'd hurt her. Yeah, he'd fucked up royally. God, had he ever.

But what was she doing in his bed in the first place? It seemed every time he woke up lately, she was in bed with him, or sleeping in a chair nearby. How was he supposed to keep her at arm's length when she plastered her body against him?

Don't go there, shithead. You are completely responsible for what happened. She was an innocent—until you came along.

Truth be told, if his memory wasn't totally faulty, it sure seemed like he was the one plastered against her hot little backside.

When he sat up, the muscles in his back and neck protested loudly. He sat on the edge of the bed waiting for his head to clear, and then stood. Slowly, trying not to pull any maimed and healing muscles—if he hadn't already done so while pumping his dick into Karla with so much enthusiasm—he walked into the adjoining bathroom to clean himself before returning to the bedroom. He pulled from the dresser a clean pair of sweats and a USMC T-shirt.

Between having sex and being out of bed for the first time in more than two weeks, he was as weak as a kitten.

Kitten.

He'd called her Kitten. Where the hell had that pet name come from? *Oh, yeah.* Her friend, Cassie, had called her Kitty when they were hiking down the mountain looking for Angelina. He'd wondered all those years ago in the Chicago bus station what nickname she hadn't wanted to reveal to him. Kitty.

He preferred Kitten. *His kitten.*

Aw, fuck that shit.

Hell, he needed to check on her. He crossed the hallway and knocked softly on her door. Was Cassie still sleeping next door? He hadn't ventured out of his bedroom since he'd gotten home from the hospital. Karla's best friend would find out soon enough what he'd done, but he wasn't ready to face the accusations of being a pervert yet. He needed to regain more of his strength first.

"Karla." He hoped his voice carried through the room's solid oak door.

No response. He should just go back to bed and leave her alone. Or maybe he should get Cassie up. Karla might be more comfortable talking with a woman at a time like this. Then the sound of sobs coming from Karla's room undid him, twisting his gut into knots tighter than the ones he used in rope suspension. *Aw, hell.* He'd made her cry. He opened the door and found her lying across the bed wrapped in a towel. Her long bare legs stirred his dick back to life.

Fuck it all to hell, old man. Can't you control your little head anymore?

"Karla?" Her body tensed and she rubbed her hands against her eyes, but didn't turn to face him. "Hon, we need to talk."

"Not now, Adam. Please, just don't say anything more."

More? What had he said? He tried to think back, but came up blank. Damned pills. "Hon, I can't tell you how sorry I…"

She rolled over and glared at him, dashing more tears away from her cheeks. The towel loosened to expose her beautiful breasts. His dick throbbed harder. Until she came along, he could go months without having sex, and now he was eager to go at it again in what, less than an hour? What the fuck was the matter with him?

Judging by the glare in Karla's eyes, having sex with him was the furthest thing from her mind at the moment. *Good girl.* At least one of them was thinking clearly.

"Adam Montague, I don't want to hear another word about your regrets."

She sat up, ignoring her bared breasts. Well, *he* certainly couldn't ignore them. Their dusky pink areolas begged to be touched. Sucked. Bitten.

Whoa! He wouldn't be having rough sex with Karla—scratch that thought. He wouldn't be having *any* kind of sex with Karla ever again.

"What happened in your bed a little while ago was the most beautiful thing that's ever happened to me, and I won't let you cheapen it or make me feel dirty because I didn't stop you when I should have."

When *she* should have? Hell, he was the one on top. Wasn't he?

Karla stood and came closer to him, first stabbing him with her angry gaze, and then poking his chest with her finger. At least she finally pulled the towel up to cover her breasts. "I've wanted you to make love to me for months. Now all I want is for you to get the hell out of my room."

Shit, he'd not only hurt her physically, he'd hurt her emotionally. Total clusterfuck.

Adam reached out and pulled her closer, rubbing his hands up and down her bare arms. "Karla, I never wanted to hurt you. If I hadn't been on all those meds…" The flash of pain in her eyes told him he'd just hurt her again. Okay, he needed to steer clear of that tack. "Hon, your first time should have been with someone who can make a commitment to you…" *Shit.* Now tears. A woman's waterworks always wrenched his gut, but he'd rarely seen Karla cry. He reached out and wiped them away with the pads of his thumbs, then pulled her against his chest.

"Aw, Kitten, I'm so sorry. Please believe me. I wish I'd made your first time so much more special."

"Adam, it *was* special. Please don't make it ugly now. Don't apologize anymore for making love with me."

Christ. What did she need to hear from him?

Adam wanted to lift her into his arms, but didn't have the strength, so he sat on the edge of the bed and pulled her down into his lap. She laid her head against his shoulder and he stroked her gorgeous thick hair, remembering how incredible it had felt to finger comb and bind it in the hair corset at Marc's— that evening seemed like a year ago.

He nearly lost his resolve to do right by her. He wanted nothing more than to press her into the mattress and make love to her the way he should have the first time, but he wasn't going to make anything better at this point with more sex. Time to regroup and form a new plan. Assess the situation on the ground, figure out how to put this behind them, and move forward. He just had no fucking clue how to do that.

"What do we do now, hon?"

She reached up to brush away her tears. "Don't make me leave, Adam. Please don't send me away."

What was she talking about? He didn't know what all he'd said in the bedroom exactly, but didn't remember any talk about sending her away. At least not that he'd spoken aloud. Had he? Oh, hell, maybe he had. Damn it, he hated having his head on so many fucking drugs. How was he supposed to navigate these dangerous waters when he was under the influence of narcotics? He wasn't going to take another damned pain pill from now on.

"I'm sorry, hon." She stiffened, and he added quickly, "If I said I wanted to send you away, it must have been the pills. I don't want you to go anywhere."

I need you.

Whoa. Sure, he wanted her, but it wasn't a need. He didn't need anyone. He'd never needed anyone.

Karla pulled away and her tear-stained face tore at his heart, her long eyelashes clumping together. He'd put those tears there. "Adam, I can't go on the way we've been living, though."

"What do you mean?" What was wrong with the way they'd been living?

She placed a hand at his hairline, just above the scars at the nape of his neck, and pulled him toward her, letting her other hand stroke his cheek. *Oh, God, no.* He couldn't resist her when she used tactics like that. He groaned and turned his head, but his mouth sought out her sexy lips instead. He grabbed the back of her head and deepened the kiss, his tongue delving into the sweetness of her mouth. His dick came to a full salute.

Shit. No. This needed to stop. Now.

She moaned, making him aware that his hand was cupping her breast. Those firm breasts had been begging to be touched for months, and he'd lain awake many nights imagining what it would feel like to do just that. Now here she was in his lap, his arm around her, hand touching her.

Yeah, he needed to stop this shit. Now.

His lips trailed down her neck, and her head dropped back giving him better access as she gasped for air. He'd never been so out of control.

God help him, but he didn't want to stop. Ever.

"What do you need from me, Kitten?" he whispered in her ear.

"Love me, Adam. Please, just love me."

Oh, God. Don't ask for the one thing I can't give you or anyone. He pulled away and searched her eyes, watching the sparkle fade as realization dawned on her. What a fucking heel he was. "I'm sorry, Karla. I can have sex with you, but there can never be anything more than that."

"Because you still love your wife?"

He closed his eyes and pressed his forehead against hers. No. Because he didn't want to hurt Karla the way he'd hurt Joni. "I made a lousy husband, Karla. You deserve someone who can love you one-hundred percent, twenty-four/seven. I'm not that man."

"Bullshit."

He pulled back and opened his eyes to find her glaring back at him again. Well, it sure beat tears. This woman was not the meek Karla he'd encountered in the hallways in this house, or at the kitchen table, all these months, but the one he remembered as a sixteen-year-old. The one he'd corresponded with for almost nine years. Feisty, stubborn, and full of life. For some reason, she seemed to have rediscovered that feistiness while he'd been in the hospital. That seemed to be when everything went south and her demeanor had changed.

"Come again?"

"You heard me. I said 'bullshit.' Joni loved you and I know you loved her. You still do." Karla's hand reached up to stroke his cheek and her voice softened. "But she's been gone a long time, Adam."

He winced. Guilt assailed him at how he'd treated Joni, never able to love her the way she wanted and needed to be loved. Guilt at how he would hurt Karla, too, if she tried to get that close to his heart. Guilt—the useless emotion that threatened to consume him before he tamped it back down. Guilt didn't help anything. He couldn't remedy anything about his relationship with Joni. But Karla was another matter.

"What would a young woman like you see in an old man like me?"

"Would you get your head out of your ass for once, Adam, and see what's been in front of your face for months? You need a living, breathing woman who can warm your bed and your heart. You need me, whether you're fucking ready to believe it or not."

"Watch your language."

"Excuse me? I'm only a few years younger than Grant and she swears like a…well, a Marine."

"Grant *is* a Marine—you're not. What's Grant's age or swearing got to do with you anyway?"

Adam had no clue what was getting Karla so riled up, but he stroked her arm to try and calm her down, surprised when it seemed to work.

"Adam, I don't know what we have in common, because you won't let me close enough to get to know you. But I know you served in the military, as did my brother. I know you like to eat, so I'm having Angie teach me to cook, mainly for the joy of watching you eat whatever I make."

"You don't have to go to all the trouble…"

"Don't interrupt."

Damned bossy woman.

"I *want* to, Adam. I want to please you."

His mind zeroed in on the words "please you" and raced to images of Karla restrained for his pleasure. His dick needed no further encouragement. Having her sitting in his lap was better than anything he could imagine. Then again, maybe not. Big mistake.

"I know you're brave and kind and noble and that you *care* about me or you wouldn't have bothered to send me all those letters for nine years—"

"Being a pen pal isn't a reason to fall in love with a guy."

"I. Said. Don't. Interrupt." She glared until he gave her a nod of the head. The woman had Domme written all over her. A relationship between them would never work.

"I know you got a mountain lion to chase after you just to save me. And I know you're my hero." The intensity in her eyes and catch in her voice caused his gut to clench.

"I'm nobody's hero. Anyone would have done the same when they saw you were in danger."

She winced. He'd hurt her again, damn it, but he needed to divest her of the notion there would ever be anything more between them.

"Adam Montague, you will not degrade what you did on that mountain any more than you will degrade what we shared in your bed, or I'm going to be the one wielding the whip and striping your ass the way Damián does his masochistic subs."

"Sorry, hon, but I don't swing that way." *Oh, yeah.* Definitely a dominant. *Shit.* No fucking way was she coming after *him* with a whip. "See? We don't even have kink in common."

His kitten leaned toward his ear and said in the sexiest purr he'd ever heard, "Adam, when you bound me with those ropes in Marc's playroom, I was never so turned on in all my life." His dick was about to explode.

Damn. Adam had known that demonstration had been a mistake from the start and still didn't know how he'd ever gotten roped into it, so to speak. Karla had seemed as surprised as he was when Angelina suggested it.

He rubbed his hand over his face. This conversation was going south fast. When had he lost control with Karla? The damned cougar attack. How soon could he regain the upper hand with her? Maybe when the fog cleared completely? At least he'd sworn off the damned pills now.

Time to regain control. "Hon, it's not like you seem to have had a lot of experience with being turned on."

Karla pulled away and her eyes, reddened from her recent crying jag, became narrow slits. "Not true. I've been turned on by you for a long time. You just chose to ignore me." She cupped his cheeks in her hands, forcing Adam to stare into her eyes again. "The only person I ever wanted to turn me on was you, Adam."

If she didn't stop whispering like that, he was going to embarrass himself.

"When I saw you in my parents' kitchen without your shirt—oh...my...God. I was ruined for any other man right then and there." She grinned.

He'd turned on a sixteen-year-old? Hell, he'd thought she'd been embarrassed, not excited. If her mom would have let him put his damned shirt back on, maybe none of this would have happened. Karla definitely took after her mother. Two strong, dominant women.

He needed to get Karla off his lap. It was wrong to take advantage of a naïve, innocent—well not as innocent as she'd been an hour ago—woman who was just discovering the joys of love. No, not love. Sex.

Wrong to wrap his arms tighter around her.

Wrong to want to kiss her.

He knew all that, so why was he ignoring his inner compass and doing those things anyway?

Chapter Three

Adam's arms tightened around her. A charge of electricity ripped through her. Still holding his face in her hands, she moved her face toward his, brushing her lips lightly against his, enjoying the tingling sensation. She wanted to savor this moment. His lips were firm and soft at the same time. She kissed his upper lip, then his fuller lower one. He didn't reciprocate, but that was okay. They had hours before daylight would bring the house to life again. With his walls of resistance still lowered, she had no doubt how her first seduction scene would turn out.

Adam Montague, you are doomed to be loved by me forever, whether you choose to accept me or not.

With the tip of her tongue, she traced the line between his lips, and he groaned, his hand moving up to cup her breast. Her bare breast. The towel must have slipped down again. She hadn't even noticed. Nor did she care.

Yes. Touch me, Adam.

"Oh God, Kitten."

The special endearment was growing on her. He rolled her nipple between his finger and thumb, sending another zing straight to her clit. She squirmed on his lap, his erection pressing against her thigh. Karla smiled. What a feeling of power. Now to move in for the kill. Thank God she'd watched a lot of romantic movies, or she might not have even known how to kiss him like a woman would. She'd fantasized about this for many, many years, but most especially since seeing him again last July.

Karla took her fingers and splayed them over the very short hairs at the nape of his neck, then held his head firmly as she pressed her tongue against his lips, breaking through and delving inside his mouth. His hand convulsed over her breast and nipple at her gentle, but persistent, invasion.

He pushed her away, and she looked at him through half-lidded eyes. Both of them gasped for air. Then he pulled her toward him with a groan that sounded an awful lot like surrender.

His tongue met and welcomed hers, teasing, stroking, dancing. Her clit throbbed. *More.* She wanted more but she needed to go slowly. God, she'd die if he pulled away from her again. He invaded her open mouth and assaulted her senses. Air became a precious commodity, and she gasped, trying to fill her aching lungs.

Throwing her head back, she gave him access to her neck, and he pressed kisses against the throbbing pulse there. His whiskers scratched and tickled at the same time. Her clit throbbed in response. As a teenager, she hadn't imagined him with whiskers. She stifled a giggle. What a giddy feeling. At last, Adam was kissing her, loving her.

Well, maybe love was too strong a word. He wasn't ready for that. But she definitely hoped he would make love to her. Again. Slowly. With great feeling.

His lips nuzzled into the hollow of her throat, and her girly bits grew wet. Her entire body tingled at the awareness he awoke inside her. *More.* Dragging her hands from around his neck, she touched his chest with trembling hands, wishing he wasn't wearing a T-shirt now. She wanted to see his chest in the light coming from her bathroom door. She hadn't been able to see much of him before in the darkness of his room.

Adam's hand moved from her breast and grasped her wrists, pressing her hands against his chest. Confused, she lifted her head and watched him close his eyes as he leaned forward until his forehead pressed against hers. He took several raspy breaths, apparently having as much trouble breathing as she was.

Don't pull away from me, Adam. Not again.

He sat up and opened his eyes, a look of pain on his face. *No!* Her heart squeezed tight before he even spoke.

"I can't do this to you, hon."

"I want you to do this *with* me, not *to* me."

"You deserve better than me."

Her voice sounded hoarse when she spoke. "Adam, they don't come any better than you."

"You don't know anything about me."

"Bullshit. I know you're a good and honorable man. I know you would lay down your life for someone you love." *Yes, including me.* "And I know you have a lot of hurts buried deep inside you that are fucking with your brain." When his eyes grew round at her second f-bomb, she continued. "When are you going to stop thinking of me as a child? I'm not sixteen anymore, Adam. And

I'm not crushing on you like I did back then. I came to you this summer because I needed you to help me deal with Ian's death. When I saw you again, I realized how much I've loved you all these years. But when you were lying in that hospital bed, it became clear to me how much you need me, too. Please don't shut me out. I can help slay your dragons."

Adam pulled further away as if she'd struck him. "What are you talking about? I don't have any dragons left. I've slayed them already."

"I'll be good. Don't lock me in there, Mommy!"

Karla remembered Adam lying in the hospital bed, feverish from infection, and screaming those words out in a high-pitched child's voice. She reached up to stroke his cheek, wondering how to get him to open up to her about the pain buried so deep inside he didn't even know it was there.

"I want to know you better. Tell me about yourself, Adam. Where did you grow up?"

He seemed wary, as if uncertain of her motives. "Minneapolis."

"Any siblings?"

"No."

This was going to be like pulling teeth. She needed to ask open-ended questions that would elicit more than one-word responses. Karla tried to stifle a grin. "What was school like for you?"

"Fine."

She sighed. "Which subjects did you like—and *why*?"

"History and math."

When he didn't continue, she coaxed, "Why?"

He drew a deep breath. "History because I liked reading about wars and military campaigns. I figured even as a teenager it was good to learn from past mistakes and not repeat them. Unfortunately, that's easier said than done." He paused a moment, lost in thought, then blinked himself back to the present. "Math because it's like a puzzle, a challenge. I like finding ways to solve problems using predictable mathematical rules that don't change on a whim. The way to the answer is the same yesterday and today as it will be tomorrow."

Ah, so math was safe for Adam. No wonder he enjoyed running the club's business so much. She imagined that skill had served him well in the Marines, too. Procedures. Duty. Code of Conduct.

"Why did you choose to join the Marines and not another branch?"

"Family tradition. There's been a Marine in the Montague family since back to the Civil War when my great-great-grandfather served."

"Wow, that's a long history. I don't think I know what my family did before World War I even."

"Well, sometimes the blood gets watered down through the generations. You have to go further back to find someone to be proud of."

Oh, here we go. Best to avoid his mother at this point, given his nightmare in the hospital. "Tell me about your dad." His body grew rigid, and he went straight on the defensive.

"He was a shi…scumbag. Drank too much. Abused my mother. Is that what you wanted to know about me, hon?"

Had his father abused Adam, too? "Oh, Adam, I'm so sorry you had to go through that. But you aren't your father and you're not responsible for the choices he made. Is that why you don't drink?"

In a flash, he placed his hands around her waist and tried to lift her off his lap. He grimaced in pain at the exertion.

"Don't lift me! You'll hurt yourself. I'll get up."

She scooted off his lap and sat down beside him on the edge of the bed.

"I'm fine." His tensed jaw told her he was in obvious pain, but she watched him stand and make his way toward the door. Why had talking about drinking set him off? "Get some sleep, Karla. I plan to do the same."

But I want to sleep with you, Adam.

"Adam." She waited for him to stop and turn toward her, his hand resting on the doorknob. "You might win this battle with your retreat, but you haven't won the war—and you won't." *I'm the most formidable foe you've ever encountered.* "Run, if you must, but you can't hide from me."

He blinked once, twice, and then turned the knob and left the room, softly closing the door behind him.

Adam Montague, I am going to hunt down all your ghosts, including Joni, and put them to rest so you can get on with your life.

Your life with me.

* * *

Had Karla just declared war on him? Over what—not telling her more about his fucking childhood? Or how his drinking had turned him into the very monster he'd been running from his entire life?

Adam remembered the night he'd gotten drunk with some buddies at the enlisted men's club and scared Joni so badly she'd threatened to leave him if he didn't stop drinking then and there. They'd only been married a few months.

Hell, they were still practically strangers, given how quickly they'd married after meeting. He wasn't even sure what had set him off, maybe her telling him he had to quit drinking. He did remember spanking her, harder than ever before. Not an erotic spanking, but a damned near abusive one. He'd lost control and struck her in anger, something a Dom should never do.

He'd stopped drinking the next day, after he'd sobered up and had seen how hurt Joni was, emotionally, if not physically. He hadn't touched a drop again until after Joni died, when the thought of life without her scared the shit out of him and sent him on a two-week, self-pity drinking binge. In the early years of their marriage, Joni had pulled him back from the brink of disaster. She'd even helped him decide to make his career with the Corps, when he could have just finished his first stint and moved on to something else. She'd sworn she was proud of him for making that decision, but her input had a lot to do with coming to that decision. If she hadn't promised to wait for him, to be there for him no matter what, he probably wouldn't have been strong enough to make the Corps his career.

Adam made his way back to his room, reaching up to rub the back of his neck and finding a new scar from one of the cat bites or scratches. Imagining Karla's delicate skin ripped open by the cat's teeth and claws caused his gut to churn.

The day of the attack, Adam and Marc had left the girls behind with Luke when Angelina told them where to pick up her hogtied ex-boyfriend. Damián hadn't been able to negotiate the steep trail as well and had stayed a little further up the trail. They'd almost met up with Karla's group again when he'd heard Angelina scream, "Karla! Watch out!" His heart had jumped into his throat as he dropped the kidnapper and ran down the trail only to find Karla, scared and pale, pinned against a boulder by a cougar. She'd looked to him to help her. To rescue her.

He'd never get that image out of his head as long as he lived. All he knew to do was to distract the big cat and get it to go after him. It did. Thank God.

He wouldn't have done anything differently on that mountain, but just wished he hadn't added to her hero-worship fixation that had begun when he'd fought off a pimp and his buddies in that Chicago bus station. He'd done what anyone would have done if they'd seen a young runaway in trouble like that.

Adam had a long fucking way to go before reaching hero pay grade. Men had died because of him. Joni had chosen to suffer alone until the very end, rather than ask for him to return from Kandahar. He'd never been able to protect his mother, either.

But Karla just kept getting herself into situations where she needed rescuing. Looking to him to be her hero. Now he'd repaid that trust by doing what? Attacking her himself.

His dick throbbed as he slammed the door and walked over to the bed. *Oh, Christ.* The bloody stain showing the aftermath of his assault on her innocent body stared him in the face. He went to the bed, removed the blanket and comforter and stripped the sheets.

Cold water and soap removes bloodstains.

The voice of his mother invaded his head for the first time in…forever. Damn her, why had Karla made him think about his father and those dark days of his childhood? It was no one's business where he'd come from. He'd left that nightmare behind more than three decades ago and had no desire to dredge any of it up.

He carried the bloodied sheet into the bathroom and scrubbed away the evidence of what he'd done to Karla. So why had she declared war on him? She should *want* him to retreat from her. Why the sudden interest in knowing more about him? About his past? Some things were better left buried.

Adam's mother had been able to protect him when he was young, but as he'd grown older his father's rages had grown more violent. He'd used Adam as a punching bag a couple of nights a week. At least on those nights he wasn't punching on Adam's mom. A new image flashed across his mind. Even though it was there for only an instant, the memory would be imprinted on his brain forever.

Blood.

The floor was covered in blood. Adam's father lay face down on the carpet, his mother lying next to him, shaking uncontrollably, dazed. Adam looked again at his father's lifeless body. This man had pummeled Adam so badly last week his mother had to take him to the emergency room. Now he looked weak, inconsequential, his life's blood draining from a gaping hole in the back of his head—and Adam didn't care.

He looked down at his side and saw the bloodied baseball bat gripped in his hand.

So much blood. What had he done? He let the bat fall from his hand.

Adam's hands began to shake. Instinctively, he knew this wasn't a dream or fiction. Hell, he recognized everyone in the scene. *Jesus fucking Christ.* What had he done? Had he killed his father? Not that the bastard didn't need killing. But how could he have forgotten or blocked out a scene like that?

Is that why he'd been running his entire life?

At some point, he found that the stain on the sheet in his hands was long gone and stopped scrubbing. Twisting the excess water out of the sheet, he wadded it up and tossed it in the hamper, wishing he could discard the bloody memory as easily. He washed his hands, but the blood wouldn't wash away. It never had.

He'd had blood on his hands for thirty-four years.

Too exhausted to make up the bed, he stripped off his shirt and sweats and stretched the top sheet out, easing himself down on the pillow and avoiding getting anywhere near Karla's side of the bed—*Wait.* Karla didn't have a side of the bed. It was *his* fucking bed. *Only* his. That was just the way he intended to keep it.

He covered his eyes with his forearm and tried to force himself to relax. To sleep. After a few minutes, he groaned and wrenched his arm down, pushing himself up as he swung his legs over the side of the bed. The pull of the muscles in his back told him to slow down.

But sleep wasn't going to come, no matter how exhausted he was. Just as well. The long-buried demons had been unleashed and would consume him if he dreamt anymore tonight. They were just too close to the surface. They'd even brought reinforcements this time.

He put his sweats and shirt back on and walked to the French doors, opened one, and stepped out onto the balcony patio. The cold blast of mid-October air shocked him awake, which was just as well. He wanted to feel again, be on full alert for the first time since he'd been attacked on that mountain.

Adam toyed with the idea of getting into the hot tub to release some of this tension under the extreme pressure of the jets, but he'd be damned if he'd risk Karla seeing his old scars, much less the fresh ones. Fortunately, she bought the argument that Marc would be better at cleaning and dressing his wounds, with his Navy corpsman and SAR training, so he'd kept her from seeing them so far.

Standing at the wrought-iron railing, he looked up at the sky but could barely make out a few stars—or maybe they were planets—dimmed by the glow of the city's lights. An ambulance siren sounded in the distance, sucking him right back into the nightmare of that night again.

Adam tried to help his mother up, but she screamed in pain. She'd been injured. He needed to call an ambulance.

"Just bring me the phone. Then take the money in the bureau and leave."

Adam looked at his father again. No sign of life. Dead.
He'd killed his father.
No wonder his mother wanted him gone. He followed her instructions to a T and left.
He ran.

* * *

Watch over him. He needs you.

Sitting up in her bed a short while later, Karla couldn't ignore the voice that had first come to her mind nine years ago. It was a woman's voice, but she didn't recognize her as anyone she'd ever known. No matter. Getting out of bed, she pulled an oversized T-shirt over her nakedness and left the room to cross the hall. She knew what she had to do.

When Adam didn't answer her knock, she eased the door open and her gaze swept the master suite. No Adam. Maybe he'd gone downstairs for something to eat or drink. She should have gotten it for him; some nursemaid she was turning out to be. An image flashed across her mind of Angelina in the sexy nurse's outfit Adam had bought for her two weeks ago, following Marc's explicit instructions in the man's efforts to win back the woman he loved. What would Adam think if she showed up in his bedroom wearing something like that? She giggled as she imagined the strangled look he'd give her—right before he ordered her to go home to Chicago.

Seeing the bed had been stripped of its bottom sheet, her face grew warm. Her virgin blood. She should have been the one to strip the bed and clean it up. Wanting to provide him with clean sheets to sleep on when he came back to bed, she went to the hallway cabinet and pulled a set out. Knowing Adam, he hadn't wanted Marc to see the telltale bloodstains when he came in to check on his friend in a few hours. Good thinking. At least one of them was still thinking clearly.

Standing taller after completing her task, she glanced toward the patio doors and saw the shadow of a tall figure. Her heart jumped into her throat for a moment, until she realized who it was. *Adam.* Where was his coat? Didn't he know it was freezing out there?

She picked up a fleece throw from the back of the glider chair she loved to sit in, usually when Adam was sleeping, and carried it toward the balcony door. The door hadn't been closed completely, so she pushed it open on silent hinges, slipped outside, and closed the door quietly before crossing the expanse of the balcony patio. Adam hadn't acknowledged her presence, but he had to know she was there. He was always on full alert and his pain pills had to have worn off by now. He clearly was ignoring her, just wishing she'd go away.

No such luck, love.

Lord, it was frigid out here. Felt like snow in the air.

Karla placed her hand on his shoulder. In a blindingly fast and fluid movement, he turned and swung his elbow at her temple. Her self-defense training kicked in automatically. Before she realized she'd even moved, she had executed an up block, grabbing his arm in a firm grip, then pushed him against the wrought-iron railing. He winced, causing her to remember too late his wounds. But if she let him go, he might still strike out at her blindly.

"Adam, it's me. Karla."

The glazed look in his eyes scared her, and he continued trying to escape her hold.

Fear. Anger. Disgust.

Her breathing came in short, rapid bursts. "Adam, look at me." When he quit struggling, she relaxed her hold. Both of them struggled to fill their lungs. She reached up to smooth the lines from his forehead.

Slowly, his focus cleared and he reached up to stroke her cheek. "God, woman, don't you know you should never sneak up on a Marine? What are you doing out here?"

He'd called her woman. She smiled.

"I didn't sneak; you were just a million miles away. I didn't want to disturb you, but you need to stay warm. It's freezing out here, and I don't want you to get another infection."

"I'm always too warm. Besides, I don't need a mother hen."

No kidding. What you need is a wife. You need me.

She wanted to wrap the throw across his shoulders, but he was too tall. "Bend over."

"Come again?" He grew rigid and stood even taller, placing his fists on his hips, elbows jutting out, to further intimidate her, as if his six-two frame and broad shoulders didn't already dwarf her five-ten skinny one.

She grinned. "Oh, relax, Adam. I just want to put this around your shoulders to keep you warm."

"I said I'm not cold."

A shiver coursed through her own body, and Adam took the throw from her hands and cocooned her in it instead. Always taking care of her. She decided to take advantage of his nearness and wrapped her arms around him, forcing him to reciprocate to keep the blanket from falling off. She touched the scars on his back through his thin shirt.

"Oh, God, Adam. I didn't hurt you did I?"

"I'd like to see the day when a little thing like you can hurt me, Kitten."

She smiled, but was extra careful to hold onto his lower back, avoiding the bandages. She rested her head against his shoulder. God, it felt so good to be in his arms.

However, he remained tense. She slipped her hand under the loose tail of his shirt and rubbed the hot skin on his lower back. His skin always felt warm, but there was a hot spot just above the base of his spine that felt like an oven.

After the longest moment, his arms tightened around her and he held on tight, as if she were his lifeline.

Trust me, Adam.

"I'm here for you, Adam."

"I didn't hit you, did I?"

"Oh, Adam, quit worrying about me. I'm not made of porcelain. Remember, you made sure this woman could defend herself against anyone who might try to do her harm." In one of his letters after he'd returned from Iraq, he'd insisted she take martial-arts training before she moved to New York to attend college. She wasn't sure if he was more worried about violent thugs on the streets or amorous boys in the co-ed dorms.

"God, if I'd ever hurt you, I...just make your presence known next time, even if you have to hit me over the head."

"Yes, sir."

He tensed. Did he think she was calling him Sir as a Dom? She smiled. Maybe they should talk about that next—but not while she was standing out here freezing. "Let's go inside. I've got your bed all made up. You need to get some sleep."

"I can't sleep."

"Then we'll talk."

Adam held his breath. Ah, so he didn't want to talk either. Too bad, because it definitely was what he needed to do.

"Talk about what?" His defensive tone made her grin, knowing he couldn't see her.

"I'll tell you when I get you inside." She released her hold on him and took his hand, holding the throw together over her breasts with the other, and led him toward the door. The fact that he followed willingly surprised her.

Whether he knew it or not, he needed someone to talk to. He'd been alone with his pent-up emotions for too long.

Inside the room, Adam halted. "Maybe I could catch some shut-eye, after all."

Karla bit the inside of her lower lip to keep from grinning and looked up at him. "Fine. I'm tired, too, but I don't want to be alone right now. I'll join you."

The trapped expression on Adam's face nearly sent her into a fit of laughter, yet she managed to keep herself from gloating over his growing discomfort.

"Look, Karla, I don't think—"

"You aren't going to keep running from me, Adam. Talk or sleep. Either way, with me. Your call."

His gaze went from the empty bed to the armless glider. Yeah, the glider would be less threatening for him, because he didn't know where Karla intended to sit. She took his hand and walked with him to the cushioned glider. "Come on. Sit down. We can start here."

He sat and looked up at her. "We?"

She gave him a moment to sweat, and then sat in his lap.

"I don't think this is a good idea."

"Am I hurting your back?"

"No."

"Well, then, I do. I like sitting in your lap." She'd wanted to do it again ever since he held her on the loveseat in his office when she'd first come to the club. Now she'd sat in his lap twice in one night.

Thoughts of what had brought her here wiped the smile from her face. Adam's hand stroked her back in long sweeping movements. This wasn't supposed to be about her sharing about her past hurts, but a sudden and overwhelming ache lodged in her heart for Ian, her dead brother.

"Does it ever get better?"

"What's that, hon?"

"The pain you feel when you think about someone you've loved and lost."

He wrapped his arm around her and pulled her head against his shoulder. "A little bit. The pain never goes away, but it dulls with time. Just takes a very long time."

Karla laid her hand over Adam's heart to feel it beating, giving her strength. Losing a spouse had to be an even greater loss than losing a sibling. She'd never heard Adam say much about Joni. From what she'd read online about the stages of grief, while trying to cope with her own grief over Ian's death, talking about the loved one was important to help someone get through the process. Was Adam as stuck in the grieving process as she was? Maybe he needed to talk about Joni. He kept so much bottled up inside. That wasn't healthy. "Express, not repress."

"What?"

She must have quoted the movie line out loud. "In one of my favorite movies, *French Kiss*, Kate tells Luc that he needs to express his feelings, rather than repress them and let them fester."

"Chick flick."

"Yeah, but a good one. We'll have to watch it together sometime."

He grunted in a noncommittal way. Somehow she doubted Adam would be into watching it with her. No biggie. She'd rather French kiss him than watch a movie by that title. She suppressed a giggle, but soon sobered as she remembered why she was sitting in Adam's lap.

"Tell me about Joni." His heartbeat sped up. *Don't run from me, Adam. You can do this.* Maybe she should start with something safe. "What did she look like?"

He paused for so long, she didn't think he'd answer. Then he laid his chin on her head, put the glider chair in motion with his foot, and began to open up about the love of his life.

"She was a tiny little thing. Barely five feet tall."

Oh, God. Karla could never make herself petite for him no matter how hard she tried.

"Short curly hair, strawberry blond." Adam stroked Karla's long, jet-black hair. Maybe she could cut her hair short, but she'd never be able to dye it strawberry blonde. She remembered how much her hair had annoyed him when he'd had to tame it before he could bind her hands and arms behind her back in the "gun" rope technique he'd demonstrated at Marc's house. That had been the only time he'd engaged in any BDSM activity with her—so far. She wondered if he'd ever use rope bondage on her again. She hoped so.

"She liked to wear short skirts and had the sexiest legs. That's the first thing I noticed about her."

Well, at least short skirts Karla could manage, but she didn't have a clue if her legs were sexy to Adam or not. "Where did you meet her?"

"I was on a short leave after boot camp and went home to Minneapolis to check on some…thing."

She could feel his heartbeat accelerate again, and he almost stopped breathing. He obviously must still be affected by the memory of how sexy she was. Pain stabbed her heart. Karla might not be strong enough to let him continue reminiscing about the ghostly rival for his affections.

"I found her working as a waitress at a diner in Saint Paul. I guess she could tell I was interested, because she just plopped down in the booth seat next to me to take my order, rubbing her..." He tensed and froze the motion of the chair, lifting his chin from her head and leaving her feeling cold. "We were married a couple weeks later. November eighth."

There was a long pause. Karla couldn't bring herself to ask about Joni anymore, but she didn't want to end this rare, intimate time together. She wanted to know so much about Adam.

Adam cleared his throat. "Tell me about Ian." When she stopped breathing, Adam put the glider in motion again and stroked her arm, up and down in long, slow strokes, keeping time with the motion of the glider. "It does help to talk about them."

Karla had planned to talk with Cassie about her loss of Ian when they'd gone on their annual campout. They'd even planned a fire ritual to help her memorialize him and release some of the pain. The anger. Unfortunately, the cougar attack had put an end to their night on the mountain—and had almost put an end to Adam's life.

"Deep breaths, Kitten. Now."

The use of the nickname he'd used in her bedroom earlier warmed her in places she wasn't used to feeling warm. His hand brushing lightly up and down her arm made rational thought difficult. Knowing he didn't mean anything sexual by it, she pulled her thoughts back to Ian. She needed to let go of her crushing grief. To let go of Ian. Tears filled her eyes and she choked back a sob.

"Oh, God, Adam. I miss him so much. It hurts more every day."

He wrapped his arms around her and pulled her tightly against him. "I know, baby. Just let it out. I have you." The gliding motion of the chair, his arms around her, his soothing words all came together to break down her defenses. She'd tried to be strong, especially when Adam had distanced himself from her.

"What are you thinking, Kitten?"

"Why doesn't it get any better?"

"Just takes time, hon. Give yourself time. The first year is the worst. Lots of anniversaries to get through. Talking helps. Tell me what he was like growing up. Your mom said he got himself into a number of scrapes."

"Yeah. And he was always so mean to me." She giggled and felt Adam grow tense. "He liked to tease me—and I was an easy target, because he always got a rise out of me. You should have heard what he thought of my pink hair."

"Neon pink." Adam shook his head and she heard the smile in his voice. "Most god-awful hair I'd ever seen, too."

"Yeah, well, that's about what he said. You two are a lot alike. I was trying to show I was my own person. He just told me I was a freak."

"Well, I've been called a freak because of the kink I enjoy—but never for pink hair. Definitely different. You sure drew a lot of attention with it."

She didn't want to remember attracting the pimp's attention at the bus station, but maybe her streaks of hair color also had attracted Adam to her. Okay, maybe it wasn't the hair, but her plight. In her predicament, she'd roused his protective instincts.

"I like it better this way." He stroked her hair and butterflies fluttered in her stomach. He liked her hair, even if it was the total opposite of Joni's? She smiled.

"What else did he tease you about?"

"That I liked to wear black clothes all the time."

"Black's fine on you, but you looked really nice in that red blouse at Marc's house."

Adam liked red on her? She didn't imagine Joni would wear red, not with strawberry blonde hair. Karla's heartbeat accelerated a bit. She needed to go shopping.

"How about when you were older?"

"I didn't see much of him after he went into the Army." One of her greatest regrets. "We e-mailed each other a lot while he was in the service."

"You always were a faithful correspondent."

His words made her feel good, because she'd certainly written enough letters to Adam while he was in Iraq—and afterward, too. For almost nine years, they'd written to each other. She returned her thoughts to Ian.

"He changed after the war."

"Most people do after serving in combat."

She wanted him to reveal something more about himself, without seeming too obvious. "In what ways?"

"Too many to name." He paused. "A big one is that some come back with

Post Traumatic Stress Disorder."

"Did you?"

His arm tightened, pressing into her back. "Some. Nightmares mostly. It scared Joni to sleep with me at first when I was home on my medical leave. Sometimes I'd lash out at her. Well, not at her. Not intentionally, at least. I'd just lash out. She just happened to be there." He paused, lost in his memories. "But they're gone now."

No, they aren't, Adam. She stroked his forearm, remembering his yelling for someone to report during one of the nightmares he'd had in the hospital. Marc must have been one of them, because she remembered the name D'Alessio.

"Ian served two tours in Iraq during his enlistment. Then he got out. I was in college by then, so we didn't see much of each other. He was in Chicago and I was in New York. Then he started traveling overseas for some kind of business. Every now and then, he'd show up unannounced at the club or my apartment in New York. I didn't even know he was back in the States the night he was…"

She couldn't say the word, but continued in a whisper, "I miss him so much. Oh, God, it hurts." Karla buried her face into the crook of his neck, breathing in a woodsy scent and Adam.

He held her closer, stroking her hair. "I know. It hurts like hell, hon, but it's only been a few months. I promise you, it'll get easier with time. You can't just blink and expect it to be all better."

Being in Adam's arms sure made it feel better, even if for just a little while.

Safe.

Home.

Chapter Four

Adam could shoot himself for not getting her to open up about Ian more over the last few months. He'd been trying so hard to avoid her, he hadn't been the friend she'd come to Denver looking for when the walls of grief had started closing in on her. He had experienced that same feeling when he decided to retire from the Corps. The walls he'd put up to ignore his grief started caving in right after the firefight in Fallujah. The grief had nearly crushed him before he decided to start the club with Marc. Damián joined in later, also needing a lifeline to hold onto. His friends may not realize it, but they had helped him keep his sanity when the reality of a life without Joni had finally sunk in.

He pulled her closer and stroked her hair. God, he loved her hair. So silky. Like her skin. She reached up to cup his jaw, then lifted her head from his shoulder and turned his face to meet hers.

"Kiss me, Adam." Her breath against his mouth set his dick to throbbing.

"Let's not go there again. If I kiss you, I won't stop." He reached up to brush a strand of hair away from her eyes. "Hon, I care too much about you. I'd just hurt you."

"You could never hurt me. Not intentionally. You're the gentlest man I know."

The unsettling flashbacks he'd experienced earlier jarred him, and he pushed her away, speaking more harshly than he'd intended. "You don't know anything about me."

"I know everything I need to know. Maybe there are a few things you need to learn about me, too, Adam." She sat up straighter, but her gaze never left his. "I *am* an adult—twenty-five."

"Exactly half my age."

"Don't interrupt."

"Yes, ma'am." He grinned in spite of himself. She was so damned sexy when she stood up to him. Everyone else buckled under to his authority, but not Karla. Well, she'd kept her distance from him the last few months, sensing his foul mood, but since he'd awakened to find her lying in his arms in his hospital bed, she'd let him know she wasn't going to take any more evasive shit from him.

Her declaring war on him tonight did nothing but conjure up fantasies of getting her to submit to him when he finally conquered her. He had no doubt he would conquer her, either, if he allowed this to continue—which he had no intention of doing. Karla was strong, but she was no match for him when he was back in top condition. *Fuck.* Even though he didn't want her to submit to him, he couldn't banish the image of Karla kneeling before him, her long black hair covering her bare breasts, waiting to do his bidding. His dick throbbed even more—directly against her ass. She smiled. Damn her.

Damn him. Having her sitting in his lap was no better than having her in his bed. Exponentially worse. At least the bed was king-sized and he could keep her at arm's length. *Yeah, like that worked for you before, shithead.* No, his body deep in sleep had gravitated toward hers earlier, until he'd accosted her in her sleep.

"I know you want me, even if you try to tell yourself you don't."

He looked into her sparkling blue eyes. "You're beautiful, Karla. Any man would be attracted to you. But you need me to be your guardian, not your lover."

"I *want* you to be my lover, Adam, more than anything. I want you to teach me to be your submissive."

"Hell, no."

She pulled back, wrinkling her forehead. "Why not?"

"First of all, I think you might *need* a submissive more than you need to *be* one."

"I loved it when you tied me up. I felt so…free. That doesn't make sense, but that's how I felt."

Hell, it made perfect sense, *if* she were a submissive. She wasn't. Besides, he didn't need to be thinking about tying her up at the moment. The one time he'd done so before, she'd managed to get her claws in too deep under his skin.

"And I've seen some people in the club who top one time and bottom another. Maybe I'm one of those."

"A switch?" The thought of watching her playing Domme with anyone at the club didn't sit well with him either—and no girl would ever top him.

However, the thought of seeing her dominated by anyone else churned his gut. But being her Dom wasn't an image he would entertain either. She had no natural interest in the lifestyle. She only wanted to get close to him because of her damned hero worship—in spite of his doing his damnedest to keep her away.

Except at this moment. What were they talking about again? Her full lips consumed his thoughts as he acknowledged how much he wanted to kiss her right now. Damn it. She'd done it again—short-circuited his brain.

"Adam?"

He returned his focus to her eyes.

"What?" he barked.

"I said maybe I'm a switch."

He needed to put an end to any discussion about bondage, discipline, domination, or submission with Karla pretty damn quick. "You're a singer. That's your role in the club—the only one you need to worry about." Something in her eyes told him she wasn't planning to let the matter drop. Damned stubborn girl. "I think we'd both better try to get some shut-eye, or we aren't going to function very well tomorrow."

His hands spanned her tiny waist, before he remembered he couldn't lift her, so he took her hand and helped her to her feet. Karla then held out her hand to him, but he ignored it and stood under his own steam, even though the effort left his back muscles sore and his legs shaking with the effort. He needed to wean himself off "Nurse Karla" here and get his life back on an even keel. The fleeting image of Karla wearing one of those skimpy nurse's outfits like the one Marc had wanted Angelina to wear for the first costume night at the club this month, right before the cougar attack, sent his dick bobbing inside his sweats.

God, would he ever be able to get his life or his dick back under control, given what had happened earlier tonight? Not fucking likely.

Karla went to his side of the bed and turned down the sheets for him.

"I think I can take it from here, hon. Thank you for taking such good care of me." He reached out and stroked her cheek, until she closed her eyes and leaned her face into his hand. He pulled his hand away quickly.

Keep your fucking hands off her, old man.

Rather than look hurt, she just smiled and walked around the foot of the bed. He expected her to continue toward the door into the hallway. Not Karla. Instead, she surprised him by walking to the other side of the bed, turning down the sheet and blanket, and climbing in.

"Karla, what the f...heck do you think you're doing?"

"Going to bed. I'm exhausted." She smiled again, and he could see where she thought this was headed. Well, not if he had anything left to say about it.

"Go to your own bed."

"I don't want to be alone tonight. You don't mind if I stay here with you? I promise I'll stay on my side."

What was this "my side" shit? Now *she* was saying it?

Without waiting for a response, she pulled the covers over her and curled onto her side, presenting her curvy backside to him. Adam stood and stared a moment. If his strength hadn't been so compromised, he'd have picked her up and carried her to where she belonged. However, the thought of dropping and hurting her put an end to that plan.

He glanced at his side of the bed, not certain what to do. Maybe he should go sleep in her room. That thought wasn't very satisfying. Not that he planned to get any satisfaction—or even sleep—tonight.

"Turn out the light and come to bed, sweetheart."

Sweetheart?

If Karla had declared war on his heart earlier tonight, then she'd just now entered the occupation phase of her campaign. Not just of his bed, but occupation of that cold place inside his chest he'd vowed to never let anyone in. They didn't make tactics charts to deal with this kind of combat.

Maybe he could think more clearly after he'd gotten some sleep. Hell, like he was going to get any sleep with Karla lying a few feet away.

Times like these, he wished he hadn't quit drinking. Or given up those pain pills. He wouldn't get any sleep tonight.

Fuck.

But there was no way he'd let his sleeping body naturally gravitate again toward the warm—and willing—girl lying in his bed. He took the few steps to the nightstand and switched off the light, crawled into bed, and turned onto his side, with his back toward her.

Adam stared at the window, even though it was still pitch black outside. He planned to stay on full alert until she got out of his bed.

* * *

Karla smiled. She was sleeping in Adam's bed—and he knew it this time. He hadn't demanded that she leave, well, not forcefully enough to get her to obey, although he'd clearly wanted her to do just that. Adam's resolve wouldn't always be impaired by the recent ordeal he'd barely survived, so she needed to breach his defenses every chance she could. Perhaps she'd win a place in his life before he would send her back to her parents' home in Chicago.

But he'd said he wasn't going to send her home. She believed him, but if he became too threatened by her, he'd put the walls of resistance up even higher. She'd only managed to break through them this time because he'd been injured and sick. She'd never be able to batter the walls down again unless his body and mind were severely compromised. She shuddered. She'd rather lose him emotionally than to ever have him be that vulnerable again.

Still, she wouldn't be deterred from her mission to win a place in his heart.

She fought to stay alert, in case Adam needed her, but soon her eyelids became too heavy to keep open. She'd just rest them for a minute…

Karla awoke sometime later, shivering from the chill in the air. On her bed across the hall, she had a warm quilt and two blankets. Her body was always cold. Adam's was just the opposite—always warm. Tonight there was only a blanket and a thin comforter over them, not enough to keep her warm at all.

She turned over to find Adam's back to her, moonlight streaming across his body from the skylights. His massive back and muscular arms strained against the black T-shirt he wore. The sound of his rhythmic breathing told her he must be sleeping. Maybe if she just moved a little closer, without touching him, she could benefit from his body's built-in heater. Careful not to disturb him, she rolled over very gently onto her other side, but still found a wide gap between hers and Adam's bodies.

Too far to feel his warmth, she scooted herself toward him until she began to feel the warmth emanating from his back and legs. The urge to reach out and run her hand along his arm had to be quelled, along with the intense desire to get him to turn toward her. To kiss her. Okay, clearly she hadn't thought this plan through to its logical conclusion. To be so close and not be able to caress him was torture.

If he didn't need his sleep so badly, she would have pressed herself against him. Instead, she filled her lungs with a slow, deep breath—just the kind Adam always urged her to take when he needed to calm her down. His woodsy scent filled her nostrils. Her skin grew warmer. Talking with Adam tonight had filled a hole in her heart she hadn't even been aware was there. She wanted so much to get to know him better, to share secret hopes and dreams. Did Adam even have dreams for himself anymore? He'd been married so long and had lost his wife to cancer. He'd served his country about twenty-five years, making a career of the Marine Corps. Now he seemed content to run his private kink club and live for the friends he'd brought into his life through the club. But he was only fifty years old. Surely he still had goals to achieve, activities to experience, places to see.

"Karla?"

Her heart tripped over itself as the whisper of her name hung on the early-morning air. She whispered back, "Yes, Adam?"

She watched his shoulders rise and fall with some slow, deep breaths of his own. Then he turned onto his back, now just inches from her. She remembered that military men didn't sleep very soundly. Once, when she'd gone in to wake Ian for breakfast in her loft apartment in the city, he'd nearly jumped out of the bed and tackled her when she'd touched his arm.

Thoughts of Ian put a damper on her libido and brought tears to her eyes. Without waiting for an invitation, she took Adam's wrist, lifted his arm, and burrowed against his warm skin, laying her head against his shoulder. Her cheek rested on his pectoral, and she wrapped his arm around her. How could something as simple as lying against him make her feel so safe?

"What's wrong, hon?"

She shook her head, not wanting to talk about Ian anymore. "Just hold me, Adam." He didn't hesitate and wrapped his other arm around her, pulling her closer.

"I'm here, Kitten."

She was becoming accustomed to the sweet endearment he'd begun calling her. But how long would he be here for her? How far would he allow their relationship to go?

Did they even have a relationship?

* * *

Adam hadn't woken up to find a woman in his bed in nearly a decade. Now, with Karla, it was becoming a regular occurrence. Why was he finding it so damned enjoyable, when the last thing he wanted was a relationship with her?

He stroked her arm, comforting her from whatever thoughts had disturbed her sleep this morning. He couldn't believe he'd fallen asleep. When he'd woken to feel her moving toward him, he'd expected another assault on his senses, but none had come. Now why did he regret that?

He'd be glad when he was one-hundred percent strong again. He and

Karla had turned a major page tonight. Retreat may no longer be an option. So now what? Hell, she was half his age. What would her parents say if they knew he'd slept with their daughter?

Hell, not only slept with her, but taken her virginity as well.

Fuck, fuck, fuck.

Nine years ago Thanksgiving morning, they'd taken him in. This past summer, they'd trusted him to watch out for their daughter when she'd come running to him in Denver.

She reached out to stroke his chest. "Are you in pain?"

Only around my heart.

"I'm fine."

"Would you admit it to me if you *were* in pain?"

He smiled. "Hell, no."

"I didn't think so." Her fingers traced the USMC lettering on his T-shirt, bumping into his hard nipple. "Maybe you'll feel like coming downstairs today. Angelina's been dropping by and whipping up the most wonderful meals. And Cassie's promised a Peruvian feast when you're feeling better. You need to start eating more."

"Damned pills killed my appetite, but I'm through with them."

"I hate to see you in pain, Adam. Please take one if you need to."

She took her thumb and brushed the nail against his hard nip. His hard-on grew even stiffer. Taking her hand, he moved it away from his pec and laid it on his upper abs.

Her hand slipped from his grasp and moved over his abdomen, then further south. His dick throbbed even more.

"Karla, you're heading into dangerous territory."

"I've never been one to play it safe, Adam. I just don't want to go there alone."

Why he didn't stop her, he couldn't say. When her tiny hand wrapped around his dick, his hips raised up to welcome her.

"You want me, Adam. Admit it."

"Every man wakes up with a hard-on. It's natural."

Her hand froze and she pulled away. Her body stiffened against him. He hated that he'd hurt her feelings again, but her little exploration needed to stop. Now. He couldn't let her know how much she turned him on, because he wasn't about to allow things to go too far this time—or ever again.

"Teach me about being a submissive."

Again? He thought they were talking about his woody. "We've been over this before. You aren't submissive."

"Try me."

"No."

"Why not?"

He sighed. "Because, when I see your parents at Thanksgiving, I want to do so knowing I didn't introduce you to my world of debauchery." There. That ought to make her stop and think a minute. When Karla had shown up at his club and he'd called Carl and Jenny to let them know she was okay, he'd promised he'd bring her home for Thanksgiving if she was still working here. The thought of sharing the meal with them knowing he'd debased their daughter didn't sit well with him now. It would only get worse if he continued.

Now maybe she'd lay off him about BDSM and let him go back to keeping his distance from her—emotionally and physically.

Karla began to giggle, which only made him stiffer, if that were possible. Soon she was laughing so hard her breasts jiggled against his chest, causing his balls to tighten.

"What's so damned funny?"

"You."

Ah, just what every man dreamed of, having a sexy woman lying in his arms laughing hysterically—at him. The very least he wanted to know was what she found so fucking funny.

She reached up and stroked his cheek. "The apple doesn't fall far from the tree."

What apple? Whose tree? "Come again?"

"I came home from college a day early for Thanksgiving my sophomore year to surprise Mom and Daddy. I didn't find them downstairs, so I checked upstairs. I didn't have the nerve to knock on the door when I heard what definitely sounded like moans of passion and what I now know was a flogger, thanks to the education I've gotten here at the club. I just knew from the sounds Mom was making that whatever was going on in there was none of my business, so I snuck back out of the house and froze my ass off for an hour before 'arriving home' again."

Jenny? Submissive? If that were true, then he'd have to concede that maybe...

Karla smiled, then whispered, "Try me, Adam. No, even better, *tie* me. I want you to tie me up again."

"Karla…"

"If you won't, I'll ask Damián to train me for you."

Like hell. He'd have to have a talk with Damián ASAP to make sure he didn't touch her. She wasn't going to coerce Adam—topping him from the bottom and trying to control or direct him. If she wanted him to be her Dom, he'd…

How could he convince her she didn't want anything to do with this? She might want him to restrain her with ropes, but he was certain submission wasn't a deep-seated need for her. It wouldn't take long for her to realize that.

Well, maybe he just needed to speed up the process a bit—to show her how much she'd hate taking orders, even from him. Sure, she liked restraints, but she hadn't experienced a punishment yet. Hell, if she'd seen the orgasm-torture demonstration he'd done on Grant in the medical theme room at the club—showing an inexperienced Dom his technique for multiple, back-to-back forced orgasms—she'd change her naïve view of BDSM. All she ever saw was what went on in the great room while she was performing.

Remembering how pissed Grant had been, he'd have to make sure he didn't mess around when it came to restraining Karla for such a session. Grant would have kicked the shit out of his balls and dick if she hadn't been strapped to the table as well as she had been. He valued his private anatomy and his life too much to mess with her. But Karla also had some serious martial-arts training before college, judging by her moves earlier on the patio.

What he needed to do was make being a submissive sound like the most onerous thing in the world to her so she wouldn't want to have anything to do with pursuing a BDSM relationship with him. He knew exactly how to do that.

Adam grinned. Hell, when he was finished spelling out the details of his proposition, she'd steer clear of any Dom who ever came near her in the future looking for a sub.

* * *

Karla waited, her fingers playing with his nips. God, they were hard. She wanted to remove his shirt, bend over, and bite one, but didn't want to break his train of thought. Was he going to let Damián train her? She hoped not, because it would be extremely uncomfortable for her to submit to a man who wasn't much older than she was. Someone she thought of as more of a brother.

"You will address me as Sir, Master, or Master Adam at all times."

Karla's heart throbbed in her ears. He was agreeing to train her? Wow.

Where had that come from?

Who cared? She smiled.

"Yes, Sir."

"If I tell you to jump, the proper response would be 'How high, Sir?'"

Adam wouldn't ask her to do anything she didn't want to do. Besides, she could do anything for the short-term. How long did scenes last? An hour or two at most? The thought of having Adam's focus on her for that long sent a thrill through her body.

"Yes, Sir." Her breathy whisper sounded sexy even to her ears. She hoped it sounded that way to him, too.

"I will tell you when and what to eat, when to dress, what to wear, when and where to kneel, sit, lie, or stand. You will focus all of your time and energy on pleasing me because, as a submissive slave, meeting your Master's needs and wants is the only thing that will bring you pleasure and satisfaction."

What did he say? "Slave, Sir?" Wait a minute. Who said anything about slave? She just wanted to play at being submissive. More to the point, she just wanted to play with Adam.

"Yes, what I'm proposing is a Master/slave arrangement, which is what I had with my wife for a number of years."

A shaft of coldness ran through her at the mention of his dead wife. The woman had agreed to that kind of relationship for *years*? Was she some kind of doormat?

"It'll be twenty-four/seven. In the lifestyle, this is known as a Total Power Exchange, or TPE. A slave's main purpose and duty is to be faithful and obedient to her Master and respectful of her Master at all times. You'll make no decisions for yourself. Everything you do, think, say, feel, eat, wear, etc., will be my responsibility and require my approval. You will respond to my every command without question and will learn to look for ways to please me once you know more about what I enjoy. In addition to what I've already said, I also will tell you when to wake, when to sleep, who you can talk to, and what topics of discussion are permitted, when and how to service my sexual appetites and any other needs I want serviced, including housekeeping, yard work, running errands, and so on. I will even have to approve your song list at the club. In other words, I will be in control of everything about you—all day, every day— as long as the agreement is in effect."

Karla's heart pounded in her ears. Total submission? Slavery? The words had such negative connotations. Was he for real? How could anyone agree to live like that? How could he *want* her to agree to that? She thought he liked that she stood up to him, well, to a point.

He reached over and pinched her nipple until she gasped. "Your body will be my sexual toy to do with as I wish. You will become disciplined in pleasing me and I will take corrective measures until you learn to do so. If you willfully disobey me, you will be punished. I will let you express your hard limits and, if I am in the right mood, won't exceed them—right away. But, as your Master, it will be my pleasure to push your limits fast, hard, and often."

Back up. What did Adam mean by punished? She shivered at the images of some of the things she'd seen in the great room at the club—everything from severe whippings to hot wax dripped where it didn't belong to public humiliation. Yet, images of being bound again with ropes, the way he'd done at Marc's, caused her to grow wet. She hoped he wanted to do more of that.

"If there's something I'd like you to do, may I ask?"

"No. You'll learn to like whatever I tell you to like."

Whoa! Did he just say what she thought he'd said? Angie talked about communication being the key. Negotiation. The submissive held the control in the relationship. But that didn't sound at all like what Adam was proposing. He wasn't even going to listen to her, take her preferences into consideration?

"How will you know what I like?"

"I repeat—you'll like whatever I tell you to like."

Had Joni been like this for Adam? Is that what turned him on? Maybe that's why Karla hadn't gotten him to notice her in all these months. She was too strong-willed. She'd thought he admired that.

She'd only ever seen him engaging in rope-bondage scenes with Mistress Grant in the great room. Adam certainly didn't demand total submission from that Marine, as if he could get it from the kick-ass Domme. Karla had just assumed that meant he was attracted to strong women, like Grant, even though she'd been his subordinate in Iraq.

Of course, he did scenes with some of the bottoms at the club, as did all of the Masters at Arms owners. It was one of the membership perks and brought in unattached members, which made it easier for other members to find new partners. But she didn't observe those scenes that often took place in the private theme rooms used to fulfill various fantasies. Who knew what happened in there? Besides, if it involved Adam being with some other lucky sub or bottom, she'd certainly had no desire to watch.

Could Karla become a slave for Adam? She took a deep breath and looked up at him. His moss-green eyes stared back. No hint of a smile. No crinkle in the lines at the sides of his eyes. He wasn't joking. How could she give up all of her freedom and personality to become that...subservient?

His intense gaze bore into her, sending a strange warmth spreading throughout her. How could she not? This might be her only chance to get Adam to teach her what he loved so much about this lifestyle. Short of selling her soul, there was a lot she could withstand, especially if it would help him see that she was the perfect woman for him. Of course, the thought of a lifetime gig where she had to perform as the perfect slave, well, no deal.

But maybe she could learn to like some of it, if this was what made Adam happy.

"I could try being your slave, Sir."

His body tensed. Surprised? Had he just been testing her? Well, clearly he had no idea how much she wanted him.

And Karla had no idea what she was getting into, but wasn't there always a choice in BDSM? If she couldn't do it, she could safeword, couldn't she? Then again, maybe she'd better make certain, because she'd never spoken to anyone before about becoming a slave.

"What if I need to stop? Call it off at some point? You won't really own me. I mean, this *is* the 21st Century, after all... Right?"

"Yes, Kitten, you can safeword if you decide it's too intense. That will put an end to the arrangement."

She wasn't sure she wanted to know the answer to this question, but had to ask. "If I safeword, then what about the relationship?"

"Relationship isn't the right word for what we'll have. This is a TPE arrangement between two consenting adults who want to explore the Master/slave dynamic." He made it sound like some kind of adult-education course, only what she'd be learning from Adam was much more adult than anything those schools had ever listed in their curriculum.

"I'm not offering anything other than a Master/slave arrangement. If you safeword, then it ends."

So, it was slave or going back to what they had before—which was nothing.

Karla pulled out of his arms. When she turned back to look down at him, she thought there was a bit of a smirk on his lips, as though he'd won some battle. She knelt beside him, resting her butt on her heels, keeping her back straight. She held her hands palm upward on her thighs, as she'd seen countless subs do in the club, and cast her gaze down upon them.

"I am your willing slave, Master Adam."

She fought the urge to look him in the eye, but didn't think that would be allowed. Dear Lord, how was she supposed to learn the rules for something like this? Did they have tutorials or books available? Maybe she could go online or seek out a slave at the club to answer her questions. But how would she know which were slaves and which were just subs, or even bottoms just out to play slave girl for the night?

"Eyes on me."

Ka-thunk!

The sensation of having her stomach drop into her pelvis caused her heart rate to speed up. His commanding voice definitely excited her. She lifted her gaze to meet his.

"Are you sure about this, Karla? There's no going back to what we were, once we make this commitment."

Thank the gods, Sir. She never wanted to go back there. She wanted to move forward. To be in a relationship with Adam, no matter how difficult the transition and learning curve might be. As long as she and Adam were happy, who cared what anyone else thought?

"Yes, Sir. I'm sure."

Chapter Five

What the fuck did she mean she was sure? She couldn't want this any more than he did. Did she even have a fucking clue what she was getting into with a TPE, a Master/slave arrangement? Karla, as his willing slave? *Bullshit.* Karla didn't kowtow to anyone—man or woman.

"Sir, may I speak?"

Fuck, fuck, fuck. What had he just gotten himself into? He remembered those early days after Joni had asked him to be her Master. Disciplining her in the ways of a slave, he'd watched her lose herself and her autonomy in the bargain. He'd never quite understood why she'd wanted to go to that extreme in the first place. It had killed something inside him, too. After a couple of months, he'd slacked off on the rules a bit to make it more palatable for himself. Luckily, she'd still gotten whatever it was she needed from giving up control like that.

Joni, at least, was submissive to the core. But Karla?

"Sir?"

"Speak." She flinched at his tone. *Fuck.* Did he have the energy for this?

"This is totally new for me. Could we start training right away? And will you be patient with me until I get the hang of it?"

Damn. Why did she have to take to this so enthusiastically? His cock throbbed as he looked at Karla kneeling on the bed beside him, her breasts pressed against her thin T-shirt, nipples erect and poking against the fabric. How was he supposed to train her as his slave and not want to take her to bed? But that was on *his* list of hard limits. No sex with Karla.

"Choose your safeword." The sooner he could get her to safeword and end this arrangement, the better it would be for them both.

She furrowed her brows, whether from confusion or worry, he wasn't sure. He waited.

"I've never really thought about having one before, Sir."

"Why don't you use red, then? Red like the stop light or stop sign." Red for stop this asinine arrangement.

Her smile wavered, but she nodded. "Yes, Sir. Red will be fine."

"Remove your T-shirt."

Fuck. Where had that come from? He wanted to rescind the command as soon as the words left his lips, then found his gaze riveted to her hands, waiting for them to move, to do his bidding. Maybe he wanted to see how much she'd take before she safeworded. She sat upright, off her heels. He relaxed. *Good girl.* She'd come to her senses and was going to leave now. At least one of them still had their wits about them. This hadn't turned into the total clusterfuck he'd imagined a few moments ago when she'd agreed to be his slave, of all things.

Fuck, no. As if in slow motion, her slender fingers wrapped around the hem of her thigh-length shirt, and he watched as she slowly pulled the tee up, exposing her sexy thighs, the springy black curls of her mons—*Her naked mons? Shit!*—on up to her flat abdomen. His dick bobbed. She continued to lift the shirt until her pert young breasts bounced free of its confines. Sweat broke out on his forehead as his heart hammered hard. In oh-so-painful slow motion, she continued to strip until she'd pulled the shirt over her head and discarded it onto the bed beside her.

Adam stared up at her, watching her nipples grow even more erect than they had been under the shirt, whether from the cold morning air or because she was as excited as he was, he didn't know or care.

"Straddle me."

He would go straight to hell for this, but he couldn't shut his fucking mouth if he wanted to. Maybe he still thought he could send her running to safety.

Maybe he didn't want her to run.

She smiled. *Fuck.* Before he realized he'd started to move, he'd slid over half a foot from the edge of the bed to give her room for her right knee. He needed to touch her again. Just his hands. He wouldn't let it go too far. No way. Her thighs clamped against his sides like a vise, her pussy pressing against his dick, and all control fled from his mind. Adam reached up and spanned her tiny waist, then let his hands roam up her sides until he cupped her firm, high breasts.

Sweet Jesus.

She reached down and touched his nips. "Stop. I didn't give you permission to touch me." He hated the look of uncertainty that crossed her face, but if she touched him like that, he'd be on top of her in no time, driving his dick...

When his erection throbbed against her ass, she smiled. What the fuck was he doing? Had there been a point to asking her to straddle him? Hell, he'd thought she'd run for the door and hide in her bedroom. Why was she following his commands like this?

Why were his hands squeezing her tits? Pinching her nipples?

Jesus.

* * *

Karla moaned as Adam pinched her nipples. Straddling him gave her a sense of power, but she'd quickly learned who was in control. Learning what she could and couldn't do was going to be a challenge, but she was a fast learner. Rule Number One: Touching him was out, unless he gave her permission.

Training to be his sex slave wasn't going to be the easiest thing she'd ever done, but she might as well face it—nothing about Adam had ever been easy. Then again, the slave role certainly eliminated the guesswork. For someone so new to sex, being a slave relieved the pressure of trying to figure out how to please him. She could just wait for him to tell her what he wanted.

She didn't have to wait long.

"Lean over me and prop your elbows on the headboard."

Bending at the waist, she reached out and grabbed the headboard with her hands, then positioned her elbows along the top of the wood. Her breasts dangled over Adam's mouth, and he lifted his head off the pillow and took one nipple and areola into his mouth.

Heat! Breath hissed from Karla's throat like a steam vent. *Oh, Lord.* Her pussy clenched and she wiggled against his erection. His mouth broke away as he growled.

"Do. Not. Move. Not unless I give you an explicit command. Do you understand?"

She gulped air into her lungs. "Yes. Yes, Sir."

His teeth latched onto her other breast and he nipped at the peak. "Ahhh!" His hand brushed the sensitive side of her breast as he cupped her almost reverently. But his mouth was anything but reverent as it ravaged her—nipping, sucking, licking.

"Oh, Adam! Yes!" Biting. "Ow!" He pulled away again, and she groaned. "What did I do now?"

"How do you address me, Kitten?"

Karla didn't even remember speaking. "Sir or Master."

"Don't forget it, or I'll find creative ways to help you learn discipline. To remember. I'll do the same if you move again without permission."

"Yes, Sir." Karla just wanted him to suck on her breasts again. *Please, Sir!*

Adam's teeth grazed her left nipple, and then tightened around it, pulling as he lowered his head. She gasped and fought the urge to curve her back to relieve the tension. *Don't move. You don't have permission to move.* When she thought she'd break out in a sweat, he released her and her breast sprang back, then dangled above him once more like an apple on a tree.

"Good girl."

Adam's praise made her smile and a strange heat spread throughout her. She'd pleased him. She waited for another command.

"Your breasts are so beautiful. I know just how to bind them." Her nipples tightened at the thought. "I see that excites you."

"Yes, Sir. I'd like that." Her words came out on the breath of a whisper. When would he put her in rope bondage again? Soon, she hoped, but he hadn't given her permission to ask questions. She'd just have to be patient. Having gotten this far with him was more than she'd dreamed of a few hours ago.

"You do enjoy the embrace of the rope, don't you?"

She sighed. "Very much, Sir."

"Tonight, then. Right now, I want you to go to your bedroom."

Karla couldn't hide her disappointment. He was sending her away? Earlier, when she'd laid siege to his bed, she could just ignore his command. If she was going to be his slave, she needed to obey him. Even when the order pissed her off, like now. How could he leave her waiting and wanting like this?

"Sit up." She did. His hands cupped her breasts once more, but regret shone in his eyes. He spanned her waist and strained as he lifted her off his lap and set her beside him on the bed. She knelt as she had earlier, hands in her lap. "I want you to wear one of your band T-shirts and black jeans today. No corsets or bustiers except when I ask you to wear them in the bedroom or on stage."

"Yes, Sir." She thought he'd found her sexy clothing hot, but apparently not.

"For tonight's Shibari session, you'll wear a blouse and skirt—something loose and frilly—and a bra and thong."

She nodded. That sounded a little sexier at least.

"You are not to talk to anyone about our new arrangement."

"Not even Cassie?" Adam scowled, and she added a hasty, "Sir?"

"Especially not Cassie. She won't understand. It would freak her out."

That was an understatement, but Karla wasn't sure *she* understood the arrangement herself, so maybe it was best she didn't try to explain it to her best friend. Still, surely Cassie would see the change, if Karla went all docile and obedient out of the blue.

"We'll need to communicate silently when others are around. For permission to begin eating, raise your fork or spoon and look at me for my nod; same with your glass, when you want to drink. You'll never begin eating before I do, however."

"Yes, Sir." She'd have to think about every movement she made, it seemed. Well, that's certainly what he'd laid out for her—what she'd agreed to do. "Do I need permission to breathe, Sir?"

Master Adam reached out and smacked her ass cheek with the open palm of his hand, the sound like the crack of a whip. "Don't be insubordinate." Her ass still stung when he reached out and picked up her T-shirt. "Put this on and go to your room. I'll meet you in the kitchen in twenty minutes. Make breakfast for whoever shows up. Marc will be here to pester me about my back soon, I'm sure."

Karla looked out the window and saw daylight. When had the sun risen? She'd been so focused on Adam, she hadn't noticed.

"I plan to be dressed and out of bed before Marc gets here so he'll lay off me with the Doc shit from now on. It's gone way beyond getting old."

Karla smiled. Adam definitely was on the mend.

"Yes, Sir. Would you like your slave to help you get dressed, Sir?"

His eyes opened a little wider before he scowled again. "I can dress my damned self. Now, go do the same."

Karla hid her grin until she had scooted off the bed backward and turned away from him. She would definitely have to find ways to push the envelope with this slave role. For some reason, she didn't think he'd expected her to take to it. Well, she was going to be the best slave he'd ever had.

Even better than Joni.

She hoped.

* * *

Later that evening, Karla walked down the hallway, past the theme rooms, and into the club's great room where Adam had told her to wait for him. For tonight, based on his instructions, she'd chosen to wear a black-lace bra and thong panties under a see-through red blouse with a long wrap-around skirt. Loose and frilly, just the way he'd ordered.

Thank God Cassie was in her room working on sketches tonight, because Karla would die if Cassie happened upon her in a slave scene with Master Adam. Not much was private in a BDSM club, she'd learned since being hired here. She'd also seen Cassie's odd glances in her direction at the dinner table when Karla had cursed under her breath the times she'd messed up by not looking to Adam for permission before starting to eat or drink at the beginning of the meal.

She'd hoped Cassie didn't think she was cursing her wonderful native meal, though. The pork loin was tender and juicy and the spicy rice such a treat. It seemed everyone could cook like a pro, except her. Now cooking was one of the duties Master Adam expected of her. Did he even have a clue what he was going to get as a result?

But she needn't worry about being seen here by Cassie. Her sexually repressed friend wouldn't be caught dead in this part of the house, even on nights like tonight when everything was quiet. Karla looked at the dark, empty stage. She'd missed several performances while Adam was recovering but figured she'd be up there again tonight. Fridays were their busiest nights.

Now, however, the room was quiet. Karla's heart pounded as she anticipated having Master Adam's warm, strong hands on her again. Where should she wait? Should she kneel, sit, stand? There were so many things she wasn't sure about in pleasing him as a slave. She really should have asked more questions, and wished Adam was more forthcoming about what he wanted and expected.

Kneel for him.

The voice in her head was becoming quite familiar, and at the moment it gave her the direction she needed. She looked around the room and decided the rope station would be the logical place to wait. She crossed to the darkened corner where a large steel ring looking like the ones used by male gymnasts was suspended from a ceiling beam.

Nearby, several short wall shelves held a number of various-hued ropes of multiple thicknesses. Hanging from the bottom shelf was a black curtain. The rope didn't look scratchy like twine or some other types of rope might be, but soft and silky looking instead. To test her observation, she couldn't resist reaching out and touching one of the bundles. Soft and silky, indeed. Her nipples grew tighter just thinking about the rope against her skin.

Would Adam bind her over her blouse or ask her to strip? The Shibari-demonstration videos on the internet usually involved clothed women. She'd find out soon enough. Knowing her Master would be here at any moment, she walked over to the large, square cushioned pad on the floor underneath the dangling ring. She'd observed subs in "the position" often enough in the club—head down, gaze on the floor in front of her, hands on her thighs. She knelt and posed for him. Perfect. She hoped.

She hoped her Master would find her position pleasing. What if a slave was supposed to pose differently than a sub?

The time stretched out, and she wondered if he would see her kneeling here in this dark corner. Nervous, she glanced up and across the great room to find Master Adam standing near the center post, staring at her. He wore shiny black leathers and a black vest, his muscled chest otherwise bare.

Ka-thunk! She could see from the bulge in the front of his leathers that he liked what he saw and felt a warm glow seep into her bones. Without meeting his gaze, she returned hers to the floor in front of her.

And waited.

Why didn't he come over to her? Was she doing something wrong? Insecurity assailed her; her confidence drifted away. Pleasing Master Adam was all she'd ever wanted to do. But what if she couldn't be what he wanted?

Please, Sir. Accept me as I am.

His body's warmth reached her first. He knelt behind her on the mat and his arms came around her. His large hands cupped her breasts as he nuzzled her neck. "I told you to wait for me here, but I didn't give you permission to kneel. You were to wait for my instructions."

But the voice…oh yeah, tell him you're hearing voices, Kitty.

She'd displeased him, even though she hadn't meant to. "I'm sorry, Sir. I'll do better next time."

"Yes, I'm sure you will." He trailed kisses down the column of her neck. "But it's fucking hard for me to be upset when you looked so beautifully submissive kneeling here for me. When I came into the room and saw you there, waiting gracefully for me… Well done, Kitten. Thank you."

His mixed messages threw her off guard, but he seemed pleased now and that's all that mattered. Karla's head leaned back and rested against his chest, giving him easier access to her neck and breasts.

"Remove the blouse."

Here we go.

With shaking hands, she straightened her spine again, pulling away from his warmth with reluctance. He didn't remove his hands from her breasts so she began unbuttoning the blouse from the bottom. When her hands met his, he released her breasts and unfastened the first two buttons for her. His wrists brushed against her erect nipples, causing them to grow even more rigid. He opened the blouse and cool air hit her skin; her nipples puckered with need. Before she could finish removing the blouse, his hands moved up again to cup the undersides of her lace-covered breasts. Warm fingers and thumbs latched onto the hard peak, squeezing hard.

"Ahh!" The sensation sent all thought fleeing from her mind. *More.* Her head lolled back against him and he bent down to nuzzle her neck once more. His beard stubble abraded her tender skin and sent bolts of electricity to her clit. The pulse in her neck beat so strongly, surely he could feel it against his lips.

His right hand released her nipple and glided down over her flat abdomen and the filmy skirt. He found the opening flap of the wrap-around skirt, and his hand slid between her thighs as he moved up to the juncture where she grew even wetter. Karla held her breath. When his fingers came into contact with the bit of fabric barely covering her pussy and clit, she gasped. *Touch me there.* Instead, he followed the wide lace waistband to the thin thong strap in the back.

"Good girl."

Did he think she wouldn't follow his instructions? "Thank you, Sir." The breathy sound of her voice sounded seductive. She enjoyed being sexy for her Master.

"Keep the skirt and thong on."

"Yes, Sir."

"Let's lose the blouse and bra, though." He placed her arms at her sides and pulled the blouse further open, sliding the sleeves down and off her arms. The feel of the warm silk and firm fingers against her skin sent a shiver up her spine. She glanced up and was surprised to find their reflection on a wall mirror she hadn't noticed before. Ah, the curtain below the shelf had been moved aside to reveal a mirror. He brushed her hair aside and unhooked her bra, tugging on a loose strand of hair. He left the scrap of lace hanging from the straps as his warm hands slid around her and under the lace to cup her bare breasts. She hissed when he pinched her nipples again.

"I love touching your tits, Kitten."

"Your kitten loves to have her tits touched by you, Sir." Her face grew red at speaking of herself in third-person and using a word like tits, but she smiled anyway. She'd read online that slaves often referred to themselves this way. She and her breasts—or tits—were his property now.

She hoped he was pleased with her body. Her breasts weren't overly large, but oh-so-sensitive when he touched her now, as if he'd awakened them or something. She loved that he loved having his hands on them.

Master Adam released his hold and stood behind her, then went to the shelves where she'd seen the bundles of colorful rope. She waited. Warmth enveloped her; he'd turned on a space heater.

"Rope bondage is hard for someone who's cold, and you seem to be cold-natured, so I placed a space heater here to keep you warm. Let me know if you're too hot or too cold."

"Yes, Master. Thank you." That he had thought about her comfort pleased her, too. He wasn't only concerned about what he would gain from their scene. She'd seen some postings online from some egomaniacal Masters who got into humiliating their slaves and treating them like objects, but Master Adam didn't seem that way at all.

A few moments later, he knelt behind her again and dropped several rope bundles onto the mat beside her thigh. She resisted the urge to turn and look at them, but red and blue ones were visible out of the corner of her eye.

"Hold your hair up out of the way." Once again, he sounded annoyed about her hair, just as he had been at Marc's house. Maybe she needed to consider cutting it. Only now she would have to ask for Master Adam's permission. Her hair was his, too.

She reached up to do as he instructed, and he surprised her by reaching around in front of her, holding a black leather collar lined with sheepskin fur. A dog collar? She blushed at being treated like a pet, but she supposed that's what she was now. His toy. His pet.

His kitten.

But she didn't want him to treat her like a baby anything. She'd been trying to get him to see her as a woman all this time and now she was just doing whatever he told her, like a good little kitten. A child.

He placed the collar around her neck. "This is a playtime collar. The D-rings on it can be useful for bondage, and the collar is a reminder to you that you're my pet. My plaything." His hands wrapped around her collar, fingers on either side sliding inside and pulling it away from her skin.

"That isn't too tight, is it?"

"No, Sir."

"Good." His hands slid to her shoulders and he eased the bra straps down her arms, his calloused hands gently abrading her skin. He tossed the scrap of lace aside. She felt exposed and vulnerable until Adam's hands reached around her again, so warm against her cool skin.

"I can't keep my fucking hands off your tits."

Karla smiled at his earthy language. A sense of power came over her. Master Adam saw her as a woman at last. Her nipples reached out to greet the pads of his palms.

He tugged her hair from her grip and let it cascade over her shoulders and back. "I also love touching your hair."

A burst of pride welled up inside her. He liked her hair?

Then his fingers splayed out, his palms covering her ears as his fingertips brushed upward across cheeks and into her hairline. He raked his fingertips over her scalp, massaging her with a firm, gentle touch. The muscles in her legs and back gave out; she slumped against his body for support.

He chuckled.

Her clit throbbed as he continued his sensual massage of her scalp. Who knew this was an erogenous zone for her?

Master Adam.

She moaned.

"That's right, Kitten. Surrender to your Master, completely."

I did that long ago, Sir.

After several more minutes, he began finger-combing her curls, from her scalp to the ends of her tresses. He fanned the long strands over her shoulders and breasts. She continued to lean against him, as if she could have moved if she'd wanted to. Why did she always melt like butter on a hot stove when he touched her?

"Clasp your hands behind your lower back, just above your ass."

The abrupt command sent her erotic nerve-endings back on full alert. She straightened her back yet again and did his bidding.

He released her and picked up a red-dyed bundle of rope, unwrapping it and finding the ends. She lifted her butt off her heels and knelt taller for him, her breasts jutting out, erect and proud. She watched in the mirror as he shook out the strands of red rope, preparing to begin binding her.

Instead, he took the strands, threading them between his fingers, and rubbed the cold rope and his warm hands over her bare breasts. The sensual feel of the rope, along with the pressure of his hands, elicited a moan from deep within her throat. This was so different from the demonstration at Marc's house. For one, her breasts were bare this time. But he seemed to be spending so much more time preparing her.

"That's right, Kitten. Embrace the rope."

"Yes, Master," she whispered. Her heartbeat fluttered. Waiting. Wanting. Needing.

"Breathe, baby." Master Adam's voice reminded her of the need for oxygen. She took a deep, relaxing breath. He continued to rub the rope over her breasts, abdomen, mons, even pressing it against her thong-covered clit and pussy, causing a delicious friction there that sent heat radiating throughout her body. Her breath hitched as her nipples became even more engorged. The rope and his hands moved up her arms leaving a trail of gooseflesh in their path. She fought to maintain her kneeling position, but the sensory overload left her wanting to puddle at his feet.

"Breathe, Kitten."

Once more, she did as he commanded. His hands returned the rope to her breasts and her breath caught when he brushed the rope across her sensitive nipples. No longer able to fight gravity, she sagged against him, her head lolling to the side. His body enfolded hers. His lips kissed the curve of her neck, and then nipped at the tender flesh there. She caught her lower lip between her teeth and panted. *Now.* She wanted him to touch her now.

"Stay."

How could she do anything else?

He rose, and she knelt straighter, planting her butt against her heels for support. She watched the rope dance in his hands as he prepared it for the binding to come. Her eyelids drifted shut. All of a sudden, the rope lashed her torso, licking repeatedly at her tender nipples. She opened her mouth to scream only to realize she wasn't experiencing pain, just surprise. He walked in a circle around her continually flogging her with the ends of the rope—touching every exposed area, shoulders, breasts, arms, thighs, hands, butt. The nerves rose to the surface to welcome the sensual lash of the rope.

Just as suddenly, the flogger ceased its stinging motion, and he knelt behind her again, separating her hair into two shanks and letting one fall over each shoulder to cover her breasts. Apparently, this time, he wasn't going to bind it in the hair corset as he'd done at Marc's house.

"Bend your elbows behind your lower back at ninety-degree angles and grab the opposite elbows with your hands. Your inner wrists need to be flush against your forearms."

Karla hoped she did everything he'd ordered in his list of rapid-fire commands. Where did he want her elbows, hands, wrists? Had she done it right?

"Good girl."

Her body warmed and relaxed at his praise. Her breasts jutted out even further in front of her, making them seem larger than they were.

"If you feel any tingling, especially in your arms, and eventually your legs, I want you to tell me immediately. Understand?"

"Yes, Sir."

He tied her forearms together, midway between her wrist and elbow, and with bone-melting movements, Master Adam's hands wrapped, twisted, and threaded the rope with quick precision around her upper arms. She remembered countless scenes of his club demonstrations where he created what looked like a box out of the model's arms, wrists, and hands. Occasionally, he tugged at her arms and the ropes, checking for tightness or comfort, maybe both.

She'd also suffered through watching Adam bind Mistress Grant many times in demonstrations for other Doms wanting to learn the art. Those demos had been so torturous for Karla that sometimes she'd had to turn her attention to other scenes happening in the club's great room, because watching him touch her so intimately hurt too badly.

Of course, he'd never been as intimate doing Shibari with Mistress Grant as he had been with Karla just now. Tonight he wasn't performing for anyone but the two of them, wasn't touching anyone but her. She smiled.

Soon he had her upper arms and torso tightly secured by the rope, her arms pressed snugly against her sides. She tested the bindings to see how much movement she still had in her arms; very little give.

"Don't move, unless you need to flex your hands or fingers. Don't shift your body. The ropes will be placed on your torso, hips, and arms in very precise ways so that, when I suspend you, I won't put a strain on your arms."

Suspend? She remembered the ring hanging above her. *Oh, my!* His explanation made sense. She didn't feel any sense of panic, though. She trusted Master Adam not to harm her. He'd been her guardian and protector in many ways since she was sixteen.

Again, he worked in rapid motion behind her back. She wondered if there was a name for this design but if he told her the Japanese word, she'd forget it anyway. He reached around in front of her and threaded a blue rope above and below her breasts, adjusting the tension and attaching these ropes to the red ones on her arms. Her breasts were squeezed between the ropes, but not so tightly they hurt. He pressed a kiss against her right shoulder and she shivered with need.

Rather than analyze what he was doing, she closed her eyes and surrendered to the ropes and Master Adam's hands once more, letting him push and pull the rope through the bindings, moving her torso left and right, forward and back, while he manipulated her body as if she were a rag doll. Her head fell forward as she lost the ability to hold it upright. Her loose hair cascaded over her breasts and swung in the air in front of her as he bound her. Time ceased, and Karla felt as if she were levitating off the floor, floating above her body.

Free.

When Master Adam took a shank of her hair and slowly pulled her head back, her eyes fluttered open to find herself staring upside-down into his mint-green eyes. "I've never worked with anyone so responsive to the rope, Kitten." He smiled.

That sounded like a good thing. She smiled, feeling half drunk, before her gaze settled on his lips. All she wanted was to feel them on her—anywhere. His smile faded. "Up you go, pet."

His strong hands gripped her tightly bound upper arms and lifted her to her feet. He walked around to stand in front of her and stared down at her breasts, which had become swollen and turned red between the blue rope bindings. When Master Adam bent to brush his tongue over one of her protruding nipples, she gasped at the hyper-sensitivity.

"Oh, my God!"

He chuckled. "I'm flattered, but you know better how to address me."

"I'm sorry, Sir. I'm a little…disoriented."

"If I didn't know better, I'd say you'd gone into subspace."

She'd heard Angie talk about the time her mind and body separated when the abusive Dom beat her. "I thought you have to be in lots of pain to go into subspace."

"No, it can happen anytime a sub or slave so completely surrenders and is able to move outside her conscious mind. It's like going into a trance—or being stoned."

She smiled. "I felt that, Master. I floated. Time disappeared."

He chuckled and stroked her cheek. "Thank you, Kitten, for your sweet surrender. Those are the sweetest words a D—a Master can hear."

Master Adam was pleased, which pleased her. She'd been a good slave for him. All she wanted was to be what he wanted. To give him herself.

"Time to heighten your senses even more."

She grew wet at the threat in his words—or was it a promise? She bowed her head. "Thank you, Sir."

He reached out and squeezed her tender nipples until they were hard and even more sensitive, which didn't seem possible a moment ago. From the right pocket of his leathers, he pulled out a chain with clamps on either end. Master Adam took her left breast in his cupped hand and bent down to place her erect nipple between his lips. His teeth bit down gently and she sucked in a sharp breath, feeling as if her knees would collapse under her.

He stood tall again. "Perfect." Still cupping her breast, he took the clamp with his other hand and placed her nipple between the pincher-like ends, then slid a tiny ring along the shaft closer to her nipple, causing the pinchers to squeeze tighter and tighter onto her nipple. "Tell me when it's too tight."

She tried to hold out as long as she could to show she could be a good slave and take what her Master meted out, but when she could stand it no longer, she screamed, "Now!" Rather than stop, he pushed the ring just a little further sending a raging fire of pain burning through her nipple, until her knees buckled. He grabbed her arms to steady her, chuckling.

Sadist.

"How do you address me?"

Oh, shit. She hadn't called him a sadist to his face, had she? Then she remembered what she'd forgotten when she'd tried to get him to stop squeezing her nip. "I'm sorry—Sir."

How was she supposed to remember protocols when he did such mind-blowing things to her body? Would addressing him as Sir ever be a natural response for her? When he went to attach the other clamp to her right nipple, Karla instinctively moved away from him.

"Do. Not. Move."

Ka-thunk! Her stomach dropped into her pelvis at his stern words, which left her feeling even more skittish. He bent down and bit her nipple, causing it to double in size, and placed the other clamp over it and began to tighten the pinchers. She decided not to let the pain go beyond her tolerance level this time and quickly shouted, "Now, Sir!" But he continued to adjust it to about the same tension as the other. *The pain! Oh, God!* He hadn't even asked her this time to tell him when it hurt too much.

Karla's breaths came in shallow hisses as the burning pain in both her nipples consumed her mind. She looked down at her squashed nipples and wondered how she'd be able to stand it much longer. She took a deeper breath, hoping it would relax her. The pain receded to a tolerable level and she was able to breathe normally again.

"Good girl."

Why did those two words of praise and his gentle touch make her feel as if she could stand so much more for him? Because she wanted nothing more than to please Adam, her Master.

He stroked her breasts, avoiding her tender nipples. When he pinched the sides of her breasts, he took her focus away from the nipples and made the pain more tolerable. *Strange.*

While this Master/slave relationship—arrangement—had begun as a game to get him to notice her, it had very quickly gone so much further than she'd ever intended. Karla already felt herself morphing into the docile slave Adam wanted. The independent, headstrong Karla should be bothered that she was losing herself as she became someone else's property, but she'd wanted to belong to him for so long. No wonder he hadn't been attracted to her before. Her personality was too powerful. She was too independent.

However, since they'd entered into this arrangement, he'd focused more on her every need. Being his slave stopped being a game. She was growing to need him as her Master.

She wanted nothing more than to become his slave, totally and completely.

Chapter Six

Adam had just tested her pain limits and Karla hadn't whined. He'd even tried to go beyond her limits, hoping she would safeword and put an end to this goddamned arrangement. Nothing. Oh, at one point, she'd glared at him and he'd seen the old Karla shining through—the one who wouldn't put up with anyone's shit. Then she'd surrendered to his will.

Why didn't she tell him to go fuck himself?

Her complete surrender was a helluva turn-on. Had he been wrong about her? Was she submissive? The thought of being her Dom made his dick grow hard, no doubt about that. He may not be into the extreme of the Master/slave relationship, but he sure as hell was dominant to the bone—and her telling him he'd put her into subspace just made him rock hard.

Oh, hell, who was he kidding? Karla was no sub. He'd just need to make the arrangement even more onerous for her to get her to see this wasn't the lifestyle for her. But first, he had a raging need to suspend her and plant his mouth between her legs, because he'd wanted to go down on her since he'd touched her wet, thong-covered pussy moments ago.

He went to the shelf and grabbed a bundle of natural-colored hemp that he hadn't dyed like the others, and grinned as he thought about his plans for his little kitten. He'd have to be sure to photograph her when he finished. He wished he'd decided to do this scene in the rope-suspension theme room, where he could have videotaped her to watch her expressions later. He'd been able to glance at the nearby wall mirror a couple of times while he worked, but her hair obscured her face. Besides, his focus needed to be on what his hands were doing, because a mistake could cause nerve damage or serious injury.

He knelt beside her and took her bound arms in his hands. "I'm going to lower your body to the mat now. You'll be lying on your left side at first." She relaxed into his hands—so trusting—and he laid her gently on the mat.

"Stretch out your legs and relax them." She did so.

Taking the hemp bundle in his hands, he loosened the ends and stroked her abdomen, mons, and thighs with the rope. She moaned, causing his balls to tighten. He'd never worked with anyone before who had him so turned-on. Her responses and surrender just about made him come undone. He'd wanted to give her pussy time to heal from her first-time sex acts, but damn, it wasn't going to be easy to deflect his dick from its prime target.

"I'm going to tie your ankle and pull your foot back until it touches your upper thigh." Adam began binding her right thigh and calf in Futomomo fashion, with a single-column tie just above the ankle, leaving it smooth in the front, but loose. Taking the end of the rope, he pulled the heel of her foot firmly against the back of her thigh and spiraled the rope around her calf and thigh four times before finishing off with four knots in the outer trench formed there.

Rolling Karla over to her other side, he bent down and brushed his lips over hers. "Still with me, Kitten?"

Her heavy-lidded eyes and sexy smile told him she was incredibly relaxed. The girl did love the rope. "If you feel a charley horse cramp, you tell me immediately and I'll get you out of the ropes and massage it out. Understood?"

She nodded meekly and he tweaked her nipple clamp playfully. Her eyes opened wide as she hissed in a gasp of air. He chuckled. "Soon, pet." She creased her brows at him, but he didn't elaborate.

Picking up another bundle of the neutral-colored hemp, Adam made his tie just above her right knee and left the remainder of the rope lying beside her for the moment. He added a rope just below her waist circling her body at the top and bottom of her hips, then cross binding it, finishing with multiple strands together on the upper side of each hip for the suspension points.

"I'm going to lift you up now."

"No! I'm too heavy! You'll hurt your back!"

He glared at her.

"Sir."

Her lack of his title wasn't what pissed him off. "Kitten, I'll be the judge of how much weight I can lift. Now, relax your neck and head, until I can prepare a sling to support them after I have you suspended."

He stood and ran the end of the rope up and through the steel suspension ring overhead. He lifted her using the suspension points at her hips and chest and checked her weight distribution, then added the ropes that would support her legs. He found the perfect height for what he planned and adjusted her bindings until her head was slightly lower than her torso, to give her a nice blood rush to the head. Later, he would invert her completely for a short while to test her endurance, but he didn't want her fainting and putting an end to his play before it had even started. She could remain in this position for hours.

Her hair fell toward the floor in a cascade of shiny black curls, leaving him wanting to run his fingers through the locks again. She'd been practically catatonic when he'd massaged her scalp earlier. Definitely needed to play with her hair more, not just pull it.

The gauzy wrap-around skirt fell open to expose her thong. He couldn't wait to taste her. But first, he needed to add neck and head support. He went back to the shelf and picked up a long, wide silk scarf and fashioned it into a small hammock for her head to rest on by folding it into a stretched diamond shape, with the wide part under her head and the ends roped onto the ring.

"Are you comfortable, Kitten?"

"Yes, Sir. I don't even feel the pull of the rope."

"Good."

Taking the rope attached to her right knee, he pulled and tightened it until her leg was spread open for him. *Very soon.*

"Oh!"

"Are you okay, Kitten?"

"Yes, Sir. I just wasn't expecting that."

He chuckled. "Well, I find this the best position for when my beast needs to feed—like now."

He heard the sweet hitch in her breath and saw her nibbling her plump lower lip. She knew exactly what he intended to do, but he'd let her anticipate his mouth on her pussy awhile longer. He stood back to admire his sub…no, his slave.

"So beautiful."

"Thank you for making me beautiful for you, Sir."

Oh, Karla. You were always beautiful.

Adam wasn't sure why he couldn't speak the words aloud. He wondered what kind of expectations she had for what he'd be doing to her. He supposed she could have seen some of his scenes in here over the past few months. But he liked to change things up and improvise. He walked over to his toy bag, which he had stashed in here earlier. Opening it, he pulled out the Wartenburg wheel. Her tits and legs were going to be very sensitive, not to mention some other parts of her anatomy. He also pulled out two sixteen-inch floggers. Might as well warm her skin up a bit before applying the wheel.

He set the items down on the mat and stared at Karla, suspended above the floor, face up, totally helpless and vulnerable. She began to squirm under his silent scrutiny. *Oh, I definitely intended to take my time, Kitten.*

He removed the skirt that not only obstructed his view, but soon would block him from impacting some of the places he wanted access to. The bit of gauze fluttered to the mat, and he kicked it away. Now, time to make his kitten dance. He reached out and cupped her breasts.

"Are you ready?"

"Ready for what, Master?" The anxiety he heard in her voice caused his dick to harden, not to mention heighten his own anticipation.

"For me to remove the tit clamps?"

"Yes, Sir. If that's what you want to do, then I'd like to have them removed."

He grinned. That docile mood would soon disappear. She apparently had no idea how much this was going to hurt. But he'd left them on long enough. This wasn't a punishment, after all.

He smiled and took the first clamp between his fingers.

"Hang on, Kitten."

* * *

Hang on? To what? I'm hanging from the ceiling!

"I don't understand, Sir. My hands are bound."

Instead of answering, he took the clamp on her left nipple and began loosening the ring. She'd be glad to have the tight things off. But immediately after the pincher was removed, her nipple began to swell as blood and feeling rushed back into the peak. Pain!

"Owww!" She jerked, which sent her swinging from the rope above her. "Sir, make it stop! Oh, fuck. Goddamn it. Don't touch me!" Karla tried to move away from Adam's hands, but could only make awkward, jerky motions with all the ropes he had her tied in. She danced on the ends of the rope like a marionette, her body bouncing off Adam's.

Adam's hands halted her movement, steadying the ropes, and he bent over her and took her aching nipple into his mouth. "Sir. No! Please, don't bite it!"

He raised his head and met her gaze. "Kitten, are you telling your Master what to do?"

Yes! No! Don't displease him. "No, Sir. I'm sorry. I forgot myself." Tears spilled from the corners of her eyes as his tongue brushed against her sore nip. She fought the urge to scream at the torture her nipple endured, first from the clamp and now his mouth. She'd never felt anything so intense in her life. Oh, dear Lord, he still had to take the other clamp off. She wanted to run from him, but there was no escape.

She choked on a sob. Adam's mouth gently licked her nipple before he sucked her hard nipple into his mouth. Her clit stirred to life. The pain receded, replaced by an intense heat warming her entire body. *More!* "Oh, Sir!" What was happening? "That feels so...Oh, my God!" How had she gone from pain to pleasure as fast as a *glissando* on a keyboard?

He removed his mouth and reached up to remove the other clamp.

"No, please, don't!"

Adam's hand cupped her swollen breast and squeezed her numb nipple, but didn't remove the clamp yet. "What did you say?"

Karla looked into his eyes, begging him not to hurt her again. "Please, Sir. Don't take it off."

"You mean you want to keep it on? Forever?"

Okay, she hadn't thought this through. The clamp had to come off. He grinned, knowing she now understood her predicament.

"Beg me to remove it, Kitten."

Beg him to torture her? Why didn't he just take it off? Now!

"Master, please..."

"Please what, Kitten?"

"Please don't hurt me anymore." A shadow passed over his eyes. She'd disappointed him by being a wimp. "I'm sorry. Please, Sir, remove the clamp."

Karla closed her eyes tightly and tensed her body.

"Slow, deep breath, and hold it, Kitten."

How could she breathe when she was steeling herself for the pain to come?

"That wasn't a suggestion."

She took a deep, ragged breath.

"Good girl. Be brave for me, Kitten. I'll make it better soon."

Adam's fingers deftly loosened the clamp. Pain engulfed her again and she screamed as her tortured nip was released. "Ackkkk! Oh, shit. Oh, God, no. Fuck, fuck, fuck! Make it..." Karla blubbered something incoherent, then Adam's warm, sweet tongue licked her swollen, aching nipple. He sucked hard.

Even faster this time, the pain turned to ecstasy, perhaps because she wasn't fighting it as much. Perhaps because of his exquisite mouth.

He released her nip with a plop and grinned up at her. "That's my girl."

She wanted to be brave for her Master. Thankfully, he took her nipple between his lips and sucked again. "Oh, ohhh, ohhhhhhh! Don't stop, Sir!"

But he did stop and stood. She groaned in frustration.

Leaving her nipples wet in the chilled air surrounding them, his hands began stroking her body, his fingers tracing the circles of her breasts. Then one hand went underneath her to her back as the other blazed a trail to her mons, but no further, teasing her mercilessly.

"Touch me, Sir!"

"Where would you like me to touch you, Kitten?"

"Everywhere. My pussy. My clit. My breasts."

"That's a lot of area to cover. I might need some help."

She quirked a brow and looked around the great room to make sure they were alone—she'd seen lots of threesomes in the club. *Alone. Thank the gods.* Then she watched him bend down to pick up with one hand two objects that looked like cheerleader pom-poms—only these looked like they were made of soft leather or suede. She held her breath.

Floggers.

Oh, those could be very painful from what she'd seen in here on club nights. Marc was wicked with them, leaving red marks that remained on Angelina the rest of the night. Why would Adam want to punish her? She'd been brave for him? Hadn't she?

"What was that thought?"

She forced her gaze to leave the floggers and focus on Master Adam. "Did I displease you, Sir?"

"Absolutely not. Why would you ask?"

"Because you're going to flog me."

He grinned. "Trust me, love, these aren't only used for punishment. They can also kiss the skin just enough to bring the blood flow to the surface, heightening your senses."

But he'd heightened her senses with the nipple clamps and it had hurt like hell.

Without asking if she was ready, he stepped back, took one flogger in each hand, and began twirling the strands in the air between their bodies until the floggers were a frenzy of continuous motion. He didn't strike her skin yet. *Oh, dear lord*. She'd told him she wanted him to touch her clit and pussy. *Surely to God he wouldn't…not with those…oh God.*

The flogger first caressed her left ass cheek and thigh with light thuds. As he repeatedly hit the same spots, the skin grew warmer and more sensitive. She tried to jerk away, but only sent herself into a half-spin. With Adam standing farther away, he wasn't there to stop her, and she spun in a full circle. Out of nowhere, his hand gave her thigh a gentle push, sending her spinning even more.

Oh, God. Don't puke, Kitty.

"Close your eyes, Kitten."

Now the floggers began hitting any exposed area that happened to come into their path—breasts, abdomen, arms, legs, soles of her feet, and…oh God, that last lash hit her directly on her pussy and clit. Pain!

"Oh!" Her clit zinged. Maybe not pain! But she'd spun away again before the next blow fell on her breasts and abdomen. The whooshing and thudding of the floggers mesmerized her mind. She kept her eyes closed and surrendered to the sensations, becoming lightheaded. Time stood still as she floated. The thudding continued, but she no longer wanted to avoid the blows. Euphoria. Floating. Free.

A kiss to her lips caused her eyelids to flutter open. His hands on her tingling breasts eased her back to reality. Where had she been? She only remembered the exquisite sense of euphoria. Nothing existed but this sublime ecstasy.

"Back with me, Kitten?"

"Back?"

"You were floating again. I thought I'd let you enjoy subspace a while longer this time, now that I'm sure that's where you're going. You've been out of it for about thirty minutes."

"I think I still am." Her breathless voice sounded like a siren's. She giggled. Heady stuff.

"Ready for more?"

"There's more?"

He chuckled. "Oh, yes, Kitten. I have much more planned for you."

He disappeared from her vision for a moment and when he stood by her again, he'd lost the floggers. Now he held what looked like her mother's pattern-tracing wheel, with a dozen or more sharp, steel points. Before she could wonder what he intended to do, it pressed lightly against the sole of her right foot, which was bound tightly behind her thigh.

"No, Sir! I'm ticklish there!"

He chuckled again, sadistically, and continued to run the wheel over her sole until tears filled her eyes. At last, he moved on to her leg, which had turned red and looked slightly swollen inside the bindings. Oh, that was going to hurt when the blood rushed back in—she hoped not as badly as her nipples.

The wheel continued up her calf, over the bumps and knots of the ropes, then up onto her thigh.

"You still want me to touch your clit and pussy, Kitten?"

"No, Sir! I changed my mind!"

He laughed out loud this time and the wheel moved closer and closer to her pussy. She tried to evade him, but he was between her legs now, not allowing the ropes to spin her away, moving closer and closer to her thong. With his other hand, his finger traced the outline of the waistband, over the triangular scrap of lace, and down the crack between her legs. She shook her head as the wheel came closer. Closer.

The wheel squeaked as it rolled onto the side of her mons and into the valley between her thigh and pussy. The spikes grabbed at her pubic hair and wouldn't let go. "Ow!" Master Adam bent over and kissed the place where her hair had been pulled, then leaned away and let the damned wheel roll right over the lace triangle, applying more pressure as he went over her clit.

"Oh, my God!" Her clit zinged to welcome the device of torture. Where would it go next?

His lips brushed her right thigh between the ropes and sent delicious tingles through her. He slowly nibbled his way to the vee between her legs, then his teeth skimmed over her lace-covered and now very erect clit. How was he going to get the thong off with her legs tied like this? He should have thought about that earlier. Somehow, though, she was certain he'd figure out something. Right now, all she wanted to do was lose herself in the feel of his mouth approaching her pussy.

He stood, and she heard the wheel hit the floor. He seemed to be reaching into his pocket for something, and she saw him coming at her with a pocket-knife. One slight tug of the string between her butt cheeks and another at the waistband and the thong fell away. Well, she guessed he'd purchased the expensive thong, so it was his to cut away if he wanted to.

The knife went back into his leathers, and he bent down to spread the curls on her outer lips with his thumbs. The tip of his warm, hard tongue pressed against the side of her clit hood, removing all rational thought from her mind. Lightheadedness only added to the sense of euphoria rushing through her.

"Oh, Sir! Yessss!" His finger slid down the cleft to her pussy and entered her in one swift motion. Dripping wet. He plunged another finger inside her and curled them around to press that bundle of nerves she'd never known existed.

She couldn't contain her screams, no matter who might hear. "Oh, please, yesssssssssss!" His tongue stroked both sides of her hood, teasing her clit to become more erect, without touching it directly. When it responded inevitably, he flicked his tongue against the sensitive nub. So intense. Suddenly, she felt like crying and laughing at the same time.

"Oh, Master Adam! Yessss!!!"

Karla grew even more weightless, hanging on the edge. She flew. A strange euphoria engulfed every part of her body. She floated, literally this time, as she tumbled over the crest. Her screams laced intermittently with panting filled the room, and she tried to clamp her thighs around his head to hold him closer, but, of course, she couldn't move. Then his head was gone. Suddenly, the world spun on its axis and went topsy-turvy. She was hanging knees over head, staring at the bulge in Master Adam's leathers.

Totally at her Master's mercy.

Totally surrendered to him.

Totally Master Adam's.

* * *

Hearing Karla's screams sent his dick into painful spasms, aching to get out of his leathers and have some fun, too. She excited him more than anyone had in a very long time. Shock and awe. But he needed to get her down out of this inverted position now, before she blacked out. Her body shook from the after-spasms of her orgasm. For a novice to the lifestyle, she certainly had intense responses to submission, going into subspace twice during the scene. He usually had to work with a sub for quite a while to get her to trust him enough to let go, but Karla…

Trusts you completely, jarhead.

Fuck. Her trust was better than just about anything she could have given him. What was he going to do with such a special gift?

He adjusted the ropes to move her torso into a horizontal position again, and lowered her carefully to the floor. He knelt, immediately loosening and untying her right leg.

"M-Master Adam?"

"Yes, Kitten?"

"Th-thank you. That was…unbelievable."

"I loved hearing you scream my name, little one."

Her trembling had lessened as he released the rest of the ropes, then scooped her up in his arms and carried her over to the loveseat where he grabbed a blanket from the basket on the floor and wrapped her in it. He stroked her hair, loving the feel of her body curled against him.

"I didn't know I would be so loud, Sir."

He chuckled. "Most men enjoy hearing a girl in the throes of passion. I know I do."

Her hand reached up and stroked his leather vest, then ventured inside to his pec. "Sir?"

"Yes, Kitten?"

"If I do something wrong as your slave, you'll tell me, won't you?"

"Yes. It's my responsibility to make you aware of those things so you can correct them. That's what we refer to as discipline."

"Am I in trouble for forgetting to call you Sir or forgetting to get the signal to eat, Sir?"

He tilted her head back into the crook of his arm and stroked her cheek, smiling down at her. "Karla, this is just your first day. You're still in training. I don't expect perfection. I also won't inflict punishments unless you willfully disobey me. That would be true, whether you are my slave or my sub. I'm just pleased to see you trying so hard to be a good slave for me."

Even if I don't want you being my slave.

Why was he having such a hard time accepting her as a slave if she wanted to be one? He'd tolerated the arrangement to make Joni happy. It was just that being a Dom came more naturally to him. Regardless, he missed having Karla challenge him, talk back to him, even engage in conversation about things not related to BDSM and sex. Why had she shut down that part of herself?

Because now she was his slave.

Because you effectively killed it.

"Sir?"

"Yes, Kitten?"

"Don't you want to come, too?"

He smiled, pleased that she was concerned about him. "No, hon. The experience of restraining you with ropes and giving you that screaming orgasm is all I need to satisfy me right now. A lot of BDSM play doesn't involve sex."

"But I thought…"

He waited, and when she didn't continue, he prompted, "You thought what?"

"Never mind, Sir."

"Kitten." Her body grew rigid at his tone.

"Well, I just thought…that was the goal. Why do BDSM if you don't have sex?"

"For me, BDSM is about control. When I had you swinging from those ropes, I had total control over your body. You couldn't escape. I manipulated you any way I wanted and there was nothing you could do to stop me—well, except safeword."

"No, I didn't even think about safewording. Even in the middle of the most intense pain, there was…"

"Finish the thought."

"Pleasure. And I was so relaxed. But when you suspended me in the air, I felt like I could fly. Then you tilted me upside down after I came and…all I could think about was falling at first, but…" She nibbled her full lower lip.

"Kitten, stop making me coax the words out of you."

"I'm sorry. I…I just trusted you not to harm me."

Yeah, I know you did. Those words should make him feel elated. She trusted him not to do physical harm, but what about emotional harm? He could inflict great damage there, as he'd done with Joni. Hadn't he? Joni hadn't said so but…

He needed to get Karla to fucking safeword before it was too late.

* * *

Karla felt safe and protected in Master Adam's arms. She wished they could stay like this forever.

"Karla, tomorrow I want you to take Cassie home."

"Slaves can drive, Sir?"

"Slaves do anything their Masters tell them to do. Many of them hold jobs, some of them in pretty high-powered management and executive positions."

Really? She had no idea.

"You'll take Cassie home and be back here in six and a half hours from when you leave. Stop for a quick lunch before you head home. Nothing else."

He was putting her on a time limit? She'd always enjoyed visiting with Cassie at the cabin for hours, but he was only giving her a thirty-minute window outside driving time, which included time to stop and eat? Well, she could skip lunch and drive a little faster…

"You will obey the speed limit, and you will eat because if you disobey me, Kitten, you will suffer the consequences when you get home." Had he just read her mind, or had he just come to know her so well—finally? She shivered.

Why did his telling her what to do outside the house bother her so much? She'd been independent since college. Maybe his hiring her, giving her a place to live, and taking care of most of her living expenses had given him the idea he owned her. However, she'd loved submitting to him a short while ago. He had commanded her every move and she had never had such an emotional and physical connection to anyone before.

But that was different. Could she really let him control everything about her, the way he wanted to? Could she even think about saying no, when he was holding her like this, focusing on her alone? Of course not.

"Yes, Sir."

Karla heard footsteps behind her but was too tired to lift her head to see who had arrived. She wished she could have Master Adam all to herself.

"Sorry, Dad." Damián sounded drained. "Didn't see you here. Didn't mean to interrupt. I'll come back later."

Adam's arms around her grew tense. "What's wrong?"

"Nothing. Bad day. I just dropped by to work out some…tension."

"Wait for me in the kitchen."

Karla began to sit up, but Master Adam held her firmly in his arms. "This is our special time, Kitten. Aftercare. Damián will wait."

Our special time.

For him to choose her needs over Damián's was sweet, but Damián didn't sound very good. He needed Master Adam, too. Karla hated to let go, feeling a little fragile right now, but Damián needed him more.

"I'm fine, Sir." She pulled away from him and, this time, he let her go. He took her chin and turned her toward him, searching each eye in turn. She smiled.

"You're sure?"

She nodded, unable to speak past the knot in her throat. He helped her up and walked across the room to retrieve her clothing, helping her dress. She felt cherished and nurtured. If only they could have more special time together. She liked that.

* * *

As the hour approached midnight, Karla started down the hall to Cassie's door. She was naked under Master Adam's terry-cloth robe, which nearly came to her ankles. She should have asked for his permission to use the hot tub, but most likely, he wouldn't even know they'd been out there.

When they had gone into the kitchen earlier this evening, Damián had looked as if the demons of hell were on his heels. He'd headed home without talking, but her Master had insisted on following him to check on Damián. He told her that, on nights like these, the two of them usually talked things over for hours on end. She assumed it was about the war, which he wouldn't talk with her about. He'd told her not to wait up for him, so he probably wouldn't be back for hours.

Karla blushed to think Damián might have been in the house when she was screaming as Master Adam brought her to the most explosive orgasm of her life. There was no privacy in this house. When she'd moved in, he'd told her she had free run of the house, too. She'd just avoided his bedroom, until after he'd returned home from the hospital over a week ago. Surely Master Adam wouldn't object to her wanting to make use of his hot tub.

Cassie would be going home soon. Realizing this might be their only opportunity this year to have their cleansing ceremony—something she'd been looking forward to as a means of releasing some of her anger and grief—she'd asked Cassie if they could do it tonight. Angie had also been on the disastrous Mount Evans camping trip earlier this month. They'd planned originally to have their ritual around the campfire, before all the drama had happened. So, Karla had invited Angie, too, and she was on her way over. The three of them all had things from the past they needed to heal, and Cassie promised this ceremony would help.

"Sorry it took so long," Angie said, out of breath as she reached the top of the stairs. She carried her bathrobe over her forearm and a covered tray in her hand. "Got here as soon as I could. Had to stop downstairs and get…something. I'm so glad we're going to get to do this. I think I'm more focused now than I would have been two weeks ago. Where should I change?"

Angie's energy and enthusiasm made Karla chuckle. Master Marc must be getting her to verbally express herself.

"Just go in there," she said, pointing to the master bedroom. "Bathroom's on the right. Just don't leave anything behind for Mas...for Adam to find."

"How about the food tray?"

"Here, I'll take it." Karla took the tray of the items Cassie had requested—something green and something sweet to eat after the ceremony.

Angie hurried away just as Cassie opened her door, dressed in a robe as well. Karla saw she had her own tray of items—candles, dried and twisted sage, matches. "You're sure Adam's okay with this?"

"Oh, sure." *More or less.* "We'll be finished long before he gets home."

They padded on slippered feet across the hall and into Adam's room. Karla held the French patio door for Cassie to precede her onto the deck. Adam's oak-scented body wash filled the air. Karla thought it provided the perfect ambiance and replaced the woodsy scents they were missing this year. She'd been careful to only use a bit, not wanting a bubble bath fiasco in his hot tub. Master Adam might not appreciate that.

The mall's bed-and-bath store chain seemed the last place she'd expect Adam to buy his shampoo and body wash. Who had bought it for him? She tamped down the jealous thoughts that ran through her head.

Angie came outside dressed in her robe, and the three of them looked at each other. Karla and Angie giggled. Cassie set about preparing for the ceremony. The night was dark—no visible moon—but the hot tub lights cast a greenish light over them. Karla just hoped the lack of moonlight would give them even more privacy from the prying eyes of neighbors, especially later, when they got stark naked in the middle of downtown Denver. She didn't want to give any of Master Adam's neighbors fits if they looked out or up and saw them performing what looked like some kind of pagan ritual.

Okay, it *was* a pagan ritual. But every year since Karla had been visiting Cassie out here, she'd derived such peace from them that she didn't want to miss the ceremony this year. Especially not this year. Karla's family had never been religious and she hadn't really gone to church much, except with friends like Cassie in college. Cassie had a mixture of Peruvian Indian and Catholic backgrounds, which gave her all kinds of ideas for ritualistic ceremonies. The woman was a bit of a mystic, too. The drawing she made of Luke's dead wife and baby at the hospital two weeks ago—neither of whom had Cassie ever met—still gave Karla chills.

Angie had been raised Catholic, too, and had been enthusiastic about participating when Karla had told her about it before the fateful camping trip.

"The hot tub is perfect for the cleansing stage in the ceremony," Cassie said.

Karla smiled. "Definitely warmer than some of the streams we've cleansed in."

Cassie nodded, and then stood taller as she grew more confident, deep in her element now. Of course, there were no men around, which helped. "Did everyone bring a symbol of what they want to release?"

Karla and Angie nodded and pulled the objects from their robe pockets. For Karla, it was a miniature motorcycle. For Angie, the mask Marc wore at the club—did he know Angie had it? That must have been what she'd retrieved downstairs. For Cassie, it was an airline-sized bottle of rum.

Cassie cast the circle around them and invoked the spirit watchers. She instructed the women to close their eyes. "Now, imagine a circle within the circle, like a chain-link fence with posts. This will keep the negativity from escaping our circle. We don't want to send it out into the universe. But any negativity we express or that comes at us will be deflected by those fence posts into the ground, like lightning rods. Don't absorb any of the negativity into yourselves either. When one of us is expressing our hurt, just ask for blessings to heal those negative thoughts as they swirl around in the circle, and then send them on their way to a fiery hell. Don't let it stay within our circle, or within us."

Cassie asked them to take a deep cleansing breath and to keep their eyes closed. "Now, we will take turns expressing the hurt we want to release. I'll go first, so you'll see what to do, Angie."

With her eyes closed, Karla heard Cassie take a deep breath and slowly release it. For the longest time, there was silence. They waited. Then Cassie released a keening cry that bordered on pain, expressing and releasing her anguish and sorrow over what was taken from her in that Peruvian bar four and a half years ago. She spoke in a mixture of Spanish and English. This wasn't the first time Cassie had been working on releasing this hurt. God, Karla hoped and prayed she would succeed this time. Her friend needed to heal and move on with her life without all the fear and anger.

Tears burned Karla's eyes as she absorbed some of Cassie's pain, then she remembered not to let that negativity remain inside her. She asked for blessings and sent it to the grounding poles and away from them. The air among them grew warmer, lighter.

Breathing heavily, Cassie paused. "Please open your eyes." Karla looked across the small circle at her friend, who had tears shimmering on her cheeks from the shine of a distant street light. "I denounce the pigs who raped me," she gritted out between her teeth. "I denounce the alcohol they drank that kept them from choosing right over wrong. I denounce the bar where such attacks on women are condoned as male sport. And I denounce my homeland that allows such things to happen to its women in the name of *machismo*."

She held up the bottle of rum. "This bottle is a symbol of my attack and my attackers. I denounce it as well." She threw the bottle outside the circle, and Karla heard it roll to the edge of the deck and over the side, falling to the shrubbery below. Cassie's chest rose and fell as she breathed rapidly. Gradually her friend's breathing slowed to normal, as she relaxed.

With what Karla was learning about BDSM now, she wondered if there was anything in the lifestyle that might help Cassie regain control of her life, but this wasn't the time or place to discuss it.

Cassie dashed the tears from her cheeks and turned to Angie. "Would you like to go next?"

"Not until I give you a hug, if that's okay."

Cassie nodded and opened her arms; Angie wrapped her arms around her. Karla joined in, surprised Cassie was letting someone she barely knew hold her. That was progress, at least. After a moment, Cassie stiffened, signaling that it was time to pull away.

"Please, Angelina, just get in touch with the feelings, especially the anger, then let it go."

"This is silly, really, compared to yours."

"No! Don't downgrade the emotions you feel, Angelina. I'm glad it's not like mine, but the pain you feel is just as real as mine—just as valid."

Angie blinked and looked down at the wolf mask she held in her hands. She brushed her fingers over the fur on the mask. "I'm falling in love with someone who...lied to me about who he was. At first, he just didn't share that we'd met before, because he didn't expect that he'd ever see me again. But things happened, and now we're exploring the possibility of a long-term relationship. It was a silly lie really, and I don't know why it bothers me so much..."

"Angelina, how did the lie make you feel?"

"Like I can't fully trust him. But I want to trust him. And he's never done anything that's made me question giving him my trust, except for this one lie of omission. He also brought other people into it with him—Karla, Adam,

Damián, Luke."

"Oh, Angie. You don't know how much I hated that I was a part of that. Please forgive me."

"I have, Karla. And I've forgiven everyone else, even Marc. He's apologized. I know he's sincere, but I just can't forget. If he did it again, it would be over."

Karla reached out to stroke Angie's sleeve. "What do you want to say to him, Angie, that you haven't been able to say yet?"

Angie took a deep breath, staring at the mask again. "Marc, I want you as my Dom, maybe in more than just the bedroom and the club. But how can I trust you not to lie to me about something else? How can I let you put me in even more vulnerable situations, where I have to totally rely on you for my well-being, and know you won't let me down again? I guess I still don't understand why he perpetuated it so long."

Silence fell between them as Angie's words drifted away on a frigid breeze. Her heart ached for Angie, because she and Marc really were so good for each other. Karla had thought everything was going well with them, but apparently Marc's lie had caused some damage to their budding relationship.

"Angie, maybe it's because you're so new as a couple. When he has a better track record over time with no more lies, it won't seem as monumental."

Angie nodded, but she didn't say anything more. Just stared down at the wolf mask. After a pause, Cassie cleared her throat. "Tell us about the mask, Angelina."

"He continues to hide behind a mask." Angie looked down at it again and a tear slid down her cheek and into the soft fur on the edges. There was more going on here than Marc's lie.

After a moment, Angie continued. "Family is everything to me, and I know Marc's close to his parents and siblings, too, although not quite as close as I am to my Mom and brothers. He's asked me to go home with him for New Year's dinner, because he knows I need to be with my Mom at Christmas. I've never missed a Christmas at home."

Angie's father had been killed in an avalanche a number of years ago, a SAR worker trying to rescue Luke's pregnant wife, who also died in the tragic accident. Karla had met Angie's mother and four brothers while Adam was in the hospital.

"Here at the club, Marc hides behind this mask because his Mama is afraid he'll run into someone from her Aspen social circle here, which would embarrass her." Suddenly, Angie crushed the mask in her fist. "But if they're embarrassed about Marc's connection to the club, then will they be embarrassed about me, because Marc and I first met here?"

"If Marc's family won't accept me, I'll have to let him go, because I will not come between them. So I'm scared, because I don't want to lose Marc. We've become very close in the past two months, and I really think he's the one for me, but the thought of being rejected by his family just petrifies me. I'm dreading the thought of spending New Year's Eve with them."

Karla reached out and patted her friend's back. "Angie, I'm sure they'll love you, just as much as Marc does. But I think you need to tell him how you feel. Open and honest communication is so important in any relationship."

"I know. I really should. And I will." She looked from Karla to Cassie, as if to convince them, rather than herself. "Soon."

Cassie smiled. "Why don't you put your emotions, the fear and the hurt, into the mask and then toss those emotions and the mask from the circle?"

"Oh, yeah. Sorry. I forgot that part." Angie smiled and shook her head. "He's not going to be too happy to see what I did to his club mask." Angie stared down at it a few moments more before flinging the mangled mask outside the circle much like Cassie had tossed away her bottle.

"Just keep the lines of communication open. I'm sure you'll be able to work through this anxiety."

Cassie was so intuitive, so wise. Karla thanked the gods she could count her as a friend.

"I hope you're right. I had no idea how worried I was about it. I've just tamped it down, because we're such a new couple. I really do love him, but I want the kind of love my parents had—the kind that lasts forever, even beyond death. Anyway, thanks, Cassie. I think this has helped a lot."

Angie grinned, and Karla relaxed a bit. She reached over to her and, once again, they were in a three-way group hug.

When they separated, Karla's heart pounded harder. She looked down at the tiny Honda motorcycle in her hand, trying not to picture Ian riding on it, the semi crushing him, his mangled body flying through the air to land with a thud against the pavement. *Major fail.* That's all she could think about.

"Why'd you have to ride that stupid thing, Ian?" Tears burned her eyes. "You always thought you were invincible. That nothing could pierce your super-human armor." A tear splashed onto her hand, then rolled off onto the tiny bike. His casket had remained closed at the funeral. She and her parents hadn't wanted to see the reconstructed face the morticians had tried to make look like her beautiful, handsome brother.

"Why'd you stop coming to see me at the club those last months? We used to be so close." She squeezed her eyes shut as pain tore through her stomach. *Don't puke, Kitty.* A tear trickled down her cheek, the cold air nearly freezing it against her skin. She held the bike up above her head, shaking it at the heavens.

"Why, Ian?" she screamed. "Why did you fucking leave me? Why don't you ever talk to me, send me messages, communicate with me?" Her voice grew louder with each accusation, but she no longer cared what the neighbors thought. Cassie and Angie disappeared. This was between her and Ian. "How could you leave and not come back? I hate you for dying on me, Ian! Do you hear me? I hate you!"

She flung the bike so hard it careened over the wrought iron fence at the other end of the deck and fell toward the driveway.

Chapter Seven

Adam closed the door of the SUV and ran his fingers through his hair. When was Damián going to be able to rid himself of the images that still plagued him? Fucking PTSD. Tonight the boy had been consumed by memories from that rooftop in Fallujah. Memories of Sergeant Miller's crushing weight on his chest, his bloody brains spilling onto him. When talking hadn't helped, Adam had gotten him to take a sleeping pill and he'd finally drifted into a peaceful sleep. But how long before…?

"I hate you for dying on me, Ian! Do you hear me? I hate you!!!"

Karla? His heart pounded harder. Was she in the throes of her own nightmare? It sounded like she was up on the deck. He looked up in time to see a tiny projectile spinning end over end until it banged against his chest and bounced off. He bent down to pick it up. A toy motorcycle?

Taking the steps to the porch two at a time, he unlocked the back door, raced up the stairs, and ran across the bedroom to the French doors in time to watch Karla's naked ass as she stepped into the hot tub to join Cassie and Angie. *What the fuck?*

Concerned and more than a little confused, he hurried to the doors and opened one to go out on the deck. "Karla, are you all right?"

She turned, her dangling breasts lit by the shimmering glow of the candles on the edge of the hot tub and the lights inside. She looked like Venus rising from the sea. He refused to look anywhere near her Venus mound and still felt his balls tighten and his dick spring to life.

"Mast…Adam," she said, looking down at her friends, then back at him. "You're home earlier than I expected."

"Obviously. What the fuck's going on?" *Why were you screaming like that?*

He took in the candles, smelled burning sage, something one of the men in his unit—a Shoshone—had done as a religious observance on base when he'd wanted to cleanse some thing or some place. He also could swear he could smell the "Oak" body wash Joni's mom supplied him with every Christmas.

Karla began shivering, her nipples becoming harder and more erect. "Sit down in the damned water, Karla, before you freeze to death."

"Yes, Sir." She sunk into the water, her face appearing shaken and a bit dejected. He noticed the stricken look on Cassie's face and a glare from Angelina, who then cast a worried glance in Karla's direction. Angelina's eyes opened wider. Hell, she'd probably caught onto the submissive responses Karla had given and figured out the two of them had been playing at dominance and submission. Only it was something much more intense than a Dom/sub relationship, actually.

But right now, he was more concerned about Karla screaming her hatred for her dead brother a few moments ago. Where was the rage and anger now? She seemed almost serene, although still very unhappy.

"Is someone going to tell me what's going on? Karla, what's this all about?" He held the broken toy in the palm of his hand, and she looked down at it as if she'd seen a ghost from the grave.

"Take that horrible thing away from Kitty!" Cassie glared at him, the most emotion he'd seen on her face in, well, ever. Very protective of her friends, something he admired, but didn't appreciate at the moment.

What the fuck were they doing out here?

Cassie wasn't finished with him yet, either. "We're trying to have a cathartic healing. You need to take your negative energy and leave."

"I and my negative energy own this deck, this bedroom, this house," he said, spreading his arms to indicate the entire deck and house. "I'm not the one who needs to leave."

A choking sound from Karla brought his attention back to her, only to find her in tears. *Fuck.* What the hell was wrong? Before he could go to her to comfort her, the other two women were moving to her side, obviously as naked as Karla was, and reaching to put their arms around her. She obviously didn't need him.

"Fine. Stay as long as you like. I'll be down in my office. Karla, when you and your friends are done doing…whatever it is you're doing…come downstairs. We need to have a talk."

Without waiting for a response, respectful or otherwise, he turned to walk back inside and made a beeline to the sanctuary that was his office. At least he didn't have to worry about anyone laying siege there.

First his bed. Now his deck.

Women. If he lived to be a hundred, he'd never understand them.

* * *

"What's his problem, Kitty?"

"What's with the Master and Sir stuff, Karla? I had no idea you two were…"

"We just started this morning, well, yesterday morning now, I guess." Karla looked from Cassie to Angie. "Look, it's complicated and I'm not supp…ready to discuss it. But I'm so sorry he took out his anger on you two, especially after we'd worked so hard to cleanse ourselves from our negativity."

"Don't apologize for him. He's responsible for his feelings, not you."

But I made him feel that way. She remembered her mother's words to Ian, when he'd lose his temper. "No one can make you angry, Ian. You *choose* to become angry." Well, maybe, but Karla knew she needed to go to him, and she dreaded the confrontation to come. Why had he been so angry at her for using his deck and hot tub? Or was something else going on?

Cassie insisted on finishing this part of the ceremony, but Karla's thoughts were on the man downstairs, waiting for her. Would he punish her for not asking to use his deck?

A tray was passed in front of her and Karla blinked back to the present, reaching down to take one of each of the two items Angie had prepared and ate them, but couldn't say what they were. Her stomach was in knots worrying about what Master Adam would say and do. Sometime later, she had no idea how long; Cassie stood and blew out the candles. The time had come to face the music—the most discordant music she could imagine.

Karla trudged down the stairs, through the kitchen, and into the hallway leading to his office as if she'd been sentenced to the gallows. The drumming of her pulse did nothing to allay her tension. She knocked on his door.

"Come."

She wished he'd been commanding her to come another way, but that wasn't going to happen this morning. When she walked into the room and saw the look of concern on his face, she thought maybe she'd been wrong. He wasn't angry anymore?

"You wanted to see me, Master?"

At her words, a change came over his face. She almost thought there was reluctance, but he commanded, "Close the door." She did as instructed and walked toward his desk. "Kneel." His gaze went to a mat at the side of his enormous desk, and she went there without question, falling to her knees. She kept her back straight, her eyes downcast, and her hands, palm up, on her thighs.

"Strip."

She was still wearing his terrycloth robe, because, oddly enough, her Master's scent in the fabric had given her some much-needed courage. But she slipped it off her shoulders and let it puddle around her knees and legs at his command.

"If I don't want you to look at me, I'll blindfold you. Eyes on me."

Ka-thunk!

She closed and opened her eyes slowly, drew a deep breath, and raised her head. Adam still wore his black leathers from their earlier session but had on a white dress shirt, open at the collar and tucked into his pants. Seeing him sitting in his office, the memory of a fantasy stirred inside that surprised her, but she wouldn't go there. Tonight wasn't about fulfilling fantasies. Master Adam wouldn't play when he was angry. She'd seen him stop scenes in the club when he thought a Dom wasn't in control of his anger.

"Explain yourself."

The vulnerability of her naked and subservient position, coupled with having her emotions lying right at the surface from the ritual ceremony with her friends, weren't a good combination. Tears welled in her eyes and her lower lip quivered.

"I'm sorry, Sir. I didn't think you would be home so early." His brow furrowed, but he waited for her to continue. "Cassie will be leaving today and I thought it was the last chance we'd get to perform the ritual we'd planned to do up on Mount Evans two weeks ago."

He relaxed and leaned back in the swivel chair, spreading his legs open. She tried not to look at his tight leathers, but they had some kind of hypnotic effect on her. He had a bulge in his leathers telling her he was turned on. Well, that made one of them.

"Eyes." She looked up at him again. "Do you mean to tell me you and Cassie get naked every year and do pagan rituals during your camping trips?"

She thought she saw him bite the corner of his lip. Was he teasing her? She took another much-needed deep breath, but maintained her rigid posture. "Yes, Sir. It's a time to release past hurts."

He closed his eyes as if in pain and his lips twitched. "Stand up, Kitten." She stood, naked, raw, and vulnerable. "Put the robe on and come here." She did as he instructed, her hands shaking. He wasn't angry anymore? She didn't want him to be displeased with her.

He held his arms out to her and she crawled into his lap, tugging the robe tighter around her neck to keep herself warm. She held herself upright and rigid, not sure what he wanted her to do, until his hand on her cheek guided her head to his shoulder.

"I'm sorry, Kitten. You scared the fuck out of me when I came home and heard you screaming at Ian. Then, when I found you and the girls in the hot tub, well, I..."

"Don't apologize, Sir. I didn't ask permission to use your hot tub. You were right to be angry."

"Fuck that shit. This house is as much yours as it is mine. I wasn't upset about your using the hot tub. I thought you were...hurt, or hurting." He stroked her hair, and his voice softened. "I was worried about my little kitten."

The dam broke, and a sob tore from her chest at his words. She clutched the front of his shirt and held on tight.

"Shhhh. I have you."

He rocked the chair and held her while she cried, until she began hiccoughing and sniffling. "Tell me about the ceremony."

She waited until she had regained some of her composure. "I'm so angry at him, Master. He left me. He left me even before he was killed on that damned motorcycle. Why didn't he come to see me at the club those last few months? And why doesn't he come to me now to let me know he's okay?"

He continued to rock back and forth in the chair, the motion providing her with some comfort. "I can't answer those questions, but I know anger is about the toughest part of the grieving process to get through. But you do have to get through it; have to let it go. Having your ceremony will probably help."

"Were you angry with Joni?"

Oh, shit. Why had she brought Joni into their special time together?

* * *

Still am.

Now where had that brainfart come from? She'd been dead and buried for nine years now. What could he possibly still be angry about?

Then it hit him. He'd expected honesty from Karla. He owed her the same.

"Yeah. I think she knew her cancer was back when I was home on medical leave earlier in the year she died. She didn't say anything, so I had no fucking idea. I went back into combat not knowing she may not be there when I got back."

She reached up and stroked his cheek. "Oh, Master, I'm so sorry. But isn't a slave supposed to share everything with her Master?"

"We weren't in a TPE arrangement then. Those relationships are hard to do long-distance, although lots of people do it on the internet now. Internet access was pretty limited in Kandahar back then. Besides, I couldn't maintain an intense relationship like that and also keep my focus on combat." He'd always put combat zones and military conflicts ahead of Joni.

Karla's fingernail scratched his whiskers, seemingly fascinated by the sound. His dick stirred again. Damn. This wasn't the time or place.

"What's your favorite fantasy, Master?"

Whoa! Clearly, her thoughts had strayed into similar territory. How could the two of them be so different and still have times like this when they were in sync with each other? "I have a few. Having a beautiful harem girl is one."

She giggled, making him grow hard.

"What's so funny?"

"I think I can…I mean, I can't really picture you being into the sheikh or sultan thing."

He chuckled. "Maybe I spent too much time in the Middle East. Not that I saw any harems or would like the responsibility of that many slave women." God, no. Just having three naked women on his deck had been enough to stop him in his tracks.

"How about you, Kitten? What do you fantasize about?"

She reached out to stroke the collar of his shirt. "Promise you won't laugh?"

"It can't be any further out there than mine, can it?"

"Well, no. It's boring as fantasies go."

"Tell me."

She glanced over at his desk, ignoring the photos of Joni. "I think it would be really hot to have sex on a desk like this." Her fingers stroking the smooth wooden surface of his desk gave him a raging woody now. "Maybe even to be spanked—" She looked up at him and clarified herself. "Not too hard; just for fun."

He chuckled at her stipulations before he caught himself. "Your Master decides how hard and how long, Kitten, and whether it's time for play, discipline, or punishment." She grew stiff in his arms. Both of them needed to blow off some steam tonight. That she'd shared the fantasy with him was enough for him to know she needed to experience it. Now.

"Stand up."

She did as he instructed without hesitation, but he noticed the hem of the robe she wore shaking as she stood before him.

"Strip."

Karla let the robe glide down her arms. Her erect nipples, no doubt still sensitive from their nipple-clamp play in the great room last night, called out to him, but he fought the urge to touch them yet. Clearly, she was as turned on as he was. He stood and began removing items from the top of the desk—his laptop, photo frames, desk blotter. No, he'd leave the blotter. Probably part of the fantasy. He walked to the corner of the room and picked up his leather toy bag, where he'd left it last night.

"Give me your wrists."

She held her slender wrists out in front of him, and he cuffed each one before reaching back into the bag to pull out four utilitarian cuffs and an equal number of chains, laying them on the blotter. She flinched. Well, he'd let her think he planned to use the chains on her backside for a bit. A little fear and anticipation would heighten the senses and her responses to what he would be doing to her body. He pulled out two more padded cuffs like the ones on her wrists and worked his way around the desk, bending to attach the utilitarian ones to each of the legs. When he stood, he noticed Karla's gaze hadn't left the chains and her eyes were as wide as saucers.

Fantasy time. He sat back down in his chair. "Miss Paxton. I'd like you to take a memo."

Her gaze tore away from the chains and settled on him. He watched her pupils dilate, and his dick throbbed seeing her fear mixed with excitement.

"Y-yes, Sir." She looked around, as if to find a steno pad, and turned back at him with a question in her eyes.

"Don't tell me you came in here again without your pad and pen."

She paused only a moment, before she clicked into the fantasy with him. "I'm s-sorry, Sir, but I'm afraid I did."

"If this were the first time, I think we could just forget it. But this isn't the first time, is it, Miss Paxton?"

"N-no, Sir."

"What should I do about this latest infraction, so you won't forget next time?"

Her gaze returned to the chains, then back at him. A pleading look besieged him. He was afraid she'd back down from the fantasy, instead she raised her chin a bit—showing him the old Karla was still inside there somewhere—and squared her shoulders.

"I need to be spanked, Sir."

He looked down to see her nipples grow even larger, more erect. Her breathing became shallow and her lips parted slightly. She certainly seemed turned on and ready for the next phase. Just to keep her in the dark a little longer, he needed to play with her head a bit more. Standing, he reached into his toy bag and pulled out a man's silk tie.

"Turn around."

She glanced at the tie before presenting him with her curvy backside. He held each end and reached around, securing the tie tightly around her eyes and head. "How does that feel?"

"Fine, Mr. Montague."

He grinned. She was getting fully into the fantasy now. "Good girl." He smacked her ass lightly, and she squeaked. So sensitive. Was she sure she knew what she'd gotten herself into? Well, they'd both find out soon enough.

* * *

Her ass stung where he'd smacked her. *Oh, dear Lord.* If it stung from a light smack, what on earth was she going to be feeling when he used those chains on her? This wasn't quite the fantasy she had in mind. Just a bare-handed spanking is what the bosses used on the secretaries in any of the fantasies she'd ever seen or read about.

Leave it to Master Adam and his BDSM kink to ramp things up. But she wouldn't turn back now. Adam knew how she felt about extreme pain—didn't he? She still could safeword if it got too intense. But this was only a fantasy. Just for fun. Surely she wouldn't have to worry about a safeword. Of course, she supposed everything was just for fun with Adam. He didn't have to be on the receiving end of the pain. Ever.

"Lie face down on the desk." She heard the rattle of the chains as they hit something softer, then felt his hand on her arm and back, steering her toward what she hoped was the desk. "Bend over." *Trust him.* She leaned forward until she would have fallen on her face, but one hand remained steady and supportive on her arm with the other just below her breasts as he eased her down onto the cold, hard surface. Her nipples bunched, but the blood thrumming through her veins left the rest of her feeling anything but cold.

He adjusted her backside to where her hip joints were right at the edge of the desk and tapped at the insides of each of her ankles, indicating she should spread her legs open. The vulnerability of the position left her shaking, but needy.

Adam won't harm you. True. But why did he want to beat her with chains?

His hands glided over her ass and down the backs of her thighs to her knees, then shifted to her inner thighs and came back up until his right hand slid inside her intimate vee and stroked her pussy.

"So wet for me, Miss Paxton." She smiled. Master Adam was pleased. "Did I give you permission to get wet?"

Oh, no. She was in trouble *again*.

"Answer me."

To hell with it. She was supposed to be honest. "No, Sir. But I've dreamed about this for months, and I…can't help myself." *Oh, no!* She was mixing fantasy with reality. In July, when she'd come to Denver and inadvertently wound up auditioning at his sex club, she hadn't even known about this part of his life. Of course, in their years of letter-writing, he continued to think of her as a sixteen-year-old kid, which she had been when they'd first met.

Since he'd held her in his lap on the loveseat in this very room, she'd dreamed about being taken by Adam on his desk. But in her virginal fantasies, she wasn't cuffed and lying face down on the desk—and there most definitely weren't any chains.

He removed his finger. The heat of his body warmed her, even though he was no longer touching her. When his fingers entered her pussy swiftly and without warning, she gasped. Raising herself onto her tiptoes, she settled back against his hand as he pumped in and out of her pussy. She moaned.

"Silence. Don't move."

Karla nodded. She'd said enough, as it was. His fingers continued to fill her, pull out, and then fill her again. She was primed and ready for anything he dished out. An image of Master Adam's penis taking her in this position caused her clit to throb. She moaned again.

Smack.

The sharp sting of the palm of his free hand against her left ass cheek caused her to jump, pulling up and away from his fingers. His fingers didn't enter her again. Fighting the urge to groan, she wiggled her ass. *Touch me again, Sir.*

Smack.

"Do. Not. Move."

Ka-thunk!

His firm hand grasped her left ankle and pushed it further out. She heard Velcro and something cold around her ankle. He slipped a finger inside the cuff. "How's that? Too tight?"

"No, Sir. It's fine."

He did the same with her right ankle. So open, exposed, vulnerable. Thank God she did hip exercises or he might have torn her apart at this angle.

The rattle of the chains put her senses on full alert. *Oh, dear Lord.* The heavy, cold metal pressed against her back as he ran one of them down the valley of her spine. By the time it reached the curve of her ass, the metal was no longer cold. Her hips tilted up to embrace it.

"Do you like the feel of the chains on your ass, Miss Paxton?"

Direct question. Answer him.

"Um, yes, Sir. Well, like this anyway. It's…exciting."

He chuckled. "Good to know."

What would he do with that information? She didn't think she wanted to know. The man had a diabolical mind when it came to making a woman beg. Making her needy. She hoped she didn't sound as needy as she felt. She was too vulnerable to him already.

The chains rattled, and she heard a click. Then he touched the cuff on her left leg and she heard another click. *Damn him!* The chains were just for restraining her to the desk. But her annoyance soon turned to relief. Her body turned to mush on the desk as she sank against the wood. He was just messing with her head.

He made quick work of restraining her right ankle to the desk, then picked up more chains and moved to the other end of the desk. "Hands open. Palms down." She did as he instructed and felt the tug of her right arm as he attached a length of chain to the wrist cuff. He pulled it until her hand was outstretched. *Oh, God.* Did her sweaty palm just squeak against the desk? The chains rattled, and she heard another click. She pulled and found no give in her arm.

"Is that too tight?"

"N-no, Sir." *Not yet.*

"Tell me if your arms hurt or get numb."

He restrained her other arm similarly, then she heard him digging through his leather bag again. What other means of torture did he have hiding inside there?

"Tell me again, Miss Paxton. Why are you needing a spanking?"

"Because I forgot my pad and pen, Sir."

"You remember your safeword?"

Oh, no! He wouldn't spank her hard enough to need it would he?

"Miss Paxton?"

"Y-yes, Sir. Red, Sir."

"If you use it, the safeword will only apply to this scene, not our TPE arrangement."

Relief flooded her, and she relaxed.

He brushed his hand over her butt and gooseflesh rose in his wake. "I think five swats will suffice in getting you to remember your duties next time, Miss Paxton. Count them for me."

Five smacks of his hand didn't sound so bad. He'd already smacked her a few times. Definitely do-able.

Swat!

Oh, God, no! That wasn't his hand. Whatever he'd swatted her with stung like a wasp, the burning increasing as the cool air hit her. He was blowing on her ass cheek? Oh, what had she gotten herself into?

"Miss Paxton."

"I'm sorry, Sir. One!"

"Faster next time."

Swat!

This time the paddle or whatever it was smacked her other cheek. "Two, Sir!" Her ass was burning after only two swats. *Dear Lord.* This wasn't the fantasy she had in mind.

Swat!

"Three, Sir!" She clenched her hands.

"Hands flat on the desk."

She complied as quickly as she could force her fingers to open.

Swat!

"Ow! I mean, four, Sir!" Her voice sounded ragged and tears wet the tie. More cool air blew over her burning butt and the rising gooseflesh just made the stinging even worse. *Sadistic bastard.*

Swat!

"Jesus!" The last blow landed against her pussy lips and her erect clit. *Oh, God.* How could she be excited by this kind of pain? *Count, Miss Paxton!* "Oh, five, Sir!"

"Good girl."

Relief flooded her that she'd pleased him—and that they were finished. Those emotions made sense. What she didn't understand was the unexpected cathartic feeling of relief washing over her. The paddling had released something that had been embedded deep inside her, something she'd clung to since Ian's death.

A strange mixture of a sob and a giggle escaped from her raw throat. It was over. She waited for him to remove the cuffs and chains.

But she waited in vain. Instead, she heard a familiar foil packet being torn. He wouldn't. Not like this! His warm, hard penis pressed against the cleft of her pussy, rubbing up and down from her pussy hole to her swollen and sore clit. Yes, he would.

She squirmed, not sure whether she wanted to get away from him or line him up better. When he bobbed his erection repeatedly against her clit, teasing it to become even more erect, she knew the answer.

"Oh, yes, Sir! Right there!" She gasped for breath. *More.* She needed more of him. "Please, Sir. I need you inside me."

"I will determine what you need, Kitten."

She groaned. How could he work her up to this and leave her hanging—like a rag doll over his desk? He continued to tease her clit. Holding her right hip, he lowered his penis to her pussy hole. *Yes. Please, Master!*

He pressed inside her then pulled out. She whimpered. Needy. Not caring. "Please, Master."

"Please what, Kitten."

She drew a ragged breath that did nothing to fill her starving lungs. "I need you, Master."

He took hold of her hips and drove himself deeply inside her. "Oh, God, yes!" He pulled her hair until he lifted her head off the desk. Her clit throbbed for more, her mons slamming against the edge of the desk providing torturous stimulation. She was being battered and rammed. So rough. Oh, God. She loved it.

"More, Sir."

What had gotten into her? She couldn't hold back the build-up of emotion. His love-making was raw, gritty, elemental. And she was begging for more. Luckily, he gave her what she asked for. His fingertips dug into her right butt cheek, still sore from the paddling, and he bent over her, biting her shoulder.

The pain and pleasure mixed, and her clit felt as if it were about to explode.

"God, Karla. You feel so fucking good."

Yes, I do! "So do you, Sir! Fuck me harder." *Oh. My. God. I didn't just say that.* Then all thought left her mind as he pounded her to an earth-shattering orgasm. She screamed, something incoherent, her vaginal muscles clenching against his hard penis.

"Come with me, Kitten."

I already did. Then she came again. "Yesss, Sirrrrrr! Oh, please. Oh, God. Ohhhhhhhhhhh!"

His earthy grunt and the pulsing of his penis deep inside her told her he'd joined her, and she hurtled over the cliff with Adam holding tightly onto her.

Chapter Eight

Adam woke in the middle of the night to find himself spooned against Karla, his arm wrapped around her waist. He should have taken things a lot more slowly with her, but having her close like this was even better than having sex with her.

Not that he didn't enjoy the sex. Her initial enthusiasm for sex, including the rough stuff, had led him to forget she'd been a virgin until less than two days ago. He'd pushed her too far, too fast, but when was the last time he'd dealt with a virgin and newbie sub in one person?

Joni.

Karla moaned in her sleep, waking with a start. "It's okay, Kitten. I have you." Her hand came to rest over his, as if to reassure herself he was there. Then she curled into him further and promptly went back to sleep. God, he'd forgotten how nice it was to hold a woman like this. Too fucking long. He hadn't even realized he'd missed that, until he had Karla in his bed. In his arms.

In his life.

A sense of contentment spread over him. He hadn't felt that in a long time either.

He must have dozed again, because he woke to find two sparkling blue eyes staring up at him from the pillow beside him. She smiled. "Good morning, Sir." Her breathy greeting sent his dick to throbbing. Damned morning woodies.

He reached up to smooth a loose strand of hair from her face. She didn't notice his stiffie, thank God, because he wasn't touching her there. "Good morning, beautiful."

Her hand came up to stroke his cheek and he heard the scratch of his whiskers against her fingertips. She reached up to rub a finger against his temple. He throbbed for her. How could such an innocent gesture set his little head off like that?

"I'll be right back."

He went to the bathroom to relieve himself and returned to set and light the fireplace to chase away the morning chill in the room. Karla padded into the bathroom, her long T-shirt doing nothing to hide her long, sexy legs.

He tossed a bigger log on the fire. Was he ready for winter to set in? Soon he'd be in Minnesota for his annual visit. Most years, he looked forward to going back to visit Joni's mom and spend some time at his wife's grave on their anniversary. This year, he dreaded the trip. For one reason, Marge was downsizing—moving to an apartment—and had told him to be prepared to do something with the stuff Joni had left. He'd put off dealing with that huge box in the closet for almost six years, since he'd retired from the Corps.

He stood, walked around the bed, and sat on the edge, waiting for Karla. When she came back, her erect nipples bounced under her long T-shirt as she walked. He tried not to notice. *Yeah, how's that working for you, old man?* Maybe they were stimulated from the cold. The room sure felt warm enough to him now, though.

She smiled down at him and he reached for the hem of her tee, making sure she wouldn't be sitting on it when he pulled her into the cradle between his thighs. So right.

She giggled. Damn her. He moved away from the edge of the bed to put more space between them. He placed his hands on her shoulders, figuring that would be a safe place to touch her. Soon, his hands drifted down and he lifted her T-shirt and began removing it, watching her arms go up without having to tell her to do so.

"Relax now." He took her long black curls and pushed them out of his way to cascade over her left shoulder. He tried to keep his touch firm, but gentle, as he began to knead the knotted muscles in both shoulders. God, her muscles were bunched up.

She moaned as if in pain.

"You'll feel better once we get the kinks out."

"I thought it was all about the kinks, Sir." She giggled and he fought the urge to pull his brat's hair and throw her onto the bed underneath him. Damn her.

Karla's pale skin felt like satin in his hands, as he massaged her neck and shoulders. He couldn't keep himself from bending forward and pressing his lips against her shoulder blade any more than he could have denied himself water in Iraq. He kissed the hollow of her neck. Air hissed from her lungs, making him aware of his scratchy five-o'clock shadow. But her head lolled to the side and she moaned again, definitely not from discomfort. He took her submission as an invitation for him to trail more kisses along the column of her long, slim neck, then nibbled on the fleshy part of her shoulder.

"Oh, Master. Keep doing that."

"Are you telling your Master what to do, Kitten?"

She tensed again and he regretted teasing her. Hell, he wanted to know what she liked, what she wanted. He let his hands glide down her arms, pulling her tighter against his chest. Her eyelashes fanned just above her cheekbones and her head lay against his shoulder. He reached around to cup both of her high, firm breasts in his hands. He'd loved clamping and binding her tits and nipples. He gently rolled each between his thumb and forefinger and squeezed, then twisted.

"Oh, God!"

Her breathy gasp and the arching of her chest toward his hands told him all he needed to know.

"Tell me what you need, Kitten." He nuzzled her neck as his right hand ventured south until he cupped her Venus mound and his middle finger stroked her wet slit. Her pelvis tilted to allow him access, but he waited for her to say the words.

She moaned in frustration.

"Tell me, Kitten."

"I need you, Sir."

"You need me to what?" He could feel the heat rise from her face.

"I need you to…make love to me, Sir."

What Adam had in mind had nothing to do with love; her romantic words made him feel a little guilty. Sure, he had intense feelings for her, but he'd never be able to love anyone. He needed to keep things on the level with her, keep her from entertaining any fairy-tale notions.

"Your Master plans to fuck you hard and fast again, Kitten. Are you ready for that?"

She tensed and he heard that sexy hitch in her throat. "I…um, I think so, Sir."

God love her. He chuckled. "Well, I think maybe we need to start a little slower, Kitten." He could restrain her and she'd take whatever he dished out, but he wanted to see how she would submit and give of herself without restraints. "Stand up." She barely hesitated before standing. "Turn around."

She turned to face him and he lay back on the bed. "Take them off." His gaze went to his black skivvies.

Karla hesitated a bit longer this time. She looked down at him and the outline of his rock-hard penis straining against his skivvies. Her tantalizing teeth gave him another idea.

"Take them off—with your teeth." God, he'd regret this for the rest of his life, but having her sexy mouth that close to his dick was all he could think about right now.

She glanced down at him and smiled a shaky smile, then bent over him, bracing herself by placing her hands at either side of his waist, and damned if she didn't take his waistband between her teeth. *Shit*. Her fingers warmed on his bare skin and her grip tightened, whether to hold herself steady or both of them, he didn't know. His dick bobbed against her chin, causing her to stop, pull back, and reassess the situation. So fucking sexy. Then she bent down and took the waistband between her teeth again, pulling it up and over his erection until the head of his dick poked out.

She pulled back yet again, her face taking on a playful expression. "My, what have we here, Sir?" Her hand reached down to cup his still-covered balls, and then moved up the length of his mostly covered dick until she brushed her thumb over the bare head.

"Karla, no hands."

Ignoring him, her thumb pad rubbed over the notch in the head of his cock, which eagerly bobbed its welcome. "Oh, Sir, it feels like velvet."

Fuck. She'd apparently not even touched one before. He was going straight to hell for letting her continue down this path to debauchery, but he couldn't have refused her now if he'd wanted to—which he most certainly didn't want to do.

"Do you want your first punishment, slave?" Her hand pulled away, as if his dick had become a red hot poker. "Good girl. Now remove them completely." He gave the command through clenched teeth.

"Yes, Sir." Her upper teeth scraped against his dick as they wrapped around the waistband again. All the air left his lungs, but he didn't have the wherewithal to replace it. So close. What would her hot mouth feel like sheathing his cock?

Don't go there, old man.

The tip of his dick brushed against her nose as she pulled his skivvies a little further down, nearly causing him to lose all control. Rather than take them all the way off, she got sidetracked yet again, which made him throb for her even more. With one tentative hand, she cupped his balls.

"Augghh." His hips lifted toward her face. Sweat broke out on Adam's forehead and he closed his eyes. Sweet Jesus, her hand felt so good on him, the combination of innocent naïveté and hesitant touch an incredible turn-on.

Rather than tell her what to do or reprimand her, he decided to wait and see what she'd do of her own volition in her first carnal exploration. Her sweet, warm breath on the head of his dick had him straining toward her. For the longest time, she merely stared at his dick with uncertainty. When she wrapped her tiny hand around his girth, over his skivvies, she applied the sweetest pressure. Torture. The girl was fucking torturing him, whether she intended to or not. When had he lost control of this scene?

She squeezed him and seemed surprised by the strength and muscle in his dick. But she didn't squeeze his balls or go straight to pumping his cock, as an experienced woman might. Instead, her thumb began stroking the exposed ridge on the head of his cock, back and forth, and he had to reach out and grasp her hand to stop her. Now *he* needed to slow things down. When she looked up at him, stricken with insecurity and fear, he smiled his encouragement.

"Kitten, what you're doing feels so good, I'm afraid I might explode before I'm ready. Let's take this a little slower, okay?"

She smiled. "Yes, Sir." He loved the sense of newfound power she exuded. This girl would make some man very happy someday with her erotic mix of kitten and tiger.

She latched onto his skivvies again and pulled them down further as he lifted his hips to aid her, but she released them again just below his balls and returned her attention to his now aching dick. Her wide-eyed gaze stared at the length and thickness of his erection, and she furrowed her brows.

"How did we…?"

"Don't worry, Kitten. We fit together perfectly." She looked up at him for reassurance. "We sure did last night and yesterday morning, didn't we?"

She smiled and turned her attention back to his equipment, her thumb continuing to make that enticing motion along the ridge. He wanted to let her explore a bit more, but damned if he could hold on for what he'd originally had in mind if she kept touching him like that. When pre-cum lubricated her thumb, increasing the ease with which she could flick over his notch, her eyes opened wider in fascination.

His cock pulsated in her hand. *Slow, deep breaths.* He tried to practice the techniques he'd learned in martial arts to slow down his heart rate, hoping it would lessen the pulsing in his dick. When she surprised him by letting the tip of her pink tongue tentatively lick him where her thumb had been moments before, he groaned, balling his hands into fists at his sides to keep from thrusting his hips up and ramming his cock down what obviously was her virgin throat.

As if she were giving him a news bulletin, she paused to look up at him and announced, "You taste salty, Sir."

"Karla," he ground the words out, "get my fucking skivvies off—now."

He heard her giggle, which made him even harder, but she obeyed. *About damned time.* He'd have to work on obedience with her soon, although he had to admit he wouldn't have missed this slow tease for anything. Even if it was the fucking slowest one he'd ever experienced with a girl.

"Just use your hands." Having her head anywhere near his at the moment was a tactical disaster waiting to happen. When she finally stripped them the rest of the way off, she knelt on the floor, head between his thighs, waiting for further instructions.

"Open the drawer in the nightstand and get a condom." She turned without hesitation and did as he instructed, holding her foil-wrapped find out to him like a trophy.

"Open it and put it on me."

She carefully tore the edge of the foil, as if afraid she might damage its contents, and then gingerly pulled the rubber from the pouch. Discarding the foil on the nightstand, she took the rubber in both hands and looked up at him with uncertainty.

"Just press the center against the tip of my head…dick…penis." God, he didn't know what term she'd be comfortable with. *Shit.* He'd forgotten how new everything would be to her. "Then just roll it down the length of me."

Her tiny hands went to work, her deliciously pink tongue protruding from her lips as she concentrated on the task at hand. His bobbing dick didn't make this any easier for her. But soon she had managed to sheath him, then stood and smiled down at him as if she'd just conquered Mount Evans.

Not sure how much longer he could hold out, he ordered, "Straddle me." He held his hands up to her to help position her on top of him. She stood and climbed up onto the bed. Her knees pressed against the juncture of his waist and hips, her sweet pussy hovering over him. He wasn't sure how much natural lubricant she had, so he took his dick in hand and tilted his hips up to rub it along her cleft. He moved between her slick folds without impediment, watching as she closed her eyes and threw her head back with abandon when he began to slap his dick against her clit.

"Ohhh!"

She was ready. "Now, sit on it."

Her eyes flew open and she looked down, searching his face. "Sir?"

"You're in control of how fast and how deep. Just ease the tip inside, bob up and down on it a few times, taking me deeper with each stroke until your sweet ass is plastered against my pelvis."

It took everything he had not to thrust up and into her when her tight pussy slowly began to envelop his head. His upper lip grew wet with the strain to remain still, but he wanted her to get used to him again at her speed, not his. This angle was different from what they'd done before.

"Oh, my Lord, I feel so full."

Sweet Jesus, don't give me a blow-by-blow. You're killing me here, girl.

As she took him deeper, she lowered her upper body over his and rested on her forearms, her hands combing through his short-cropped hair. Her face came down onto his and her tongue licked the rim of his mouth before he opened up and sucked her tongue inside. She soon took control and her tongue stroked in and out, deeper each time, simulating what her pussy was doing to his dick.

Unable to stop himself, his hands reached out to cup the curves of her ass. He didn't try to set the pace, but he wanted to enjoy feeling the rise and fall of her ass in his hands as she took him deeper and deeper. At last, her upper thighs brushed against his hips. She'd fully seated herself. Her face pulled away and she grinned down at him in triumph.

His little innocent was not looking particularly innocent at the moment. His dick pulsed, and her pussy answered by squeezing around him.

"I need to move inside you, Kitten. Are you ready to ride?"

Her pupils dilated and she grinned. "Giddyup, Sir." She lifted herself up, raised her hand in the air, and shouted, "Yee-hah!"

Damn, girl. Clearly, she was off in her own little fantasy world now. Time to rein her in. He pulled her hips back down at the same time he thrust himself deep inside her.

The smile left her face. "Oh!"

"Are you okay?"

"Oh, yeah." Her breathy whisper was sexy as hell. She smiled. "Don't stop…Master Adam."

He smiled that she nearly forgot how to address him. He liked that he made her mind turn to mush just about as much as she did his. Needing no further encouragement, he gripped her hips harder and pulled her off him, then impaled her again. She grunted and closed her eyes as he repeated the movements again and again. Soon, she matched his rhythm. Her pussy squeezed him like a vise, released him, and then squeezed again. He increased the tempo even more, slamming her against him. Knowing he was about to come, he reached his right hand between the juncture of their bodies and placed his fingertip over her erect clit.

"Oh, my God!" Karla stopped moving for a moment, but he continued to piston her pussy until soon she was meeting his strokes again. Her incoherent mewling told him she was nearing the crest.

"Come with me, baby tiger."

On cue, her clit hardened even more. Her pussy clenched around him, and she screamed her release just as his dick exploded inside her. He'd never felt anything so mind-blowing in his life and didn't want the moment to end. For what seemed like forever, his dick twitched inside her as the spasms from her velvet sheath sucked him dry.

"God, Kitten. You're killing me."

She collapsed against his chest. "How can that be? I think I died first."

"Just the little death."

"*Petit mort*. Now I know what they mean."

"That's the one, Kitten. Best way to go."

He stroked her hair with one hand and her back with the other. Her weight on top of him felt so fucking good. His cock still throbbed inside her. Her pussy continued to pulse with tiny, intermittent aftershocks. It wouldn't take much for him to be ready to go again, but that wasn't a good idea.

He didn't want to break contact just yet, but he wanted to get rid of the condom before they went back to sleep. "I'll be right back." He tried to roll her off of him and pull out of her warm sheath, but she moaned and her body grew heavier. She'd fallen asleep. Damn.

He stroked her hair. "That's it, Kitten. Sleep now." He reached out and pulled the sheet and blanket over her naked body and soon fell asleep with her.

* * *

"Get the fuck off me, you son of a bitch!"

Karla's eyes opened as her world spun out of control. She was thrown onto her back and looked up to find Adam holding her hands above her head, his fingertips biting into her wrists. His body pressed hers into the mattress. The crazed look in his eyes told her this wasn't the Adam she loved. He must be in the middle of some kind of nightmare.

"Adam, wake up! It's me, Karla." Her heart thudded against her chest. The rage on his face terrified her. What if he didn't wake up? Would he hurt her? She needed to get through to him. "Adam, you're dreaming. You're safe. No one wants to hurt you."

He blinked several times, his breathing harsh to her ears. At last, his focus cleared and intensified. She expelled her pent-up breath.

"Adam? Are you okay?" He continued to suck air in and out through his mouth, then looked up at her hands and loosened his grip. She might not have gotten bruises from their BDSM play in the last couple of days, but she'd certainly have them now.

"Oh, God." He rolled off her and stared up at the ceiling. "Did I hurt you?"

"No, Master. You were dreaming."

"Fucking nightmare." He rubbed his hands over his eyes as if to wash away the images. "I need to hit the head and get rid of this condom."

Karla couldn't believe she'd fallen asleep on top of him right after they'd made love. She'd never felt so relaxed and safe. But was her weight on him what triggered the nightmare? Or was it more than a nightmare? Did Adam suffer from PTSD? When he returned from the bathroom, naked and beautiful, she turned onto her side and propped herself up on her elbow. "Maybe if you talk about it..."

"Not now. I don't want to talk about it." He rounded the bed and lay back down, but kept his distance from her.

She rolled over, closer to him. "It can help sometimes. Take away its power. Just like you got me to do when I had nightmares about Ian."

"This is different."

"How so?"

"It's me." He grinned over at her, but she ignored his attempt to deflect her concern.

She reached out and stroked his cheek. "Adam, I'm a good listener. Try me."

He placed his hand over hers, squeezed it, and then moved her hand away from his face. "It was just a dream. It didn't mean anything. It didn't even make any sense."

"Tell me about it. Maybe I can help sort it out. What did you dream about?"

"Karla, I'm not going to talk about it with you. Now drop it. That's an order."

His words stung, and she pulled her hand back. Clearly, he didn't want to open up to her about anything personal. He never did.

"I'm sorry, Sir."

"I think it's best if you sleep in your own bed the rest of the night."

Tears filled her eyes. He didn't want her here. A knot formed in her throat and Karla needed to get away before she embarrassed herself with tears. She reached for Adam's robe and started toward the door.

"I'm sorry, Karla. It's not you. I just don't want to hurt you."

She opened the door and turned toward him. "Too late for that, Master Adam. You already did." Not waiting for a response, she exited as quickly as she could.

By the time she reached her room and opened the chest of drawers to pull out a long T-shirt, she was shivering. She turned on the baseboard heat, donned the shirt, and crawled under the quilts, but even the flannel sheets Adam had bought to help keep her warm didn't come close to the warmth she felt when curled against his body.

Sleep was a lost cause at this point, so she piled the pillows up behind her and picked up the spiral notebook and pencil she kept on the nightstand for journaling, song-writing, rambling, and list-making. Propping the pad against her tented knees, she started scribbling the lyrics to some songs that had begun rattling around in her head. The songs were far grittier than anything she'd sung in the New York Goth club or even the Masters at Arms Clubs before. Some of the songs glorified inflicting pain, spoke of rough sex, but mostly it was about control—the surrender and acceptance of control.

A soft knock at the door pulled her away from her work several pages later, and she looked over at the clock. Four-forty-three. She'd been working for more than an hour, so consumed by the composition that time had stood still. She hadn't had a writing session like this since before Ian died. Maybe her creative fog was lifting. Or maybe writing a song about her frustration with *Master* Adam Montague was just the thing she needed right now.

The knock came again; Adam wasn't going to go away. He must have seen the light under the door.

"Come in."

The door opened and he stepped inside. "Are you okay?"

"Fine." Karla didn't look at him, keeping her steady gaze on the idle pencil in her hand, trying not to show that he'd hurt her. "And you?"

"Other than being a royal pain in the ass, you mean?"

Karla turned toward the doorway to see Adam grinning. Why did he have to be so damned adorable when she really wanted to stay mad at him? "Yeah, well, that's a given."

"A good slave wouldn't agree so quickly." He sobered. "Come here." He gave her a smoldering look that caused her stomach to go ka-thunk again. "It wasn't a suggestion, Kitten."

With a sigh, Karla laid the notebook and pencil on the nightstand, wincing at the strain in her neck muscles from the awkward position she'd held for the last hour. She stood and closed the space between them, looking Adam in the eyes. She wasn't quite ready to submit totally again just yet. Maybe he'd cut her some slack, her being such a new slave.

Adam's hands reached out and cupped her face. "I know you care. I don't mean to shut you out. All I can remember are random bits of nothing. They don't make sense. I can't even make enough sense out of them to describe them to you."

Karla placed her open hand against his bare pec. Wasn't the man ever cold? "Were you a child or an adult?"

"What?"

"In the nightmare. Did you feel like you were a child or an adult?"

Adam looked away. "A teenager."

"Who were you pushing away?"

"My father."

"The alcoholic?" The one who abused his mother.

"Look, I know what you're trying to do, but I just want to forget about it."

"Sounds like your mother wasn't the only one who suffered his abuse, Adam." She reached up to cup his cheek and brushed her finger across his lips. The slight tremble told her he might be fighting to maintain control. Good. He needed to lose it for once.

Adam's grip tightened on her face and he pulled her closer. "I really don't want to talk about it." He paused. "Follow me, Kitten."

She stepped toward him—what choice did she have? He grinned and took her hand, turning to leave. But she wasn't ready to let go of this conversation. Well, her mind wasn't ready; her body, on the other hand, had gone right back to doing what Adam said.

"Adam, I think if you faced the trauma of your childhood, you'll free yourself from what's haunting you right now."

Adam turned and she could tell he was pissed by the glare in his gaze, but she stood her ground. "One fucking nightmare doesn't make me haunted."

"It wasn't the first one, Adam."

His hand jerked involuntarily. "What are you talking about?"

"In the hospital, while you were feverish, you said some things…"

"What kinds of things?"

Karla glanced away. How could she repeat those words he'd spoken about his mother doing something so unspeakable? Wanting to comfort him—and perhaps herself—she wrapped her arms around his steel-banded waist and pressed her cheek against his hard chest. His heart was beating fast and hard against her face. She ached for the little boy inside Adam who had been treated so badly as a child.

Just when she thought he wouldn't return the hug, at last Adam reached around her and held her, giving her the courage to speak the words. "You were begging your mother not to lock you in something. You were telling her you'd be good, begging not to be…" Tears stung Karla's eyes, but when Adam tried to break off their embrace, she just held him tighter. "Oh, Adam. I'm so sorry. No child should have to go through that kind of torment."

"I don't need your pity."

Again, he tried halfheartedly to remove her arms from him, but he'd have succeeded if he really wanted to. She held on even tighter. "I'm giving you my love, Adam, not my pity."

His body grew even more rigid. This time, he reached for her arms and pushed her away from him until he could look down into her eyes. "That's even worse, Kitten." He turned and walked back across the hallway, closing the door to his bedroom, blocking her out. Again.

"Oh, Adam. What did they do to you?"

If Adam wouldn't talk, then she'd have to find out on her own. If she ever found his parents, she'd be sure to give them a piece of her mind, because the way they'd treated him as a boy made Adam, the man, unable to accept her love. She wouldn't leave it up to him anymore. She may be the first slave ever to declare war on her Master, but she would take no prisoners in her effort to win Adam's heart.

Chapter Nine

Karla curled into a ball under the quilt, fighting the urge to cry. *Fail.* She felt as if a wet blanket had been thrown over her. Cassie had described that feeling during one of her bouts of depression after the attack during college. But why should Karla feel depressed? Adam had finally begun seeing her as a woman.

But Master Adam doesn't want me.

After their argument over his nightmare, he'd sent her to sleep alone here in her room. She'd cried herself into a restless sleep for the last hour or so. She needed to make amends. How? She didn't even know what she'd done to displease him.

Clearly, he didn't want her anymore. Tears spilled over the bridge of her nose and onto her pillow. The stabbing pain in her chest smothered the air from her lungs. She should go wake Cassie to try and talk this through, but her friend hadn't gotten a lot of sleep last night either. No, Karla needed to fight through this, whatever *this* was.

Go to Adam. He can help.

Not now. She didn't want to deal with the mysterious voice of the woman who kept telling her what to do. It was enough that she had to take orders from Master Adam. Besides, he'd made it clear he didn't want her. He'd rejected her. Another sob tore from her throat; she curled up even tighter, trying to lessen the area these feelings could bombard by making herself a smaller target.

Go to Adam.

She groaned. *All right, already! I'm going!*

She threw the quilt and blankets back and swung her stiff legs over the edge of the bed. She grabbed Adam's robe; his lingering scent made her want to cry even more. She didn't want to throw herself at him if he didn't want her, but she did want to feel his arms around her again. She needed him to make this awful pain go away.

Problem was, he was the reason for her pain.

Karla's heart pounded as she crossed the hallway to Adam's bedroom and heard his bathroom door close. She opened his door and peeked inside the bedroom. No Adam in sight. She glanced at the hot tub and cringed. Adam said he understood what they were doing out there. Did he, or was he still upset with her?

The shower spray started, bringing her back to the present. Wasn't a slave supposed to find ways to please her Master? Surely her Master would welcome having his dutiful slave wash his body, even if he hadn't ordered her to do so. Then maybe he would hold and cuddle her again. She needed him to touch her.

Maybe taking care of his needs would help her not feel so abandoned and alone.

Oh, Lord, if he rejected her offer, though, something inside her surely would shrivel up and die. The shower door opened and closed; she reached for the bathroom door handle. Her hand stilled with it turned down only halfway. She leaned her forehead against the cold doorjamb.

Move, Kitty! She wasn't going to complete her mission standing outside Master Adam's bathroom door. She didn't have a lot of time. He took quick showers; must be his Marine training.

She wanted him to love her with his whole heart, the way he'd loved Joni. Perhaps this was just another pipedream, like her recording career. Master Adam may never be able to love another woman, if he couldn't let go of Joni. His long-dead wife still controlled his heart with an iron fist.

She opened the door and peeked inside to see if she would be approaching him without being seen, or if she needed to go on a frontal attack.

Singing? The last thing she'd expected to hear was Master Adam singing in the shower. He kept his voice low, but he definitely was singing in a voice that sent shivers over her. The man was full of surprises. She hoped she'd have many years with him to discover every one of them. Then she heard a couple snatches of the lyrics.

"Under my thumb. The girl who once pushed me around."

What girl? Her? When had she pushed him around? She smiled. Maybe there still was hope. Taking another deep breath, she poked her head the rest of the way through the door, her long loose hair dangling toward the floor. His face was in profile and turned toward the spray with his eyes closed. Perfect.

She resumed her full height and pulled her shoulders back. To achieve her goal in that shower stall, she'd need to approach him from a position of power, even if she was supposed to be his slave and under his total control—and felt like worthless crap at the moment.

She let the robe slip from her body and walked across the tiled floor to the shower stall, encased on three sides by clear glass. She'd never seen one like this before. Very open. Very revealing. Her breath caught at the sight of Adam's gorgeous chest again. His pecs made her knees nearly give out. And those nips called to her like a siren's song, just as they had when she was sixteen. His six-pack abs also looked as firm as when she'd first seen them nine years ago. The man took care of his body.

Lickable. Even as a teen, she'd fantasized his body would be delicious to lick. He reached out, picked up a bottle of body wash, and squirted some into his hand. A familiar woodsy scent permeated the air. *Adam.* He rubbed a lather into his hair.

Before he finished his shower, she'd better get inside to help. Master Adam was naked and hers for the pleasing. She only hoped he'd accept what she had to offer him.

* * *

Adam heard the shower door open and felt someone soft, warm, and naked press against him. His eyes were closed to avoid getting shampoo suds in them—not that he had any doubt who had joined him. Now she was invading his shower? "What the f…?"

"Good Lord, Master, this water is freezing!" Karla must have adjusted the temperature, because the water soon turned very warm, not that he needed any help warming up with her in here with him.

He groaned, rinsing off the shampoo, and quickly dried his eyes on the towel hanging over the shower door. Karla stood looking up at him like some innocent Alice who'd just taken a wrong turn in Wonderland and wound up in the shower with him. Damn her. He needed that cold water again to keep himself from stirring awake, because his willpower was nil when it came to Karla.

"Karla, what the fuck are you doing in my shower?"

"Shhh, Master. Don't mind me. Your slave just needs to…wants to help bathe you."

"I've been bathing myself since I was a kid. I don't need any help."

"But you haven't been bathed by me before, Master."

Her sultry smile left no doubt he wasn't in the shower with a little girl. He definitely caught a glimpse of his feisty Karla again. His balls tightened. She squirted the Oak body wash into her hands and lathered them, running her sexy hands over his chest and abdomen. Gooseflesh rose along her treacherous path. That wasn't all she raised. He also felt his nips harden into tiny pebbles beneath her fingers, and his… She balanced herself on tiptoes and pressed her lips against his.

Adam pushed her away, holding her steady by her forearms when she might have lost her balance. Last night, he'd abused her body in a way he never should have. She was practically a virgin, and he'd taken her rough and hard, and then had taken her again an hour later. Even if she'd said she wanted it, she didn't know what she was unleashing.

"Don't. Kitten, you need to go back to your room. Now."

The wounded look in her eyes did him in. Her chin quivered, and she turned to reach for the stall's door handle. He growled and pulled her back toward him, grinding his lips against hers in a gut-wrenching kiss. He should stop there, but his tongue delved inside her sweet mouth. Their tongues mated in a sensual dance, sucking, retreating. His cock throbbed against her abdomen.

Cool it. You aren't getting any this morning.

Karla broke away, gasping for air. "Sir, I think you're trying to distract your slave from her duties." She turned him toward the spray to wash the soap away. The tip of her pink tongue stuck out between her lips as she focused on her task. His dick bobbed, aching to bury itself inside her sweet pussy again.

Goddamn it, he'd promised himself that wouldn't happen again. How did she keep short-circuiting his brain?

"Karla, I want you to…"

Her pink tongue traced a path toward his left pec and laved his nipple. He wouldn't have thought it could get any harder, but it did. Shit, her tongue felt so good. What would it hurt to let her explore him a bit? He could stop her before things went too far.

After washing his other nipple with her tongue, she pulled back and smiled up at him. "I've been fantasizing about doing that since I was sixteen."

Thank you, God. All he'd needed was that reminder of how young she was. Now he'd be able to kick her out of here.

Karla rubbed her nipples against his chest until her nubs turned to stone against his water-slickened skin. *Fuck.* The girl didn't play fair. With a groan, he grabbed a fistful of her hair and pulled her head back, then bent down to take her erect nipple into his mouth. He nipped playfully at first, then bit down harder.

"Ahhhh!" Her moan of ecstasy, coupled with the jutting of her hips toward him, caused his dick to harden even more. He released her hair just as her fingers threaded through his and pulled him closer. He sucked her further into his mouth, and then pulled away taking her tit with him.

Sweet Jesus.

She gasped for air. "Sir." The breathy word made his dick bob. "I haven't finished washing you. Turn around...Sir." Somehow he didn't think adding the title made her words any less of a command. Clearly, the girl was just playing at being his submissive...his slave. She'd more naturally swing toward being a Mistress, if given half a chance. Not that he'd allow her to top him, of course.

Her hands reached up to his shoulders, and she tried to turn him. Her touch and those incredibly sexy blue eyes made him forget himself for a moment, but he halted. No way was he going to let her see his back.

He needed to re-establish his place as her Master. He needed for her to fucking safeword.

"Turn around, Kitten."

She looked up at him, her eyes wide, pupils dilated. When she didn't respond, he reached down and slapped her ass. Hard. The surprise on her face made him even harder as the sting of his hand against her wet butt grabbed her attention, the sensory memory of their time in his office a few hours ago now front and center in his mind. Minutes ago, he'd intended to march her out of the shower, but now all he wanted was to bury himself to the hilt inside her tight pussy. She might as well learn that with him, it most often would be rough sex.

"I. Said. Turn. Around." She complied, but more slowly than he'd like. "When your Master gives you an order, Kitten, you need to discipline yourself to respond more quickly or risk his displeasure—and your punishment."

Grabbing a fistful of her hair again, he pulled her head back with one hand, while he pushed her roughly against the shower stall glass. He wished he had a mirror positioned where he could see her breasts pressed against the glass, but at the moment, all he wanted to do was touch her pussy. He reached down, and his finger zeroed in on her clit. Slick. He slid down her cleft and shoved two fingers inside her without impediment. Her gasp made his balls ache. She was ready for him.

He took her hands. "Use your hands as a cushion." Prying her fists open, he laid her palms flat against the glass, in front of her face. This scene was about to get rough; he didn't want her banging her head on the glass while he was banging her pussy. "I'm going to fuck my slave, fast and hard, and she isn't going to come until I tell her she can. Is that understood?"

He heard the hitch in her breath that told him her excitement level had raised, too. She nodded. Damn it. She wanted it rough?

"Answer me." He wanted to be sure she wanted him to do this. He didn't get off on non-consensual sex.

"Yes, Sir."

Her breathless response told him all he needed to know. He stepped back, grabbed her hips, and pulled her toward him until her head and hands slid down the glass. He had her back bent at a perfect angle for leaning over and grabbing one of her tits between his finger and thumb. With his teeth against her shoulder, mindful not to bite in the same place he'd bitten her earlier, he rammed his stiff cock into her tight sheath.

"Oh, God!"

Hearing her words and feeling her pussy spasm around him was all the encouragement he needed. He stood and began pumping hard and fast, just as he'd promised. When he heard her head hit the glass, he slowed the pace and released her tit.

"Hands in front of your face." She adjusted her hands, and he began pounding his pelvis against her firm ass again immediately. She'd surrendered herself to his control. His hand moved to her clit again. He took the erect nubbin between his finger and thumb, much as he had her nipple, pressing until she screamed in pain.

"Ow! Stop!"

"Did you just tell your Master to stop, Kitten?"

She sucked air in and out of her lungs, and he watched her shoulders rise and fall with the effort to regain control. No chance. He pinched her again and her pussy clamped onto his dick like a vise. *Shit.*

"I'm sorry, Sir. Please, use your slave as you wish."

Hearing her referring to herself in the third person pissed him off. He didn't want her to see herself as his property. His slave. Was that what she wanted?

No way. Not Karla. *Safeword, damn it.*

"I don't need your permission, Kitten. I'm already using your body as I wish." He released his hold on her clit and began stroking her rapidly until her mewling whimpers told him she neared the peak.

"Please, Sir. May I come?" She gasped for air.

"No."

Her groan of frustration made him throb. He removed his hand and grabbed her hips again, pounding into her mercilessly. "Oh, Adam. Please don't make me wait!"

"What did you call me?" He ground the words out between clenched teeth, but didn't slow his pace. She felt so fucking good sheathing his dick.

"I'm...sorry, Master. Your slave forgot herself."

What would it take for her to call off this ridiculous arrangement?

Deprivation. If she enjoyed everything he threw at her when it came to BDSM and rough sex, then deprivation was the next weapon in his arsenal. He was about to come, but first ground out the words for her discipline. "Kitten...you are not permitted to come." His balls tightened, and his shaft began to pulsate as his hot cum spurted inside her.

"Sir. I don't understand."

He heard the confusion and need in her voice as he slammed into her, harder than before, and he heard her head bang against the shower wall again.

Shit. Go easier on her, jarhead.

He couldn't let her get under his last defense. He hated himself for it and didn't understand his need to push her away while at the same time bury himself inside her.

"A slave never questions her Master. If you don't want this arrangement any longer, then safeword." With a few more strokes, he finished shooting his load inside her hot pussy. His hand shook as he fought the urge to reach down and give her pleasure, too. But depriving her of one orgasm wasn't going to kill her. He needed to show her being his slave meant he had total control of her body. He needed to continue to show her how bad this arrangement was for her until he could get her to fucking safeword.

"Yes, Sir."

Fuck it, girl, why won't you call this off? He already regretted how he'd just used her body. He'd lost control. What the fuck was wrong with him? He pulled out of her, reaching down to pull off the condom. *Goddamn it, no!* His dick was bare. He'd fucked her without protection. Again.

She turned to face him a hesitant smile on her face.

"This shower is over. Get dressed." *Before I go back on my word.*

Her smile vanished. "But, Sir, I haven't washed your back."

"You aren't going to, either." She stood her ground, raising her chin, and they locked eyes. He shivered at her sudden power over him. "Go get dressed, Karla. Now!"

Shit. He could have sworn he saw tears in her eyes before she turned away and opened the shower door to leave. He felt like a scumbag for raising his voice and treating her that way. Only a poor excuse for a Dom or Master raised his voice to command attention, which obviously made him one. He'd totally screwed up with Karla and didn't see how to undo the damage without getting himself more attached emotionally. That wasn't going to happen.

But at least she wasn't standing in front of him with her sexy tits, hot pussy, and those big blue, soulful eyes. He reached over to the faucet and turned the hot water off. The cold spray washed over him full force. He needed to regain control of his overactive libido before he set foot outside this shower and came anywhere near Karla again today. He should have called her back, told her she's doing a fine job as his slave, that she's just so young and inexperienced, and that he's…he's what? A complete shithead for taking advantage of her surrender to him, of her complete trust in him, of emotions that a scumbag like him didn't deserve.

* * *

"You okay, Karla?" Cassie asked.

Karla kept her eyes on the road, not sure what to say. Adam had told her not to mention their Master/slave arrangement to Cassie—Karla didn't really want to share that anyway. How could she explain what the fuck was the matter with her? Her friend would never understand that she enjoyed being taken to the edge of pain, then tumbling over into some strange world of ecstasy. No, Cassie would think she was a freak.

But he hadn't ordered her not to talk about their relationship in general.

"Adam and I had sex." *Lots of sex.* She couldn't really call it making love. It was raw, rough, and rugged sex, no doubt about it. "It was pretty intense." *And frightening. I feel so empty now.* The feeling of melancholy she'd woken with this morning hadn't left her, but she wouldn't give in to tears.

"I guess he's doing better then, Kitty."

Karla couldn't resist a glance at her friend, who smiled at her, but with sadness in her eyes. Unable to look at her friend's pain-filled eyes, she returned her attention to the road ahead.

"I'm just glad your first time was better than mine."

Oh, Cassie. Karla reached across the seat and squeezed her friend's hand. "Those bastards should have been strung up by their balls."

"Well, I'm afraid that would never happen," Cassie said. "Not in Latin America. They just won bragging rights for life."

Karla ached for her friend. When Cassie had come back to New York to start their senior year, Karla had known at first glance something awful had happened to her roommate and friend. Dealing with the devastating aftermath of her friend's horrific gang rape had gotten both of them placed on probation as their grades tanked that fall semester. However, Cassie was so incredibly strong and had fought her way back. Well, up to a point. She'd never be the fun-loving, carefree Cassie again, especially not around men.

Cassie squeezed Karla's hand. "Adam scared me last night. I thought he was going to hit you."

"No, he'd never take his anger out on me. He'd heard me screaming at Ian during our cleansing ceremony and was just concerned about me."

"Well, he has a funny way of showing it."

Actually, he has a wonderful way of showing it, when he lets his guard down. She remembered how he'd held her after the Shibari session and how he'd cuddled her in his lap in his office before they came upstairs.

"So, what happens next, Kitty? Have you convinced him he can't live without you?"

Her black mood descended again. "No. I'm not sure what will happen next. I don't think he wants me with him anymore." She remembered being kicked out of the shower this morning, and her eyes blurred. She found a pull-off and parked.

Cassie reached out to her. "Want me to drive?"

Karla shook her head. "Just give me a minute. I'm having a really pissy day."

Cassie released her seatbelt and leaned over to give her a hug. More tears fell. "I can't make him love me, Cassie. I've tried to be what he wants, but it's never enough."

Cassie pushed her away and reached into her bag to hand her a tissue. "Karla Paxton, you don't need to change who you are for any man. If that's not good enough for him, then kick him to the curb. You're awesome and if he can't see that, then he's not the man for you."

Karla had been so focused and determined on getting him to eventually want her that she didn't see she'd been closing her emotions off from herself. Maybe that's why she'd been feeling so numb and lost. Whatever was happening to her, she just wanted it to end. Maybe she needed to stop chasing Adam. After three months, she really wasn't any closer to him emotionally than when they had reunited in July. Sex wasn't enough.

"Thanks, Cassie. I think I know what I need to do." She just didn't want to do it.

Taking a deep breath, she got the SUV back on the road and drove on. Soon after they'd come through the pass, Karla turned onto the gravel road leading down to Cassie's cabin. The blue spruce trees closed in around them on the narrow, rutted drive. Thank goodness Adam's SUV was high enough not to hit bottom. After bouncing along for nearly a quarter-mile, they came out of the woods into a clearing where Cassie's cabin sat nestled among aspens and evergreens. So Cassie.

Beautiful. Lonely. Detached.

Which could describe Adam, as well.

"Come inside for a cup of tea."

"Um, I can't really stay long. I promised Adam I'd get right back."

"You always visit a while. He'll understand."

Karla hated not being able to tell her friend why she couldn't stay, but she was still his slave until they had a serious talk about where they were going, if anywhere. Still, talking with Cassie on the drive up here had helped lift the wet blanket that had been over her since Adam left her early this morning after their fight. They really hadn't had a lot of time together this visit, what with all that had been happening over the last two weeks. Karla had about thirty minutes before she really had to get back on the road. "One cup of tea, then I need to head back to Denver."

Cassie smiled. "You've got it bad, Karla. Can't even stand to be apart for a few hours. I hope it works out. I hope he's good to you."

You and me both, Cassie.

* * *

Adam closed the lid to the laptop and looked at his watch again. Forty minutes late. Was she testing him already? He'd told her he'd have to punish her if she willfully disobeyed. Goddamn it, why was she putting him in this position? Hell, they were only finishing the second day of their TPE arrangement.

What had ever possessed him to propose this damned arrangement in the first place? He'd tested Karla's limits, thinking each time he'd gone further than she'd ever agree to go, but goddamn it, she just accepted whatever he dished out and asked for more. She'd changed, too. She wasn't the Karla who'd fucking made him insane for the past three months. This morning, she'd seemed a little lost. He'd never wanted to alter her personality, but that's what had happened with Joni at first, too.

He missed the feisty Karla who would stand up to him, tell him to his face he was full of shit, fucking declare war on him, even. How could he get her back? Did she even want to come back? She seemed to be enjoying the role of slave. She sure enjoyed rough sex—but she didn't need to be a slave to get that from him.

Not that he should be having any kind of sex with her. She was twenty-five years younger than he was. She needed to find someone closer to her own age, get married, raise babies, and share a nice long life together with him.

He looked at his watch again. Forty-seven minutes late. He should call her and read her the riot act. Why had he given her a deadline for returning anyway? Oh, how could he fucking forget? He was her Master and needed to exert his will over her. To get her to put an end to this arrangement, he also needed to try to make her life as a slave miserable.

He rubbed his hand over his face and rolled his chair away from the desk. The sore muscles and tendons in his back pulled as he stood, but he wasn't going to take another damned pill. He'd need his full faculties if he was going to navigate these waters with Karla. Besides, he needed to set up for their Shibari suspension session tonight. He'd planned to videotape her this time.

Now it looked as if there would need to be a punishment session as well. How should he punish her? She'd enjoyed being paddled last night. Maybe some other impact play? Orgasm torture? Deprivation? Well, he could call off the play scene. She enjoyed Shibari. She'd gone into subspace during their session last night—twice. Maybe deprivation would be the best way.

Except he'd been looking forward to that session all day and wasn't interested in punishing himself.

On his way to the suspension theme room he wanted to use, he heard a squeal coming from the kitchen. Maybe Karla was home. Although he'd never heard her squeal like that before, certainly not since she'd become the slave he'd created. Walking into the room, instead he found Angelina over Marc's lap, getting her ass spanked.

"Can't you two wait for the club to open tonight?"

Marc looked up and grinned. Angelina kept her gaze on the floor, her hair hiding what he was sure was a very red face at the moment. Adam was happy Marc had finally found a woman he was evenly matched with, after such a long spell of being so miserable. Before either could respond to his question, Adam's cell phone began playing the tune "This Girl is a Woman Now," one of Joni's favorite songs. How the hell did that ringtone get on his phone, and who the fuck was calling? He looked at the caller ID. Karla?

About goddamned time.

Adam's heartbeat picked up as he turned away from Marc and Angelina and pressed the accept button, putting the phone to his ear. "Where are you?" His barked question sounded harsh, but he didn't appreciate her making him worry about her like this.

Silence.

He held his breath. "Karla? What's wrong?"

"I'm sorry, Sir." She was crying.

His throat closed in fear. "Karla, tell me what's wrong. Now."

He heard her draw a ragged breath. "I wrecked your SUV."

Adam had to remind himself to breathe again. Images of Karla's battered and bloodied body flashed across his mind, and he had to lean against the doorjamb to keep himself upright.

"Are you okay, baby?" This question barely came out in a whisper.

She choked on a sob. "Oh, Master, I'm so sorry. I was tired and driving too fast. It was snowing. I didn't see it."

"See what?"

"Oh, God, she's dead." She began sobbing even harder.

"Who, Karla? Talk to me." Had Cassie been killed? *Jesus Christ, no.* What the fuck had happened? She should have gotten Cassie home more than five hours ago. How long ago had she had the wreck?

"She just jumped out in front of me, Adam."

"Cassie?"

"Cassie? No, she's home."

"Who jumped out in front of you?"

"The doe, Adam. I didn't have time to swerve."

She'd called him Adam. Even though he hated that she was so upset, he liked hearing her call him by his given name again, though he knew it was only because she wasn't thinking clearly right now.

He expelled his pent-up breath, relieved Cassie hadn't been hurt. Karla wouldn't have survived that. Thank God she'd hit the deer, rather than swerve off the road. Picturing her plunging down the side of a mountain or plowing into a tree made him even weaker in the knees. "Tell me where you are. I'll come get you."

"They brought me to the ER in Littleton."

Oh, God, no. She *was* hurt. Adam felt as if he'd just been roundhouse kicked in the gut.

"How badly are you hurt, Kitten?"

"Bruises, mostly from the seatbelt and airbag. The doctor said I may have some neck and shoulder strain tomorrow. No concussion, though. They gave me something for pain, but it's not working."

Her plaintive voice pulled at his heart. Adam needed to get to her, to hold her, to make sure she was okay.

"I'm on my way, hon." He walked over to the mug rack where he hung his keys and retrieved the set for his truck. "Just take deep breaths and hang on."

"Sir?"

"Yes, Kitten?"

"Please don't be mad at me."

"I'm not mad at you, hon."

"But I disobeyed you, Sir."

His command that she return home within a certain time rewound and played again in his head. What had he done? This damned TPE arrangement could have gotten her killed. "Kitten, stop worrying." He cleared the gravel from his throat. "I'm leaving right now. I'll be there within thirty minutes. Are they taking good care of you?"

A pause, then a meek, "Yes, Sir."

"Just do whatever they tell you. Everything's going to be fine, Kitten."

Another long silence. She said they'd given her something, maybe a sedative. "Yes, Sir. Please hurry. I need you."

Her plea broke his heart and left him feeling so fucking helpless. "I'm coming, baby."

Adam disconnected the phone and turned to find Marc and Angelina looking at him with worried expressions on their faces.

"What happened?" they asked in unison.

"Karla hit a deer. She's a little banged up, but she says she'll be okay. I'm going to go get her in Littleton."

Marc took the keys from Adam before he had time to react. His damned reaction times were slowed down by his recovery. "When's the last time you took a pain pill?"

"Two nights ago. I'm fine. Give me my fucking keys."

"Why don't you let me drive so you can hold her on the way back? She'll probably be shaken up."

Well, fuck. Of course, Marc was right. Adam wasn't thinking clearly. It would be better if he could focus on Karla on the way back and not the road. He took the keys from Marc again, though. "You can drive on the way back. Let's go."

"I'll call Damián and Grant and ask them to get some others in to help cover for you two at the club tonight," Angelina said, putting her hand on Marc's forearm. Marc nodded. "Just be careful yourselves. It was snowing when we headed over here this evening. The roads may be slick now."

Marc leaned down and kissed her cheek. "We'll be fine, *cara*. Maybe you can prepare something light for tonight, in case Karla's hungry. I doubt anyone's going to have much of an appetite."

"I know just the thing." She paused and added, "I love you." She brushed a kiss across Marc's lips, and then Adam and Marc headed out the back door.

Kitten, I hope you know I love you, too.

I just can't love you the way you need to be loved.

Chapter Ten

Karla lay curled on her side in the narrow hospital bed. The pain in her chest and shoulders radiated into her neck. Her head had begun to throb in the last quarter hour, matching the beat of her heart. Why hadn't she listened to her Master and come straight home? When Cassie had wanted to show her the painting she was working on, Karla lost track of the time until she was already half an hour late. She'd only sped a little before the snow started, and she'd decided it would be better to slow down and be a little late than to get hurt. She'd gotten hurt anyway, killed a deer, and probably totaled Adam's SUV. With limited, restless sleep last night from her uncharacteristic downer, perhaps her response time wasn't what it could have been. *Oh, why did the deer have to...*

"Just a minute, sir! Only family members are allowed back here with patients!"

"Karla, where are you?"

Sir! "Here!" Tears sprung to her eyes as she tried to rise, keeping her gaze riveted on the opening between the curtains and feeling the strain of already stiff muscles. *Please hurry, Sir. I need you.* She struggled to push herself upright and winced.

"Lie still." Adam's tall, broad frame filled the entrance to her cubicle, relief barely edging out worry in his eyes. She'd caused him to worry; he didn't need that right now. Oh, dear lord, he was the most beautiful sight in the world.

She choked on a sob. "Hold me, Sir."

He hurried the few feet to get to her and scooped her into his arms, then sat on the edge of the narrow bed. "Oh, baby. I'm so glad to see you're okay."

"I am now. I'm sorry."

"I've got you, Kitten. Don't worry about anything."

Safe.

Karla's body began shaking. Another sob broke deep within her. She'd been on the verge of crying all day, only now she had no reason to cry. What was wrong with her? Everything was going to be okay. Adam was here, holding her.

He held her tighter against his chest. "Shhh, baby. Everything's going to be okay."

"I made a mess of everything. I didn't mean to be so late."

"We'll talk about it later, hon. Just rest now. Slow, deep breaths."

"I stayed at Cassie's too long…"

"I said we'd talk about it later."

Sir was angry. Wanting to please him again, she took a shaky breath, then another a little deeper and the shaking lessened. "Please, Sir. Don't send me away."

"Who said anything about sending you away?"

"I haven't been a very good slave."

Adam picked up the thermal blanket from the bed and wrapped it around her. He tilted her head back, and her mind grew fuzzy. The pain pill they'd given her must finally be having an effect on her, now that she didn't have to hold herself together, wound tighter than a snare drum. "So sleepy."

"Good girl. You just sleep now. I have you."

"But I don't have you, do I?" she whispered. Adam's body grew tense. A tear trickled from the corner of her eye. She'd disobeyed him. How would he ever be able to love her if she couldn't respect him enough to obey a simple command?

"I'm sorry, baby," he whispered.

What did he have to be sorry about? Sorry he'd asked her to be his slave? Sorry she'd disobeyed him? Oh, God, sorry she'd disappointed him? Or sorry that he had to send her away?

"Relax, Kitten. Get some sleep."

Her head hurt too much to sort it all out. She rested her cheek against his shoulder and drifted off to sleep.

Home.

Safe.

* * *

Adam held her closer. Seeing Karla so scared and vulnerable ripped his guts apart. He'd put her in the situation that led to this accident. If he hadn't been so intent on making her life miserable as his slave, hoping she'd put an end to this asinine arrangement, she wouldn't have been hurt.

"I'm so sorry, Kitten."

She moaned and stirred against him, making him realize he'd spoken aloud. He laid his chin on the top of her head and just held on. Nothing had ever felt as right as holding her like this.

Yet he had never been so wrong.

What was he going to do with her? Why couldn't she see he wasn't the right man for her? All she'd know with him would be pain, frustration, regret. He couldn't give her what she needed most—his love. He'd never been able to love anyone. Why couldn't he convince her she didn't need him?

Karla was the first woman since Joni he'd wanted to love him. But if he couldn't love her in return, what kind of life would that be for her?

Regrets over Joni seeped into his mind as Karla's breathing slowed and grew steady. He'd never been there when Joni had needed him, either; the worst being when their baby had been stillborn and he was somewhere in Kuwait. How Joni had continued to love him 'til the day she died was a mystery to Adam.

Now Karla. How had he rated being loved by these two wonderful women? Make no mistake, he had no doubt Karla loved him, as much as he'd like to pretend she didn't. It was written all over her face and in her actions.

What the fuck was he going to do with her?

Love her back, jarhead.

Adam grew tense. His mind was playing fucking tricks on him, but Joni's voice was as strong in his ear as if she were sitting on this bed beside him. When she'd been upset with him, or teasing him, she called him by that common, but sometimes derogatory, Marine nickname.

How convenient—getting the first wife to approve the second. *Whoa! Who said anything about a wife?* He would enjoy having Karla as his sub, maybe, but nothing more permanent.

He hadn't felt Joni with him since the weeks right after she'd died. Of course, he'd closed the door on any such feelings, heading back to war soon after he'd lost her.

I'm sorry I was such a disappointment to you, Joni.

He looked down at the beautiful, but very different, woman sleeping in his arms. "Forgive me, Karla, but I can never be the man you need. I'll do everything in my power to shelter and protect you until you find that man."

"Excuse me, sir." Adam looked up to find the same nurse who'd tried to keep him from Karla glaring at him over her clipboard. "The doctor has released Ms. Paxton, but I'll need to go over her discharge papers with you if she'll be staying with you."

"She will be. You can give me the instructions." After the nurse had gotten him to sign the release, he'd asked her to tell Marc to bring the truck around. Okay, maybe *ordered* was more accurate; once a master sergeant, always one, he guessed. Adam stood, cradling Karla in his arms as he made his way out of the hospital.

In the passenger seat of the truck, he continued to hold her in his lap. Marc drove slower than usual. Adam and Karla shared a seat belt, but Adam didn't want any jarring or sudden stops to put pressure on her already sore neck and shoulders.

Back at the house, Marc held open the passenger door and walked ahead of them to the back door to hold that one for them, as well. They entered the kitchen to the smell of strong Italian seasonings. *Damn, Marc's girlfriend could cook.* Some of Damián's edgy music spilled from the hallway leading to the club, where pre-recorded metal music entertained the members tonight. He was grateful he could trust Damián and Grant to step up when he couldn't oversee the club the way he usually did.

Angelina turned away from a large stock pot on the stove and came over to them, her hand reaching out to stroke Karla's hair and whisper, "How is she?"

"Sedated. I'm going to get her into bed."

"I have a pot of minestrone on the stove. Great comfort food. Can I fix you a bowl, Adam?"

"No, thanks, hon. Smells great, but I'll wait and enjoy it later with Karla. Thanks for going to all the trouble of making it."

"No trouble. I can make it in my sleep." Angelina reached up and cupped Adam's cheek. "I'm glad she has you, Adam."

He cleared his throat. *It's not like that.* However, he didn't owe any explanation to Angelina. He turned to his buddy. "Marc, thanks for your help tonight, too. You two stay as long as you like. Sounds like the club's hopping, if you're in the mood, but we're going to bed. Good night."

Karla raised her head and snared him with her sleepy gaze, then smiled. Adam didn't care if Marc and Angelina knew he'd slept with her already or not, but Karla wasn't going to be anywhere other than beside him in his bed tonight. He wouldn't be able to sleep unless she was nearby. Truthfully, he wouldn't be able to *sleep* with her regardless, but at least he wouldn't worry as much as he would if she slept across the hall.

He grinned back at her and proceeded down the hallway toward the stairs. "How are you feeling, hon?"

"Like the coyote in the *Road Runner* cartoons. Only better, because you're holding me." She laid her head against his shoulder again, and his chest swelled with pride that he'd made her happy with such a simple thing. He wished he could go on making her happy forever, but that wasn't the wise thing to do. He'd already learned that, where Karla was concerned, his self-control was nil.

All he would do was hurt her. Like he'd done tonight.

He carried her into his bedroom and laid her down. She moaned and reached for him, wrapping her surprisingly strong arms around his neck, but he managed to extricate himself from her grip long enough to remove her shoes and jeans. He tossed the covers aside before coaxing her to scoot over to his side of the bed so she wouldn't be lying on top of the comforter. Watching her curl onto her side, he undressed and crawled in on what he'd come to know as her side of the bed. Once he'd covered them both, he pulled her backside into the spoon of his body, wrapped an arm over her midsection, and held onto her.

"Sleep now, love."

Adam closed his eyes. What was he going to do to make things right again? How could he have fucked everything up so badly? All he'd wanted to do was protect her—from himself.

Yet all he'd managed to do was hurt her.

Big fucking surprise.

* * *

Karla had never felt so safe. Warm. Cocooned.

Adam.

His woodsy scent surrounded her; he held her again. He wasn't angry. Maybe he would forgive her for willfully disobeying him. She needed to turn around and face him, ask his forgiveness, but she didn't want to put an end to this rare intimate moment with him.

When he eased his arm away and slowly got out of the bed, though, the same sense of abandonment overwhelmed her that she'd felt when he'd walked out of her bedroom after they'd argued. When was it? Yesterday? So much had happened. Tears pricked her eyes. She tried to turn onto her back, but her neck and shoulder muscles screamed in protest. Remaining on her left side, she listened as the door opened and closed softly.

Adam was gone.

The tears filling her eyes just made her head pound even more and her sinuses clog. He wouldn't want to be her Master anymore. How could he? She was an awful slave. If she loved him enough, wouldn't she be able to give Adam herself, totally and completely? But her stubbornness wouldn't let her sell her independence, not even for Adam.

Karla didn't know how long she lay there feeling sorry for herself and miserable before she heard the door open again and the smell of…cinnamon? Had Angelina been baking this morning? Her stomach growled and she moaned as she tried to turn over.

"Lie still, Kitten."

"Adam? What have you…?"

"I've brought you breakfast—or tried. Fucking stove…"

Adam brought her breakfast in bed? He couldn't even boil water! Determined to see what he'd made, she ignored the pain and turned onto her back to find him standing there in his sweats and a USMC T-shirt, carrying a plate stacked high with gooey cinnamon rolls in one hand and a glass of orange juice in the other. The only thing sweeter was the sight of Adam, smiling at her. Fresh tears filled her eyes.

"Hey, I may have burnt the bottoms a little, but I don't think they're worth crying about." He grinned. She couldn't help but smile back as she scooted up against the headboard. Adam set the glass and plate on the nightstand. "Lean forward." She did as he told her, oddly happy he was giving her orders again. He positioned two pillows between her and the headboard. "There. Lean back."

"Yes, Sir." Those words helped to right her world somehow. Everything was going to be okay. Adam hadn't left her. Yet.

Adam picked up one of the sticky rolls, noticed the blackened bottom, and tore a piece off the top. He held it up to her mouth. "Open." Like a little bird, or a young child, she did as he instructed. He placed the doughy treat in her mouth. Next to pancakes, this was her favorite breakfast. Of course, if Adam continued to feed her like this, it just might become her favorite.

After Karla had devoured three of the eight rolls, she glanced over at the juice. He licked the sticky sweetness from his fingers. "Sorry. Forgot the napkins." His sheepish grin melted her heart like the icing on the cinnamon rolls. He picked up the glass of OJ and held it to her lips at just the right angle so she could drink without choking. No one had taken care of her like this since she'd been fifteen and sick with the flu.

After she'd indicated she'd had her fill, he placed the glass next to the plate. "You should eat some, too, Sir. I could never eat all of those."

"Try one more."

For Adam, she did and he seemed pleased, then he went into the bathroom and she heard water running in the sink. He came out carrying a balled-up wet washcloth and brushed the still-warm cloth against her mouth as he cleaned her up. Again, that feeling of being cared for, cherished, nearly overwhelmed her. Maybe she'd been wrong. Maybe he wasn't going to send her away after all.

After he returned from putting the washcloth back in the bathroom, his face grew serious. *Oh, no!* A stabbing sensation right over her heart took her breath away.

"Do you remember what happened last night?"

"We had sex."

Apparently reminding him of better times only made him grow even more somber. "No. I mean the night after that. On your way home from Cassie's."

An image of a beautiful doe springing out from the woods into her path caused her to bolt up, and the room began to spin. "Oh, no! The deer."

"Lie back." His hand on her shoulder was firm, but tender, and he settled her back against the pillows again.

"I wrecked your SUV, Sir."

He waved his hand away. "It's insured. The main thing is you weren't hurt more seriously." He stroked her hair, tucking a strand behind her ear and cupping her cheek. "You had me so fucking worried, Kitten."

"I'm sorry I was late. I'm sorry I didn't do—"

"Kitten, no more apologies."

She couldn't even apologize right. He wasn't happy with her.

Adam stood and shucked his sweatpants, but kept his T-shirt on and crawled back into bed. "I need to hold you right now, Kitten."

He wanted to hold her? She scooted back down into his warm arms under the covers. He adjusted the pillows for his head while he guided her head into the crook of his chest and shoulder.

"You're home with me now—safe and sound. That's all that matters."

Home with me. Was her home with him? Did he still want to be her Master?

"Sir?"

"Yes, Kitten?"

She paused, not sure how to ask. What if she just gave him ideas he hadn't considered yet? Maybe she should just keep her mouth shut until...

"Say what's on your mind, Karla."

Oh, it usually wasn't good when he called her Karla. She wanted to be his kitten again. At least he didn't sound super annoyed with her. She rubbed her temples, trying to formulate a lucid sentence. The normally soothing hunter-green walls in here failed to make her feel calm.

"Do you want to take one of the pain pills? Marc had the prescription filled before they went home last night."

"No, thank you, Sir." She was having enough trouble thinking clearly as it was. No sense mucking up her brain any more than it already was. His hand stroked up and down her arm, warming her a bit. "Sir, please don't give up on me yet." Her raspy whisper embarrassed her, revealing how raw her emotions were right now. So vulnerable. "I'll do better next time. I promise, Sir."

"I don't want to hear any more apologies..."

She hated the pleading tone in her voice—the neediness—but she couldn't stop the flood of words spilling from her heart. "I feel lost, Sir. Even before the accident—ever since you left my room—" She paused, trying to gather her thoughts. "I know you aren't pleased with me as a slave...that you want me to leave...that I disobeyed you—willfully. Oh, Sir, I'll take whatever punishment you want to give if you just let me..."

Adam sighed and slid away from her. She shivered without his warmth. He *was* going to leave her, or more likely ask her to leave. This was his house, not hers. If she could blink the tears away before they fell, at least she wouldn't look so pathetic. *Fail.* They trickled down the sides of her face, into her hair, and onto his pillow where her head now rested. Ashamed to face him any longer, she turned away and curled into a ball, keeping her gaze on the window and realizing for the first time she was on Adam's side of the bed.

Adam's warm hand reached out, and he took her upper arm, guiding her gently onto her back. "Eyes on me." She blinked rapidly, futilely hoping he wouldn't see her tears. She just didn't have any fight left. She gazed up at him.

"Why didn't you tell me you were feeling that way the next morning?"

She took a deep breath, not wanting to reveal something so personal, but he'd asked her a direct question. She must answer if she wanted any chance at remaining his slave. "I was embarrassed. I didn't want you to think I'm emotionally fragile. I know this makes no sense, but I went to you in the shower just because I wanted you to hold me. When you told me to get out, just as you had earlier, I..."

She felt his body tense and saw him close his eyes. She finished on a whisper. "I just felt so abandoned. Unwanted. Alone."

"Karla, about our Master/slave arrangement—" She reached up and pressed two fingers against his lips, hoping to stop the words before it was too late. Tears spilled from her eyes, but she no longer tried to hold them back.

"Please, Sir, give me one more chance..."

"Read."

Karla furrowed her brow. "Have I read what, Sir?" Why was he talking about reading all of the sudden? Was her brain still fuzzy from the narcotic or banging it in the SUV last night?

"Red, the color. Red, our fucking safeword."

"Yes, Sir. I remember my safeword. But I don't need it. Really, Sir, I'll do bett..."

"Silence." Adam pressed his finger against her lips. "Kitten, I'm the one trying to fucking safeword here, if I can get a word in edgewise."

What did he mean? Angie said subs have a safeword. She didn't say anything about Doms, or Masters in this case, using them, too. "Masters can't safeword. Can they?"

"Masters can do whatever the hell they want to do." As if to soften his words, he smiled, and the lines at the corners of his eyes crinkled just the way they had when she'd first met him at the bus station in Chicago. Why didn't he smile more now? She loved seeing those crinkles.

"Either partner can safeword, Kitten, when things get too intense or painful, or they need to stop for any reason."

Finally what he was saying sank in. *Oh, no!* He was releasing her. Permanently.

"I didn't mean to hurt you, Sir." Oh, God. But she had! She'd displeased him! "I'm so sorry."

"If I hear you say you're sorry one more time, I'm going to take you over my lap—just as soon as your injuries heal—and wallop the daylights out of you. Haven't you heard a word I've said?"

"You safeworded. You don't want me to be your slave anymore."

He smiled with satisfaction. "Exactly."

Adam's face swam before her eyes. The stabbing pain she'd felt earlier sank into her stomach now. "I'm so sor…I mean, I hurt you, didn't I, Sir?"

"Not intentionally, but…" He closed his eyes as if in pain.

Oh, but she *had* hurt him.

His gaze returned to hers, and he cleared his throat before continuing in a whisper. "I could have lost you last night, all because of my stupid command that you return within that tight window of time, without regard to weather or anything else. I should be horsewhipped."

But where would Karla be if he called it off? Adam liked his women to be slaves, didn't he? Joni had been his slave. If Karla wasn't his slave, she'd lose him.

"Please, Sir, you don't have to safeword. I really will do better. If I'd just done as you'd told me—"

"Enough, Karla!"

His raised voice caused her chest to constrict again. Damn it. How would she ever be what Adam wanted? *Could* she ever be? Apparently not.

"I'm sorry, Sir."

She heard his growl, but didn't care. At least if he spanked her, he'd show he cared for her. Clearly, she was going to lose him. The thought of not having him in her life caused the sob she'd tried to tamp down to come out in a gasp. The one person she'd wanted to love her more than anyone didn't want her.

"Please don't send me away. I can't lose you. Not again." She hated the neediness in her voice. God, how had she become so fucked up?

He gazed down at her mouth. Okay, she was rambling. He probably wanted to get one of those mouth gag things and…

"Karla, when did you say you started feeling abandoned, depressed?"

She shook her head. "I'm not depressed…" Well, maybe she was, but she didn't want to admit it to Adam.

"Answer the question."

"When you walked out of my room yesterday morning."

"I'm a fucking idiot."

Well, I'll admit you certainly are slow at figuring out how badly I need you.

"Kitten, you're experiencing subdrop."

"No, Sir, this isn't anything like what I felt when you tied and suspended me in the great room. That was incredible…"

"No, that was sub*space*. I know you've been bombarded with a whole new vocabulary lately, but subdrop is about the polar opposite. It usually happens after an intensely good scene. Can be up to a week later, but the feelings you're describing—abandonment, unworthiness, depression—those are all signs of sub*drop*. In the vanilla world outside BDSM, it's the equivalent of the feeling you get after going on the best vacation ever, then having to go back to the real world again. You tank. Hit rock bottom. For a sub/slave/bottom in the lifestyle, though, it's even more intense."

That sounded exactly like what she was feeling.

He reached out to stroke her cheek. "My guess is the drop is associated with the Shibari session. Your mind went into subspace—separated from your body—twice. That's pretty intense for anyone, let alone someone in one of their first BDSM scenes. Then our aftercare session was interrupted by Damián."

"You didn't want to get rid of me?"

"No, hon. As much as I should, I don't think I can. What I'm trying to do is get rid of this goddamned twenty-four/seven Master/slave arrangement. It's just not right for either one of us."

"But you…"

"I fucked up. Screwed the pooch. However you want to say it, it was wrong of me to offer you that. You're never going to be a slave, Karla. And that's okay."

Adam's gaze became fixed on her lips. He lowered his head and brushed his lips across hers, sending jolts of electricity to ground somewhere near her clit. She reached up, wincing at the pain in her neck muscles as she interlaced her fingers at the nape of his neck. No way was she going to let him get away this time until she was ready.

Karla opened her mouth and Adam's warm tongue delved inside. Her hips bucked up in response. *Touch me there, Sir.* Unfortunately, she couldn't ask while their lips were locked together. She moved her left hand down his arm until she found his hand and pulled it up to lay across her breast.

Touch me there, too, Sir.

He chuckled against her mouth but cupped her breast and pinched her nipple. Again her hips convulsed and she sucked Adam's tongue deeper inside her mouth. He groaned. Was he in pain, too? The coarse hairs on his leg caused gooseflesh to rise as he kneed her bare legs apart. When had he removed her jeans?

Who cares? She was just glad there was very little to get in his way.

Adam's hand released her breast with a ragged breath. "Wait. We aren't having sex. You were just in a major accident."

Karla groaned. How could he pull back now? She needed him. "Please, Sir. Don't leave me like this."

"I promise to take care of your wants later. Right now, you need sleep."

He pulled her against him and held her close, laying his chin on the crown of her head. She tried to regain her equilibrium. How was she supposed to just fall asleep when he'd stirred her body to life like that?

Wait a minute. Adam held her—tightly. He didn't want to leave. Not at the moment anyway. She wasn't his slave anymore—maybe she wasn't his submissive either—but he was holding her, and that was more than enough for her.

She turned onto her left side and scooted back against him, spooning into the curve of his body. His erection against her ass made her smile. At least she wasn't the only one turned on this morning.

Karla sighed as Adam's hand splayed open on her belly, and he pulled her closer. Maybe everything was going to be okay after all.

Chapter Eleven

Three nights later, Adam lay awake, holding Karla in his arms as he'd done every night since he'd nearly lost her. No closer to figuring out what the hell he was going to do to fix the mess he'd created, he thought back over the last few days.

Since Saturday morning, they'd laid in bed, lounged around, ate Angelina's minestrone soup to the last drop, and curled up in front of the fire to talk about…well, nothing earthshattering. Just ordinary stuff, sharing stories about their lives, catching up on the mundane facts of life they used to share in their letters over the years.

Adam had given Karla daily all-body massages. He'd even pulled the TENS unit out of his toy bag and used the electrical stimulation to help relieve the whiplash pain in her shoulders. He smiled at the thought of using the unit on even more sensitive areas.

By last night, they'd played a card game, laughed, watched some sappy chick flick about a town full of matchmakers in Ireland, and he thought the lingering effects of subdrop had disappeared. She'd reported that her muscles weren't as sore either.

He ought to be horsewhipped. What kind of Dom—technically he was her Master then, which made it even worse—was he not to anticipate subdrop?

He'd put her into subspace twice during their Shibari scene. Hell, that was intense even for an experienced sub, but he hadn't explained to her anything about it or told her to watch for the telltale emotions of a drop. The girl might have spent more than three months singing in a kink club, but her knowledge of BDSM was limited to what she could observe from the stage in the public area.

Joni had suffered from it often and he'd made her promise to seek him out in those times so he could take care of her needs until the feelings passed. Hell, Karla had done that instinctively—coming to him in the shower seeking comfort—and he'd jumped her bones and none too nicely, either. Karla hadn't shown the more obvious symptoms he was familiar with, but if he hadn't sent her off to take Cassie home, not to mention to distance himself from her a bit, he could have been around to observe and recognize the signs.

He hadn't been an attentive Master. Not wanting to be placed in that role was no excuse. Once he'd accepted it, he had a responsibility to her to make sure all her needs were met. He'd screwed the pooch royally. He'd have to watch to see what her signals were in the future.

Wait a minute. There was no future for them. What the hell was the matter with him?

You're running scared, jarhead.

"Yeah, you can say that again, Joni."

Joni? What the fuck was going on with his head?

Running scared. Well, the voice in his head had that right. He didn't like the feeling now any more than he had over the last three decades. After that blow-up with Karla over his nightmare or PTSD or whatever the fuck it was, he'd needed to put some distance between the two of them.

His only thoughts since last week were how to get himself out of this damned TPE arrangement—well, when his little head wasn't thinking about how to get back inside her pussy.

What was he going to do about her? Seeing her so helpless and hurting at the hospital Friday night had nearly killed him. He needed to be her protector, her guardian. But damned if he wasn't starting to feel he needed to be something more…something he couldn't quite name.

The side of his thumb idly stroked her abdomen. She wore her long T-shirt and he'd insisted on panties after discovering she preferred to go commando. Well, so did he, but he'd taken to wearing skivvies himself, hoping the combination would cut back on temptation for both of them. He stroked her hair and she moaned in her sleep, causing his woody to bang against her ass.

Stand down. You're not getting any.

Karla sure had changed since she'd arrived at his club. The girl had fascinated him ever since she'd shown up here last summer. She'd grown up. Many trips to the shops on Broadway had helped him transform her stage wear—getting rid of those chaste, dull Maid Marian dresses—and he'd spent many a night at the club ogling her. Even her music had drawn him in, her voice a mixture of sultriness and grit. He'd seen other men at the club watching her, too, and had to fight the urge to rip their throats out.

Possessiveness wasn't what a guardian should be experiencing, was it?

Admit it, jarhead. You want her. All of her.

But he didn't want to own her. He wanted to…what?

He sure as hell didn't want to send her away. She'd begged him not to ever since the hospital. He must have said something to her in his delirium or under the influence of pain pills to make her think that. Hell, he'd never known Karla to be insecure. He couldn't even blame that stinkin' thinkin' on the Master/slave arrangement, because it happened before. The subdrop intensified it, but its roots were deeper.

The TPE also had eroded other parts of her personality as if she'd tried to become what she thought he wanted. In the future, he'd need to be extremely careful in revealing his wants or asking her to do anything, because clearly she was going to sacrifice herself and her own needs in order to meet his. That might turn some men on, but that wasn't the Karla he was falling in love with.

Whoa! Fuck that shit! He wasn't falling in anything—except maybe a pile of horseshit. Man, if he didn't rein in thoughts like those, he'd hurt her even more. He may be attracted to her and care about her, love having sex with her, but "falling in love" wasn't in his vocabulary.

Sure, he did care about her. A lot. Big fucking deal.

Somehow he didn't think that's what Karla wanted…or needed.

Later that day, after dinner, they sat in front of the fireplace again, watching the flames licking the wood, Karla sitting upright against his chest, dressed in her long T-shirt. Her knees were tented in front of her and he fought the urge to take his hand and…

Cool it, old man.

Instead, he buried his face in her tangled curls, breathing in her citrus-y scent.

"Adam?"

"Yes, Kitten?"

"Thank you for taking such good care of me."

He hugged her tighter. The thought of not having Karla in his life anymore caused a sharp pain in his chest, not much different from the pain he'd felt after Joni died. How had she gotten under his skin so deep?

Adam rested his chin on the crown of her head. "I'm just glad you're feeling better. You scared the shit out of me."

She laughed. "I won't break, you know?"

"What?"

Rather than answer, she took his hand from around her waist and moved it up to cover her breast. His balls tightened. Her tit fit his hand perfectly. He chuckled and pinched her nipple until it became as hard as a pebble. He loved that little hitch in her breathing that signaled her sexual excitement.

"Demanding little kitten, aren't you?"

"Well, if I had to wait for you to take the initiative again, Sir, I might be an old lady."

His fingers stilled. She'd never be old to him. No matter how long he lived, she'd always be a quarter-century younger. Why, all of the sudden, didn't he care anymore? Karla was mature for her age. He'd just have to work at maintaining his health and be sure to keep his body in shape so she wouldn't grow tired of having an old man for a…

Dom. That's all they were going to have, a Dom/sub relationship. Don't even think about anything else. Hell, maybe she didn't want any kind of BDSM arrangement with him. He'd messed up badly before. Would she still trust him to care for her needs like a good Dom should? When she came to her senses—tomorrow, next month, next year—she'd find someone closer to her own age. But think of the memories he'd create in their time together, however long it might last. He wanted to make those memories.

His hand skimmed down over her abdomen, pulled up the tail of the T-shirt up, and slid inside the waistband of her panties. Her hips bolted upward and she stretched her legs out as his finger slid between her very wet folds. "Eager, little one?"

"Yes, Sir." Her breathy whisper sounded almost sultry. "You left me hanging twice now—once in the shower and once after the accident."

"That I did, didn't I?" He was pleased to know she'd felt deprived enough to miss those orgasms.

Adam's mouth brushed against her temple and her head lolled to the side, allowing him to trail kisses along the column of her neck as his finger parted her nether-curls and found the opening of her pussy, pressing inside. She gasped.

"Tell me if anything hurts. Your pussy and mons may be bruised from that rough session in my office Friday morning, not to mention other areas injured in the accident that night. We're going to take it slowly this time."

"Please, Sir, not too slowly. I need you!"

He groaned at the urgency in her plea and his wet finger pulled out of her quivering hole and stroked between her folds to her clit hood. She tilted her pelvis against his finger.

"Don't move. I will control how fast I let you come, Kitten."

She shivered, but he didn't think it was from the cold. She hadn't balked at obeying. Did she still want him to be her Dom?

* * *

He was going to let her come. Thank the gods.

His finger and thumb pinched her clit and she tried to squirm away, but he held her tightly against him. Why had she gone bratty on him immediately, though? Would she jeopardize her orgasm as a result? He didn't seem too upset. But he'd ended their Master/slave agreement, hadn't he? She wasn't sure what her status was now.

Trying to keep her hips still was a challenge she hadn't expected to be so difficult. She concentrated on his fingers, reveling in the intense feeling of having his large hand on her small pussy. But shouldn't she be touching him, too, giving something back? She reached out to run her fingers over his leg.

Adam sighed and pushed her away from his chest, removing his finger from her clit. She groaned in frustration. *Don't push me away again, Adam. Please!* She turned around to face him.

His scowl told her he definitely was not happy. "What did I tell you?"

What had she done wrong this time? He wasn't pleased with her. "You told me not to move my hips, Sir."

"I told you not to *move*. Period. If I'm going to take this slowly, I can't have you touching me."

"But I only touched your leg, not your…" Her gaze flicked down to his crotch, and her face grew warm. She looked back up at him. How could such innocent touches have that much of an effect on him? She smiled, feeling a sense of power she hadn't known she possessed. "Please, Sir. Tell me what you want. But don't stop doing what you were doing."

"Are you giving your Dom orders, Kitten?"

Crap. "I'm sorry, Sir. I wasn't sure if…" Her eyes opened wider as his words sank in. "My Dom?"

His other hand reached up to cup her breast in a possessive display that made her feel like she was his, but in a way she enjoyed.

"I may not want to be your Master, but being a Dom is ingrained in me. Can you accept that? Submit to me sexually?"

"I…I think so."

"You'll have to do better than 'I think so,' Kitten. Yes…or no?"

I can do this. Whatever "this" is.

"Yes, Sir. I can submit sexually." Being so new to sex, it certainly was easier to submit than to take charge. She had no clue what to do most of the time.

"We'll see." He stood and held a hand out to her. She winced as she began to rise and he bent down to scoop her into his arms.

"Whoa! What are you doing? Put me down, Adam!"

"You'd better correct yourself, and soon."

"Master Adam, Sir. Sorry. But you shouldn't be lifting me."

"I'll lift whatever I damned well please and right now, it pleases me to lift you."

He carried her out of their room and down the hallway. Was he going to take her down to a theme room and restrain her? Her clit zinged even as her heart rate tripled. But instead of going down the stairs, he continued to the end of the hall and opened the door to one of the club's private bedrooms. She'd never been in one of these. They were used by members wanting a little more privacy than the theme rooms allowed with their observation windows.

"Damn, it's colder than a motherf…than a mother in here."

He could say that again—and for Adam to be cold was saying something. He carried her to the side of the bed and lowered her to her feet, then pulled the sheet and comforter down. "Get under the covers while I start a fire in here. Better enjoy it, too, because I'm not going to let you burrow under those covers for long." Her nipples tightened, more from excitement than the cold, she suspected, and she crawled into bed to watch him light the gas logs in the fireplace. Soon, the heat of the fire warmed her face.

"Sorry it's not a wood fire, but I can't run the risk of some careless or distracted club member burning the place down trying to light a fire." After the fire began to roar, she watched him go to a closet and pull out a black leather vest. Her heartbeat increased again, pounding blood loudly through her ears. He turned toward her and removed his T-shirt. The firelight flickered across the muscles and planes of his chest and she ached to run her fingers over him. His muscular pecs and abs begged to be licked, but she wouldn't displease him again by taking the initiative. If he wanted her to touch him, he'd tell her. He donned the vest.

The room warmed quickly, probably not as a result of the flames in the fireplace, and Adam glanced at the blankets. "Kick the covers off and remove your shirt."

Her clit stood at attention. She sat up and stripped down to her thong. Adam's intense gaze as he watched her follow his command caused her nipples to peak. She'd gone braless today and wondered if he would strip any further himself, but he kept his button-fly jeans on and walked over to the bed and reached toward the headboard bed post. She heard the jangle of chains.

Again with the chains?

Well, it was a BDSM club. *Adam's club.* He'd brought her to this bed because apparently he didn't have his own equipped with chains, which made her smile. Maybe that meant he hadn't restrained any other slaves, subs, or bottoms in his bed. Somehow that made her feel more special and to appreciate their time in his bedroom even more.

"Give me your wrists."

Ka-thunk! Obediently, she raised her arms toward him. He took the right wrist and wrapped it in a soft leather cuff.

"What if my arms aren't up to strenuous contortions yet, Sir?" She really hadn't noticed any pain since yesterday morning, so she'd probably healed already.

"Who said anything about restraining your arms?" The look in his eyes caused heat to pool in her pelvis. Her pussy grew wet. He cuffed her left wrist and laid both hands on top of her abdomen. Were the cuffs just for decoration then? His warm hands curved around her shoulders and gently massaged the muscles before his hands slipped down further and cupped her breasts. He pinched and twisted her nipples.

"Ackkk!"

Her pelvis strained toward him as her nipples tightened and swelled beneath his fingers and thumbs. He released her and watched as her nipples grew bigger, straining toward him. Her breasts swelled, begging for his hands, his lips, his touch.

Adam smiled. She wasn't quite sure she liked what that wicked smile held in store for her. He went to the nightstand and pulled out a bundle of soft-looking white string or very thin rope. How could tying her arms with that be less painful?

"Scoot toward the middle of the bed." She did as he told her, not noticing any soreness in her muscles. The colder sheets caused her nipples to bunch even more. "Perfect."

For what? But her body warmed quickly under his praise. Adam straddled her hips, lightly resting his denim-clad hips above her knee, then bent over and took her left nip into his mouth, between his teeth. She hissed when he bit down and pulled.

"Oh, God, Sir! Do that again!"

He growled. Damn. She was telling him what to do again. She needed to remember her place. After working so hard at being his slave last week, you'd think she could enjoy a little more freedom now, but there didn't seem to be much difference between a slave and a sub, other than the time frame in which she had to submit. If she wanted to keep from getting gagged, she'd better keep her mouth shut.

"I'm sorry, Sir. I'll remember myself. It just felt so good."

He grinned at her, then took the other peak between his teeth and did the same. She clenched the sheets in her fists and bit her lip to keep from crying out. When he sat up, resting most of his weight on his knees, she watched him unravel the bundle of rope and determined the midpoint. Pulling a pocketknife from his pocket, he snipped it into two long lengths.

"In my toy bag, I have a pair of nip nooses we'll have to play with sometime. But I'm sure we can improvise tonight, rather than postpone your fun while I go get the bag."

Nip nooses? They sounded like a death sentence for her poor nippies. He lowered the rope to her chest, pulling it taut and teasing her nipples with the cool strands for several minutes until gooseflesh rose on her skin and her nipples grew even harder, if possible. What did he plan to do? She didn't have to wait long to find out. Pinching one nipple between his thumb and forefinger, nearly to the point of pain, he took the rope, formed a knot, and laid it in a circle on her areola. She felt his gaze on her face, but her eyes were riveted to her breast, watching as he slowly pulled the end of the rope and the circle grew smaller and smaller until it surrounded her nipple like a lasso. Then he tightened it even more.

"Ahhh!" The exquisite pain caused her clit to throb and her knees and hips would have bucked upward if his hips weren't obstructing them.

He did the same with the other nipple. Even though she knew what was coming this time, she still gasped when he tightened the noose. He pulled on the ropes, lifting her nipples into the air and stretching her swollen breasts.

"Oh, God!" The sensation of pulling her up by her nipples nearly made her come. They were so hypersensitive. Now she just wanted his mouth and hands on her again. But the feel of her nipples embracing the rope, as he put it, was too erotic for words.

When he lifted his leg and got off of her, she was curious as to the purpose of lassoing her nipples. Then he took the string tied around her left nipple and pulled tighter and tighter, stretching the string toward the bed post. Surely not. No way.

Yes way.

Within seconds, he'd expertly tied the string to the bedpost, restraining her by her nipple. He walked around the bed, took the other string, and performed the same maneuver. She tried to move, but that only caused the slip knots around her nipples to tighten even more. Her clit throbbed, her nipples ached. She wasn't going anywhere.

"How do your arms feel now?"

She glared up at him, but when he grinned at her, she couldn't stay angry. Besides, if she expended too much energy or made the wrong movements, she was going to cause some serious pain to her nips.

Adam straddled her again and bent over her to kiss her lips, his chest rubbing against her distended nipples. When she opened her mouth to invite his tongue inside, he ignored her and instead trailed whiskery kisses down her neck. He moved down her body until his tongue flicked over one of her engorged nipples. When he took it into his mouth, even his lips felt razor sharp and she strained toward him, then away. So sensitive. He gave the other bud the same attention, and then continued to scoot down the bed, blazing a trail over her abdomen and pelvis.

Her clit zinged and his hard cock throbbed against her inner calf, as if in response.

Adam reached up to cup her breast, loosening the strain of the rope. "How does that feel, Kitten?"

"Fine, Sir." *Really hot, actually.* Who knew Karla Paxton would get off on being restrained to a bed by her nipples?

"Not too tight?"

"No, Sir. I'm fine."

"Fine is not what I'm looking for here, Kitten."

Oh, my.

"I don't want to restrain your arms, because of the whiplash in your neck and shoulders, but I want you to find something to hold onto with your hands so I don't have to. If they get in my way, I just might tie them to the nipple restraints and you'll be feeling some serious pain every time you move or jerk your arms. Understood?"

"Yes, Sir." She nibbled her lower lip. "I'm not into pain, Sir." It wouldn't hurt to remind him every now and then.

"You have the control over the amount of pain you feel, Kitten. This is called predicament bondage because you certainly are in a predicament, aren't you?" He grinned. "If you move, there's pain. If you don't move, less pain."

Either way, pain, but if he hadn't restrained her like this, she'd certainly have a lot more control, wouldn't she? Like getting him to start already. If he didn't hurry up and do something, she'd be screaming in frustration.

Helpless. Hopeful. Horny.

"Please, Sir. Don't make me wait any longer."

"Is my kitten running this show, or is her Dom?"

Feeling bolder than she ever had, she couldn't resist teasing him. After all, kittens were supposed to be mischievous, not obedient, weren't they? "Your kitten wants her Dom to pet her pussy. Now, Sir." Karla raised her head off the pillow to snarl at him.

"Sounds like I have a baby tiger trying to intimidate me." The smile faded from his lips as his gaze smoldered, and he covered her body with his pressing her into the mattress. The strings holding her nipples to the bedposts pulled and her hips bucked up in response. She clutched the sheet to keep from moving her hands.

His fist grabbed a shank of her hair and he forced her head back, positioning his face mere inches above hers.

Karla's gaze settled on his mouth and, without a thought toward the repercussions, her mouth clamped down on his full lower lip in a playful nip. Adam growled playfully and pulled her head away by the hair he still held in his fist.

"I should have warned you, baby tiger. I bite back."

He lowered his mouth to hers, but instead of kissing her, took her lower lip between his teeth and bit down, hard. The sting of pain caused her eyes to water, but the promise of his erection poking against her mound left her breathless and wanting more.

She pressed her tongue against his teeth until he chuckled and sucked it into his mouth. *Ohhhh!* She could scream with the frustration at not being able to direct his mouth where she wanted him to be. He still maintained the control.

He ground his lips over hers, taking possession of her mouth. When she would have moaned in pain from her bruised lips, he forced his tongue inside smothering the sound. She pulled at the sheets, trying so hard not to wrap her arms around him, wanting to touch his hair, his face, his shoulders—to pull him even closer. He tore his lips away and moved off her to lie beside her, then bent over her breast and took one hard, captured nipple between his teeth again.

Frustrated, she tilted her pelvis toward him and he answered by trailing his hand down slowly over her other breast, her quivering abdomen, her thrusting hips, until he reached her mons, where he slid his palm inside the triangle of her thong.

At the same time, his teeth clamped onto one rigid nipple and tugged, causing her to arch her back when she thought he might not stop pulling. Oh, God! The pain! He released her nip and bent over the other, biting down again. When cold air touched the first wet nipple, it became even more painfully erect, the noose-like rope biting into her nipple.

Better to keep them lassoed as long as she could. When he removed those strings, she could only imagine the howl of pain he would hear his "baby tiger" emit.

She watched Adam's head slowly move back and forth as his teeth tugged on the peak, making it even harder this time.

"Ahhhh!" Now the pain was delicious. How could that be? *Oh, dear Lord!* She wanted more.

He released her nipple. "Like that, do you, Kitten?"

She opened her eyes, panted for air, and looked down to find Adam staring up at her, smiling. "Oh, yes, Sir."

"Well, I may just have to find some other way to discipline you for being so insubordinate until you learn to behave. Who knew my near-virgin little kitten would like it so rough?"

Who indeed?

She gasped to fill her lungs before he assaulted her senses yet again. Adam cupped her right breast and pinched her nipple. Hard.

"Thank you, Sir. May I have another?"

He chuckled. "Absolutely bratty."

"Only for you, Sir."

He covered her again with his body and grew serious as he lowered his mouth to her bare peak, taking it between his teeth. His teeth released her only to have his lips latch on. He sucked, flicking his tongue against the peak as he pulled his head back, taking her rope-captured nip with him.

"Oh, dear Lord!" She reached out and grabbed his head, wanting to drag him closer before he pulled too hard, only to realize her mistake too late. She tore her hands away and latched back onto the sheets, groaning in frustration.

His penis throbbed against her leg and she tilted her hips against him until he groaned with equal frustration. She smiled. Maybe he hadn't noticed. Maybe he would take her as she wanted to be taken.

Instead, he broke contact with her mouth. The evil grin on his face didn't bode well. What was he going to do next? Obviously not what she wanted him to do.

"I think you need to be restrained, my baby tiger."

"I am restrained, Sir." Her breathy words sounded sexy to her ears. When had she become such a siren? *When she'd answered the call of her own siren—Adam.*

"Not as completely as you need to be, it seems." He slid off her body and knelt near the bottom of the bed, reaching for the waistband of her thong. "First, I think we need to lose this. It'll just be in the way of where I intend to be in a few minutes."

Karla's clit throbbed at the promise in his words. Soon. He was going to make love to her this time, totally and completely, and in just a few minutes. She had to remind herself to breathe. Whatever had happened to get Adam to see her as a sexy woman, rather than too young for him, she hoped the spell would never break. Having him making love to her was…

Adam got off the bed and returned to the nightstand, which seemed to be equipped with everything an adventurous Dom might need. He pulled out a silk scarf and indicated with his come-hither finger gesture for her to lift her head off the pillow. Karla pleaded with him silently not to blindfold her, but within seconds the light from the room grew dim, then black. Pleading would only make him want to do it more. She needed to try harder to obey. Just because he wasn't her Master anymore didn't mean she wasn't supposed to obey her Dom.

The sound of chains left her wondering if she was going to be able to withstand the strain of over-the-head restraints, but she wouldn't displease him by complaining. If she needed to, she could safeword. She waited for him to restrain her cuffed wrists, steeling herself for the pain to come.

Nothing.

He didn't touch her arms, but instead took her legs and tented them, her soles now flat on the mattress near her butt. Maybe he was going to restrain her ankles. She heard the chains again, but the sound came from above her head. What did he have in mind? She turned her head, listening, as a chain scraped against the headboard. Gee, this had looked like such a romantic little bedroom when they'd first come in here tonight. Now it was sounding like a torture chamber. Of course, Master Adam wouldn't harm her. Anticipation of the orgasm and sex to come kept her from becoming overly frightened.

He fiddled with the chains and she heard him take a few steps away. The smell of leather permeated the room and soon he returned and wrapped something warm, almost hot, around her left thigh, then something similar around her right one. He must have warmed the leather by the fire. *So considerate of you, Sir.* The chains rattled once more and he placed his hand under her thigh and spread her leg toward the side of the bed and up in the air. She heard a click and he let go, but her thigh remained in the air.

She wasn't so sure about this. "Sir..."

"Silence. You do not have permission to speak except to safeword or answer a direct question."

He repeated the motions with her right thigh and soon she was splayed open on the bed, nipples and thighs restrained, feeling like a butterfly mounted on a specimen tray in her freshman biology class. She heard the dreaded drawer open again and the smell of leather once more. "Lift your head." She did so, feeling a slight pull from her strained muscles, but not groaning or showing any sign of weakness.

Warm leather wrapped around her neck. Another collar.

"Good girl. Lay your head back again." She did so and his warm fingers slipped inside the collar. "Not too tight?"

"No, Sir." He kneaded the tensed muscles in her shoulders and she moaned in pleasure. "Be sure to tell me if you get a cramp or if your muscles get too tight."

She nodded.

"Because you don't know if I am looking at you, I want you to respond with a 'Yes, Sir,' or 'No, Sir,' when I ask for that kind of information. Don't just nod or shake your head."

"Yes, Sir."

He took her left wrist and stretched her arm straight out on the bed. More chains and soon she was restrained. "Any pain?"

"No, Sir."

"Good." He quickly stretched her right arm out and the snick of another clamp to a chain told her she was fully restrained. His finger slipped inside each of the cuffs. "Any pain?"

"Not yet."

He chuckled. "Such a pessimistic answer." He reached out and tweaked her nipple, which apparently had relaxed a bit while her attention was focused elsewhere.

Inexperience left her confused, though. She thought men like to have women do more than just lie there when they have sex, although he certainly hadn't complained when he'd taken her on his desk the other night. She didn't suppose this could be misconstrued as the boring missionary position by anyone's definition, even if she was on her back.

"Permission to speak, Sir."

"Granted."

"How can I participate if I'm trussed up like this, Sir? Don't you want me to be able to move?"

"Oh, I expect your full participation, Kitten. Your screams will let me know you are fully engaged in the scene."

Her heart thudded against her chest and came to a stop for a moment. "Screams, Sir? Wait! I don't think…"

"Exactly. You don't need to be thinking anymore. You just need to focus on feeling all the things I'm about to do to your beautifully submissive body."

Oh, dear Lord.

Was he going to beat her like this? Have sex with her? Hell, he could do anything he wanted to, couldn't he? Fear mixed with excitement. She'd never had a pain fetish. Still, she felt more excited than fearful, perhaps because she trusted Adam completely. Pain was just a part of his scene, wasn't it, along with rough sex? Her biggest worry was how she would respond to pain. What if she disappointed him by not being a good submissive?

Opened so fully to him, she felt so exposed. The mattress dipped as he joined her on the bed again. When he sat on the mattress, the nipple nooses stretched and pulled her nips.

"What's wrong, Kitten?"

She didn't want to give voice to her concerns.

"I asked a direct question. Are your arms sore? Are you in any pain?"

"No, Sir." She nibbled on her lower lip. "I just…don't want to disappoint you, Sir." She ended on a whisper, afraid to speak the words too loudly.

He stretched out over her, his warm breath against her cheek, and whispered, "Why do you think you're going to disappoint me, Kitten?"

"I'm not sure I like pain, Sir."

"Who said anything about pain?"

"You said I'd be screaming, Sir."

"Oh, make no mistake, Kitten. You'll be screaming. Just not from pain."

With that, he crawled back down the bed, between her open legs, and pressed his lips against her inner knee. *Oh, no!* Karla tried to clamp her legs together, but, of course, they didn't move.

"No, Sir. Not that." The other night, she'd taken a shower just before their Shibari session. But she hadn't taken a shower since this morning.

"What did you say to me?"

"Sir, please, it's just that I don't want you to…"

"It doesn't matter what you want right now, Karla." Oh, no. He was upset with her. "You do not have permission to speak unless I ask you a question. Do not give me any more orders, and, most definitely, do not tell me to stop anything I'm doing, unless you want to safeword. Is that clear?"

Tears pricked the backs of her eyelids. How was this different from being a slave? She still wanted to please him—and she'd failed yet again.

His lips pressed against her thigh and moved upward, the stubble of his beard abrading her sensitive skin, causing the opening of her pussy to clench and release in anticipation. What a traitor her body was. She didn't want him to kiss her *there* and yet her pussy was ready to roll out the welcome mat.

"I…um…, Sir, please. I need to wash myself first."

He sighed. "Don't force me use a ball gag on you, brat. That would make me unable to hear your delightful screams."

Her pussy clenched again. She remembered how loud she'd gotten during the rope suspension scene. She hoped no one was wandering around the house tonight.

"Stop worrying and give in to the explosion that's about to hit your senses, Kitten, while I delight in the taste of your pussy."

"No, Sir!" She needed to stop him before she grossed him out. She pulled against the wrist cuffs, hardly rattling the chains on her thighs and wrists. No use. She couldn't move.

Adam growled. "Did you just tell your Dom no again?"

"No. I mean, yes, I did, but I really, really don't want you to do this, Sir."

"You're in no position to disagree with me, are you?"

With herself splayed open and bound so tightly, she certainly wasn't.

"Women worry too much about how they smell or taste. I assure you, I love to taste a woman's primal essence on my tongue."

Something melted inside her. He liked it? "Really? You're not just being polite, are you, Sir?"

"No, Kitten, when it comes to sex, I don't have a polite bone in my body. Now, I have a very hungry beast that needs to be fed—by devouring your sweet, sexy pussy. But make no mistake, you will be punished later for being so willfully argumentative."

Punished? She remembered the pain of the nipple clamps and wondered if he had something similar in mind. But he was torturing her nipples already—not nearly as much as they'd feel tortured when he removed the nooses, though. Would the pain be worse if associated with punishment?

His lips pressed against her thigh again and his teeth nipped the tender skin as he continued to move ever closer. Karla held her breath and steeled herself for the onslaught of sensations to come, still worried about his reaction.

Adam nipped her skin again and again. Closer and closer. What if he bit her clit? Oh, surely he wouldn't. Dizziness overcame her. *Breathe*. She sucked a huge amount of air into her lungs. Her nipples grew taut, causing the ropes to tighten around the swollen buds. Letting her head fall back onto the pillow, she willed her body to relax into the mattress.

Feel.

Give in to the explosion.

Chapter Twelve

Her clit throbbed, aching for some kind of contact, but he didn't provide the stimulation she craved. Instead, his fingers spread her labia open and his tongue pressed insistently against the opening of her pussy, then stabbed inside her.

"Ohhh!" She couldn't move her hips very well, but used her vaginal muscles to strangle his tongue, eliciting a tortured groan from him.

He pulled away. "You are determined to make me come undone, aren't you, baby tiger?"

She gasped for air, panting like the pet she was. "Payback, Sir. For torturing me like this."

"Oh, Kitten, I haven't even begun to torture you. But I think that would be appropriate, in due time."

Adam was teasing her? She nearly let out a giggle, before the threat of torture registered in her muddled brain. His mouth descended once more. At least she hoped he was teasing about the torture part, too. He pressed the backs of his hands against the juncture of her thighs, then used his thumbs to spread open her outer pussy lips. The cool air from the room, along with his breath against her exposed vulva, caused her clit to tighten, seeking in vain the warmth it had known within its sheltered hood. But his mouth soon spread warmth from her pussy to her clit when his flattened tongue licked her as if she were a melting ice-cream cone.

"Oh, God!" The chains clanged as Karla fought against the restraints. Thank God he'd used the restraints, because she'd have tried to escape him otherwise, or closed herself off to his mouth. He'd taken away the ability for her to deny him access to her most private self. He'd removed her need for modesty or shyness.

Karla prepared for her personal explosion.

Rather than grant her the release she sought, though, the tip of his tongue teased along one side of her clit hood, flicking lightly over her tiny erection, and then teased the other side of the hood. He nipped the inner flesh of her larger labia, and his teeth nibbled at her inner lips.

"Oh, my God!"

The intense sensation caused her to struggle against her restraints again, but whether to get away from him or to position herself where he could finally give her clit the attention it deserved, she wasn't sure.

"I can't last much longer, Sir. Please!"

His mouth left her pussy. *Shit.* She'd spoken again. Was he making a list of all her naughty transgressions? What kind of punishment would he devise? She waited, but he didn't reprimand her again.

"Give you what, Kitten?"

Direct question. Okay to answer. "You know what I need, Sir."

"Yes, but I want to hear you beg for it. Tell me what you need."

Beg? He'd reduced her to a quivering mass of raw nerves and now he wanted her to beg for more? Oh, sure. She could do that. Not a problem.

"Please, Sir. I need your fingers inside me, your hot tongue on my clit devouring your kitten's pussy, and then I need you to drive your penis inside me over and over until you have taken total and complete control of your subbie's body and mind."

Adam's breathing became labored. Had she gone too far? Well, he'd asked her to beg for what she needed—and that was exactly what she needed.

He didn't say a word but he moved and, this time, when his lips encircled her clit, he drew it into his molten mouth. His teeth grazed the ultra-sensitive nubbin. Two fingers plunged deep inside her.

"Oh, God, yes, Adam! I mean, Sir Adam." Karla fought to escape the restraints as her body tried to jettison off the bed. "Please take me. Please make me come. I need you inside me. Now!"

His fingers plunged in and out of her vagina, then entered her more deeply and curled toward her pubic bone until he touched a bundle of nerves that had been her undoing in the Shibari suspension scene. "Sweet Jesus, yes! I can't take anymore. Oh, please, Sir! Oh, God, please! I need..."

She thrashed her head back and forth on the pillow. Her incoherent rants filled the room as his mouth released her clit and his tongue began flicking rapidly over the sensitive nubbin. The combination of intense sensations caused all thought to flee her mind.

His fingers pulled out as the spasms just began to build. She nearly sobbed.

"No, please don't stop!"

She heard a foil packet. Oh, they were going to have sex. Finally! Her euphoria was short-lived. Something cold pressed against her asshole. "No! Not there!" She tried to pull away, but could go nowhere.

"Karla, it's just my finger with a lubricated condom. We're going to try anal sex sometime, but tonight we're experimenting. I won't be putting my penis there yet. Do you want to use your safeword?"

She panted, hanging on the edge. Dear Lord, he couldn't leave her hanging like this. Not again. She needed release. "No. No, Sir." A sob escaped her. "I need to come, Sir."

"I know you do, Kitten." Without giving her time to tense again, he pressed his finger just inside her tight, still-virgin hole. "Relax your muscles, baby. As much as you can, move against my finger."

Was he kidding? He held his finger still just inside the now burning ring, waiting for her to adjust to him. The burning soon receded a bit, leaving a feeling of fullness different from what his penis felt like inside her vagina. Even fuller. His finger moved deeper inside her and the burning increased again as he passed a second ring of muscles she didn't even know were there, then began pressing a second finger against her overfilled opening. She shook her head back and forth, but fought the urge to tell him no again.

Master Adam would never harm me.

"Relax. Press your ring against my fingers. Don't fight me, Kitten. Let me inside you." His words sent heat spreading throughout her abdomen and relaxed her. She tilted her pelvis as much as she could in her restrained position, wanting to please him more than anything. "That's my brave kitten. Your Dom is well pleased."

She relaxed further and he plunged his two fingers fully inside her. "Ahhhh!" Her clit pulsed as his fingers filled her completely, then Adam's tongue flicked over the ultra-sensitive nubbin.

Her suspended orgasm spiraled up inside until, in a flash of white lightning, she exploded against his mouth and fingers. "Ohhhh, ohhhhhh, yesssssss! Oh, shit. Oh, dear Lord. Yessssss, Adam!" She convulsed and shook as spasm after spasm, wave after shocking wave, wracked her lower body. "Don't stop! Please, Sir, don't stop!"

He didn't disappoint her. On and on the waves of passion flooded her senses, one bigger than the last until she crested the highest wave and tumbled face first into the bliss-filled abyss below, floating free of any bonds he might have placed on her body.

Adam continued to flick his tongue against her. Suddenly, the sensations of him touching her clit became painful. Didn't he know she'd already come?

"Stop! No more! Ow. Ow! Please, stop, Sir!"

Adam pulled away. "What did you say?"

"Stop…tonguing me, *Sir*! Please!" Tears filled her eyes. "It's too sensitive."

* * *

Hearing Karla order, then beg, him to stop made Adam harder than ever. He'd planned to go slowly with her, even if it killed him, but he knew what he needed to do next. Orgasm torture. He needed to punish her for disobeying and arguing with him, or she'd never be able to truly submit to something her mind told her she shouldn't want to try, like anal sex. She needed to learn discipline. Forced orgasms would be easier to tolerate for her than some other punishments he might inflict.

"That was incredible." Her breathy whisper made his dick and balls tighten.

He discarded the condom in the wastebasket stood at the side of the bed, pulled the sash off her eyes, and pushed it up into her hair. She looked up at him with languid eyes indicating she was one satisfied woman. Hell, he hadn't even started to satisfy her. Well, satisfy might not be the word she'd use.

"Not nearly as incredible as hearing you scream when you came. Good thing you took Cassie home. She might think I was killing you in here."

"Oh, but what a way to go."

He closed the space between their faces and kissed her, trying not to pull at the ropes on her nips too hard. When she tensed up, he pulled back to try and gauge what was the matter. Her cute little nose wrinkled up. "What's wrong, Kitten?"

Her face turned as red as the bustier she'd worn at Marc's house several weeks ago. "It's weird, tasting myself on your lips like that." She nibbled her lower lip, making his dick throb, anticipating having those teeth and lips around him. "How did I taste, Sir? Was it gross?"

He sighed. Why the fuck did women worry so much about how they tasted? "Kitten, you tasted as sweet as sugar."

"You're just saying that."

He took her chin in his hand and gave her what he hoped was his most stern Dom look. "No, Kitten. I wouldn't lie to a sub about something that important. There's nothing more sexy than the scent and taste of a woman's pussy."

"So, you've...uh...tasted a lot of them?"

Adam chuckled. "I don't taste and tell. Don't worry, though. I'm very selective."

Karla smiled. "Thank you, Sir."

"For what?"

She looked away, then back at him. "For...making me explode like that. For making me try things I didn't think I would like to try. That orgasm was...well, awesome."

"Not nearly as awesome as the next one will be."

Her eyes opened wider. "Again?"

"Yes, Kitten. Again and often." He brushed a hair off her cheek. "Remember when I promised I was going to torture you? Well, I believe there's the matter of disciplining you for willfully telling your Dom no a couple of times tonight."

Her body tensed, eyes narrowed, and she scrunched the sexiest little worry lines along her forehead. He let her fear the worst a moment longer, because what she conjured up in her head would be worse than any punishment she'd ever receive from him. Yet, he couldn't resist thinking about pulling a total mind fuck on her. Hell, she'd been so easy with the chains in his office the other night. He grinned.

"Y-yes, Sir."

"One of my favorite ways to teach a sub to behave is called orgasm torture."

"How could an orgasm be torture?"

"You're about to find out. Now, tell me why you're being disciplined."

Her eyes filled with regret. "Sir, I'm sorry that I told you no—repeatedly—and didn't believe you that eating pussy was...tasty."

Karla seemed genuinely sorry and a little bit bratty with that "tasty" remark. If she wasn't totally submissive, she sure as hell knew how to please this Dom. Something made him wonder if she'd try just as hard if he wasn't her Dom—if she just simply wanted to please him, Adam Montague, Dom or not? Was that why she'd agreed to become his slave?

He cleared his throat. He needed to keep his mind on the task at hand. He could sort out the puzzle that was Karla later.

Yeah, right.

"What have you learned?"

"That my Dom knows best. That he'll take care of my needs no matter how uncomfortable I might be. That I should trust him."

Hell. She'd thought it through more than he'd expected. Her sincerity pleased him. "Good girl. Thank you for trusting me, Kitten." He smiled and bent to kiss her again. When her lips began to quaver, he pulled away. She looked up at him, a silent plea in her eyes.

"What's wrong now, Kitten?"

"If I've learned my lesson, do you still have to punish me?"

He fought the urge to grin. "Discipline isn't the same as punishment. I'm trying to help train your mind to automatically do what your Dom has told you, without question or hesitation, and to stop trying to argue about everything I say. I am doing this for your own good, if you truly want to be my submissive. Besides, a good Dom always follows through on his promises—and his threats—because a sub needs consistency and to know what is expected of her."

She seemed to ponder that a moment, then nodded. "I'm ready, Sir." She laid her head back on the pillow and closed her eyes, looking much like a virgin about to be fed to the lions. This time, he failed to suppress his chuckle. She grew even more tense, if possible.

"Keep your eyes closed." Adam reached up and pulled the blindfold back over her eyes. When she nibbled her lower lip, his balls tightened. He couldn't wait until he was buried inside her to the hilt. But first, he needed to make sure there would be no flying body parts that could prohibit him from performing later.

He slid off her and walked over to a closet to find some of the toys he'd need, as well. He kept each of the public bedrooms stocked with new sex toys, sexy costumes, condoms, batteries, and other items members might need. His clientele certainly paid enough to be able to afford the perks. Pulling several packages off the shelf, he returned to the bedside and laid them on the nightstand.

Surveying her position, with her hands outstretched and secured and her thighs and knees in the harnesses, anchored by chains to the sides of the bed, he only had to worry about her kicking him. He picked up two leather cuffs and attached one to each ankle, then restrained them tightly with chains to the bottom of the bed. No doubt her upper body would remain still, with the nooses as an incentive. She should be ready. Well, restraint-wise, anyway.

"How does that feel, Kitten?"

"O-okay, Sir."

This position would leave her more exposed than she might like, too, but would keep him from being attacked by his baby tiger.

Adam walked over to the nightstand and opened the packages, added the necessary batteries, and picked up the tube of lubricant he'd used earlier.

He glanced down at her. "Karla, do you trust your Dom not to harm you?" He held his breath as he waited for her response.

"Yes, I do, Sir."

He relaxed a bit. Her surrender to him—and trust in him—made him feel like a king.

* * *

Cool air chilled her pussy and tender asshole, and then she heard Master Adam ripping open packages and wondered what a tortured orgasm would be like.

"Relax for me, Kitten."

Relax? Was he fucking kidding?

"*Watch your mouth.*"

Like hell.

"*Calm down.*"

The running dialogue in her head didn't help calm her, not in the least. Karla tried to relax by taking slow, deep breaths and felt herself sink into the mattress. Then she heard him open that damned drawer and wondered what else he had up his sleeve. Her shoulders and arms hurt from holding herself so stiffly. She'd become so tense.

His finger slid against her cleft from her pussy up to her clit, spreading the moisture from her orgasm to the now dry clit. Her hips bucked when he touched the nubbin. It wasn't as sensitive as it had been right after she'd come. She grew warm with excitement as she thought about coming again. Sex definitely was addictive.

He thrust his fingers inside her pussy and she jumped at the unexpected invasion. Her mouth dropped open as she panted. The sensations began to build; much quicker than before, and her breathing became rapid and shallow.

His fingers pulled out and she groaned. *More, Sir.* Then something hard and cold pressed against her pussy's opening. Too cold to be Master Adam's penis. The hard object began to press inside her. A dildo? Her face flushed. She'd bought some toys at a party during her freshman year in college, but had opted for a clit vibrator, rather than something to put inside herself.

Adam inserted the object as far as it would go, she supposed. It pressed against the bundle of nerves Adam's fingers had curled around earlier when he'd given her the orgasm. Then his hand was gone and she waited.

"Deep breath and hold it."

She did as he instructed, and felt something cold and wet pressing against her asshole. "N…." *Noooo! I can't say no or it'll just make it worse. I trust him. He won't harm me.*

"Good girl. Now, deep breath again and hold it this time."

She drew a ragged breath, dreading what he planned to do with whatever was about to enter her anus. "Release your breath slowly." As she began to release the breath, he pressed the object into her. She held her breath again and steeled herself.

"Exhale the entire breath, Kitten. Now."

How could she push the object away if she was exhaling? But she did as he instructed and the object pushed against her rings, burning her asshole, until she was stretched almost as much as when he'd put two fingers inside her. Then the object made a plopping sound and he quit putting pressure against it. But it still burned like hell. Her two holes now were filled to the max. So full. But she'd rather have Master Adam's penis inside her, not some impersonal plastic dildo.

"I'm going to go easy on you, Kitten, since this is your first real taste of corrective discipline. Three forced orgasms. Count them for me."

Forced? He should know by now he didn't have to force her to have an orgasm. She heard a click and the dildo became a vibrator pulsing against her vaginal walls. He increased the speed and that delicious nerve center inside her, as well as her clit, all vibrated at once. She even felt it pulsate against whatever was in her ass.

Touch my clit, Sir!

Then she heard another click and the object in her butt whirred to life as well. "Oh, my God!" Sensory overload! Every muscle tingled and quaked throughout her pelvis. She squeezed her hands into fists, grabbing onto the bed sheet and holding on. She'd gone from zero to eighty like a sports car. Adam's tongue flicked against her clit and she screamed, trying to clamp her legs together but unable to move. Her torso lifted off the bed, then slammed back down as she contorted and twitched at the pain in her nipples from the ever-tightening nooses. To be right at the edge so fast was too intense.

She screamed again. "Yes! Please! Don't stop! Please, Sir!"

When he took her swollen clit between his lips and sucked, she let out the loudest, shrillest scream yet. Dear God. Could the neighbors hear? *Who cares?* "Ohhhh! Ohhhhhhhhhhhhh! Shit, please don't stop!" Her shoulders and hips bucked in alternating rhythm as she catapulted through the air then came shattering to earth again.

She gasped, sucking air into her lungs, panting like a dog on a sweltering day in the desert.

Adam turned off the two vibrators. "Karla, did you come?"

Was he blind and deaf? "Oh, yessss, Sir. I did."

"Isn't there something I told you to do?"

Do? "Come three times?"

"And?"

She gasped for much-needed oxygen. *Oh! Count!* "That was one, Sir."

"Very good, Kitten. Are you ready for the next?"

"Not yet, Sir. I still need to catch my breath."

He turned on the anal plug first, and then quickly followed with the vaginal one. The pain in her clit was excruciating. "I can't yet, Sir! It's too sensitive."

Without saying a word, his tongue flicked against her hard, hyper-sensitive clit. "Owww! Please, Sir. Not yet! It hurts."

He ignored her and when his teeth clamped onto her clit, her torso started to rise off the bed until the nipple nooses tightened and pulled. The pain there became excruciating again. She couldn't reach out to push him off her. Tears wet her blindfold. "Please, Sir. I can't take any more!"

His hand reached up and pulled one of the ropes attached to her nipple. Following the rope downward, he flicked her erect, sensitive nipple still suffering from being strung up, and then his thumb and finger rolled the tender peak. *Oh dear Lord!* The orgasm began to build again, only she didn't want this one. She tried so hard to evade this assault on her tender flesh, but there was nowhere to go. She reached the precipice and just hung there. As hard as she tried to will herself to tumble over the cliff, release wouldn't come. She groaned, "I can't, Sir. Please stop!"

His hand pressed against the object in her anus and her hips bucked, pressing her clit against his teeth and lips. He turned up the speed of the anal vibrator and she hurtled over at last. "I'm coming! Oh, my God! No. Yes!" She bucked against him for an eternity, before collapsing on the bed like a puppet whose strings had been cut.

"Thank God it's over." She didn't feel the euphoria she'd felt before, though. This was painful. Torture. Oh, God. Now she knew what he meant. She would never disobey him again if only he would promise never do this to her again. How could he ruin such a good thing as an orgasm by making it punishment?

He turned off the two devices inside her. "Karla."

Oh, shit. "Two, Sir." *Jesus.* That meant there was still another one to go. She'd never survive another one. Her skin became chilled where sweat had broken out and cooled, sending a shudder through her body. Her blindfold was wet against her face, from a mixture of tears and sweat.

She dreaded the build-up beginning again. How could she possibly be ready to come again? She never wanted to come again—ever. Getting over that crest a third time would be impossible.

Then the vibrators began again, one right after the other, and she whimpered. *Nooooo. I can't do this, Sir.* She groaned.

Master Adam pinched her nipples, tongued her clit, pressed hard against the anal vibrator moving it to hit different places in her asshole. She tried to ride the crest again, but as hard as she tried, no sooner did she near the peak than her mind intruded and she could go no further. Frustrated, she released a sob. "I can't, Sir. Please. Can't you spank me or something instead?" She hated sounding so whiny.

"That's enough, Kitten."

Apparently, he hated it, too. Now he was disappointed in her because she couldn't come on command three times in rapid succession. Her chin quavered and she bit her lip to keep it from showing. He placed pressure against the vibrator in her vagina and its speed increased, jump starting her clit. The anal vibrator increased in speed, too. How many speeds did the damned have?

"Ready to free your tits, Kitten?"

How could he think of that while her pelvic area was vibrating out of control? She shook her head frantically. "No, Sir. I like them tied, thank you."

He chuckled. She remembered when he'd released her from the clamps before. Leaving the vibrators doing their job, she heard him come nearer, reaching down and cupping her left tit. She hissed a breath in and held it, tense and waiting. He lifted her tit and weakened the tautness of the string, loosening the slipknot.

"Oh, dear Lord!" She screamed and fought the restraints as blood rushed back into her nipple. He bent over and sucked the tortured nipple into his mouth, providing counter-pressure and sucking motions to help ease the circulation back into the peak. "Oh, God. Stop! Oh, please, stop! It hurts, Sir."

She half-sobbed, half-laughed with the polar extremes in what her body was feeling, then he reached for the other nipple. Her smile faded immediately.

"Deep breath, Kitten. Now."

He removed the string and extreme pain blasted her nipple. Between the pain in her nipples and the vibrations pulsing through her vagina and anus, she was at the edge, ready to come. Again, it was elusive. She couldn't get there. He massaged her nipple with his fingers, letting the blood back in more slowly this time. He flattened his tongue against her hard nipple and licked her until her whimpers ceased.

He pressed something soft and squishy against her clit.

"Hang on, Kitten. Here it comes."

No! She wasn't going to come this time. Why didn't he give up on her?

She heard a click and the rubbery, gel-like thing on her clit came to life, vibrating directly against her clit. Karla bit down on her lip, tasting iron, not even realizing her teeth were there. Her hip bounced in the air, straining the cuffs on her ankles.

"Ohhhh, Goddddd!" The intensity of the vibrations shot tremors through her body and she went straight to the crest and hovered there only a few seconds, her entire pelvis a mass of quivering flesh. Pain. Pleasure. She didn't want to come again. No! Yes, she did! She needed the release. Torture! "Stop! Oh, please don't stop! I'm coming!" The relief of tumbling over at last was dampened by the intense pain in her overused clit. Then the pressure built to a crescendo and spread throughout her. "Oh, God! I'm coming! Shit! Don't stop! Three, three, three!"

Master Adam laughed. "That's it, baby tiger. Ride the wave. Ride it for all it's worth."

She was his baby tiger. A giggle erupted, bordering on hysteria.

The euphoria plummeted like an out-of-control roller coaster and a sob tore from deep inside. Her body began to shake from head to toe and tears filled her eyes, further dampening the blindfold. Were the vibrators still on or was it just her body vibrating like that? Another sensory overload consumed her and she plummeted down to the depths of hell.

"Adam! Turn them off! No more! Please! You promised only three!"

"Aw, fuck. Not again."

Chapter Thirteen

Adam had never had a submissive drop this fast on him before. Her last subdrop had been emotional, but this had to be primarily physical.

"Hang on, baby. I'll have you in my arms in a minute."

Karla's intense reactions—both positive and negative—to their scenes must be her body and mind's response to all that had happened recently. She'd been through a lot. Or did she just experience everything at a more intense level than anyone he'd been with before?

He turned off and removed the vibrators and tossed them into the wastebasket until he could clean them later. He unhooked the ankle cuffs, releasing her shaking legs and lowering them to the mattress.

"Ackkkk!" Her anguished scream tore at his gut. "I can't stop shaking."

"I know, baby. It's only temporary." He reached into the bowl of bite-sized, dark-chocolate bars on the nightstand and unwrapped the foil, bringing the candy to her lips. "Open your mouth, Kitten." Her jaw remained clenched as her body was wracked with shivers. "Karla. Open. Now." She fought hard and managed to open enough for him to slip the chocolate inside her mouth. He patted her under the chin. "Good girl. Suck on that, hon. It'll help, too. You'll be okay after we have our special time together."

He went to the other side of the bed and released her right thigh. The intensity of her orgasms—all four of them—must have overwhelmed her. He didn't know if she was into pleasuring herself, but she was new to coming with someone else controlling her orgasms, especially when the last few were forced on her.

"Oh, God! Make it stop!"

"I'm sorry, baby. It'll be better in a minute. Slow, deep breaths. I'm going to have you out of these restraints in no time. Promise." He quickly released her left wrist, then her right and removed the cuffs.

She moaned, biting her lower lip to keep from crying out. Lowering her shaking hands to her abdomen, she clutched them together.

"That's my brave girl."

She smiled up at him through her quivering lips. Something melted deep inside him. So willing to please. So trusting. So giving.

After the collar had been removed, he wrapped the comforter around her and scooped her into his arms. "I have you, Kitten." He lifted her off the bed.

"I'm t-t-too heavy!"

"Good lord, woman. You hardly weigh anything. You need to eat more." He'd see to that—starting tomorrow.

"But your b-b-back!"

"My back is fine. I'm all healed up." He carried her back to his room and sat in the glider chair, Karla curled in his lap against his chest. She shook to her core. "Shhhh. You're going to be okay." He stroked her hair, gently setting the chair in motion with his foot.

Her hand reached up to clutch the front of his vest. "Hold me, Adam."

"I have you, Kitten." He held her tighter against his body, hoping to infuse some body heat into her. Despite the fireplace in the other bedroom, her temperature had dropped like a rock. She was too thin for one thing.

"Next time, remember to tell me if you feel tingling."

"I didn't notice until the end, but I just thought it was n-n-normal. I haven't been chained to a b-b-bed before, Sir."

Damn. Was he going to get anything right with her? First the Master/slave fiasco, now he couldn't even make sure he'd cuffed her to the bed comfortably. It had been a long time since he'd been with Joni. With Grant, well they'd usually just hooked up when he needed sex; both of them had only been interested in a quick fuck. Never in here, though. Karla was the first.

"I'm sorry, S-S-Sir."

"You have nothing to be sorry about. You did everything perfectly, baby."

"I c-c-couldn't c-c-come that last time."

"But you did. They get harder and harder to reach each time. That's why it's called torture. But you came for me. Your Dom is very pleased with how well you've done in such a short time."

He held her closer, laying his chin on the top of her head. Her body grew heavier and she gave in to sleep.

A sob tore from her throat that nearly broke his heart. "I want to be good for you. I promise, I won't say no to you ever again."

He grinned, doubting Karla would be able to keep that promise. Secretly, he hoped she couldn't. One of the things he loved most about her was that she could tell him no and be her own person. Once she bounced back from the Master/slave fiasco, he had no doubt she'd be back to her old self again.

Adam sure hoped so. He'd missed the feisty brat he'd come to love.

Love?

No.

Enjoy. Appreciate. Cherish.

Not love.

* * *

Karla waited for the club's most popular Domme to finish pouring a green martini for a club member. The woman often filled in as bartender at the club and worked as hard as any of the co-owners. Her tall, muscular build made it clear she could take care of herself in any situation. There was a hard edge to her that made most men defer to her strength and control.

I'm not going to kowtow to you, though, even if I am Adam's sub at the moment.

Damián had told Karla the blonde Marine had shown up at the club about six months before Karla. She'd wasted no time getting close to Adam. Well, Karla had to admit Grant also was good friends with Damián and Marc, who had served in her unit. But she had a special "friends with benefits" relationship with Adam that Karla didn't really want to think about.

"Mistress Grant, do you have a minute?" In the club, she had to show respect, but that didn't mean she would bow to her.

"Sure, Karla." She smiled as she wiped down the bar. "What can I get you?"

"Nothing. Well, nothing to drink. I'm sorry to bother you, but I need to talk with you about Master Adam."

The smile left Grant's face. "What about him?"

Karla could almost feel the hackles go up in the woman, reminding her of the costume night earlier this month in the club when Mistress Grant came dressed as Catwoman with a malesub Robin kneeling at her feet and licking her over-the-knee stiletto boots. She'd seemed totally bored, though. No spark. No sexual chemistry, like what sizzled between her and Master Adam during their demonstrations.

Another club regular came up to order a Guinness and Mistress Grant left Karla waiting. Maybe trying to have this conversation in between music sets wasn't a good idea.

Karla wondered idly what the woman's first name was; Damián said he had no clue. She was just Grant, one of the guys.

Yeah, right.

Mistress Grant returned to stand in front of her at the end of the bar.

Karla drew a deep breath. "I wonder if we could have lunch or something tomorrow where we can talk more privately, since we're both pretty busy tonight."

"I'm not sure there's anything to talk about. I won't discuss our private relationship. Was there something else you wanted to know?"

The acknowledgement Grant *had* a relationship with Master Adam caused a pain in her chest. Karla looked across the room to where Master Adam was teaching Luke to use a Shibari technique on Angie. Master Marc was on an overnight camping expedition tonight and had asked his search-and-rescue partner to escort Angie to the club.

Adam's strong, gentle fingers working the ropes made Karla's skin tingle and her nipples grow erect. She'd do anything for that man, even talk with his former mistress—God, she hoped Grant was a former one. But first she needed to reassure the woman she wasn't looking for her to kiss and tell.

Karla zeroed in on Mistress Grant again. "Adam's been having horrible nightmares." The raised eyebrow told her the Marine probably didn't know Adam had been sleeping with Karla. Would she be angry or jealous that Master Adam was interested in a new woman?

Then Mistress Grant smiled briefly before growing serious again and asking, "What kind of nightmares? The war?"

"No, his childhood."

"He never talked about his childhood with me."

No doubt. Although Karla was pleased to know he wasn't more open with Grant. "Me either. But I need your help in tracking down his parents or finding out what happened back then. I don't want him to hang onto those images that keep haunting him. He needs some closure."

One of the subs serving drinks tonight laid a tray of empty glasses on the bar and Mistress Grant stowed them in the bins underneath for cleaning later. "What do you want me to do?"

"Master Damián said you...had connections with federal law enforcement." He'd actually hinted at some connection with the CIA or covert operations or something, but Karla thought that sounded a little too cloak-and-dagger to be real. "I thought maybe you could have someone run a background check."

"Spy on Master Adam?" Karla thought she heard Mistress Grant growl.

"No! Well, not really on *him*." Karla leaned forward, lowering her voice. "His parents were pretty abusive from what I can tell and he's buried all these feelings so deep that I don't think he's ever going to be able to…" *love me*. No, she wouldn't bare her soul to this potential rival. "…to get on with his life until he has some answers or confronts the past in some way."

Mistress Grant sized her up for a long moment before she relaxed as much as Karla had ever seen the uber-controlled woman relax. "I'll help if I can."

Karla let the air out of her lungs with a whoosh and nodded. "Thanks."

"I'm not doing this for you." Mistress Grant looked across the room toward Master Adam with what looked like longing.

Mine.

The green-eyed monster flared up, but Karla tamped it down. She needed Mistress Grant's help right now.

The bartender laid the towel on the bar and leaned forward, tearing her gaze away from Karla's man. "I'd go to hell and back for him. He's the finest master sergeant a Marine could ever ask for." She returned her gaze to Karla. "If what we find would just cause him more pain, I don't want him to know. You'll need to screen whoever we find before we let them anywhere near Adam again."

Karla smiled. Grant cared about Master Adam, too, and wanted to protect him. As long as they both had his best interests and welfare at heart—and Mistress Grant kept her hands off him—they'd be able to work together just fine.

"Great. Do you want me to see what information I can get on him for you? I don't expect it will be much."

"That's okay. My contacts can check into his military files."

Damián was right. The woman did have connections. Karla wondered just what she'd done after her stint with the Marines had ended, but that wasn't any of her business.

"Give me a few days."

"Absolutely. Now, I'd better start my next set." She turned to go back toward the stage, but spun around again. "Thanks, Mistress Grant."

The woman winked at her, which confused Karla. Maybe she wasn't a threat to her and Adam, after all.

* * *

Adam parked the rental along the winding roadway with two wheels in the grass so as not to impede others visiting loved ones today. With a heavy sigh, he opened the door and got out, not wanting to have this conversation. Most years, he looked forward to his time here with Joni, telling her about what he'd been doing and how much he wished she were with him to share it.

But now he needed to tell her about Karla. What the fuck was he going to say? He felt disloyal.

A crust on the top of the snow crunched under his boots as he walked up the slight hill. At first, he avoided looking at her tombstone while he busied himself with clearing snow from the marble bench he'd had placed there for Joni's mom to make use of during her visits in better weather. Marge always left him his privacy for his first visit to Joni's grave, on their wedding anniversary, but he'd bring her out here tomorrow before he headed back to Denver. She probably wouldn't get out here again for a while as winter set in with a vengeance.

He sat against the frigid stone and looked down at his hands. Memories of his twenty years with Joni played like a movie in his head. They'd been separated a lot by his many deployments, but the times they'd had together had been good ones. For him, at least. He hadn't ever been able to give Joni what she wanted most—a child. Or his love.

The backs of his eyes burned as he looked up at the cold, hard granite stone with the Montague name etched across the surface and a lighthouse carved to the right of her name.

Joni, beloved wife.

"Joni, my beloved li'l subbie."

She'd given him one-hundred percent of herself. He'd only given about eighty percent back, at best. Would he have been able to surrender the remainder if they'd been together after he'd retired from the Marines? Could he open that part of himself to any woman?

"I'm so sorry, baby." His raspy words were whipped away on the wind. "You deserved so much better than you got with me."

The guilt that had been eating at him ever since he'd come home on hardship leave from Afghanistan to find her in the last weeks of her life, hanging on through the pain just to have him beside her, assaulted him once more. Toward the end, he'd begged for God to take her. He couldn't watch her suffer any more. Her mom had told him she wouldn't let go as long as she thought he needed her, so he'd released her and promised they'd be together again. Then he'd held her in his arms as the final breath left her ravaged body.

Her body had begun to grow cold before her mom had forced him to let go physically. Joni had been his anchor for twenty years. She'd taught him a lot about love, honor, and commitment, lessons he hadn't learned growing up. That she'd stuck by him all those years, half of them on her own while he was deployed somewhere else in the world, was a testament to what a strong woman she was. To how strongly she'd loved him.

He hadn't been prepared to be set adrift then. He'd lied to her on her death bed. He had still needed her. She'd been the only person who had ever loved him unconditionally. He'd had no fucking clue what he was going to do in a world without his precious Joni. But he'd closed off that hurt and gone back to war, this time in Iraq. He'd never opened himself up to thinking much about Joni and their time together.

"Oh, baby. If you were here, I'd…"

You'd what? Had he changed any over the years? Fuck no. He'd still be unable to say the words, because he'd learned early on they didn't mean anything. He didn't believe he'd ever be able to love anyone. That would require making himself too vulnerable to another person, and he wouldn't do that. No, never again.

But even though he'd never been able to tell Joni the words, surely she'd known he'd have gone to hell and back for her. Hadn't she? God, he didn't know anymore. Joni had never complained about his inability to say the words. She'd never begged him.

She'd just made him feel like the most perfect husband and Master in the world.

"L'il subbie, please forgive me. I never meant to hurt you."

How could he even think of replacing Joni with Karla? He'd just wind up hurting her, too, because he could never say what every woman needs to hear from the man she loves. Besides, Joni could never be replaced in his heart.

The wind picked up and something slapped against his cheek. He looked down at the ground to find a neon-pink flower petal lying in sharp contrast against the snow. Who would have a neon-pink flower arrangement on a grave in November? He reached down to pick it up and his thoughts immediately went to Karla and the first time he'd seen her and her garish hair color in the bus station in Chicago.

She'd looked so scared. Lost. He'd been drawn to her like a moth to a flame. There had been no sexual attraction on his part. No, she'd just brought out every protective instinct in him and forced him to play hero; to do the right thing, when—just two weeks after losing Joni—all he'd wanted to do was crawl in a hole somewhere and die. Karla had pulled him back from the dead that night.

So, when had his thoughts for her turned carnal?

At the club, during her audition this summer, before he recognized her. Seemed like a lifetime ago, so much had happened since then. He'd been drawn to her voice then, wresting him from his office and into the great room. Dressed in that awful Maid Marian dress, he'd still been captivated by her long black curls. Even then, he'd imagined grabbing her hair in his fists as he…

Jesus.

He looked up at the stone in front of him.

Joni, beloved wife.

How could he desecrate Joni's memory by sitting at her grave thinking about having sex with another woman? He looked back down at the flower petal in his hands and then surveyed the nearby tombstones. All he saw were decorations with autumn colors. He had no clue where the neon-pink flower petal could have come from. The wind must have carried it quite a ways.

He stood, tucked the petal in his pocket, and breathed a heavy sigh.

"I'll be back to say goodbye before I head home, baby. I…"

Fuck. He couldn't even say the words to her now, knowing she could never hurt him. What a sorry excuse for a husband he'd been.

He wouldn't entertain any more ridiculous notions of being any better for Karla. She deserved better. Anyone but him.

* * *

The next morning, Adam sat at the kitchen table in his mother-in-law's kitchen. The cheerful room with its yellow walls and white curtains covered with images of strawberries didn't do anything to lift his somber mood. Visiting Joni's grave always played hell with his mood and it wouldn't lift again until after the New Year. God, he hated the holidays from Thanksgiving to New Year's. Too many memories of Joni.

"Quarter for your thoughts."

He looked across the table at the silver-haired woman who had been like a mother to him for nearly thirty years. More of a mother than his own had been. She'd shown him acceptance and love, once she'd realized Joni was happy and the wandering Marine wasn't out to hurt her little girl. Not intentionally, anyway.

Adam forced a grin. "Inflation?"

"Yeah, it's popping up everywhere these days. A penny doesn't buy much of a thought anymore." She took a sip of her herbal tea and Adam stared into his coffee mug for a moment.

"I still miss her, Mom."

"So do I, hon." She called everyone hon, something Adam had picked up himself, well, when talking with women, at least.

Marge Winther reached out and squeezed the hand he had wrapped around his mug, and he looked up to see a tear slide down her wrinkled cheek. "I've rattled around in this house of sad memories too long. That's one of the reasons I decided to move to an apartment. Some friends from high school are in the same complex, and we've decided it's time to raise a little more hell while we still can. Our last hurrah."

Adam grinned at her. "Watch out, Twin Cities."

Marge grew serious again. "But Adam, you have so many years ahead of you. No one's earned another chance at happiness more than you. Don't you think it's time for you to find someone else?"

Adam stalled, taking a sip of the lukewarm coffee. He wasn't going to talk to her about Karla. That relationship couldn't go anywhere. But he had no interest in looking for anyone else.

"Who is she?"

Stunned, Adam looked up at Joni's mom and quirked an eyebrow. "She?"

"You were just thinking of someone. The half-smile on your face tells me it's a woman and she might be important to you."

Adam waved her off the scent. "She's important, but it's not like that. She's a young singer at the club. I first met her nine years ago when she needed rescuing." *Only she rescued me instead.*

"How young is young?"

"Twenty-five."

"Pshaw. Joni's dad was twenty-eight years older than me."

"And you've been alone how long?"

"He wasn't in as good physical shape as you are; lots of health problems and he drank too much. Even so, we had twenty-three years together. I wouldn't change that for anything. Except for the drinking. Joni was so happy you weren't a drinker."

Marge had no idea that it had been Joni who'd gotten him to give up drinking, before she'd brought him home to meet her folks. He'd have followed in his old man's footsteps, if not for Joni. The backs of his eyes burned.

"But you and Joni had twenty years with each other. Lots of couples aren't blessed with that. Would you still have married her if you knew it would only be for twenty years?"

He cleared the frog from his throat. "Hell, yeah."

"Well, you'll only be seventy in twenty more years. Spring chicken." She smiled.

"Yes, ma'am, but I'm still old enough to be her father."

"But you *aren't* her father. And from the way your eyes light up when you think about her, I'd say you don't picture yourself as her daddy, either."

Hell, no. But thoughts of what Karla's daddy would think when he found out Adam had slept with his daughter made his gut twist. When he'd talked with Carl and Jenny a few months back, after Karla had shown up at the club, he'd promised to take good care of her. Instead...

Marge leaned toward him, her eyes bright with unshed tears. She touched his hand again and said in a raspy whisper, "Adam, Joni would want you to have someone to love, and for you to have someone to love you as much as she did. Trust me on this. But if you don't believe me, look in that box she left for you."

The box. Every year for the past five years, she'd tried to get him to open it, or at least take it home with him. Every year, he'd left it untouched in the back of the closet in the room where Joni had died. Adam had avoided the room and that box every year he'd come up here since his retirement from the Corps. Joni had wanted him to have whatever was in there, but he'd been reluctant to take possession of it, afraid of what might lie inside.

"I think it's time, Adam. You need to take it home with you this time."

Adam looked into Marge's eyes, the eyes that reminded him so much of Joni's. But he didn't feel his heart squeeze tight or his lungs constrict the way they usually did. He just saw Marge, Joni's mom.

He nodded.

"Yeah. It's time."

Chapter Fourteen

Adam walked into the room and avoided looking at the queen-sized bed where he'd spent Joni's last agonizing weeks. But the images bombarded him just the same. Skin on bones. She'd lost so much weight between the spring when he'd been home on medical leave after the ambush in Afghanistan, to when he'd been called home by Marge finally, at Joni's request. Joni hadn't wanted to take him away from something as important as Enduring Freedom and the Marines who needed him to just sit helplessly by her side and watch her die. She was both a hero and a casualty of the war that no one would ever recognize or honor except Adam and Marge.

When he'd come into the room that first day back, Joni hadn't been able to speak, but had patted the mattress beside her. He'd crawled into the bed and wrapped her in his arms, holding her while she sobbed. Clearly, she'd needed him. He'd have been here sooner, if only he'd known. So fucking helpless.

Shit, helpless didn't begin to describe what he felt. He'd wished he could engage in combat with every cancer cell that had invaded her body and crush it between his fingers. Would he have been able to make a difference if he'd been here? Probably not, if the Mayo doctors couldn't find a cure for her. Where else could he have taken her? She'd held on longer than the doctors had predicted. Marge was probably right—she was waiting to hear the words from him that would release her to the next life. But saying them had been the hardest thing he'd ever done, as if he were saying he didn't want her beside him any longer.

Then, on the 6th of November, he just couldn't stand to watch her suffer any longer. He'd have liked to have held her close and kissed her one last time on their twentieth anniversary, only two days later, but her breathing had become so labored and the look of terror in her eyes scared him to death. At his request, the hospice nurse had increased the amount of morphine to the full dosage allowed. A few hours later, she'd surrendered to him one last time, dying in his arms.

A hand brushed his back, and he jumped. "I know it's hard, hon," Marge said. "I just want to thank you for making Joni so happy, right to the end."

He tried to speak, but the words wouldn't clear the lump in his throat. Then he fought to get the words out anyway. "She deserved better than me."

"Bullshit."

Adam had never heard Marge cuss before. He turned toward her and she pierced him with her big brown Joni eyes.

"Adam Montague, I don't know who messed with your head when you were young. I know, I know," she said, waving her hand as if to brush away his rote protests. "You don't want to talk about that time in your life. But you had better hear this. You were a good husband, a good provider, and, from what Joni hinted at, everything she ever wanted in a man between the sheets."

If Adam could blush, he would have. Talking with his mother-in-law about the kinky sex he'd shared with Joni was just wrong on too many levels.

"You need to accept that you're a good man, Adam, and move on." She reached up and stroked his face, her thumb brushing across his cheekbone. "Everyone else can see that. Why can't you?"

Not knowing what to say, resigned to leave her with her glorified view of him, he bent down and kissed her cheek. "Thanks, Mom. I'll try."

She wrapped her arms around his waist and held him. The image of his own mother flashed across his mind. Hugging him, just before she shoved him into the closet and locked the door. He grew tense and reached to remove Marge's hands from around his waist.

"Okay, okay. I'll let you go." She must have thought he was uncomfortable being hugged by her. Fine, because he needed to open this goddamned closet door, retrieve the box Joni had left him, and get the hell out of this room before the walls closed in on him.

When he stood frozen to the spot, Marge opened the closet doors and he stood staring inside the darkness for a moment, afraid to go inside. Adam Montague, afraid of the dark—or dark, closed-in spaces to be more exact. What would his subordinates say if they could see their big, tough, master sergeant now?

Marge rescued him from further embarrassment by walking into the closet—twice the size of the one he'd been locked in as a kid—and dragging the box out from the corner. Seeing how heavy it was, he took a deep breath and faced his fear by meeting her halfway. He pulled the box the rest of the way out. What the fuck did Joni have packed away in here anyway, and how was he going to get it home on the plane?

Bending down, he heaved it into his arms, curious now as to what she'd wanted to salvage and make him keep of their years together. Carrying the box to the guest room across the hall where he always slept when he visited Marge, he set it on the cedar chest at the foot of the bed and stared at it for an indeterminate amount of time.

"I'm going to leave you alone now, hon," Marge said. "Just take your time. I don't know what all she put in there in the first few months. She started on it while still at Camp Pendleton. But she asked me to add a couple items at the end. They're right on top. You may want to ship the other…items home before you leave, but you'll figure out what she wanted you to have most of all. She worked on it tirelessly, until she was just too incapacitated to continue. That was when she told me it was time to let you know about her condition."

Adam tamped down the anger that burned inside him because Joni hadn't called him home sooner. What was the last thing Joni had wanted him to have? He heard the soft click of the door as Marge left, and then stared at the box again. What he wouldn't give for a bottle of scotch. Well, he sure as hell wasn't going to find *that* in there. He hadn't touched the stuff since his binge in that motel, sidearm in hand, during those two weeks after her death. He'd chosen life over death.

He slit the packing tape, yellowed with age and drew a deep breath, hoping to quell a tremor in his hands as he reached to open the flaps of the box. Sitting on top of what looked like her favorite pair of leather floggers—*shit, Joni, why didn't you throw the toys away before you moved back here with your mom?*—he found five mini-cassette tapes and a recorder to play them in. The implications of what might be on those tapes scared the hell out of him. He wasn't ready to hear Joni's voice again, even though he'd begun conjuring it up in his mind lately. What would she want to say, knowing her time on earth was almost over? He picked up the recorder. Acid from its batteries had spilled onto one of the floggers.

Without a doubt, Marge had seen their sex toys when she'd placed the tapes inside. Did she know they'd been used to turn her daughter's skin red and send her into subspace? *Hell, no.* He hoped not, anyway. He didn't want to think that she would know anything about that, but he sure as hell would have a hard time looking her in the eye at the breakfast table tomorrow. Now he understood her hesitation when she spoke about the other "items" in the box.

He stroked the soft leather of the floggers, Joni's favorite impact-play implements. She must have kept them with her until just before he'd returned from Kandahar, before boxing them up for him to find after she was gone. Curious, he wanted to see what else she'd wanted him to have.

Just under the floggers were her private leather studded collar with D-rings, as well as her public collar, a silver and turquoise necklace he'd bought her on their second honeymoon in Cabo San Lucas, about the time they'd agreed to enter into a Master/slave arrangement, at Joni's request. Lying beside them were what looked like every card and letter he'd sent her from the places he'd been stationed, all wrapped up in a pale blue ribbon. Beneath those, he found an old dog-eared paperback copy of "Screw the Roses, Give me the Thorns." He smiled. The how-to classic on BDSM had been his bible as he'd tried to figure out what to do in the damned M/s arrangement with Joni, although he learned a lot about other general lifestyle matters, too, that helped him be a better Dom.

Next he found her favorite nativity scene, the one depicting Native Americans as the Holy Family. The pieces were in bubble wrap, tucked inside the crèche. She'd also saved the angel she placed on the top of their Christmas tree every year, with the flowing champagne-colored dress and its feathered wings encased in protective gauze. Images of him with his hands spanning Joni's waist as she stood on the step ladder and placed the angel at the top of the tree caused a painful stab to his chest. He could almost feel her tiny waist in his hands as she held the angel by its skirt. That was the extent of his helping her decorate the tree. He'd never been into all the hoopla about any of the holidays, not since he was a very young kid.

"I'm sorry I didn't keep up your Christmas traditions, Joni. The holidays hurt even more without you."

He couldn't picture himself ever decorating a tree, but he made a silent promise to Joni that he would get these decorations out and place them in his office after Thanksgiving from now on, to honor her love of Christmas.

He pulled out a bottle of the oak-scented body wash and shampoo she always bought him. The lid had been opened. The image of her smelling the soapy contents made the backs of his eyes sting. God, if she'd wanted to smell him, have him near her, why the fuck hadn't she called him home sooner? He'd have retired from the Corps earlier, if they couldn't give him an extended hardship leave.

Adam returned the bottle to the box. Marge had been sending him a year's supply of the stuff every Christmas since he'd retired. Good thing, because no way in hell was he going into a girly store at the mall to buy it. But using it reminded him of Joni, so he appreciated having it.

At the bottom of the box, providing the ballast that made it so heavy, were rocks and seashells Joni had picked up wherever they went. Once, she'd made him drive ten miles out of their way so she could get rocks from a beach she'd loved as a kid. Maybe he'd keep a few.

"Sorry, Joni. I have enough rocks in my head to last a lifetime."

Still have, jarhead.

He ignored the Joni tape playing in his head to pick up the next item—a copy of Seamus Heaney's bog poems collection. He'd been fascinated with Irish history, probably because of his heritage. Adam had read many kinds of poetry to Joni. If any of the Marines in his units had discovered that he'd read love poems and other types of poetry to his wife, he'd never live it down. He wasn't sure Heaney was a favorite of Joni's, but it was nice that she'd made sure the book stayed with him.

On the side of the box was something wrapped in brown paper. He pulled it out and opened it, finding a frame with another poem in it. There was a picture of a faded lighthouse in the background, reminding him of their honeymoon on Lake Superior. Over it was printed the words to a poem called "If You Forget Me," by Pablo Neruda. Adam wasn't familiar with the poet and sat down on the bed to read the words. By the fifth stanza, the words began to swim before his eyes.

Catapulted back to that cold Thanksgiving morning on the shore of Lake Michigan a short time after he'd buried Joni, memories had flooded back to him of their honeymoon and other times together as he'd told her goodbye.

I shall lift my arms
and my roots will set off
to seek another land.

"Ah, Joni, baby. Was that you coming to me on the wind and brushing my cheek? I'd convinced myself I'd imagined you. I hope you've found the land you sought."

He put the frame in the pile of things he'd take back with him on the plane.

He repeated the words he'd said to her back then.

"Safe journey, little subbie."

Adam remembered turning around minutes later to find sixteen-year-old Karla Paxton with her neon-pink and black hair shivering in a thin coat in the middle of a winter squall off Lake Michigan.

Almost as if Joni had brought them together.

Yeah, right. Dead wives don't send their grieving husbands jailbait. Not even Joni's warped sense of humor would go that far.

Almost nine years later, though, Karla had come back to him, a grown woman. Now what was he going to do about her? Them?

* * *

The theme to *Mission Impossible* jolted Karla from her thoughts.

Adam.

Karla dreaded answering this call, but she'd have to talk with him eventually. She'd promised to call him every evening, but hadn't been able to bring herself to do so today at the time they'd agreed on. Her reluctance wasn't just because of the pain she'd heard in his voice when they spoke yesterday. Damián said it was his anniversary.

With a sigh, she pressed the accept button and put the phone to her ear. "Hello?" Her heart pounded. She'd missed hearing his voice so much and waited with no small amount of anxiety for him to speak.

"Karla? Are you okay?" Tears pricked her eyes. Why did he always have to ask the question that resulted in tears? When she didn't respond right away, he added, "What's wrong?" She heard the worry in his voice.

She shook her head, trying to compose herself so he wouldn't know she'd been crying, but it was a losing battle.

"Karla? Tell me what's going on. Now."

His Dom voice gave her some confidence. She didn't want to pull Adam away from Minneapolis, where she hoped he was putting Joni's ghost to rest, but he'd be torn with a need to come home when he heard what had happened.

"Oh, Adam." She drew a deep breath, trying to find the words. There was nothing she could do but tell him. "Damián's niece...she's been raped." *By her father.* But Karla just couldn't speak those heinous words aloud.

"Goddamn it." He was silent for a few seconds. "How bad?"

"She's home. Devastated, of course. I don't know much more. Damián, um, didn't say a lot."

"How's he taking it?"

Well, other than pounding a fist through the wall at the club tonight, he's holding up as well as can be expected.

"He's pretty upset, Adam. I'm trying to convince him to fly out to San Diego, rather than ride that motorcycle." She didn't want to think about what might happen to Damián riding the bike in his current frame of mind. A shudder passed through her at the memory of Ian's death. "I'm going to fly out to be with him. He...shouldn't be alone right now."

But he doesn't need me. He needs you.

"I've also had some experience with...well, I can possibly be of some help with his niece and the family." She didn't need to go into the months she'd spent trying to help Cassie deal with her own rape.

"Teresa. His niece's name is Teresa," Adam explained. "Where's Damián now?"

I have no clue. And I'm scared, Adam. Please come home.

"I think he's at his apartment, hopefully getting ready to leave. Maybe you can convince him to fly out with me. My dad can probably get us on a flight out tonight with his airline."

"I'll call him. My flight leaves day after tomorrow, but I'll see if I can get one out tomorrow. What else do you need me to do, hon?"

Hold me. "I don't want you to leave Minneapolis until you've done everything you need to do." *Please bury your ghosts, Adam.* "Maybe then you can fly out to meet us in California."

"I'm about finished here. I have a feeling Damián's going to want to be at Rosa's for a while. His sister's kids are like his kids, but he's closest to Teresa. He helped raise her before he deployed to Iraq. Look, I'll call Damián as soon as we hang up, but if I don't get ahold of him, tell him to leave the Harley. I'll ride it out there for him. He'll have the bike in a few days."

Bile rose in her throat. "No, Adam! I don't want you riding that thing either!" *Oh, God, no.* Her heart pounded as images of Adam's body, mangled and broken from a motorcycle accident, made her stomach lurch into her throat.

"I'll be fine. I'm caref—"

"Call you right back!" She disconnected the cell phone, dropping it onto the bed, and ran to the bathroom where she hurled her dinner. She heard the *Mission Impossible* ring several more times, but ignored it as she waited to make sure there wasn't anything else coming up.

After ten minutes, without any further dry heaves, she got up and walked to the sink, brushed her teeth, and rinsed her mouth. She picked up the phone—twelve missed calls. Persistent. She smiled and hit the callback button.

"Are you okay? What happened?" The worry in his voice warmed her heart. He cared.

"Nothing. I was…I thought there was someone at the door." Why was she lying to him? A good sub would never lie to her Dom. But she was only trying to get him to worry less. Adam liked to be in control and clearly he must be feeling so helpless right now.

"What took so long to call me back?"

"Look, Adam. I'm fine. We need to focus on Damián right now."

"I'm sorry, Kitten, but you scared the piss out of me when you hung up like that."

Yes, he cared. Of course he did. In his own way.

She wasn't sure he'd have anything to do with her when he came back from visiting Joni's ghost—and Joni's mother. Damián said he came back from there every year depressed for two months, until he got through the holidays. Karla hoped to make the holidays special for him this year, but everything was up in the air. How long would she be out in California? Did he ever want to celebrate the holidays with her?

"I'm sorry I'll be missing some performances at the club."

"Don't worry about the fucking club right now." He paused and cleared his throat. "Sorry. Look, I'll talk with Marc and Luke about helping with the demonstration schedule and they can pull in some of the more experienced Doms to help, as well. I'll call Grant and ask her to hold down the fort. She's good with the business end of things."

The mention of Grant's name made her feel a little queasy again. The Marine had a relationship with Adam that Karla could only envy. Grant could be herself, strong and willful, and he still cared for her. Karla needed to be meek and submissive, which wasn't easy for someone as headstrong as she was.

"Karla?"

"I'm here."

He sighed. "I'm glad you're there for Damián. Just be careful. He may…go into a rage or something."

Um, ya think? The hole in the drywall flashed across her mind, but Adam didn't need to know about that yet. He'd just worry unnecessarily—even more than he'd be worrying tonight as it was.

Truth be told, Damián's rage had frightened the hell out of her. He'd always been so controlled with his submissives, as if he had a tight rein on whatever demons were festering inside. Until tonight, when he'd gotten off the phone and put his fist through the wall, she'd never seen his "inner beast," as those at the club called it, totally unleashed.

"Just give him his space if that happens. I don't want you to get hurt."

"I'll be okay." It touched her that he was worried about her in all of this, but she also heard the concern for Damián, who was like a son to him. "I've learned how to protect myself against Marines, remember?"

"This is serious, Karla. He can pack a punch. Believe me, I know. Just be careful. He would never hurt you intentionally, but if he's asleep or…"

"Don't worry. I'll be fine."

He sighed. "I know you'll know just what to do. I'm glad you can be there for him. I'll get out to the coast just as soon as I can."

Please, Sir, don't ride the motorcycle.

There was no point telling him not to do something, though. She didn't have that kind of relationship with him. "If you have any trouble getting on a flight tomorrow, let me know."

After they said their goodbyes, Karla speed-dialed Damián's number. No answer. Worried about him, she decided to go looking for him at his apartment. He wasn't there—or at least didn't answer her knocks. Maybe he was at the shop. Pulling the mid-sized sedan Adam had rented for her into the alley, she got out and walked through the back door of the garage.

Damián's gaze was fixed on the sheet of steel he was pounding, but she didn't think he saw it for what it was. No doubt, in his mind, he was pounding the brains out of his ex-brother-in-law. The muscles corded and rippled in his arms and chest with each blow. Karla shuddered. She wished Adam were here. He'd know how to talk him down, get him through the pain. He was experienced and wise and…*not here. Deal with it, Kitty.*

Knowing not to surprise him, she called out, "Damián!"

He continued pounding the steel. She wasn't sure if he'd heard her, but had learned not to get too close when he was so preoccupied. She remembered what had happened with Adam on his deck. "Damián!" His hand rose to strike again, but froze in mid-air. She filled the silence. "It's Karla. We need to talk. Make some plans."

For a few moments, Damián just stared at the object he'd pounded into oblivion, breathing heavily from the recent exertions. Then he turned toward her, dropping the tool to the floor with a clang. His glassy expression slowly focused on her.

"I should have killed him when I had the chance."

*   *   *

Damián watched as Karla's brows furrowed. She probably thought he'd lost it, but he'd never been more certain about anything in his entire life. He'd been a juvenile back then. Probably wouldn't have served much longer in juvie than he did for the assault. Then Julio, his bastard former brother-in-law, would never have been able to continue to torment his sister, Rosa, or her two kids. *I'm so sorry, princesa.* Poor Teresa. If he'd only finished what he'd started when he was sixteen and bashed in Julio's face after he'd attacked Rosa, Teresa wouldn't have been raped.

"Damián, we need to deal with today and the future. I've talked to my dad and he's gotten us both tickets to San Diego tonight."

"You can't leave the club."

"Everything's settled. I've spoken with Adam. He's going to…get your motorcycle out to you, but you need to be with Teresa and your sister as soon as possible. If we make the flight tonight, we'll be there early in the morning. You need to go pack now. The car's in the alley. Why don't you close up the shop now?"

Damián looked around. His head pounded the rhythm of the slapper he'd just been using. He couldn't think. There was something he was supposed to be finishing up here tonight. He couldn't just leave the shop.

"Look at me, Damián."

He tried to slow down his breathing. He gazed toward Karla, who now stood a few feet away—just out of arm's reach. Waiting. Watching. What did she think he was going to do?

He could control the beast inside. Couldn't he?

He stood taller. "You don't need to come with me." She took another step closer.

Waiting. Watching.

"I'm going with you. I had a friend who was…who went through this once. I think I can be of help if I'm there."

Damián felt his chest tighten. How was he going to make this better for Teresa? What could he say or do to undo the damage?

"Take slow, deep breaths, Damián. Now."

Karla's words echoed the familiar command Adam had used on him many times over the years. Apparently, she'd heard them, too. A bit of the tension eased, and he closed his eyes.

Karla's hand rubbed his arm in long, sweeping strokes. "Young people are more resilient than we think. If she's surrounded by those who love her, she'll get through this, Damián. We're going to help her get through this. Now, let's get going. They need us."

Karla took his hand and he grabbed her arm as if she were a lifeline. *Oh, God, Karla. I've never been so fucking scared in my life.* Even losing his foot in Iraq hadn't left him feeling this helpless and scared, and that time in his life had been pretty fucking intense. Why couldn't Julio have hurt Damián, rather than Teresa? She was an innocent. Just a kid.

He couldn't have loved her more if she were his own daughter. He'd tried to be there for her after Rosa divorced Julio, but the time between juvie and the Marines hadn't been long. Later, living half a country away, they'd mostly just talked on the phone, except for Damián's visits several times a year. *Madre de Dios*, how could he face her? Would she want to have anything to do with any man right now? Maybe she did need Karla there.

Karla's arms squeezing him tight drew him back to the present. "I know you're scared, but you're not alone in this. You have me right now, and Adam will get out there as soon as he can. We'll be there for you, Damián; for Teresa, and your whole family. Just stay focused. She'll survive this, but she'll need you to be strong for her."

Damián drew a lungful of air and pulled away. He forced himself to smile at Karla. He'd gotten close to her in the months since she'd shown up to audition at the club. She'd become like another sister to him, once he'd seen there was something going on between her and Adam and Damián had backed off. Not that his surrogate dad was moving very fast with her, well, until lately. She wasn't really Damián's type anyway. He preferred petite blondes. But he didn't want anyone else standing by his side in the days to come. Karla had an inner strength that he'd need to help pull him through—to help him stay strong for Teresa.

He gazed into her blue eyes, filled with trust and concern. "Let's get the hell out of here. I can pack my seabag in about twenty minutes."

The next afternoon, he and Karla sat in the mental health clinic's waiting room, with Teresa between them. As the minutes stretched out, Teresa reached for Karla's hand. The two had hit it off. Teresa loved Goth music and black clothing, too. After about twenty minutes, his niece laid her head against

Damián's shoulder and he put his arm around her and pulled her closer. She'd been clinging to him, too, ever since he'd arrived in Eden Gardens, the Hispanic community in Solana Beach where he'd lived until he'd gone into the Marines.

Damián was so glad she hadn't shut him out. She looked so fragile. Nothing like the exuberant teenager he'd seen less than a month ago at her sixteenth birthday party. Now Teresa waited for the appointment with a social worker to discuss a horrific attack on her person. His sister, Rosa, was a basket case and had asked Damián and Karla to bring her to the neighborhood clinic. Damián hoped to talk with the counselor about what he and his family could do to help Teresa cope and move on. He needed to get Rosa in here, too, apparently, and made a mental note to ask the counselor about her seeing someone, too. But right now, Teresa had a death grip on Karla's hand and was looking lost and vulnerable. She hadn't cried in front of him, but just stared ahead as if shell shocked. God, did he ever know that feeling.

"You okay, *querida?*" She looked up at him and blinked, but he didn't think she really saw him. "You're going to get through this, baby girl. You're stronger than you know. Just talk to the counselors and let them help you find ways to cope."

"I don't want to go in there alone. Will you go with me, Uncle Damo?"

"Sure, but if you need to talk about anything you don't want me to hear, just boot my butt out of the room. Okay?"

No smile. No light in her eye. No fire.

Just a meek nod. That goddamned motherfucker was going to suffer for what he'd done to Teresa. Damián would make sure of it, because he planned to be judge, jury, and executioner.

The door to the inner offices opened and Damián turned to watch a brunette with shoulder-length hair step through the doorway, glance down at the manila folder in her hand, and call Teresa's name. The woman's voice was oddly familiar. Her gaze flitted over him, then Teresa, but came back to him again immediately. He felt as if he'd taken a kick to the solar plexus, unable to breathe for a moment. Her hair color had changed, but he'd recognize those big blue eyes anywhere, even though they seemed happier now than they'd been all those years ago. Her unpainted lips were a dusky pink and his balls tightened at the thought of kissing her. Again.

Savannah.

Chapter Fifteen

As recognition dawned, he watched Savannah's eyes open wider as she clutched the folder to her chest. So, she remembered him. He wasn't sure she would at first. They'd only spent about twenty-four hours together, what, eight years ago? But she'd been in his thoughts or dreams every day for many years beyond that, and still invaded his dreams from time to time.

"Uncle Damo? Are you coming in with me?"

He looked up to find Teresa standing beside his chair, waiting for a response. *Madre de Dios*, he couldn't go back there and face Savannah again. He'd finally put her memory behind him and moved on. Well, for the most part. How would he be able to sit in the same room with her and not want to touch her?

"Teresa? This way, please." Savannah's voice was as sweet as he remembered.

"Are you okay, Damián?" Karla reached out to squeeze his hand and he watched Savannah zero in on Karla and wince before she masked her expression.

"Yeah." Damián stood and took Teresa's hand.

He turned toward Savannah again. He didn't like to remember the day he'd found her, tortured and broken at the hands of two Japanese sadists at the hotel where he worked. His gaze roamed her body from head to toe. Her legs were encased in tight-fitting jeans and she wore a long-sleeved purple blouse. The folder and her arms hid her breasts from view.

Good thing.

His body reacted to her in a way that was totally inappropriate for the woman who would be Teresa's counselor. Then he remembered how much Savannah had wanted to become a social worker. To help kids. He smiled. She'd made it.

Without him.

He needed her to focus on helping Teresa deal with her trauma more than anything in the world. Putting his own feelings aside, he walked with Teresa toward Savannah. For the first time since yesterday, he began to feel things were going to be okay. Savannah would make it better. She was a kind and gentle soul. The perfect person.

For Teresa, at least.

Savannah led them down the long hallway. Noise machines whirred beside each door so passersby wouldn't hear private conversations taking place inside the rooms. At the end of the hallway, she opened a door and motioned them inside. Passing by her, he caught a whiff of a flowery scent, but it was different from the flowery scent he remembered. Inside the dim-lit office, he found a desk with two wooden chairs in front of it, a rocking chair, and a loveseat in a corner.

"Please sit wherever you're most comfortable."

Teresa made a beeline for the rocking chair and began rocking, hugging herself to provide self-comfort. Damián looked around and saw that the only other place to sit nearby was the loveseat and sat at one end. Savannah hesitated a moment, then sat at the opposite end, as far away from him as she could get.

"I'm Savi Baker, a counselor here."

Baker. So, she'd married. He looked down at her left hand and saw the wedding band on her hand. No engagement ring. Just a simple band. Damián didn't want to think about why her being married caused an ache to form in his chest. Not that she'd want anything to do with him now.

"Please call me Savi. Teresa, who do you have here with you today?"

"My Uncle Damo," she whispered.

Damián reached out his hand to Savi, as she called herself now. It would take him a while to get used to calling her anything but Savannah, after all these years. "Damián Orlando." She hesitated, looking at his hand as if it were an attacking snake, before taking it in hers. He detected a trembling that told him she wasn't as unaffected by him as she pretended to be. After a perfunctory handshake, she pulled her hand back.

Damián tried to focus on the conversation unfolding, but his mind kept comparing the old Savannah to the new Savi. Not only had she changed in physical appearance, cutting her hair and dying it, but she seemed much more in control now. Her face had stronger lines. Now she exuded confidence. Back then, she'd been afraid of her own shadow. Yeah, she'd done well for herself, which made him happy, even though he wished he'd been able to be a part of the journey with her.

She definitely had a knack for putting her clients at ease, but also for drawing out the ugly details of what had brought them here in the first place.

Savi had Teresa smiling at one point, talking about Father Martine. How did a woman from Rancho know about the Hispanic community's local parish priest? Surely she didn't attend San Miguel's, his home church, although it certainly wasn't strictly a Latino congregation. But she talked about goings on there as if she was familiar with the church and its members. Maybe she just went there occasionally to keep up with the people served by the clinic where she worked.

As Savi focused on engaging Teresa in conversation, he watched her slowly coax his niece into sharing the first details he'd heard about the rape. His admiration for Savi's skill soon turned to a rage Damián had never known as he listened. He fought hard to mask his emotions so as not to halt the words Teresa probably needed to get out. The need to crush Julio's head between his hands was so strong he could barely contain the beast that fought to escape its fragile cage.

Control. He needed to maintain control.

And distance. Needing to focus on something else, he glanced over at Savi's wedding band again. Had she married her sugar daddy, or someone else? Her full name was Savi Baker. Maiden name or married one? He'd only known her as Savannah. Judging by the gallery of photos behind her desk across the room, she probably had a child. A Hispanic-looking girl looked at him with soulful brown eyes that reminded him of Teresa's. The photo in which she looked the oldest was her First Communion, so she'd be at least seven years old.

While the photos appeared to be of one little girl at various ages, Savi might have more than one child. Or the photos could be of one or more nieces or other relatives, he supposed.

Damián was happy for her that life had turned out just the way she'd wanted, from what he could tell. Thank God he hadn't found her before shipping out to Fallujah. He wouldn't have wanted her to be saddled with a cripple like him. She deserved a whole man.

Apparently she'd found that with her husband. But her sugar daddy hadn't been Hispanic, so she must have found a new man soon after their day at the beach. Damián didn't understand why that bothered him so much.

Thirty-five minutes later, after hearing Teresa tell more about what her father had done to her, rocking faster as her turmoil built, thoughts about Savannah had been replaced by more anger and torment. When Teresa began crying, he couldn't stand it any longer and got up and went over to her.

"Mr. Orlando, you might want to give her some space…"

Teresa got up from the rocker and came into Damián's arms. "Uncle Damo, he hurt me so bad."

"Shhh, *bebé*, it's over now. He's never going to hurt you again." Damián held her as she gave into the torrent of tears that probably had been stored up for days. "It's okay. You're safe now."

After a few minutes, the sobs became more intermittent, and Damián pulled away. "Let's sit down so Mrs. Baker can finish, baby girl."

"I'm not a baby anymore, Uncle Damo."

"No, you're a kick-ass warrior woman and no one's gonna mess with you ever again."

She smiled up at him and Damián sat back down on the loveseat. Teresa surprised him by curling up in his lap. Savi grew tense beside him, and he looked over to find her casting a disapproving glance his way. *Jesús*, did she think he'd do something inappropriate with his niece? What kind of sicko did she think he was?

Savi turned her focus to Teresa and began telling her what she should do for homework, as she called it. He needed to listen up, because Teresa probably wasn't hearing anything at the moment—either.

"And I'd like you to start keeping a journal. Write about what you're feeling at least once a day. If you feel numb, write about how that feels. If you're angry, sad, content—whatever you feel—just describe it in your journal. If something triggers those feelings, write what those triggers were. Try to fill at least a page every day at first, if writing comes hard, but don't stress out over quantity. I just want you to spend some time expressing yourself in your journal every day, Teresa. You won't have to share anything in there with anyone else. But always bring it with you, because it might help you remember incidents or feelings since the last time we were together. You can refer back to it to see how you were feeling at a specific time or a particular event."

"Thanks, Ms. Savi."

"Is there anything else you'd like to talk about today, Teresa?"

His niece shook her head.

Savi got up from the loveseat and went to her desk. "I want you to make another appointment for two days from now, but I'm going to give you my card. If you feel things getting to be too much, just call the number. If it's after hours, the service will get in touch with me." She paused a moment, then turned her card over, laid it on the desktop, and picked up her pen. "Actually, I'm going to write my cell number on the back," she said, scribbling on the card. She glanced at Damián, and he saw what looked like worry in her eyes.

Shit. She acted like he was going to call and harass her or something. This woman had serious trust issues. Well, she'd made it abundantly clear years ago she wanted nothing more to do with him. He'd have no trouble respecting her wishes and steering clear of her and her perfect family.

* * *

Karla worried about Damián. He'd been very quiet since coming out of the counselor's office yesterday. What had Teresa revealed? And what was Damián going to do with that information? When she was around him, his rage barely simmered at a slow burn. Maybe she should get him out of the house for a while.

He put a pan of enchiladas into the oven. She wished she could cook well enough to help out. She doubted anyone would like her specialty—tuna-noodle casserole.

There would be time before dinner was ready. "Damián, I'd like to see your neighborhood. Let's take a walk." He looked at her with an *are-you-kidding-me?* expression that brought a grin to her face.

Teresa poured the rice into a pot and opened a can of diced tomatoes with chiles. "I'll work on the rice. Go for a walk. I'm fine." Teresa seemed to like to cook and had helped him stuff and roll the enchiladas, too. It probably was good for her to keep busy.

For the first time in days, Damián grinned and a weight lifted off Karla's chest. "I'll be ready in a few." He went down the hall to his bedroom and she went to the room where she'd been sleeping and retrieved her walking shoes. When she returned to the kitchen, he was standing at the back door waiting for her.

"So, what do you want to see?"

"Your school."

They walked out of the house and down the steps, then around to the street. "Well, then, you get a two-fer, because my school and my church are right beside each other. I went to San Miguel's until…sophomore year of high school."

"Why didn't you finish?"

"My fist had a run-in with Julio's teeth after he beat up my sister. It wasn't the first time he'd beaten her—but I'd hoped it would be the last. Unfortunately, he didn't get many more years in prison than the two I got in juvie."

Karla reached out to put her arm around him in support and felt something hard in the small of his back. "You're carrying a gun?"

He grinned down at her. "*Chiquita*, a man is always carrying a gun. But today, I'm also carrying my sidearm. This isn't the safest neighborhood in Southern California."

Karla blushed as she remembered Ian telling her about the distinction military men made between their gun—or penis—and their weapon. Wanting to change the subject, she looked around at the residential neighborhood, but thought it looked like any other working-class neighborhood. Why did he expect trouble?

"It looks to me like a nice enough place to grow up."

"Yeah, but some kids here have to grow up too fast."

Her thoughts went to Teresa and what had happened to her. Of course, those things happened in wealthy homes, too. They walked a few blocks before the bell tower of a brick church came into view. Next to it was the school building, also brick, and a blacktopped playground surrounded by a chain-link fence. Teachers stood talking in a small group and children laughed and screamed as they played together. Karla remembered her own Lincoln Park grade school and the grassy playground with swings and monkey bars where she and her girlfriends had played. This one had similar equipment, but, oh, it must be hell for tender knees and bottoms to land on that hard surface. These kids had to get tough, fast.

As they continued on, she saw a gate with a padlock leading to the school yard.

"They have to keep the school locked at all times, to protect the kids and the property."

Damián didn't seem bothered by that, but Karla thought it made the school seem more like a prison.

"Come on. We can probably get inside the church this time of day. Do you want to see it?" She looked down at her jeans and T-shirt. "Don't worry. It's very casual here. They don't exclude anyone."

Karla smiled. "Sure. I'd love to."

He took her hand and led her up the front steps of the church. Karla hadn't been to church much and hadn't really been in a lot of Catholic churches. Okay, she'd been in a total of two—one when she went to a childhood friend's wedding and the other with Cassie in New York City during college. Inside the church, the coolness contrasted with the heat of the southern California sun. Damián went to a font with water and a sponge, and dipped his middle finger in it and made the sign of the cross. She followed suit, hoping it wasn't against the rules for a non-Catholic to bless herself, too.

They were about halfway down the aisle when she heard a voice from above. She stifled a giggle. Well, not *that* kind of voice. A person's.

"Let's take *On Eagle's Wings* from the top." The music of an organ filled the church. Choir practice.

And He will raise you up on eagle's wings,
Bear you on the breath of dawn...

Karla found the words comforting as she and Damián continued to make their way forward to a small altar in a side alcove where row upon row of red-glass candle-holders held votive candles, about half of them lit.

"I want to light a candle for Teresa's healing."

Her eyes pricked with tears at the touching gesture coming from a man who had so many hard edges. She decided she would light one for Rosa, to remove her feelings of guilt and shame. Somehow, this didn't seem far removed from the rituals she and Cassie engaged in each year as they put the past behind them and moved on; they hoped to better things.

Damián dropped a folded-up bill in the collection box. Karla wished she'd brought her purse, but hadn't thought of it. The choir director intruded on their thoughts as each of them stared at the flickering candle they had lit.

"That sounded angelic. I think we've got it. See you at Mass Saturday evening."

She took Damián's hand in hers and squeezed it before they made their way to the back of the church where they encountered members of the choir coming down from the loft. Damián's hand gripped hers more tightly, and she looked up to see the counselor from the clinic staring at him, then at their interlocked hands. Beside her was a beautiful little brown-skinned, black-haired girl of about seven or eight. The counselor took the girl's arm and pulled her behind her, seemingly trying to shield her from Damián's view. What the fuck? Damián wouldn't hurt anyone—well, no one who didn't want to be hurt. Of course, the first time she'd seen him, Karla had pegged him as a sadist, so maybe the woman was judging him on his appearance. His ponytail, goatee, and the tail of the dragon tat on his left bicep peeking out from his T-shirt did give him a hard-edged look.

A man dressed in black with a white reversed collar, obviously a priest, came down the stairs and into the vestibule. "Damián, my man! Good to see you home again!"

"Hello, Father Martine."

The priest took both of his hands in a warm handshake. He looked to be in his early thirties with a swarthy complexion that looked Mediterranean. His eyes were brown and warm. Welcoming and sincere.

"I was just showing my friend where I grew up." Damián formally introduced Karla to the priest and to the counselor, Savi Baker.

"Ah, I see you two know each other," Father Martine said of Damián and Savi. "Savi's been a wonderful addition to the parish."

The counselor's face turned red and she looked down at the terra-cotta tiled floor. "Excuse me, Father, but we need to be going. Mari needs her lunch."

* * *

Damián watched as Savi took the little girl's hand and started toward the doors. He wasn't sure why, maybe because Savi was so determined to shield the little girl from him, but he needed to meet Savi's daughter. As they passed by him, he knelt on one knee and addressed the little girl. "Hi, I'm Damián. What's your name?"

"Marisol."

Marisol—surf and sun. His mind went back to the cave at Thousand Steps Beach with Savannah. Best not to remember that day. "What grade are you in?"

"Third."

She was older than he'd expected from the photos in Savi's office. He looked at her face again and thought how much she looked like Teresa.

Damián stood and met Savi's gaze only briefly before she grabbed her daughter's hand. "Mari, we need to go. Now."

Savi was gone through the door in a flash. Damián stared after them until the door slammed in his face. He turned to face Karla and Father Martine again.

"So, how long has Savi been coming here, Father?"

"She came to us in her late teens. Very troubled home life."

Was he kidding? Didn't he know where she lived? Maybe she hadn't been honest with them when she'd come here. Of course, she was caught up in some kind of high-class prostitution or something at the time.

"But she really turned her life around. She's certainly a wonderful mother and caring counselor. Everyone loves her."

I could have loved her—once upon a time.

She certainly was a little on the over-protective side, but these days you couldn't be too careful. Hell, when a child was attacked by her own father...

"How's Teresa?" Father Martine asked. Uncanny, as if he'd read Damián's thoughts.

Damián shrugged. "It's going to take some time."

"I'll stop by in a few days to see her. I hope you will come to Mass this weekend. You, too, Ms. Paxton."

"Karla, please. And, thank you for the invitation."

"Please, stay as long as you wish, but I have a meeting with the bishop to prepare for." He started toward the sanctuary.

Karla called after him, "It was nice to meet you, Father Martine." Damián said his farewells and took Karla's hand. They left the church, but he suddenly had no desire to continue touring the old neighborhood. Things had changed too much. He needed to take a ride up the Pacific Coast Highway.

"I'll be glad when Adam gets here with my bike."

At Karla's gasp, he could have kicked himself in the ass. Adam had told him not to mention it to Karla, because she'd just worry. If she could get any whiter, he didn't know how. Man, he sure had screwed the pooch this time. Adam was going to have his dick on a platter if he didn't calm Karla down.

She halted on the sidewalk and turned toward him. "What do you mean?"

* * *

Karla waited for Damián to face her, dread knotting her stomach. "I'm sorry, Karla. He left late yesterday afternoon. I expect him here tonight or early tomorrow if he doesn't drive straight through."

Terror rampaged through her. Straight through? "How can he get here that soon? It's too far to drive straight through."

"He spent 25 years in the Marines. He's used to long hours without sleep."

"He's been retired for years!" Karla heard the panic in her voice, but didn't care. "He's not conditioned for that kind of endurance now." And he'd just flown home to Denver from Minneapolis sometime yesterday. He must have set out immediately, without any sleep. *Oh, God.* She was going to be sick.

Damián took her upper arms in his hands and shook her once to get her attention. "Karla, I want you to breathe." She tried to, but couldn't inhale because of the boulder resting on her chest. "Now, Karla."

"He'll die on that thing." Her words came out in a whispery gasp as she looked into Damián's eyes, desperate for hope.

"He'll be fine. Look, we'll call him on the cell phone when we get back to the house. You'll see."

The blood drained from her face, but she managed to drag in a couple breaths. "I don't want him answering a cell phone while he's riding that thing!" Wait. Adam didn't answer his cell phone while he was driving and didn't let her either.

"Karla, I'll leave him a message right now. Don't worry." He pulled the phone out of his pocket and hit the speed dial. "Dad, it's me. Give me a call when you can and let us…me know where you are."

He disconnected the phone and wrapped his arms around Karla to give her a hug. "Please don't worry. Adam's going to be okay. He won't take any chances."

"But what about other drivers?"

Later that night, Karla checked her cell phone again. No missed calls. No text messages. She glanced over at Damián who shook his head. It had been six hours since Damián had called. She'd sent a text message, as well. He should have gotten back to them by now. Surely he'd taken a break in six hours.

Something had happened. Visions of Adam's body lying mangled on the side of the road brought bile rising into the back of her throat. She jumped up from the kitchen chair and ran down the hallway to the bathroom, barely making it to the toilet before she lost the contents of her stomach.

Damián followed her into the bathroom as she flushed the toilet. He ran water in the sink and handed her a cold washcloth. "Here, *querida*."

She leaned against the wall, took the cloth in her shaking hand, and wiped her mouth, then turned it over and pressed it against her burning forehead and eyes, hoping he didn't see her tears. She hated showing weakness.

"Look, I'm sure there's a simple explanation. Maybe his phone battery died."

More tears filled her eyes. "I just have this bad feeling." Damián held out his arms and she walked into them. "Oh, God. I don't know what I'd do if something happened to him."

"I know, *bebé*. But I'm sure he's going to be fine. You just have to have faith. Adam's invincible."

"I used to think that about my brother, too. And look how close Adam came to dying on that mountain before you killed the cougar."

"I wish I'd kept my big mouth shut about the damned bike. He's gonna ream me out for sure."

"No, it's not your fault. He should have been honest with me himself. He knows how I feel about motorcycles." Yet he'd ridden the bike out here anyway.

"You need to get your mind off this. Why don't you get cleaned up and we'll take everyone down to San Diego for some fun tonight. I think we all can use a break right about now."

"But what if Adam comes and we're gone?"

"We can leave a note. I'll bring you home right away if he gets here tonight." He let her go. "I'll go get everyone else ready."

He left her there to brush her teeth, wash her face, and regroup. Her hands shook. There were dark rings under her eyes. God, if Adam did get here, he'd take one look at her and run all the way back to Colorado.

Karla didn't want to go out and wasn't quite sure what Damián had in mind, but figured it would be something active, with Teresa and her little brother, José. Staring at her open suitcase, she opted for a T-shirt and jeans. She'd just finished dressing and walked back into the kitchen where Damián's family had gathered when she heard the rumble of a motorcycle. Not just any motorcycle, either. Definitely a hog.

She glanced at Damián, her heart climbing into her throat. He smiled. "That's my baby. I'd know her growl anywhere."

Karla ran out the back door, down the steps, and around the side of the house. At the curb sat Adam astride the beastly machine, removing a dusty black helmet, and wearing a black leather bomber jacket and black leather pants, equally dusty. She had to admit, he looked like every bad-boy stereotype she'd ever seen in the movies—only he was real. Layers of dirt-mixed sweat caked around his tired-looking eyes. He was the best thing she'd seen in a long time.

Taking a running start, she catapulted herself across the postage-stamp sized lawn and was in his arms before he could even get off the bike. "Oh, Sir.

I thought you were dead."

"Whoa! What's this all about, Kitten?"

"When I heard you were riding this damned bike out here, I just pictured all kinds of horrible scenarios. Then you didn't answer our text messages or voicemails…"

With his hands on her shoulders, he pulled her away from him, then swung his left leg over the bike's saddle and pulled her between his thighs. "Where's Damián? I want a piece of his hide for telling you."

Karla's index finger stabbed his leather-covered chest for emphasis, trying to command his attention. "You should have been the one to tell me. Why did you choose to ride this damned machine when you knew how I felt? Don't pretend you were trying to take my feelings into consideration. I don't buy it. I'm pissed at you right now."

"I thought you were just eternally grateful I wasn't road kill."

She pounded her fist against his chest, but probably hurt herself more than him. "Don't you dare make fun of my fears!"

"C'mon, baby tiger. Retract your claws. You should know by now I'm indestructible. Besides, it's been a helluva long ride and I don't need you riding me, now. At least not like this."

She looked up at him and locked her jaw so it wouldn't shake. "Oh, Adam. I kept picturing you lying somewhere…"

He held his arms out to her.

Karla walked into his embrace and held on tightly, wanting nothing more than to take care of him. She never could stay angry long.

"I'm sorry I worried you, Kitten. It wasn't my intention. This was just the easiest and fastest way to get the bike out here; Damián can always handle things better when he can go for a ride and think."

"I understand. Just don't do it again."

He chuckled. "Are you telling your Dom what to do?"

"Punish me all you want, but yes, I am." Her voice filled with emotion. "If anything happened to you, Sir, I'd…"

"Enough, Karla. Nothing happened. I'm here. End of story."

Karla sighed. "Yes, Sir. Come inside. We have leftover enchiladas and Spanish rice. You can take a shower or bath first, if you like."

"I don't suppose there's room in the tub for both of us."

She leaned back and grinned up at him. "I don't think so, unless we take a shower." Memories of his taking her roughly in the shower last month made her clit throb. Hard to believe it had been less than three weeks ago.

He met her gaze. "Oh, yeah. Shower it is." He grinned.

How could she stay mad at him, when all she wanted was to be in bed—after being in the shower—with him again?

Adam grew serious as he looked down at her. "Now, before I go in there, tell me how things are going."

Karla gave him updates on Teresa and Rosa and told him she'd spent most of her time entertaining ten-year-old José, who didn't understand what had happened, but the kid knew some serious shit had gone down around him.

"How about you, Kitten? Have you been eating? You look like you've lost weight. Are you getting enough sleep?" The pads of his thumbs brushed against the circles she'd seen in the mirror this morning.

It touched her heart that he'd think about her at a time like this, even when she looked like such a mess after her recent episode in the bathroom. "I'm fine, now that you're here." She stepped into his arms again, wrapped her arms around his waist, and held on tight. Despite the road grime, she still detected a hint of his woodsy scent, along with the more potent male musk and sweat. "I missed you so much, Sir."

His arms around her "Not half as much as I missed you, Kitten." He bent down and brushed his lips against her temple, sending shockwaves through her body. She'd missed his touch, his kisses, his...

"You two need to get a room."

Chapter Sixteen

Karla broke apart from Adam to find Damián standing a few feet away, grinning at them warily as he met Adam's gaze. Adam gave him a withering stare. "Your ass is grass, son, for worrying Karla like that."

Damián grew serious. "It just slipped out this afternoon. I swear, if I could have called the words back, I would have. Immediately." Then his tone turned accusatory. "So, why didn't you respond to our messages?"

"Fucking phone died outside Las Vegas this morning." Adam looked down and scraped the toe of his boot against the curb. "Okay, so I forgot to charge it at the motel."

His sheepish grin warmed her heart all over again. "You stopped?"

"Hell, yeah. Twelve hours on the road was my limit. Pulled into Vegas this morning and decided to get some shuteye before I took the last five-hour stretch."

He did use a little common sense. She smiled, and he quirked an eyebrow at her, but she didn't explain. Instead, she wrapped her arms around him again and felt his encircle her.

"But I did win a nice jackpot playing dollar slots in the motel lobby before I left town. I'll treat your family to dinner, after I get the layers of road dirt off."

"We'll take a rain check. I'm taking Rosa and the kids down to the amusement park in San Diego tonight." Damián grinned, a twinkle in his eyes. "You two have the house to yourselves for the next six hours or so. Enjoy."

Karla eased out of Adam's embrace and crossed to the sidewalk to give Damián a kiss on the cheek. "Thanks. I owe you one," she whispered.

"Hey, it's the least I can do to keep him from coming along tonight and chewing my ass out all the way to the city and back." He gave her a hug and turned to go back into the house. Karla returned to Adam's arms, not wanting to be away from him for a second longer.

"Damián." The younger man turned to face Adam. "How are you doing?"

Damián balled his hands into fists before she watched him forcibly regain control of his emotions. "Motherfucker…" He glanced at Karla. "No apologies. That's what he is." He looked back at Adam. "Motherfucker hasn't been caught yet."

"Shit. Stay here as long as you need to, to protect your family."

"Might as well. I got fired from the shop."

Karla hadn't heard about that. Like Adam, Damián didn't reveal much. Without question, his being here was necessary. His family needed him and she could tell he served in a paternal role with them, even long distance.

"Aw, hell, I'm sorry to hear that, son. I know how much you liked working there."

Damián shrugged, but she knew how much he loved his work, too. "There'll be other jobs. My place is here right now."

"I'm proud of you, son, for taking care of your family."

Damián's voice grew husky. "Thanks, Dad. Coming from you, that means a lot."

Karla didn't try to hide the tears wetting her cheeks. These two men had such a special connection. She was so glad they had each other, even if they'd had to bond under such horrific circumstances in Fallujah. She didn't know a lot about what had happened there, but the pieces she'd overheard from them when they spoke with other vets at the club, including Marc, told her it had caused many nightmares for all of them.

"I'd better get inside. Teresa and José were pretty excited about going to San Diego. Rosa, well, she just needs a change of scenery."

"What can I do to help, son?"

Damián cast a worried glance at Karla before turning back to Adam. Rage in the younger man seethed just below the surface. She could even feel the tenseness in Adam; he harbored a deep-seated anger as well.

"We'll talk in the morning."

She had a feeling she didn't want to know what the two of them would be planning, but she was sure it had to do with Julio. She hoped the police caught him before either or both of these two men did.

Adam pulled a huge roll of bills out of his jacket pocket, the outer bill a twenty, and handed it to Damián. "Here. These winnings are for you."

Damián held his hand up, palm facing Adam. "No, I don't need…"

"Take it." When Adam used that tone, she'd never refuse him. Neither did Damián, who reached out to accept the money.

"Thanks. I appreciate it." Looking embarrassed, Damián turned and went toward the house. Thank goodness Adam had had a lucky streak. She hadn't thought about how being here was affecting Damián's livelihood, although he obviously couldn't make money if he wasn't able to go to the shop. Then she wondered if Adam had really won the money, or if this was his way to get a man with *machismo* to accept his help without appearing unable to meet the needs of his family.

Men and their pride. She shook her head, rolling her eyes.

Adam reached down and stroked her cheek. "I'm proud of you."

"For what?"

"For the whole way you handled Damián and dealt with his crisis while I was gone—better than I could have done."

"That's ridiculous. He'd have rather had you here. Besides, I just did what anyone would do." She smiled, finally able to use the line that Adam had thrown at her so many times.

"Stop disagreeing with your Dom, baby tiger."

"Yes, Sir."

He chuckled. "Just know that you made me very proud. You're strong and invincible. I'd want you fighting by my side any day."

Hearing those words warmed her more than anything he could have said. She'd felt so helpless with Damián back in Denver, and she hadn't been able to help Rosa at all despite enjoying time spent with the kids to give their mom a break. Now she was happy to relinquish authority to Adam. How he managed to stay so strong when everyone was always coming to him to solve their problems was beyond her.

Adam handed her his helmet and turned around to retrieve a small overnight bag from the compartment in the back of the hog. He turned back toward her and covered her hand with his. "C'mon, Kitten. Let's go get that shower. I've decided I like it when you bathe me—but only as my sub, not my slave."

She grinned, anxious to get to minister to his needs again. Thank God Adam had come back to her in one piece. The world had righted itself again.

* * *

Adam shampooed the sweat and grit out of his hair as Karla's hands playfully lathered his chest and underarms. Having her hands on his skin again after more than a week apart nearly caused him to embarrass himself. He didn't expect to last long the first time, but they had plenty of time to go at it again after the shower. He couldn't wait to hear her scream for him again.

When her soapy hands took his erect dick and stroked him, as if he were some kind of slick tug-of-war rope she was trying to gain hold of, he grew even harder. He leaned back against the wall and let her continue, eyes closed. He spread his legs and she washed his balls, careful not to stroke those as hard. In such a short time, she'd learned just how to touch him, how to please him.

After she removed the soap from his dick, she knelt and soaped him up from his legs to his toes. With her hands against his thighs, she positioned him under the spray so that she could rinse the soap away from his legs. Her sweet submission to him, taking care of him like this, just made him want her even more.

"I need to do this, Sir. For me." Before he understood what "this" was, she brushed her fingertips and tongue along his water-slickened cock, which practically bobbed into her mouth on its own. Taking him in hand near the base, she used her lips to kiss the head and sucked him inside her warm mouth.

Goddamn it! How was he supposed to hold up against this kind of attack?

"You don't have to do that, Karla," he said, trying to pull her up. She looked up at him and smiled, never releasing his cock from her mouth. *Sweet Jesus. So fucking sexy.*

"I want to," she mumbled around his dick.

He grinned. "Then don't talk with your mouth full."

She flicked her tongue against the underside of his cock before he could protest again, trailing her tongue along the veined shaft and pressing kisses against the length of him as she sucked his tight skin down to his balls and back up again.

"Oh, baby! Your mouth is so fucking hot."

The corners of Karla's eyes crinkled as she looked up and smiled at him, releasing all but the tip, flicking her tongue rapidly against the underside, then taking him a little further inside her mouth. Her hand let go of the base and she placed both hands on his hips, pushing his pelvis away from her face, ever so slowly.

Adam groaned with regret, although he understood her not being ready for more yet. Then she drew him back inside her mouth. "Augghhhh, yes, Kitten." *Sweet torture.* He looked down to watch the water cascading over her head. She increased the rate she pumped him in and out of her mouth. He grabbed a thick shank of her black curls in each hand, winding them several times around his fists for a better grip and, with gentle tugs to her hair, set the pace his body needed, pulling her mouth over his shaft, then releasing the tension to let her ease off before pulling her mouth onto his dick again. Sometimes he slowed the pace, just to make the exquisite sensations last longer. She encased him as deeply in her mouth as she could. He hoped he wasn't forcing himself too far into her, but he wasn't sure he could control himself anymore.

He threw his head back and moaned. She increased the depth in which she took him into her mouth on her own. Instinctively, he pounded his dick into her face harder, one stroke touching the back of her throat, causing her to gag.

Fuck!

"I'm sorry, Kitten." He looked down to make sure she was okay.

She shook her head and pulled her mouth off his cock.

"Tell me how you want me to please you, Sir."

How could he deny her when she was just trying to be his good little sub? "Take your hand and placed it at the base of my di...penis. That'll give you more control."

She did as he'd instructed and squeezed her fist harder around the base of his shaft. *Shit.*

In a strained voice, he continued to teach her how to please him in this new way. "With your other hand, stroke my balls."

She grabbed his gonads with equal enthusiasm. "Whoa, Kitten. Be a little more gentle with those. They're much more sensitive."

"I'm sorry, Sir. I forgot." She probably was nervous, not knowing what to expect. Then her hand began to stroke him, gently pulling on his short hairs. His dick bobbed, and she took his head into her mouth again. He throbbed against the roof of her mouth.

"Oh, baby. I can't hold back."

He tried to pull her mouth away with his hands in her hair, but she kept pumping her face over his dick. Did she want him to come in her mouth? He didn't want to go further than she intended, but they hadn't exactly discussed this yet. She gripped him tighter, increasing pressure both with her hands and her mouth.

"Ahh, yes, baby!" The base of his dick began to pulsate. "I'm coming, Kitten!"

He threw his head back and leaned against the wall to keep from collapsing. As he shot his load, she pulled her mouth away and stroked him faster. Using both hands, she continued to stroke his balls and pump the shaft of his cock. A guttural growl ripped from his throat as he came.

"Augghhhhh, fuck, baby." She continued to pump him with enthusiasm, but after his dick became too sensitive, he grabbed her hand. "Easy now, Kitten."

"I'm sorry."

"Nothing to be sorry about. That was fucking incredible."

When he could see straight again, Adam looked down to watch her pink tongue venture outside her mouth to taste his semen at the corner of her mouth. She'd let him come on her face. *Sweet Jesus*. His dick throbbed again just watching her.

Karla let the shower spray clean her face as she gently touched his cock, which continued to jerk in the after-effects. He let go of her hair and reached down to pull her to her feet. His lips covered hers as his tongue invaded her mouth where his cock had been only moments before.

Adam drew away and looked down at her, cupping her face. "Your Dom is well pleased. Where'd you learn to do that?" It was none of his business, but she'd come across as not having much experience with sex of any kind. Okay, so he had a possessive streak.

She glanced away. "Do I have to answer?"

Adam set her away from him so he could gauge her response. He wasn't sure he even wanted to know anymore, but he couldn't back off now. "Answer the question."

"I...um...I rented a how-to movie online that showed, well, how to do it."

"Porn?"

The blush that pinked her cheeks turned him on again. "Yeah, it looked more like porn than a tutorial."

Knowing she'd thought about him while they were apart, enough to rent a porn flick to learn how to please him, well, nearly made him want to take this relationship further than Dom/sub and sex. She'd blown his mind—not to mention his...

Don't go there, man!

The skin between her brows wrinkled. "What's wrong, Kitten?"

She hesitated a moment. Just when he was about to demand an answer, she said, "I'm sorry I couldn't let you come inside my—"

He laughed and pulled her to him. He cupped her chin and raised her face to look up at his. "Kitten, if you'd done that any more perfectly, I wouldn't be standing right now."

Karla smiled and he lowered his mouth to hers again. The kiss they shared this time was gentler. When they pulled apart, she laid her head against his chest and giggled. His balls stirred to life. *Jesus Christ.* He was like a teenager around her.

"What's so funny?"

"Nothing. I'm just happy. Really happy."

He reached for the soap and lathered it between his hands, then washed his cum off her breasts. His hands continued to rub her chest long after all of his semen had been washed away. Her nipples hardened and his hands stilled.

She felt so good. He'd missed her more than he would have thought. He handed the soap to her. "I'd better let you take care of your face." He watched as she cleaned herself up. He'd been so lonely since he'd gone to Minnesota. He'd missed sharing his days with her, not to mention his bed. She was so right for him in so many ways. Maybe Marge was right. Maybe it was time.

But first he needed to make sure she wouldn't be repulsed by him. With his hand on her shoulder, he turned her gently toward him. Her erect nipples grazed his chest and it was all he could do not to slam her against the wall and plow into her.

Not that he was ready to go again just yet.

"Kitten, I want you to wash my back." Her eyes opened wide as she searched his gaze, from one eye to the other several times. "I'll warn you again, it's not pretty."

"I don't need pretty, Sir. I just need you. All of you."

Damn. Her big blue eyes melted another chunk of ice around his heart. If he thought himself capable of it, he'd think he was falling in love with her.

"Turn around, Sir." He quirked an eyebrow at her command and she added with a smile, "Please."

Adam's heart hammered hard as he complied very slowly. This moment would tell him if she could accept him as he was. The spray of water hit him in the face and he turned the shower head downward.

"Oh, Adam!"

He squeezed his eyes shut, expecting her to run from the shower. Instead, her soap-slickened hand lathered his back, touching every inch of his scarred upper back. He wanted to know what she was thinking, but was afraid to ask. Was she washing him out of a sense of duty, as his sub, because he'd ordered her to, or because she wanted to? Maybe he'd been wrong to reveal himself to her like this, to make himself so fucking vulnerable to her yet again.

"*Gino* D'Alessio?"

Ah, she'd gotten to his tat. "Marc's older brother. He was killed in Afghanistan serving in my recon unit."

"Oh, God. When you called for them to report…"

His body grew tense as he held his breath. "Called who to report?"

She turned him sideways to rinse the soap off under the spray and looked up at him. "In the hospital, you were having a lot of nightmares. You shouted out for D'Alessio and Garcia to report and I just assumed you were dreaming about Marc. I had no idea." She wrapped her arms around him. "And Miller?"

"Iraq. He died on top of Damián."

"Christ, Adam. What hell you've all been through."

He held onto her, trying to wipe those images out of both their minds now. What had gotten him to tell her that? Marines didn't tell their war stories to civilians.

She pulled away and turned him so his back faced her again. What more could she possibly need to see? Then what he most certainly thought was the pressure of her tongue began tracing patterns among the deadened skin, over the shrapnel wounds and the cougar's bites and claw marks. Her fingertips touched the spot where the tat memorialized the three men who had died under his command.

Her fingers trailed down to his butt cheeks and his cock throbbed to life again with a need to bury himself inside her to the hilt. He couldn't wait any longer. Adam turned and pushed her back against the wall. "Spread your legs. I need to be inside you. Now."

Her pupils dilated, her breathing became shallow, and she spread herself open to him, clearly as aroused as he was.

"And I need you inside me, Sir."

He reached down and ran his wet fingers along the cleft from her pussy hole to her clit. Definitely wet from more than shower water, he slid two fingers up inside her. She gasped before her face broke out in a knowing smile. Even though he hadn't anticipated a tenth of what had happened in here already, he reached down for the condom he'd placed on the rim of the tub, picked it up, and tore the foil open before she took it from his hand and removed the rubber. With shaking hands, she bent over him and expertly rolled it down his erection, then stood on tiptoes and kissed him, her tits pressing against his chest, mons against his balls.

Fuck. She spread her legs again, without being told, and he stroked her cleft with his dick, then picked her up by her thighs, keeping her back pressed against the tiled wall, and lowered her sweet pussy onto his erection.

"Oh, Sir!"

He chuckled, loving her sexy gasp and that delightful expression of shock and awe as he slid deeper inside her, pressing her harder against the wall, cupping her ass, pumping in and out of her as she let her head loll back and forth. Her tits bounced with each thrust and he longed to touch them, suck them, but didn't want to let go of Karla. He lowered his mouth to the side of her neck instead and nuzzled, knowing he'd leave whisker burns, but not caring at the moment. He needed his mouth on her.

"Oh, Sir! Please may I come?"

"Not yet."

She groaned and panted in the sexiest way.

"I don't want this to end yet, Kitten."

She reached up to clasp her hands behind his head and drew him toward her face, where her tongue waited to plunge inside his mouth much as his dick was plunging inside her pussy. Her breath against his mouth smelled minty and he groaned, unable to prolong the ecstasy any longer.

"Come. Now, Kitten."

He couldn't let go to stroke her clit, but let his body strike the sensitive spot until her screams filled the bathroom. "Oh, ohhh, ohhhhhh. Yes, Sir! Please don't stop. Oh, my God!"

"Oh, God, Karla! Fuck me dry!" He pumped her body up and down on his dick, letting her pussy land harder against him each time.

"Acccckkkkkkk! Oh, shit! Don't stop! Fuck my brains out, Adam!"

Man, he had her swearing like a sailor now. Maybe she'd been watching *too* many porn flicks. *Oh, who gives a fuck?* The sweetest sounds he'd ever heard were coming from her mouth. Her pussy spasmed around him as she milked him for all she was worth. She howled like a cat in heat. God, would he ever get enough of her?

Not in this fucking lifetime.

He continued to hold her, impaled on his dick, pressed against the wall. His baby tiger liked it rough. How had he ever found a woman so evenly matched to him?

She couldn't possibly be comfortable in this position. He lifted her off his dick, pressed her body hard against the tile, and let her lower her feet to the bottom of the tub. When her legs gave out, he turned her around and held her against his body with his arm wrapped around her waist and positioned her under the shower spray to wash her off before reaching out to turn off the water.

He closed his eyes and lifted her into his arms. Setting her on the floor near the sink, he didn't say a word as he dried her off, then lifted her again and carried her down the hall to the room they'd be sharing. He grinned when he saw the twin-sized rack they'd be sleeping in, imaging her body spread out over his. He wasn't sure how much sleep he'd be able to get.

He might need to rack out on the floor instead. He needed some time to think. What in the hell was he going to do with her? All he knew was that the thought of spending the rest of his life without her suddenly seemed bleak.

But he had a lot of baggage he didn't need to be saddling her with, not the least of which was whatever he'd done to his father. While in Minnesota, he'd looked up his mother again, but there was no one there by that name. She could be dead by now. He didn't know why that thought made him feel sad.

Chapter Seventeen

Uncle Damo, he hurt me so bad. Fire! Help! No more, please! "Stop, Daddy! Don't touch me!"

Damián bolted up from the bed and tossed the sheet off his lower body. He needed to get to Savannah. He shook his head clear. No, not Savannah. Savi. God, he hadn't dreamt of her in forever. No, wait. It was Teresa. She needed him. He felt around in the dark until he found his prosthesis and tried to strap it onto his leg. Fucking thing. Why couldn't he get it to fasten this time?

Finally, he had it in place. "I'm coming, *bebé*," he whispered. He reached into the nightstand for his sidearm and headed for the door. Julio wasn't going to hurt Teresa ever again.

"Stop! Don't!"

Teresa's pleas filled his chest with rage. The motherfucker had come back. When Damián reached her door, he braced himself on his feet so his prosthesis wouldn't be a liability, and opened the door. In one fluid motion, he leveled the sidearm at Teresa's bed, where the screams were coming from.

She was alone. Just a fucking nightmare. *Madre de Dios*, did he ever know how real those could be.

He laid the sidearm on her vanity, turned on the lamp, and crossed to the bed. He began speaking to her in a calm, firm voice. "Teresa, wake up. You're dreaming." When he touched her arm, she swung at him. "Whoa, it's Uncle Damo. You're safe now, *princesa*."

At last, her terror-filled eyes opened, but the glazed look told him she was still in the throes of the nightmare. She pounded at his chest and shoulders with both fists. For a moment, he just let her rage, because she'd feel better after she'd expended some of the adrenaline.

"I hate you! I hate you!"

"That's it, *bebé*. Let it out."

Damn, but she packed a punch. After some targeted self-defense classes, she'd be able to fight off anyone who tried to hurt her ever again.

Suddenly, her eyes opened wide, her fists paused, and she stared into his eyes. "Uncle Damo?" Her hands opened and she pulled them back as if burned. "I'm sorry I hurt you." Tears streamed down her eyes as her body shook from the adrenaline crash and he opened his arms for her to come into them.

"You can't hurt me, *princesa*." *Not with your fists, anyway.* "But we'll see about getting you into some classes where you can gain some skills and confidence in protecting yourself."

Her arms wrapped around him and she laid her head against his shoulder and bawled until her body grew limp. He eased her back down on the pillow and brushed the loose strands of hair away from her damp forehead.

"That's it, *bebé*. Sleep now."

He eased himself up off the bed, catching himself on the bedpost. Fuck. His good leg had fallen asleep. Gingerly, he hobbled across the room and picked up his sidearm, cast one more glance at Teresa's sleeping form, and walked out of the room. As the feeling returned to his leg, he realized it had been a long time since he'd had to hobble. God, those long months of getting used to the damned prosthesis, followed by nearly a year before he could walk without crutches or a cane; seemed like forever ago.

He walked toward the kitchen, wanting to check to be sure the house was secure and no one had entered. Adam and Karla had gone up to Pendleton to spend the night on base with one of his old buddies. Damián needed to send them back to Colorado soon. They couldn't hang around here forever waiting for Julio to show up. That fucking bastard would pay eventually for what he'd done to Damián's family, if it was the last thing he did. As far as Damián knew, the bastard still hadn't been captured. Had he slipped across the border to find sanctuary with relatives in Mexico? Or was some lowlife harboring him in the San Diego barrio where he lived?

When Damián turned the corner, he saw light spilling from the doorway and found Rosa sitting at the table with a cup of coffee and a cigarette. Damn. She'd taken up smoking again. She turned to him, but didn't smile or say a word. The dark circles under her eyes told him his sister had been to hell and back. Again.

No, that bastard had better not show up here, because Damián's rein on the beast was stretched tight. It wouldn't take much for him to snap. When he did, nothing would be the same.

"How is she?"

"Sleeping."

"I'm sorry, Damo. I knew it would be better if you went to her. I can't protect her." Her hand shook as she reached for the cigarette and Damián placed his over hers and squeezed. "Oh, *Dios*."

Damián reached out and wrapped his arms around her and held her while she cried. At least she was showing some emotion again. He'd hated the haunted, hollow look in her eyes. Julio's attack hadn't only been on Teresa, it had brought up old scars Rosa probably hadn't dealt with from when Julio had beaten her more than a decade ago.

"I brought that monster into this family. I encouraged Teresa to go with him that night."

"Don't blame yourself, Rosa. He chose to do what he did."

"I wanted her to know her father. He'd never hurt the kids before. Only me." She gave a ragged sob and held on tighter.

"Shhh, sis. It's going to be all right. I'm going to make sure of it."

He needed to talk to Savi about getting Rosa into some kind of counseling. His sister had held the weight of so much on her shoulders since she was young. Anyone would break under all the shit she'd been through.

Maybe he should check in at the shop he'd worked at as a teenager and see if there were any openings. He'd need to stay out here until Rosa could handle things with Teresa again. But he needed to make some money to help support them. He'd often supplemented Rosa's income when he could, as far back as when he'd been in the Corps. Now he needed to provide for his family once more.

* * *

Karla watched the muscle in Adam's jaw clench. All the way home from Camp Pendleton yesterday, he'd been distracted and silent. Had his friends said something about him being there with someone half his age? She hadn't gotten that impression, but Adam and Master Gunnery Sergeant Richardson had spent some time separate from his wife and Karla. She wondered what they'd discussed, not that it was any of her business.

But she hadn't felt either of them had disapproved of her. They'd seemed really nice. Still, something had been bothering him since they'd left. He reached up and rubbed the scars at the back of his neck.

"I love Lady GaGa's new music video. Have you seen it?"

Karla turned her attention to Teresa in the backseat of her mother's Ford Focus.

After hearing that Teresa had suffered from another nightmare last night, Karla thought it might be fun to take the girl shopping. Trite as it may seem, new clothes could always make a girl feel better. Certainly worked for Karla—so she'd made a few purchases of her own tonight.

Adam had appointed himself chauffeur—more likely bodyguard. Everyone was on edge waiting to see what Julio would do.

After several hours of shopping in San Diego, Adam had looked ready to implode. Apparently, while he loved to shop for Karla at the kinkster stores, there wasn't quite the thrill shopping with a teenage girl at more mainstream shops. She suppressed a giggle.

All in all, though, the evening had been lots of fun and Adam had laughed along with them occasionally, especially when they people watched in the mall's food court.

Karla also had been able to get Teresa to talk about their shared interest in Goth music. The young woman was so smart, and also wanted to pursue a singing career. Karla couldn't believe it when she'd given the young girl the same advice her parents had given her—stay in school, go to college, and then, if you're still interested, you can major in music.

Gawd, when had she gotten so old?

Soon, they'd be back at the house and the weight of all that had happened a couple weeks ago would be back on Teresa's shoulders. The house had such a depressing pall over it. Poor little José had needed a reprieve, too, so Rosa had let him spend the night at a friend's house tonight. It was bad enough José and Damián had to camp out in the living room of the tiny bungalow, with Rosa insisting that Karla and Adam have her son's bedroom. Karla had tried to make it fun for him by helping him create a tent with some chairs and blankets, the same as she and Ian had done when they were young. But José needed to get back to some normalcy, too, and she and Adam had decided they'd head back to Denver on Wednesday.

That would be a week since Karla had been out here. Teresa seemed to be coping and had seen her counselor again today. There still were times when the glaze of pain came over her face and her eyes became vacant, lost in the horror of her attack. How could a father do something so horrendous to his daughter? Rape was vile in any circumstance, but to violate a sacred trust like that went beyond anything Karla could ever understand. Her own father had always been affectionate, supportive, and loving. She felt so safe with him. It was hard to imagine there were such monsters in the world.

Adam was protective, affectionate, caring, strong, and everything she'd ever imagined a man should be. Something had changed when he came out here. Had something happened in Minneapolis to make him see her differently? All she knew was that he didn't seem to be pushing her away all the time.

Even though they couldn't really indulge in their Dom/sub playtime here, she always felt that aura of control and power around him. She looked for ways to please him, because that pleased her. Last night, everyone had been watching a popular Marine/Navy investigation show on TV and, when Karla and Rosa had finished cleaning up the kitchen, Rosa had gone to bed, but Karla had ventured into the living room. The places to sit were filled and, when Adam had started to get up for her, she motioned for him to remain seated. Then she'd curled up on the floor between his knees and leaned back against his thigh.

He stroked her hair, one of her most erogenous zones. A sense of peace and contentment had come over her unlike anything she'd ever known. She'd let her guard down completely and before she knew it, he grabbed her hand and guided her up into his lap, where she curled up and relaxed against him.

Bliss.

Cassie and her other friends would have died if they'd seen her in such a domestic scene. Karla had never submitted to a man or anyone else. And yet, even though their Master/slave arrangement had been a disaster, something had changed for her. She couldn't live that extreme twenty-four/seven way, but what about on an as-needed basis? With the emotional roller-coaster everyone had been on lately, she welcomed relinquishing control and letting Master Adam call the shots. Very freeing.

But what happens next? Adam had never talked of love or anything permanent. Could she just go on living a shadow life? Would he ever be able to move on from Joni and take another wife? Being a friend with benefits or just his BDSM partner wouldn't be enough for her.

She wanted Adam's love and total commitment.

Might as well shoot for the moon, Kitty.

* * *

"Don't move, motherfucker, or I'll blow your head off—then I'll blow your fucking brains out." Both hands on his weapon, Damián leveled the sidearm directly at Julio's balls and waited. He'd show his former brother-in-law what pain feels like. His expert marksmanship training in the Marines ensured he wouldn't miss, especially at such close range. What kind of idiot was Julio, breaking the window and crawling into the utility room? Did he think Damián was fucking deaf? Or did he just think that Damián wouldn't be here to protect what was his this time?

Hands in the air, Julio pumped his palms toward Damián, as if to calm him down. But Damián was as cool as fried ice cream. He smiled. Plain and simple, he planned to kill the bastard this time. It would be slow, bloody, and painful—nothing like the way he'd been trained to kill by the Marines.

"Damo, man, I just had too much to drink. I fucked up."

Judging from the way he swayed on his feet, he'd fucked up again. Had he ever.

What had he broken in here for? To attack Teresa again? Damián felt rage building in him, but tamped it down. Remain calm.

"No, *bastardo*, you raped your daughter—my niece—and for that, you're going to pay."

Damián reveled in the look of pure terror on his former brother-in-law's face. The man's eyes bulged from his eye sockets and he lowered his hands to cover his crotch, as if they'd shield him from the first bullet Damián planned to discharge from his weapon, ensuring Julio would never rape anyone again. For the first time since he'd heard about Teresa's attack, Damián felt like he was in control.

Maybe for the first time in an even longer time—since before Fallujah. Before Savannah.

Damián heard the key in the lock of the back door and before he could wave them off, Karla and Teresa came into the utility room laughing. When she saw her father, Teresa's eyes grew round and Karla pushed the girl toward the back door, trying to keep her out of harm's way. With her back turned toward Julio, the bastard grabbed Karla in a chokehold and hauled her against him. He retrieved a knife from his boot and held the blade to her throat. A moment of sheer terror flashed in Karla's eyes as she pleaded silently with Damián to do something.

"Put the gun down, Damo, or I cut this bitch."

"Dad, don't hurt her! Go away! Leave us alone!" Teresa's voice became shrill and tears streamed down her face. She held her arms to her abdomen and began crying, then screamed. Damián watched as Adam's arm reached inside the door and pulled her outside to safety.

"No! I can stop him!"

* * *

Adam yanked his cell phone out of his pocket. "Teresa, go down to the corner and call 911. Now." He pressed the phone into her hand and shoved her toward the street. With Teresa out of harm's way, Adam glanced through the window to assess the situation. Some fucking shithead had his hands on Karla. Had to be Julio. Oh, yeah, he'd pay for touching her, scaring her—and if he hurt her, he'd pay with his life.

Damián pointed his .357 at Julio's head, but Karla was in the way. Adam motioned for Damián to stand down. She was too close to chance taking Julio out, and, even though his son could hit his target from a lot further away, neither would risk Karla getting shot if someone moved. Adam couldn't lunge at them, either, and have Julio flinch or move, because the knife was lying flush against her artery.

Karla looked at Adam then Damián, scared and maybe expecting them to rescue her. Same facial expression as when she'd been pinned by the cougar against a boulder on Mount Evans. He'd rescued her then, but this cat wasn't as predictable. When she locked onto Adam's gaze again, he tried to communicate with her nonverbally. He eased into the room, but Julio's knife pressed tighter against her jugular and he pulled her head back, making Karla more vulnerable.

"Back off, man!"

Adam raised his hands.

As if a light bulb lit, Karla's expression hardened and, just the way they'd trained on their day at the martial-arts center last month, she raised her hands.

That's it, baby. I'm ready when you are.

In a flash, Karla grabbed onto the wrist in which Julio held the knife and using both of her hands pulled his down as she pivoted and raised her left knee into his elbow. The knife clattered to the floor as Julio's elbow cracked and he screamed in pain. Before Adam could lunge forward to pull her away from danger, she completed the move, jamming the heel of her foot into the back of his knee and Julio began to crumple.

Good girl.

Before Adam could reach her, Damián grabbed Karla and pulled her away from Julio. Her scream of frustration indicated she wasn't quite finished with him yet, but once Karla was safely out of harm's way, Adam took the shithead the rest of the way to the floor and grabbed his throat, choking the life out of him.

"No, Adam! Don't kill him!"

Why the fuck not? He could have killed you. But the scumbag was no longer a threat. He blubbered like a baby, his arm lying at a grotesque angle. Karla definitely had broken it somewhere. Not taking any chance on him hurting her, he pressed on Julio's carotid artery until he cut off the oxygen to his brain. Julio's body relaxed as he passed out.

Adam looked up to find Karla gasping for breath, Damián's arm around her waist to keep her from going at Julio again—or maybe she wanted to go after Adam to keep him from killing the scumbag. Damn, that girl could fight. He left the trash on the floor and turned to Karla who broke free from Damián and ran into Adam's arms. Her body trembled as she wrapped her arms around him.

The wail of sirens sounded in the distance. He hoped they weren't up on the 5, which paralleled the neighborhood, but actually headed here.

"Oh, God. I can't believe it really worked!"

He chuckled. "Yes, tiger. You did well."

"I froze. I think I was waiting for you or Damián to rescue me. Then you raised your hands and I remembered what I was supposed to do."

"You did everything you needed to do. Didn't even need us. You'll be able to take care of yourself any time."

For the first time, Adam noticed Damián standing over Julio, his sidearm pointed at the shithead's head.

Fuck. "Stand down, son. He's not worth it. Your family needs you to not be stuck in prison right now. Let the police take care of him."

Damián stared down at the unconscious man with a cold, calculating look in his eyes. Adam understood his wanting to finish him off. Hell, he'd come close to strangling him a few minutes ago himself for threatening Karla. For what he'd done to Teresa, and now the attack on Karla, Julio wouldn't be getting out of prison anytime soon. "Damián, go meet the police and let them know they're clear to come inside."

Damián didn't move for several moments, then seemed to come to a decision and took a step away, holstering his sidearm behind his back. Adam closed his eyes in relief. He hadn't been sure he'd be able to get through to him, not after what Julio had done.

Suddenly, Damián hauled off and kicked Julio right in the nuts. Julio grunted, but remained unconscious. Adam grinned. The shithead would wonder for a quite a while why his balls and dick were so sore. Served him right; deserved a lot worse.

Minutes later, Damián led two police officers into the utility room and they had the now conscious Julio on his stomach with his hands cuffed behind his back in no time. The pain in the scumbag's broken arm or elbow had him screaming like a baby as they manhandled him. Good. He needed to feel more pain, after all that he'd caused others. They lifted him up to the sound of more howls and dragged him out the door.

Adam watched Damián grow tense when he looked toward the doorway again. On alert, in case Julio had somehow gotten loose, which seemed unlikely, Adam's gaze followed. A sobbing Teresa ran in with a petite brunette behind her. Seeing Damián, Teresa ran across the room and into his arms.

"Uncle Damo, I was so afraid he'd hurt you or Karla."

Adam felt the unknown woman's scrutiny on himself and Karla. Then she looked at Damián and furrowed her brow as if she disapproved—or was confused. Who was she?

But Adam's attention returned to Teresa. "Hon, you did well. Proud of you."

Teresa looked over at Adam and gave a quivering smile. "After I called the police, I chickened out and called my counselor to come over, too."

Ah, the stranger. The brunette stepped forward and extended her hand, giving Karla a puzzled look. Again, she stared from Karla to Damián and back again. With seeming reluctance, she offered her hand to Adam. "I'm Savi Baker."

"Nice to meet you, Ms. Baker. Thanks for coming over for Teresa."

Three more officers came in and insisted on separating Damián, Adam, and Karla for questioning. He didn't want to leave Karla, but had no choice.

Adam cleared his throat and looked at the counselor. "Ms. Baker, why don't you and Teresa wait outside?"

"Oh! Of course. Teresa, let's go find some place to talk and process some of this, sweetheart."

They left and the officers split up, taking Karla into the living room, Adam into the kitchen, and Damián remained in the utility room.

After they'd given their accounts to the officers, Adam went in search of

Karla. He found her curled up on the sofa, shivering from adrenaline drop. He walked over to her and quickly scooped her up. "I've got you, baby."

She rested her head on his shoulder, her entire body trembling. He held her tighter against him and pulled an afghan over her.

"Don't let me go, Adam."

Adam wished he could hold her forever, but would settle for this moment and as long as she'd put up with him. Seeing that sharp blade pressed against her thin, fragile neck had nearly gutted him. Thank God she hadn't been cut or hurt in the scuffle.

"I'm better now. You can put me down." He looked down at Karla, seeing a flush on her cheeks.

"No, Kitten. I need to have you in my arms right now. For me." He pulled her closer and she relaxed against him.

* * *

Karla's face grew hot from the embarrassment of being coddled like a child, but had to admit she really didn't want Adam to put her down. She wasn't sure she'd be able to stand yet, anyway. The feel of the steel blade against her throat was singed into her body's memory and her chest felt sore from how hard her heart had been pounding.

Everything had happened so quickly—and yet time had stood still. It took forever for her to even remember her training and how to respond to the attack. One minute, she and Teresa were laughing about a music video and the next she was being threatened with a knife.

"Thank God they have him. He can't hurt her anymore."

She burrowed like a lost kitten into the afghan and snuggled against his chest.

"You were incredibly brave, baby tiger."

"I was scared to death."

"But you kept a clear head and dealt with the dick—bastard—despite your fear. That's what a hero does."

"Oh, Adam, I'm not a hero."

"Nonsense." His arms tightened around her. "No one was hurt or killed except Julio, who's been neutralized for the foreseeable future, thanks to you. Hon, you're definitely a hero in my book."

Her cheeks grew warm. She remembered the tattoo on his back beginning to understand why, by his definition, he could never be considered a hero. The image of the tat's boots, helmet perched on an upright rifle, and the names of those he believed were dead because of him. She splayed her hand over his pec and felt his heart beating against it. "Sometimes a hero can't save everyone, but it doesn't stop him from trying and from saving as many as he can. It doesn't stop him from being a hero." He stopped breathing.

Oh, Adam. You'll always be a hero to me. "Thanks for helping me remember what to do in there."

With a grunt, he laid his chin on her head. If he thought he was going to shut her up, he had another think coming. "I wouldn't have remembered what to do otherwise."

"Nonsense. Your training would have kicked in. Look at how quickly you responded on my patio a couple weeks ago."

"But I was supposed to execute that move within seconds. I froze."

"You got the job done, tiger. Quit beating yourself up over it."

"Like you beat yourself up over Afghanistan?" He pulled back as if she were about to explode in his hands. "Marc told me you saved a lot of men in that ambush."

"Marc needs to keep his mouth shut."

"Why can't you admit you're a hero? You're always saying things like, 'I did what anyone would have done.'" She pulled away from the comfort of his chest and stared him in the eyes. "But not everyone would have gone into an ambush to save his Marines. Not everyone would have gotten involved in an altercation in a bus station to save a stupid teenager who didn't have the sense God gave a goose. And not everyone would entice a mountain lion to chase after him to save someone else." She poked her index finger in his chest. "You're a hero, Adam, whether you choose to accept the title or not."

* * *

The image of his father lying in a pool of blood flashed before his eyes. The walls were closing in on him. His hands became cold, despite the blanket over them. If this conversation didn't take a new direction soon, he'd need to get out of here.

"We've been over this before. I'm not going to talk about this now."

Her hand reached out of the blanket and up to his cheek, warm and comforting, but he pulled away. "You don't know the half of what I've done, the people I've gotten hurt...or killed."

"You'd never hurt anyone intentionally. You're a guardian. A protector.

You take care of those you love."

Okay, now it just got worse. "I don't have what it takes to love anyone, either. The sooner you get that into your head, the better off we'll both be."

Karla's hand that had been pressed against his cheek drew into a fist. At first, he thought she was going to deck him, but she drew it back under the blanket in a protective move.

"I never promised you anything more."

Her eyes sparkled with unshed tears, making her voice raspy. "I know."

"Let's talk about something else."

"I don't think there's anything else to talk about, except maybe what our relationship is going to be when we get back to Denver."

At least she still wanted to be with him. Didn't she?

"I'd like to get back on stage. I've missed performing."

Okay, maybe she wasn't interested in being there with him. What did she expect? Friends with benefits and Dom/sub was all he'd ever offered.

"I never lied to you."

"No. I just saw something in you that you obviously can't see."

What the fuck was that supposed to mean?

She pushed the blanket off herself. "I'm going to go check on Teresa."

She scooted off his lap and handed him the blanket, which he laid over the armrest. He watched her walk out and sat for a long time, just staring at the doorway. Why had she gotten so hung up on hero talk? Well, hell. He'd been the one who initiated the topic.

Immediately, he missed having his arms around her, but if she couldn't take him the way he was and kept conjuring up this fantasy hero, then it probably was for the best that there was some distance between them.

No way was he ever going to let himself fall in love with her. Love just led to pain. Hurt.

Not much fucking difference from what he felt right now.

* * *

Damián felt exhausted as he motioned Teresa and Savannah into the kitchen after he'd finished with the police.

"Savan…Savi, can I get you something to drink?"

A haunted expression came over her face. What? Did she think he didn't remember her?

"We've got water, tea, Kool-Aid."

Teresa punched his arm and giggled. "Uncle Damo, I don't think she's gonna drink Kool-Aid." It was good to see his niece bounce back so fast after what had just happened in the utility room.

"What's wrong with Kool-Aid? It's grape—José's and my favorite."

Teresa just rolled her eyes. "Ms. Savi, can I get you something more grown-up, like a Coke?"

"I'm fine. I need to be getting back home. I left Mari with a friend, but it's homework time." Her expression grew serious as she homed in on Teresa. "I want you to take some time to journal about what happened tonight, sweetie. Don't forget the three positives every day. We'll talk more during our next session. As always, though, feel free to call me if you need me. Any time."

Teresa crossed the room and gave Savi a hug. Damián couldn't help but feel jealous that he couldn't do the same.

He cleared his throat. "Thanks for everything, Savi. I'm glad you could be here for Teresa tonight."

She glanced at him, then down at the floor. "Not a problem."

Karla came into the room, looking like she could spit nails. Well, the way she'd taken Julio down, he figured she probably could. "Leaving so soon, Ms. Baker?"

"Please, it's Savi. But, yes, I need to get back to my daughter."

She reached into her tight jeans and pulled out her keys. After assuring Teresa she could call her anytime, she left the room. He couldn't keep his eyes off her ass, encased in those blue jeans like a second skin.

Hell, he needed to see her out. "I need to go clean up that glass and board up the broken window." He was just a couple of yards away when she reached for the door handle. "How've you been, Savannah?"

Her body grew stiff. Her fingers gripped the handle, but she didn't turn around. "Don't call me that. Savannah Gentry is dead."

Of all the things he'd fantasized about her saying to him—like 'I've never forgotten you or our perfect day at the beach'—that sure as hell wasn't one of them. Fr. Martine said she'd come to San Miguel's troubled. What the fuck else had happened to her after he'd dropped her off safely at her house? Had she continued to do tricks for that creep at the hotel?

"I tried to get in touch with you, after the beach."

She turned and looked at him. "You did?" The hopeful look in her eyes was soon replaced by a coldness that sent a chill up his spine.

"Yeah. I left letters in your mailbox. Even staked out the hotel awhile."

She became fascinated by watching the toe of her sandal scuffing against the door jamb. Her pink toenails looked like she'd let her daughter paint them. She looked back at him. "Well, it's good you didn't find me." Despite the passion in her voice, her eyes remained devoid of emotion. He'd never known anyone to be so closed off emotionally. How did she connect with her patients, if she was so disconnected from her own emotions?

Well, maybe that was her coping mechanism. How could anyone listen to tragic stories like Teresa's day in and day out and not close herself off emotionally? Probably kept her from getting burned out. He was glad she could compartmentalize her feelings that way, so she could help Teresa. But at what cost to herself?

Suddenly, he had an urge to get some kind of response out of her. He closed the space between them and nearly backed off when she cringed against the door, her hand on the handle, ready to run.

"You were the most perfect thing I ever held in my hands, *pequeña mariposa*."

His little butterfly closed her eyes, as if with regret…or pain. So there was some feeling inside. She did remember their day together. Knowing that made him feel better in some way. When she opened her eyes, there was a glimpse of some unreadable emotion before she shut down again.

"I've lived with the memory of our time in that cave every day since. But I can't have anything to do with you ever again."

Then she opened the door and walked out of his life again, closing the window of hope that there could ever be anything between them.

Chapter Eighteen

Joni's voice filled his office. He heard the strain, her sweet voice laced with so much pain. To increase the volume and improve the sound quality, he'd attached his computer speakers to the micro-cassette recorder. In retrospect, maybe that tinny radio sound would be better than having her sound so close, so real. He cringed, knowing she'd been suffering through a private hell when she'd recorded these tapes, but had wanted to tell him these things anyway. He didn't deserve that kind of sacrifice.

That kind of love.

"I was just thinking about the time we went to the Marine Corps Ball the year after you came home from Kuwait. So handsome in your dress blues. Made my heart stop for a moment. If I never told you that before, I wanted you to know how proud I was to be by your side that night and every day."

God, Joni. You always made me the proudest Marine. She was the perfect Marine wife. No, the perfect wife. Period.

He heard her draw a deep breath. "Anyway, I still remember talking with your CO and his wife and I accidentally called you Master. Her eyes became so wide." Another breath, this one ragged. "She looked from you to me. You'd think she'd never seen a slave before, which is pretty hard to imagine, because several other wives on base were collared by their husbands in twenty-four/seven relationships."

Is that where she'd gotten the idea to be collared by him? Surely not, because he'd known some of those Masters, too, and they seemed to take their wives for granted. Adam never thought he deserved Joni, but he sure as hell never took her for granted. Of course, she had her own circle of friends on base, which was good, especially when school was out for the summers and he was out on maneuvers or deployed somewhere.

The tape continued to whirr in silence a moment, then she continued, her voice barely a whisper, causing him to raise the volume. "I wish I could have been your slave to the end. I so wanted to please you. You gave me so much. Please, Master, tell me I pleased you." Her voice broke and the tape was paused. He reached out to turn it off, not able to listen to more.

How can you even ask that?

"Aww, fuck, Joni, you were the best slave a man could want. You always pleased me." Hell, all she had to do was smile and he was pleased. He rubbed his thumb and forefinger over his eyelids. Maybe she'd been able to tell his heart wasn't in being a Master, though, all those years. If he'd been honest with her, he never would have gotten into a Master/slave arrangement in the first place. Or he'd have gone back to a Dom/sub when he'd seen what it was doing to him. He didn't want that much fucking control over anyone.

"Hell, just look at the mess it was with Karla," he muttered to himself.

But he and Karla had at least been honest with each other and ended their Master/slave when Adam safeworded, as much for her as for himself. They'd gravitated to a Dom/sub instead, which seemed to work for them for a while. Now, he wasn't sure what they had, if anything. Since returning from San Diego last week, they'd just been coexisting again, most of their interactions club-related; no BDSM or sex.

Damn, he'd tried to do his best with Joni, but he just didn't want a slave. He could chalk that mistake up to being young and stupid, but if he were honest, he could see that everything about his marriage had been a lie. He'd promised to love, honor, and cherish Joni—and had only managed to succeed at two out of three.

What could he possibly offer Karla that would be any better?

He put the last mini-cassette into the recorder. They'd been numbered and dated. This one also was the last one she'd recorded. He heard the weakening in her voice. The words were slow, her breathing labored, as she struggled to get one last point across.

"Don't hold onto my ghost...Find a new subbie...Find a new wife."

* * *

Karla leaned against the wall outside Adam's office, certain her feet wouldn't support her if she tried to walk right now.

"Joni, you were the best slave a man could want."

"Hell, just look at the mess it was with Karla."

The ringing in her ears made her realize she was close to passing out, throwing up, or both. She held her forearm against her stomach and pushed away from the wall with the other, then made her way back to the kitchen, the hallway, the stairway. The sooner she could get upstairs and remove this ridiculous corset and thong and dress in jeans and a T-shirt, the better. She'd almost made a fool of herself, throwing herself at a man who wanted so much more than she could ever give him.

When he'd called off their Master/slave arrangement, she'd thought it had been because he didn't want that kind of relationship. He'd told Karla a twenty-four/seven wasn't right for either of them, but now he'd admitted he did enjoy the role of Master. With Joni, at least. He'd rejected the agreement with Karla in exchange for a Dom/sub. Clearly, he hadn't been honest with her.

Could Karla ever go back to being his slave again? She didn't enjoy subjugating herself in that way. She'd slowly lost pieces of her personality as she'd tried to mold herself into what Adam wanted. A total disaster. Now that she was stronger, both sexually and emotionally, becoming his slave was even harder. She didn't want to give up her power like that again.

But she clearly needed to do just that if she wanted to win over Master Adam.

He wants you.

Karla put her fists to her ears in an attempt to block out the voice that had given her messages since that Thanksgiving Day nine years ago when she'd been told to "watch over him" and had followed him to Lake Michigan.

It was Joni's voice.

Hearing her rival's voice on the tape just now in Adam's office confirmed what Karla had suspected lately. How could her mind play tricks on her like that? How could Karla conveniently conjure up her ghostly rival's voice and delude herself into thinking Adam wanted her and that she had the blessings of his dead wife?

Maybe she needed to go into counseling to deal with Ian's death. The worst of her delusions had started after losing him. Now she was about to lose Adam. The weight of that loss crushed her like a boulder on her chest.

No, the worst of her delusions was when she'd seen Adam standing in front of the stage during her audition. She'd convinced herself she'd come home to him at last. That she was safe with Adam. How could she have been so wrong?

"Oh, Adam. Why can't you just love me the way I am?" How pathetic was she that, even now, she wanted to try and win him over—to be what he wanted her to be? How could she give up on him? He was the only man she'd ever loved. She'd waited so long for him. Maybe just one more try to win his heart. Not everything about being his slave had been horrible. She could just find the things that both of them enjoyed and see if he would be satisfied with those, couldn't she?

Formulating a plan, she went to the closet and pulled out the red, filmy harem-girl costume she'd owned since college. How perfect that the costume and veil were red, Adam's favorite color. Hell, maybe Joni had chosen the color.

Okay, Kitty. Don't go bat-shit crazy on me here.

She pulled out her phone and called Angie, knowing she'd need the moral support of another harem girl in the club tonight. She explained what she had in mind.

"I'll talk to Marc. I'm sure he'll help."

Angie said they'd come upstairs to meet her tonight and discuss the plan of attack before heading to the club. Karla remembered how Luke, Marc, and Adam had banded together to help Marc win over Angelina again last month. What were friends for? Only now Karla was the one in need of help.

She stripped down to the skin and donned the next-to-nothing costume. The red silk bra was sequined and beaded, with strands of beads dangling all around for optimal effect at the slightest movement of her body. From one breast to the other hung strands of beads on strings similar to the chain that had hung between her breasts when she'd worn the nipple clamps. She wondered if her Master would be reminded of that night, as well. She shimmied her shoulders and watched the strings of beads dance. She hoped so.

The skirt had a black silk waist, also heavily beaded and sequined, with layer upon layer of red, opaque scarves hiding her naked mons and ass from view. She practiced some of her belly-dancing moves and caught glimpses of the dark triangle of her mons as the scarves moved. No, that wouldn't do. She took everything off again and headed to the shower.

Half an hour later, her mound smooth and bare, she donned the costume again and scrutinized herself in the mirror. Better. She brushed her hair until it gleamed and tossed her head a few times to make sure her tresses flowed the way she wanted them to. Adam seemed to have a love-hate with her hair—as much as with her—so she hoped tonight he was in a more loving mood, in more ways than one.

Having Angie and Marc seeing her in the revealing costume would help her get over her jitters about showing up at the club half-naked. She'd always worn revealing costumes, but had never worn anything that displayed her mons like this. But if she couldn't let her friends see her like this, how would she ever go down there and face the club members—and Adam?

Oh, Adam. You had better appreciate this.

And me.

* * *

Adam surveyed the great room, having already checked the readiness of the theme rooms. Until last night, it had been forever since he'd been inside his own club when it was open for members, which it would be in a few moments. In reality, it had been only three weeks, but so much had happened, it seemed like longer. Good thing he had partners and friends who could step in and keep things running smoothly when all hell broke loose, which it seemed to have done lately.

He glanced over at the stage area. Empty. Usually Karla was doing a sound check by now. He wondered if he should check on *her*, then heard voices coming down the hallway and turned to see Angelina walking down the hall past the theme rooms dressed in the skimpy harem costume Marc had told Adam to purchase for her last month, along with some other fantasy outfits. She wore a black leather collar, with a leash held by Marc. With her generous hips and breasts, she filled the costume well.

Marc followed in his sheikh's costume—or maybe he fancied himself a sultan, with that damned gold-lamé turban on his head. Adam grinned. Apparently, the two of them were exploring a fantasy theme tonight, also one of Adam's favorites. Seeing Marc happy after he'd been so miserable for the past year brought an even wider smile to Adam's face.

Until he saw a second leash in Marc's hand. *What the fuck?* Adam reached up to rub the scar on the back of his neck. The man no longer shared, not after he'd met Angelina. So who was going to play with them tonight—and how would Angelina feel about sharing?

Adam's smile faded when he saw who followed them. Karla, head down, head and upper body covered in a red veil. He couldn't see the rest of her. Around her neck she wore the black fur-lined leather collar he'd put on her the night he'd suspended her with ropes in here—the very night she'd fully surrendered to becoming his slave, in action as well as words.

Mine.

He glared at Marc, who just grinned back at him. What kind of game was the perennial jokester playing tonight? More important, just how had Karla become involved in it? Heat rose into his face as he crossed the room to stand in front of his impudent partner. He didn't have to say a word, but stood with his hands on his hips and waited for someone to tell him what the fuck was going on.

"I come bearing a tribute for you, my friend, who I understand is the sheikh of the Masters at Arms tribe." Marc grinned and held out Karla's leash.

"Marc," he growled. If Adam's no-nonsense tone didn't get the cocky bastard to explain himself soon, Adam was going to head slap him.

"You see, I'm a one-woman man now." He reached out to stroke Angelina's cheek and Adam watched as she leaned into his hand, the corners of her mouth quivering as she fought breaking into a smile. "So, I'm giving you this now unattached harem girl so she can find happiness, as well. I do believe she's attracted to you, too, Your Excellency."

Adam glanced at Karla, who kept her head bowed. Through the veil, he watched to see her lips curve into a smile, or any other acknowledgement of Marc's words, but detected only a slight tremor from the veil. Rather than appearing to be in a playful mood, she acted like a lamb headed to slaughter.

What the fuck was going on?

Adam planned to find out, but without an audience. Accepting Marc's "tribute," he took the leash, thanked him tersely, and led Karla to the vacant loveseat near the stage. His balls tightened looking at her sexy body barely covered by the veil and scarves. He'd admitted to her the other night that the harem-girl fantasy was among his favorites. He'd like to see her shed the veil and scarves to reveal her body to him slowly, but wasn't sure how he felt about her revealing herself to everyone at the club tonight.

Now why was that a problem? If she wanted to be his sub, she needed to become comfortable with her naked body, because he could order her to strip anytime he wished. He'd never had a problem with that before, although he'd never been emotionally attached to any of the subs he'd ordered to do so in the past. But hadn't he been her Dom, more or less, since they'd ended the Master/slave arrangement last month?

God knew he wanted her all to himself. But first he wanted to know what was going through her head. He sat on the loveseat. If she wanted a sheikh, he supposed he'd have to play the part.

"Kneel." He pointed to a place near his feet. Without hesitation, she complied, still keeping her head bowed. "What is it you need tonight, Karla?"

"Only to please you, Master."

How did she mean Master? They weren't back to Master/slave again, were they? God, he hoped not.

"Just how do you plan to do that?"

"In whatever ways you ask, Master."

"Remove the veil." He'd quickly grown tired of having her face hidden from him. Even if the material was flimsy and see-through, he needed to see her eyes, her mouth, her lips.

"Permission to move, Your Excellency."

Move? Of course she'd need to move in order to remove the veil. Why was she asking for unnecessary permission?

He sighed. "Granted."

She raised her hands, striking a dramatic pose, and the veil fell between them, its material continuing to shield her from his view. Without warning, passionate Middle Eastern music blared from the nearby speakers, distracting him momentarily. He looked over at the sound system to find his partner, the quasi-sultan/sheikh, grinning in his direction and executing a salaam as he bowed in Adam's direction. Then Marc returned to where he'd left Angelina kneeling beside a small stage-side table. He sat with his slave girl between his knees and gave her an order. She looked up at him warily and around at the others nearby, balking until Marc said something that had her face turning red at the same time as her hands reached out to undo his leathers. Adam grinned.

Karla's long, flowing veil flitted across Adam's face, drawing his attention back to her. She dipped and undulated to the music, alternately hiding her face and revealing it with the red veil. She looked so good in red. Why she ever thought black was her color was beyond him.

He just wished her expression wasn't so serious. Maybe she just wanted to concentrate on the moves—and him; she didn't take her eyes off him. The intensity of her smoldering, come-hither look made him feel as if she'd sucked his breath from his lungs.

What was going on in her head tonight?

She began rippling her hips, alternating between fast movements and slow ones in such a sensuous way, causing his heart rate to speed up and slow down in direct response. Her breasts spilled over the tops of the red bra cups studded with black sequins and beads, making him wish his lips were brushing over the creamy skin there he'd learned was as soft as satin. Her torso and hips rippled like waves on the ocean, commanding his attention as the beads and bangles hanging from her bra and the waistband of her skirt mesmerized him. This was one very expensive outfit, no Halloween costume.

Where had she learned to dance like that—and why hadn't he known about this talent sooner? Karla lifted the veil over her head and twirled on bare feet, her hands and arms making graceful motions that caused the veil to flutter and float around her body. When she turned away from him, he watched her hips shake to the music, her hips enticing him to reach out to her and sending the bangles into frenzied motion. She took the ends of the veil and leaned back until her gorgeous cleavage came into view, then whipped the veil over both their heads and around his neck and shoulders, pulling him closer to her tits. Just before his lips would have pressed against her jiggling mounds, she released one end of the veil and stood upright, evading his head with a sideways lunge. She pulled the veil away from him, wrapping it around herself again. His dick rose to a full salute and he adjusted himself against the loveseat to keep from strangling his little head. He nearly came in his leathers.

"Very nice, Kitten," he managed to choke out. "Where did you learn to dance like that?" He waited, not sure he really wanted to know.

She giggled, damn her. He throbbed even more.

"Columbia, Sir. A phys-ed activity elective. Cassie and I took the belly-dancing class together and we both use it for working out now." At her body's strenuous exertions, her words came out in sexy, breathy gasps that only made him harder.

"If I'd known college was this much fun…"

She smiled. He'd missed seeing that smile. She tossed her head side to side and back and forth as she danced, sending her long, gleaming curls whipping around her face and shoulders. The desire to grab her by the hair and pull her upstairs to his bed nearly overwhelmed him. *Control yourself, old man.*

Her hips undulated to the beat of the music, as she lifted a couple of the scarves hanging from her waist and he could have sworn he'd caught a glimpse of a shaved pussy. When had she shaved—or was his brain playing fucking tricks on him? She lifted the scarves again and flounced them in his face, obstructing his view without giving him the answer.

The music pulsed in time to the movement of her hips as her undulations picked up speed. Sweat broke out on his upper lip. He wanted to order her to straddle him, now, hoping she wore nothing under the scarf skirt and was as turned-on as he was, but didn't want to end her erotic dance for anything. Not just yet.

Best decision he'd made in a long fucking time, because Karla turned toward him again and came down onto her knees just inches from him, her legs spread open. He looked down to see if he could see her mound and caught what looked like a tiny glimpse of pale skin. *Jesus. Had she?*

Again, she threw the veil around his shoulders and drew him close to her tits. His head dipped toward them, but she kept moving his desired targets as she leaned further back until he would have fallen off the loveseat and onto her if he hadn't pulled himself back. He reached out to part her skirt.

Fuck. Fuck. Fuck.

There it was—her Venus mound shaved bare. He closed his eyes a moment to regain control. When he opened them once more, she had leaned back until her head touched the floor. *Christ.* He couldn't take much more. Then she gave him much, much more. Her chest and hips rippled in alternating currents, giving him an even more delightful view of her pussy. She raised and lowered her hips, simulating sexual intercourse.

"Lie still." His words sounded strangled in his own ears. She complied, looking up at him, breathing hard and waiting for further commands. "Straddle me." She glanced at the bulge in his leathers and quirked an eyebrow. "Not yet. Just straddle me."

She lifted her head and torso from the floor in one graceful, fluid motion. He reached out to take her arms and lifted her the rest of the way onto his lap. She pressed her bare pussy against the front of his soft leathers and his dick nearly ripped a new opening in his pants. She continued to move her hips and torso to the music, torturing him even more.

Adam reached out and brushed his thumb pad over her lower lip. So full and sensuous. He grabbed her hair in his fists and pulled her closer until their lips met. She didn't open for him until he pulled her head back by her hair and drove his tongue deep inside her mouth. His heart pounded in alternating rhythm with the throbbing dick pressed against her clit and pussy.

"Master, how can this lowly slave girl please you?"

The seriousness of her expression told him there was more going on here than role-playing, but he didn't want to waste time or energy processing that information. At the moment, she wanted to know how to please him. He could respond to that much, at least.

"Remove the bra."

She released her hold on the veil, leaving it draped over his shoulders, and reached both hands around to her back to unhook the bra. Watching the strands of beads dangling between her breasts made him wish he had his nipple clamps to replace them, but he wasn't going in search of his toy bag at the moment.

When the bra loosened, he reached out to pull it off, realizing he still held her hair in his fists. He released her hair and took the straps in each hand, easing them down her arms, revealing to his hungry gaze the dusky-pink areolas he could never get enough of. They looked swollen, inviting, and he lowered his head, cupping one breast in his hand as he flicked his tongue over the peak, feeling the nipple swell to twice its size against his tongue. His dick bobbed against her pussy and she squirmed in his lap. Taking the bud between his teeth, he bit down gently and pulled.

"Ow!" Her gasp of pain surprised him. He wasn't anywhere near her limit. He released her tit and searched her face for answers.

"I'm sorry, Master. They're just more sensitive than usual tonight."

She'd probably have screamed if he'd put her in the nipple clamps tonight. He chuckled. The night was still young. He did so enjoy hearing her screams of passion that followed those of pain. No doubt her screams would be of both varieties before this night was over.

He bent again and took her other nipple between his teeth, eliciting the same response. Her erotic dancing must have stimulated her, as well, preparing her for his mouth and touch. He'd have to get her to dance for him on a regular basis now, in private, as well. His own little harem girl.

Even though he'd managed to ignore them during the height of Karla's dance, the murmurs of several club members reached him now. He tuned them out and focused once more on Karla.

"Your dancing turned me on, Kitten."

She smiled like a woman who knew her power. "I can tell, Master." She squirmed against his dick.

"There's nothing I want more right now than to take you to the Arabian Nights theme room and have you feed me grapes then have you, well, eat something else."

Her pupils dilated. Clearly, she was ready to leave the public area, too. But when he reached out to span her waist and lift her off him, she placed her hands on his shoulders. "Wait, Master."

Why didn't she just call him Sir again? Must be the harem slave girl role-play she was in. Well, if she wanted to role-play, he'd give her that. "What is it, my sexy little slave girl?" She nibbled on her lower lip and closed her eyes. He placed a knuckle under her chin, and she opened her eyes as he tilted her head back. "What's wrong, Kitten. Tell me."

Her clear blue eyes met his gaze and she swallowed hard. "I want to be your slave girl again."

He hoped she didn't mean what he thought she meant. He reached up to rub the scar at the back of his neck. "I very much want you to be my slave girl tonight, Kitten. The whole harem fantasy is one of my favorites and you have pleased me by…"

She reached out and placed a finger against his lips to shut him up. Not proper behavior for a slave or a sub, but he wanted to know what was troubling her and let it slide.

"Not just tonight. I want to go back to the Master/slave arrangement we tried before. I promise I'll do better this t—"

"No, Kitten." If he'd slapped her, he wouldn't have elicited a more shocked expression on her face. Her lips quivered as she fought to control her emotions. She needed to hear his reasons. Had he even explained the reason it wasn't right when he called off their TPE arrangement before? He'd talked more about his regret for giving her that asinine command to get home from Cassie's with only a thirty-minute window to spare. Then they'd dealt with the subdrop issue. Maybe if he focused this time on why a Master/slave wasn't right for her.

"I didn't like seeing your personality change when you were my slave. It's not a healthy BDSM choice for either of us. While I would enjoy having you as my slave girl on a short-term basis, in fantasy role-playing like tonight, I don't want a twenty-four/seven slave ever again."

The look she gave him seemed to be accusing him of lying. Where had that come from? He'd never lie to a sub. She ought to know that by now. "What was that thought?"

She looked down at his vest. "Nothing, Mast…Sir."

She seemed disappointed calling him Sir again. Damn it, he needed to know what was going on in that beautiful mind of hers. "Whether you're my slave or my sub, you answer a direct question. Now, tell me what you were thinking." Eyes downcast, she opened her mouth to speak. He needed to read what was going on here.

"Eyes on me."

* * *

Karla bit down on her lip again until she tasted iron. She took a deep breath and raised her gaze to meet his cold, angry stare. At this moment, he wasn't pleased with her and the thought brought more unwanted tears to her eyes. She was failing so miserably.

"Kitten, what's going on?"

"I need to be your slave, Sir."

"Why?"

Because you love your slaves more, Sir. "Because...I need to please you."

"You've already pleased me—by being my sub."

"That's not enough, Sir. I need to please you—on a deeper level."

He quirked an eyebrow. "Why?"

She took a deep, ragged breath. "Because I love you, Sir." *Oh, dear Lord.* She'd said the words, not that they should come as any surprise to him by now. She'd never made any secret of her love. But somehow equating love with becoming his slave seemed so strange. When his expression became guarded, she knew no similar words would be coming from his lips.

Something inside her died.

Karla couldn't throw herself at him any longer. His penis no longer throbbed against her clit either. She had his answer. "I'm sorry if my love makes you uncomfortable, Sir." She choked on a sob she could no longer suppress. What was with the fucking waterworks?

"Karla, you're a wonderful sub and I'd be honored to be your Dom, but there can't be anything more than that. I hope you can understand..."

"Yes, Sir. Permission to return to my room, Sir. I don't think I can perform tonight." She hoped he understood she wasn't referring to singing. Hurt and regret filled his eyes, then he looked down at her bare breasts and she understood the regret. At least he still wanted her for sex, but that just wasn't enough for her anymore.

"Permission granted." He reached beside him and handed her the bra. "Cover yourself first."

She fumbled with the straps, but was obstructed by her damned tears.

"Here, let me." He took the bra from her trembling hands. "Hold your arms in front of you." Apparently, he couldn't get rid of her fast enough so he was going to dress her now. More fucking tears spilled down her cheeks. She hated to appear needy in front of him.

With the pads of his thumbs, he brushed the tears aside and tilted her head until she met his gaze. "I'm sorry, Karla."

Call me kitten, Sir. Just one more time.

But she was no longer his kitten. All she could be to him was the singer in his club, a friend with benefits, and a sub he enjoyed playing with from time to time. None of which was enough to meet her needs.

She braced her hands on his shoulders and eased off his lap. Before she reached her room, she'd made her decision. Time to go home to Chicago. After making a couple of phone calls, she pulled her suitcase from the closet and began emptying the drawers and closet, taking only what she'd brought with her. She realized how little she owned. He'd chosen everything she wore, and paid for it personally. Adam owned everything. God, he owned almost everything in here. So why couldn't he accept her as his slave, too?

She'd sold her soul to win Adam's love, and it had all been for nothing. She could never give him what he wanted and needed—his perfect slave, Joni, the woman who still owned him, body and soul.

* * *

Marc's vintage Porsche was parked in his spot. Wasn't he supposed to be up on the mountain today?

Adam pulled the truck into the driveway behind the rental Karla used. He'd be glad when he had time to go vehicle shopping to replace the totaled SUV. First, though, he needed to check online safety reports to find the safest vehicle possible for her. If Karla had another accident, he didn't want her to be hurt like she had been in the last one—or worse.

Getting Karla her own car would give her more freedom. Her growing dependence on him was worrisome. This wasn't the Karla he'd known a few months ago. Maybe he needed to talk with her about pursuing her recording career again. She'd been so anxious for that as a teenager that she'd even run away from home at sixteen. With her voice and her songwriting abilities, she could record CDs, MP3s, or whatever way music was being recorded these days, and market them online. Did Goth singers go on music tours? The thought of her singing in other clubs or in bars didn't appeal to him, though.

But having her own source of income other than what she made singing at the Masters at Arms Club would boost her confidence, too. He thought she'd bounced back to her old self again until last night in the club when she'd begged to go back to being his slave.

Last night, he'd realized how much he'd inhibited her by controlling so much of her life. Hell, he'd thought she'd been happy to be rid of that damned arrangement when he'd safeworded and put an end to it. Okay, so he could have used a little more tact when he refused to go back down that road. Had he sounded like he was rejecting her, not just the Master/slave lifestyle? He hadn't intended that. But what the fuck was going on in her head?

She said she loved you, jarhead.

Adam turned to stare at the passenger window, half expecting to find Joni sitting beside him. She'd called him jarhead the few times she chose to challenge his authority. He heard her voice now just as plain as if he were listening to one of her tapes. Was he losing it?

Adam picked up the hardware store bag from the seat and heard the rattle of chains. While he very much looked forward to restraining her to his bed with them, he sure as hell didn't want her to complicate things by trying to put chains on him. Why'd she have to bring love into the relationship? Not going to happen.

He sighed. He'd have another talk with her today. She'd stayed holed up in her bedroom this morning, so he hadn't been able to say anything about what had happened last night in the club. He needed to find out what was going on.

Exiting the truck, he walked toward the porch humming *Under My Thumb*. If she wanted to play the slave, he certainly could accommodate her fantasies, right up to chaining her to the chair in his office while he worked on the books, with her dressed in her harem-girl costume. He might need to buy more chains, but he wouldn't live with her in that lifestyle twenty-four/seven.

He walked into the kitchen to find Marc leaning against the counter. Alone.

"Where's Angelina?" It was unusual to find one without the other these days.

"The airport."

"Where's she going?"

"Nowhere, asshole."

What the fuck? Marc's foul mood registered for the first time. He'd never talked to him that way before. Shit, the man was pissed. What the hell had Adam done? "Come again?"

"What the fuck are you doing letting that woman go?"

"Angelina?"

"No, goddamn it. Karla. Keep up with this conversation."

Karla? Gone? "What the fuck are you talking about? She was in her room when I left this morning."

"Probably packing. So, she didn't tell you?"

"Tell me what? I just went to the hardware store, for Christ's sake. Hell, I haven't been gone ninety minutes." He'd decided this morning he needed to outfit his bed for bondage scenes with Karla, rather than having to take her to the club bedrooms or theme rooms to play. He wanted to have her closer to him. Why would she leave?

"She called Angelina last night and told her she was leaving today. She had more stuff than we could get into my Porsche, so Luke came over with the Land Rover. They've been gone about forty-five minutes."

"Why didn't you text me?"

"I did."

Fuck. He pulled the phone out of his pocket and saw he hadn't turned it on this morning. Adam sank into a chair at the table, at a loss for words. She'd left him? She hadn't even said goodbye? He'd thought she'd needed to sleep in this morning, but had she been avoiding him instead so she could sneak off like this?

She'd fucking left him? Why?

"You're a damned fool, Adam."

He glared up at Marc, who seemed to think her leaving was his fault. What had he done? Was this all because he couldn't tell her he loved her last night?

"How you haven't been able to see all these months how much Karla loves you is beyond me. She fucking wore her heart on her sleeve. Even sang her feelings out to you on club nights, and you just walked around with your head up your ass. When the cougar attacked you, I had to pull her off the cat because she was trying to wrestle it away from you."

"Karla attacked the cat?"

"Hell, yeah. Had it by the tail and wasn't going to let go until I finally pulled her off so Damián could take care of it."

Shit. He had no idea she'd been in so much danger. Why hadn't she stayed put like he'd told her? Why had she risked her life for him?

Because she loves you, jarhead.

Okay, Joni's voice was starting to mess with his head. He shouldn't have listened to the rest of those tapes last night when he hadn't been able to sleep. Only she hadn't called him a jarhead in any of them.

"When you were lying in that hospital bed unconscious for three days, the only time she left your side was when we forced her to go eat. She didn't want to leave you for a minute."

Adam had no idea she'd done that. No wonder she'd had dark circles under her eyes and had lost weight. He was a fucking shithead with his head up his ass. Just like Marc said.

Still, it was one thing saying that to himself. But being chewed out by a subordinate didn't sit well with him. As Marc's former master sergeant, Adam was more used to delivering a reaming, not receiving one.

Especially one he didn't even deserve. If he'd done something to hurt Karla intentionally and send her running, he might think differently, but things had been going pretty well between them since her accident, except for a slight glitch after San Diego. Until last night, he thought they'd put that Master/slave shit behind them and moved on to something so much better. So, what was she doing wanting to revert to being a slave?

What was she doing trying to get him to love her?

"What are you so afraid of, Adam?"

Adam met Marc's gaze head on. "What the fuck are you talking about?"

"You've been running scared since she got here. Why?"

Adam didn't need to answer to a corpsman. *Whoa.* They weren't in the military anymore. Marc was his partner and friend now. Much as it irked him, he also had to admit the younger man was dead to rights, too. Adam had been on the run from her. But all that had changed after that night he'd taken her virginity. At first, it had only strengthened his need to be responsible for protecting her—from himself. But when he'd tried to push her away, he'd only managed to pull her closer, until he'd nearly lost her in that accident out of stupidity.

That night changed everything. He didn't want to lose her. He didn't want anyone else to be his sub. He didn't want anyone else—period.

So what the fuck happened last night? What made her think he'd want to crush her lively spirit and make her his slave when their relationship had been so much more enjoyable with her as his sub, albeit a bratty one? At least she wasn't predictable and dull, the way his life had been before she came back into it this past summer.

A hand slapped the back of his head, bringing him back to the present. He looked up to find Marc glaring down at him. "I asked why you're running, Adam."

When Adam glared back at Marc's insubordination, Marc didn't back down. "You asked me the same thing not too long ago. Remember? You got me to wake up before I'd totally screwed the pooch with Angelina. It's going to take me a while to regain her trust after lying to her." Adam could see the pain in his friend's eyes. "If I'd listened to you and confessed sooner, I wouldn't have hurt her like that. She's more than I deserve, but at least she gave me another chance."

"It's nothing like that with Karla and me." Adam had never lied to her. Not that he was aware of, anyway.

"Maybe not, but you're running just as scared and as fast as I was. I didn't know Joni, but I know how much you loved her."

Adam had had enough of this touchy-feely shit. He rose from the chair. "I didn't love her the way I should have." *I've never been able to love anyone.* It just wasn't in him.

"Bullshit. Adam, you may not get all mushy about it, but the way you protect and take care of those you love is as clear as the scars on your back. Not just women, but everyone around you. Look at this bunch of misfits you rescued in Iraq and took under your wing when you took a notion to start this club. Hell, Damián probably wouldn't have survived the first week after his discharge from rehab. I'd probably be sitting behind a desk at my family's ski resort working up to my first heart attack. Even Grant's found a haven here from whatever she's running from."

Adam probably needed to have a talk with her. Grant had shown up last winter full of anger about something and filled with secrets. He'd let Marc stew about his women problems damn near a year before talking with him. He didn't know if Grant had man problems, or something else, but maybe he shouldn't wait so long with her.

Shit, he and his co-owners sure were a fucked-up mess when it came to relationships, though, so chances were good that Grant was too. As their former master sergeant, he had their six. He also continued to watch over Garcia's and Miller's families. Marines looked after each other. Didn't mean anything more.

Marc sat down at the table. "You're more family to me than my own, Adam."

"Don't turn this into a sappy coffee commercial. We all bonded in combat. That's what Marines and their corpsmen do."

"Adam, you took Karla in, too, when she was hurting and lost. Maybe you didn't intend for anything romantic to come of it, but I've seen you two together. She's so fucking right for you, and you know it. How can you just let the best thing that's happened to you in a long time walk out your door?"

Adam stood. "This conversation is over."

"What do you plan to do about her?"

Adam looked at Marc. "What I plan to do is go upstairs." He needed to be alone, to think. He picked up the bag of hardware, hating the tell-tale sound it emitted and not sure what he'd do with the hardware now.

Chapter Nineteen

In his bedroom, he threw the bag on the bed and headed for the deck, shucking his clothes as he walked. He needed a good soak in the hot tub. Maybe he could sort out what had sent Karla packing and what he was going to do about it.

As he soaked in the tub, memories flooded his brain—of her screaming a passionate release, straddling him, kneeling at his feet, washing him, wrapping her lips around his dick—of all the ways she'd submitted to him totally and completely.

He'd never expected Karla to embrace being a submissive so wholeheartedly, but she had seemed to take to it like a ship to water, especially after they'd gotten beyond that ridiculous Master/slave arrangement. She'd inexplicably tried to go back to that agreement on what turned out to be their last night. Then she'd left him.

Later, long after he'd heard Luke saying goodbye to Angelina in the driveway and Marc's Porsche speed off a short time after, he grabbed a terry-cloth robe from the heated bin beside the hot tub and stepped out of the overheated water, donning the robe to ward off the cold chill. All he'd gotten out of his hour in the tub were pruny feet and a hard-on from thinking about Karla submitting to him. Back in the bedroom he struck a match to the fire he'd laid last night, but hadn't gotten to burn because Karla hadn't joined him after the club closed.

Sitting in front of the fireplace, staring into the flames, he ached to have Karla's body cradled between his legs, wrapped inside his arms. He missed her, but the answers he sought still weren't forthcoming. With a grunt, he stood and looked at the bed where the bag of hardware mocked him. He'd been looking forward to restraining Karla to his bed tonight.

Now he wouldn't even be able to hold her. The loneliness that descended on him pierced his chest with so much lethal force it was as if he'd fallen on his own sword.

She'd left him. Every woman he'd ever loved had abandoned him in some way. Joni didn't leave him intentionally, but the others had. His mother had kicked him out at sixteen, not that his home life was anything he should have missed. But he'd missed her in those first few years. Even went back to find her after boot camp, but she'd really disappeared by then.

His mother had kicked him out in the heat of an intense moment, though. Somehow Karla's calculated decision to leave him was worse yet. Left him hurting.

Raw.

She had stripped his defenses over the past few months until his emotions had been laid bare, exposed at the surface level. The loss of Karla hurt more than any physical pain he'd ever felt. Even losing Joni failed to compare, because his self-defense mechanisms had been firmly in place then. He'd been able to block or deflect most of the pain of her loss, then spread it out over the next few years until he retired from the Corps.

Aw, who the fuck was he kidding? He'd been so fucking numb since Joni died. He'd really only begun to face her loss in the last few weeks, when he'd gone back to Minnesota this year.

He hadn't even been able to start facing Joni's loss until Karla had come back into his life and forced him to deal with his emotions; obliterating all of his defenses.

Yesterday, after listening to the tapes, for the first time he'd been able to say goodbye to Joni without the weight of all the guilt he'd carried over the years. Maybe Marc and Karla were right. He had loved Joni, even if he'd never been able to say the words to her. She'd apparently understood and accepted that, which eased some of his guilt. All these years, he'd thought he'd let her down. That he hadn't been the man she deserved. Hearing that Joni didn't see it that way helped.

Joni and Karla were so much stronger emotionally. Adam had been crippled in that area, probably because of his fucked-up childhood. But he didn't want to think about that now.

But how had he missed the signs last night that she was so unhappy? That she was getting ready to leave him? Abandon him?

Aw, Kitten. Why'd you go? Don't you know I'm lost without you?

Like Joni, Karla had become his anchor over the years, from the time she'd helped him reset his compass nine years ago and get back into the war with his head on straight, through all those years of faithful correspondence, right up until she'd declared war on his heart, then submitted to him in such sweet ways over the past month or so. His young Amazon had not only laid siege to his heart, she'd captured the damned thing. No great prize for her. No, this was a case where the captured won it all—but was too damned bitter and blind to even see what a prize he had.

Even the thought of spending time in the club without her singing to him didn't interest him. Marc had been right. He'd thought back over the months since she'd arrived at the club in July and she'd sung at least one song to him every night expressing her feelings for him. Some weren't particularly flattering, like the one describing him as poison; but filled with truth, nonetheless. How could he be so fucking blind?

And how was she supposed to know how much he needed her? Did he ever tell her?

So now what? Now what?

If he could get Karla back, would he make the same mistakes he'd made before? Could he tell her he loved her—as well as show her—every fucking day they had together? Maybe, if only she'd come back to him.

Maybe isn't good enough for her, jarhead.

He didn't need Joni's other-worldly head slaps to get his head out of his ass. He knew what he needed to do. But first he needed to get some intel. He pulled out his phone and texted, "Do U know where she was going?"

Seconds later, a beep as Marc replied. "Chicago."

Adam smiled. *Good girl.* He knew exactly where to find her. He texted back, "UR n charge while I'm gone. Leave business matters to Grant." He hit send.

The phone beeped. "No fucking problem." Adam grinned. No one hated bookwork more than Marc.

Adam crossed the bedroom to his closet and pulled out his seabag. He'd have plenty of time to figure out what he was going to say to Karla while on the road, because there was no way in hell he'd be able to get a flight the Sunday before Thanksgiving without special connections. Adam was sure Karla's father had pulled strings with his airline to bring his daughter home on such short notice.

Adam just hoped Jenny's invitation last July to join them for Thanksgiving still stood. At that time, they'd probably just wanted to be sure he brought her home to them for the holiday. He wasn't sure what Karla would have said to her parents about their relationship, but had a feeling she'd play it close to the vest.

He didn't want to show up at the Paxtons' home until Wednesday, when he knew Jenny wouldn't be able to turn him away. Karla's mom had a thing about bringing in lost souls to eat at her table for Thanksgiving. No one was more lost than he was this year. He wasn't above grabbing at any advantage that could help him win Karla back.

But this time of year, he also needed to take advantage of clear driving conditions. The closer he could get to her location geographically, the better. He'd call and see if he could swing by East St. Louis and check on Sergeant Miller's wife and kids first. He hadn't visited the Millers on the way home from Minneapolis this year, because he'd needed to get back for Damián.

Just as well Karla wouldn't be with him. He didn't like to broadcast his failures, including the one that put Miller's unit on that rooftop in Iraq, making them sitting ducks for the incoming grenade and RPG attacks that killed Miller and nearly killed Damián and Marc, as well.

Total clusterfuck.

Now he needed to engage in the war to win Karla back. If she'd still have him, he was ready to go to the mat for her, even with her parents, who probably wouldn't be thrilled to know a man twice her age was pursuing her, let alone that the two of them already had a sexual relationship.

But no one could cherish or protect her as well as he could. There still was the matter of her thinking she wanted to be his slave, but they could discuss that and agree on some compromise. Maybe there were some aspects of that type of relationship that appealed to them both. As long as the two of them could both have their needs met, they'd be fine.

The only question was how to give Karla what she needed most—his love.

Yeah, they had plenty to talk about, that's for sure. So, he'd better get a good night's rest so he could hit the road early tomorrow and he could get to her so they could start planning their future together.

But, after lying awake in his bed for hours, he'd given up and walked across the hall to sleep in Karla's old bed. Her scent lingered on her pillow, helping him feel closer to her.

God, he just hoped he wouldn't fuck things up with her in Chicago.

He needed her.

* * *

"What's going on, Karla?" her mom asked. "You seem so lost." Karla should have known keeping anything from her mom would be impossible. The woman's radar could match anything the military had in its arsenal.

"I made a huge mistake, Mom. I fell in love with a man who doesn't want me the way I am." Mom's arms came around her shoulders and the waterworks started. She hadn't cried this much since Ian died.

"Unfortunately, we can't choose who we love—and we certainly have no control over who loves us back." Her mom pulled back and looked her dead in the eye. "But if he can't accept you as you are, then kick him to the curb, Karla. You deserve someone who loves you for yourself. Don't try and mold yourself into some impossible ideal."

Her mom didn't know the half of what Karla had done trying to get Adam to love her. And yet, even though they were wrong for each other, she still wanted him.

"Oh, Mom. I love him so much. How am I going to go on without him?"

"You're sure there's no hope? You've always been a fighter. You just usually chose your battles more wisely than your brother did. He usually managed to get his butt kicked more often than not."

"Well, I'm afraid I got my heart kicked, Mom." Then stomped on. Karla shook her head. "I fought hard, but even though I put up my best campaign ever, I still lost the war." She couldn't mention the whole Master/slave fiasco, not to her mother anyway, but that wasn't the only problem Adam had with her. Karla looked down at the chenille bedspread and pulled at the threads. "He thinks I'm just a kid."

Mom put her finger under Karla's chin and raising her gaze to meet hers. "How much older is he?"

Relax, Mom. It's over anyway. Still Karla tried to break away from her Mom's scrutiny. Not a chance. "Twenty-five years."

Her mom's eyes grew wide. "Oh, honey, that's a huge age difference. Maybe he's right. You'd be setting yourself up for a lot of years alone with someone that much older."

Karla couldn't believe her mother would take Adam's side, even if she didn't know she was. "Mom, no one has guarantees about how long they'll live and love. Ian's proof of that." At the pained expression that crossed her mother's face, Karla reached out. "I'm sorry. That was insensitive. But, Mom, no one knows how much time they have. We just need to grab life by the…um, hand…and run with it." She'd been around Adam so long that she'd almost said balls to her mom. If her mother heard half the words that had become part of her vocabulary since she'd moved in with Adam and started hanging around his Marine buddies...

"But you can't force someone to run with you, honey, if he doesn't want to."

Ouch. Karla's breath choked on a sob and she laid her head on her mom's shoulder, giving in to the ache consuming her alive. Her chest felt as if someone were squeezing the air from her lungs with an iron fist. To say nothing of the nausea. She felt like throwing up all the time since she'd left Denver. Eating had become impossible, which is probably what tipped her mom off that there was a problem and sent her in here to check on her. She'd left Adam Sunday because he wouldn't allow her to be his slave, even though that's clearly what he wanted from a woman. Just not from *this* woman.

But lying alone in her twin bed upstairs the last two nights, there had been times when she'd reached for her phone to call or text him, to beg him to give her one more chance to please him.

Good Lord, she had it bad. "I don't know how I can go on without him."

Her mom patted her hair. "I know it hurts now, but time will ease the ache. This was your first love. There will be others. Trust me."

"I'll never be able to let him go totally, Mom. He'll always be the one love of my life. He'll always have my heart, even if he left it bruised. I'd be content, if he'd only give me a tiny part of his."

Her Mom's gaze shot daggers at her. "No, Karla. You aren't going to settle for a fraction of a man's heart. You deserve all or nothing. Promise me you'll accept nothing less than one-hundred percent of a man's love. Obviously, you just haven't met the right one yet."

Maybe her mom was right. But she'd accept even a small piece of Adam's heart, if only he'd offer it. Good thing Adam was a thousand miles away, because she wasn't in any position to deny him anything right now.

She needed him so badly. Her emotional fragileness could spell disaster for her future. She'd been able to walk away from him once, but her heart wouldn't withstand being stomped on a second time.

Why did love have to be so painful?

Why couldn't you love me back, Adam, even a little?

* * *

"Karla, answer the door. My hands are full of pie dough."

Karla put her notebook aside. The lyrics for songs flowed from her now so easily, she was never far from her pencil and paper. Why was it so much easier to write about unrequited love? Probably because she couldn't think about anything else at the moment, but when she was with Adam, she didn't want to spend time writing about her feelings. She just wanted to experience those feelings with him.

More fucking tears. Enough with the waterworks already! She dashed them away with the backs of her hands as she made her way to the front door, wondering who would be visiting the day before Thanksgiving. A large man's shadow filled the doorway. Karla's heart beat an erratic tattoo. Her mind conjured up images of Adam, who couldn't possibly be here. She pushed the curtain aside and peeked out.

But she was wrong.

Of course, no one else had shoulders that broad. And where was his heavy coat? It was freezing out there. Karla hurried to open the inside door, then the storm one, and motioned him inside. "Get in here before you catch pneumonia, S...Adam." *Oh, God, she'd almost called him Sir.* She gave him a quavering smile. He didn't smile back. He didn't reach out to touch her. Karla's excitement dampened. "What are you doing here, Adam?"

"Your folks invited me last summer. I accepted."

She hoped she hid her disappointment from him. Yes, dutiful Adam always kept his promises. Karla just wished he'd been able to make some kind of promise or commitment to her. He laid his duffel bag on the floor inside the door and removed his light jacket. She reached out to take it, clutching it to her chest, breathing in the woodsy male scent. *Adam.* She'd missed his scent almost as much as she'd missed him. Almost. Okay, in a moment of weakness, she'd even gone to the mall yesterday to buy a bottle of the oak-scented body wash she'd come to associate with him.

She'd never been more pathetic in her entire life.

"Mom's in the kitchen. You know the way."

Adam reached out and stroked her cheek. "You've lost weight. Have you been sick?"

"No. Just not very hungry." *Because I missed you so much I couldn't eat.* Yeah, she had it bad.

"You need to eat more."

"I don't have to follow your orders anymore, Adam." *Great. Now she sounded like a petulant child.* No, a brat. Only she wasn't Master Adam's brat anymore, which just left her feeling empty.

She continued to clutch his jacket to her chest, wishing he were in it. The look of regret that flitted across his face sparked her anger, but she tamped it back down. Anger meant she cared. She didn't want to care anymore. It hurt too much. Besides, if he cared, he would have accepted her the way she was and made a commitment to her. Instead, he chose to live with the cold memory of his perfect slave, Joni.

Karla looked down at the floor.

Adam reached up and stroked her cheek. "You left without saying goodbye."

Karla looked up at his face and definitely saw regret in his eyes—and maybe even disappointment. "Didn't you find my letter?"

"What letter?"

"The one I left on your desk."

"I didn't go back in my office after Marc told me you'd left me, Kitten."

Please don't call me that anymore, Sir. How could he have missed her in such a short time? Besides, she could never be the type of woman he wanted and needed. "Well, it was mostly a resignation letter." She'd resigned from being the club's singer, but hadn't been able to write the words that would put an end to their personal relationship, even though both must know it was over.

"It was time. You helped me get over Ian and I needed to be with my folks for this first Thanksgiving without him."

"We'd already planned for me to bring you home. Remember? We were going to drive up here together."

I couldn't face you after I embarrassed myself so badly at the club that night. "Well, it looks like we're going to be together whether we like it or not." His eyes narrowed and she wondered why her words would cause any reaction. Maybe he regretted they couldn't remain friends, but being near him without being able to touch, hug, or kiss him was more than she would be able to stand. Lord, she hoped he wouldn't be staying the entire weekend.

Karla extended her hand toward the hallway. "After you." She'd almost added Sir again. Old habits die hard. But he wasn't her Sir anymore. He wasn't her anything. She blinked her eyes, fighting back the waterworks. If she cried in front of him, she'd absolutely die of shame.

She squared her shoulders. Karla Paxton refused to embarrass herself in front of him during this visit. And she wouldn't beg for his love or his acceptance—ever again.

* * *

Adam's heart broke to see the dark circles under Karla's eyes and how much thinner she was. She hadn't been that thin in Denver, had she? Surely he'd have noticed. He'd been working hard at feeding her so she'd gain weight, ever since he'd recovered from the cougar attack.

He'd been worried about her since she'd left Denver, apparently for good reason. The girl needed a caretaker. He'd never wanted any job more than that one.

But he'd fucked up the job the last time. How would it be different this time? He'd hurt her, rather than cared for her. Now he needed to make it right again.

He just hoped he could figure out how to do that before it was too late. The thought of going back to that house in Denver without her made his gut tighten. She'd become such a part of his life and home in recent months, which hadn't hit him until he'd had to rattle around his lonely house one fucking day and night without her. There was no corner of the house where he didn't remember Karla's presence.

But the worst had been sleeping without Karla filling his arms. Even on the nights when she'd slept in her room—usually because he'd sent her there—at least he'd known she was there if he wanted her and she'd always come running if he called for her. Yeah, bastard that he was, he'd held a lopsided amount of power in their relationship. That needed to change, too.

"Adam! What a nice surprise!"

Jenny placed the rolling pin on the table and wiped her hands on the dish towel tucked into her waistband.

"Thanks for inviting me, ma'am."

"Let's not go back to the *ma'am* stuff. It's Jenny." She came toward him and wrapped her arms around his waist. "So glad you can be here with us again, especially this year."

Adam detected the sadness in her voice and put his arms around her, too. He wished he had the words to say that would comfort her over the loss of her son, but mere words could never achieve that. Ironically, he'd first been invited to join the Paxtons for Thanksgiving nine years ago, in part because they were missing Ian, who had just finished his basic training with the Army, although he didn't think the boy had been deployed to Iraq yet. But this year was worse, because they knew with certainty Ian would never be coming back. That knowledge was more raw, now that the numbness had worn off.

Jenny's arms loosened and he let her go, but as she drew away, he saw tears swimming in her eyes. "How are you and Carl doing, Jenny?"

"We're just taking it one day at a time, but it's not easy."

Karla came over to her mom and put her arm around her shoulder. She, too, had tears in her eyes. He ached to reach out and brush them away, hold her in his arms, or in his lap, until he absorbed some of her pain, but that couldn't happen. Not yet anyway. They needed to talk first.

Jenny gave in to her tears only a moment before she stood taller and stepped back to her pie dough. "Thanksgiving is my favorite holiday of the year. Nothing is going to bring my son back, but I intend to honor him this year by telling and listening to stories of some of his exploits, preparing and sharing his favorite foods, and surrounding myself with others who will do the same."

Adam felt a little out of place, not having really known Ian, other than from what Karla had told him. But he could relate to how hard Ian's death had been on the ones who loved him.

Jenny brushed her tears away with the backs of her hands and went to the sink to wash and dry them before returning to her pie crust. "Karla, take Adam up to Ian's room and help him get settled before Daddy gets home. Then we'll all go out to eat, because I don't plan to make anything but pies and a reservation tonight."

Adam watched as Karla nibbled on her lower lip, causing his balls to tighten, and then she pulled her shoulders back and turned to face him. "Follow me."

Yes, ma'am.

They returned to the living room where he picked up his seabag, and then he followed her up the stairs to the room where he'd slept the last time he'd been here. When he walked inside, he found that the room hadn't changed a lot since then. Only now, a triangle-folded flag encased in a wood-and-glass box of the same shape held the place of honor on the boy's dresser, amidst his baseball and soccer trophies. Ian's war decorations were displayed there as well, showing the boy had earned a number of prestigious ones during his short stint in the Army.

"The bathroom's through there." She pointed at the door across the room. "It's a Jack and Jill, so be sure to lock my side if you don't want me to surprise you in there sometime."

What if I do want you to surprise me? Being near her again and not being able to touch her would be hell. But he didn't want to violate Jenny and Carl's trust by jumping their daughter's bones under their own roof. He figured the only reason they'd invited him originally was to make sure he brought their daughter home for the holiday. But that hadn't been necessary, after all. She'd brought herself home.

All he wanted was to have Karla back in his home—in his bed—as soon as possible. He needed her. No better time than the present to start letting her know that. "Thanks, Karla." He reached out and stroked her cheek, but she pulled away as if he'd struck her. *Fuck.*

"I never meant to hurt you, Kitten."

She flinched. "Please don't call me Kitten."

Fuck. Fuck. Fuck! He'd done worse than hurt her. She'd enjoyed being his kitten.

"I'm sorry, K…Karla." He wouldn't call her Kitten until he'd earned the right again, because that endearment was reserved for his sub. Obviously, she didn't want to be his sub anymore.

"Let us know if you need anything. Come down to the kitchen after you get settled in. Daddy might be a few hours, though, if you want to rest a bit." She looked as though she wanted him to hole up in here as much as possible.

She turned and left the room, closing the door with a soft click behind her.

Total clusterfucking-A. This wasn't going to be as easy as he'd thought.

Chapter Twenty

Karla went into her bedroom, then into the bath, locking the door to Adam's…Ian's room, then took a washcloth and wet it with cold water. She pressed the cold cloth against her eyes, hoping to remove any traces of the hot tears that had been burning there since Adam had shown up. How was she going to get through tomorrow with Adam so near? How long did he plan to stay?

Please, dear Lord, let him leave Friday, if not sooner.

Several hours later, she sat atop one of the tallest buildings in Chicago having dinner with her parents and Adam. The conversation remained steady on any number of inane topics until Adam dropped a conversation bomb that surprised her.

"Karla, when do you plan to start recording again?"

"Recording what?"

"Your new music. I know you've been busy writing songs in that notebook of yours. You need to pursue getting your music out on CDs or MP3s or whatever people listen to music on these days."

She put her fork down. "I don't have a contract any longer."

"Well, I've been looking into it online…"

"You've been doing what?"

He smiled at her and her stomach fluttered. Must be the altitude.

"Yeah, well, I know how much you missed out on reaching that goal when…well, when you came to Denver."

Funny, Karla thought, but she'd found so much more singing in his club and being with him, she really hadn't felt that she'd missed anything. Sure, singing in a small private club didn't give her the thrill of entertaining audiences in a big Manhattan Goth club, but she enjoyed the freedom of singing whatever she wanted. The Goth club's owner had never let her stray far from the script.

Adam had threatened to make her run her song list by him when he was her Master, but that arrangement had ended before she'd ever had to actually do it. He'd always given her free rein to sing whatever she wanted. Sure, she'd bombed on a few things—having to try and keep her audience in the BDSM mood sometimes proved a challenge she hadn't trained for—but for the most part, the club members seemed to enjoy her selections.

Wait. Clearly, he was saying he didn't want her back at the club if he wanted her to pursue a music recording career. Not that she would go back—not the way things were—but some silly part of her had thought maybe, just maybe he'd come to Chicago to win her back.

The backs of her eyes burned, and she fumbled to retrieve her fork then stabbed at her plate, hoping to spear one of the buttery shrimp, and wishing a bit that she was poking Adam instead for driving her away.

"So, what do you think?"

She stuffed the shrimp into her mouth and chewed slowly so she wouldn't have to answer, not that she *had* to answer him anymore. He wasn't her Sir anymore. He could take his direct questions and shove them...

"Anyway, it seems there's quite an industry these days for indie performers. With all the iPhones and other devices people carry all the time, they're downloading music left and right. They're always looking for something new and...edgy, as Damián would put it. You'd just need to find a good studio to record in and I think I found one right in Denver."

She glanced over at him and swallowed. "In Denver?"

He looked over at her dad. "I'm sure there are good ones in Chicago, too."

Now, why was he retreating again after getting her hopes up? *Adam, you make me dizzy.* Again, maybe it was just the heights, but suddenly, her stomach churned. "Excuse me. I need to use the restroom."

Adam was up and pulling out her chair for her in an instant and she ran to the back of the restaurant. Once inside the stall, she just stood there, holding her stomach. The nausea passed and she felt like a fool, but decided to stay here a bit longer to make sure it wasn't going to happen again.

So, what was Adam saying? Did he want her to return to Denver and pursue a career from there? With him or without him? Or did he want her to stay here in Chicago—definitely without him?

And what did she want to do?

She had no fucking clue.

"Watch your language."

"Yes, Sir."

Oh, yes, she knew what she wanted. She just didn't know if she could put herself through that again with Adam unless he was sure it was what *he* wanted. She needed to wait and see. Steeling herself, she washed her hands and returned to the table.

* * *

Lying in bed the next morning, Karla tried to ignore the continued queasiness in her stomach as the smell of roasting turkey and stuffing filled her room. That had always been a comforting aroma, but now it just made her want to puke. Mind over matter. She must have had bad shrimp last night. If she just ignored it, the feeling would pass. Then she would...

Oh, God! No!

Karla tossed the blankets off and jumped up from the bed, steadying herself on the bedpost before running for the bathroom. Holding her hair behind her, she lifted the seat, leaned over the toilet, and hurled the contents of her stomach. If only it ended there, but next she was wracked with dry heaves.

"Karla, are you okay in there?"

Adam. "Yes. Go aw..." She heaved again, her sides aching as tears spilled down her cheeks.

A strong arm wrapped around her waist, pulling her against him as he held her and grabbed her hair, freeing her hand. Damn. She hadn't locked the bathroom door to his room.

"I've got you, Kitten."

Karla couldn't stem the flow of more hot tears pouring out or the gut-wrenching sob that tore from her at having him holding her again, even in this grotesque circumstance. So embarrassing.

His body curved around hers. So comforting.

His arm tightened with each dry heave and he crooned in her ear. So loving.

She felt cherished, which just made her want to cry harder, because it didn't mean anything like that to Adam.

"Shhh...It's okay...I have you, baby."

But he didn't have her. He didn't even want her. She sobbed even harder. Needing to get rid of Adam ASAP, she took his middle finger and pulled back until he released his hold, just the way they'd taught her in self-defense, then stood. Too bad they didn't teach her how to defend her heart against attack.

Before she could go to the sink and get a washcloth, he did just that. "Look at me."

Karla stared up at him. Damn. He'd taken control of her. Again. He wiped the tears from her eyes, and then wiped her mouth and chin. Exhausted, Karla let him minister to her needs like a child. How was she going to face all that food downstairs with such a sour stomach?

"Brush your teeth."

He nudged her toward the sink and she complied. It helped not having to think about what she needed to do. Her mind was mush, both from the vomiting and from the nearness of Adam. His hand made gentle, sweeping motions up and down her back as she brushed. She wanted nothing more than to curl up in his lap, but that wasn't going to happen. Never again. More hot tears. She blinked them away.

After she'd rinsed, she stood straighter and met Adam's gaze in the mirror. "Thanks. I guess I got some bad shrimp last night."

"I had the shrimp and haven't had a reaction."

"Maybe my body reacts faster." The thought of him being sick made her look up at him to assess his condition. "God, I hope you don't get it." She never wanted to see Adam sick or wounded ever again. "Do you want to shower first or me?"

"Why don't you? The warm water might make you feel better. Besides, Jenny probably needs you downstairs, if you're feeling up to it. I'll just be a fifth wheel today."

She smiled at him, remembering how he'd run away from the house that first Thanksgiving they'd shared, then blushed to remember how she'd embarrassed herself on the front porch declaring her undying love.

Well, at least Karla wouldn't make that embarrassing mistake again today.

* * *

Adam sat next to Karla at the Thanksgiving table, instead of across from her, as they'd been the last time. He'd have preferred not to have her so close. Holding her this morning, even under the circumstances, had made him want to hold her again—in bed. Jesus, when would he get a chance to talk with her?

"Adam, Karla made the ham especially for you. Said it was your favorite for Thanksgiving. Good thing not everyone agrees, so there were plenty available when she went back to the store yesterday."

Adam looked at Karla and quirked an eyebrow. How could she have known that? She smiled, then leaned over and whispered, "You told me in the cab."

When? The last time they'd been together in a taxi-cab was...*nine years ago*.

Fuck. He'd known Karla was infatuated with him back then, but that she'd remember such a small detail all these years surprised—and pleased—the hell out of him. "Thanks, Karla. That was awfully sweet of you to remember."

The look she just gave him before she visibly caught herself was anything but sweet. More like smoldering. *Damn*. Getting through this meal without groping her under the table was going to take all the willpower he had. He smiled. Maybe there was hope for them yet. Still, he was haunted by her deep blue eyes and dark lashes, which marked a sharp contrast against her too-pale skin. Karla still didn't look as though she'd recovered from this morning's bout of nausea.

Several conversations bombarded him at once, from various people at the table. None seemed directed at him and he tried to tune them out, then a flash to an earlier Thanksgiving scene flitted across his brain. It was gone in an instant, but left an indelible impression. His father was drunk. His mother, near tears as she tried to keep up a good front for her family who had been invited to the annual celebration, was on the receiving end of his brutal tirade.

Adam must have been about fifteen or sixteen. Defending his mother, he'd mouthed off to his father and was back-handed so hard his chair had tumbled backward with him in it. Next thing he knew, his dad was sitting on his chest, pounding the shit out of his face until Adam shouted, "Get the fuck off me, you son of a bitch."

With that, Adam finally managed to turn his body hard enough to send his father sprawling onto the floor. Lifting weights at school must have been good for something besides building chest muscles.

Adam had stood, nursing his wounds. The expressions of horror on his family's faces registered, causing him extreme embarrassment. His mother had tears pouring down her face. He'd embarrassed her, too. All he could do was run from the house before he did something else he'd regret later—like kill his father.

Good God, was that what had happened? Had he come back later with a baseball bat and taken out his anger and revenge?

His breathing grew labored. Karla reached out to touch his knee, then leaned over and whispered, "Are you okay, Adam? You aren't feeling sick to your stomach, too, are you?"

Yeah, but not because of last night's shrimp.

"No. I'm fine." He took her hand, squeezed it, and then removed it from his knee before he embarrassed himself at her family's table in another way. "Thanks." Knowing she cared meant a lot to him, but now he had to wonder what kind of man he was if there was even a remote chance he could have killed his father. There was no statute of limitations for murder. What if he was found out? Hell, after thirty-four years, the case was like ice now, but he read in the paper about cold cases being solved all the time. Where would Karla be if he got hauled off to prison? Karla deserved better than that.

No, he couldn't even think about starting a life with her until he manned up, stopped running, and went back to Minnesota to face the music.

Feeling someone's gaze on him, he looked up to find Jenny staring at him, then at Karla. *Shit.* He hoped she didn't suspect anything. Of course, Karla and her mother were close, so she might have told her mother about their botched relationship already. The last thing he wanted was for her parents to find out he and Karla had been intimate, especially now when he'd suddenly, horribly realized he had unfinished business to handle. He couldn't really do anything to make their relationship permanent yet. But if Jenny had known about them already, she wouldn't have greeted him the way she did last night, would she?

He'd come to Chicago hoping for a chance to assure her parents he could provide for their daughter and would love her in his way until his final breath. But if he really was going to go to Minnesota and come clean, he couldn't make them that kind of promise anymore. Not until he could come to her with a clear conscience and no felony convictions.

He laid down his fork. Damn, he should have accepted Damián's invitation to join his family in California this year. Which reminded him—he needed to check in with his son later tonight. They were a couple of hours behind him, so they may not have started their celebration yet. Last time he'd checked in on them, before he'd left for Chicago, Damián said his niece was coping better than he'd expected, but his sister wasn't dealing with reality very well and that he'd have to stay on.

Adam understood what she was going through. His own mother had often apologized to him as a kid for marrying a similar scumbag—his father.

"So, tell me, Adam," Carl began, "how is retirement treating you? Did you pick up golf or any other vices?"

Adam grinned over at Carl before returning his gaze to Jenny who didn't quite smile back. The two of them looked like they've been through hell, grief having ravaged their once-young faces. But it looked as though their marriage was solid. Having each other to weather the storm would make all the difference.

"No, sir. I haven't gone the golfing, fishing, or hunting route." He wasn't sure why he'd avoided fishing and hunting. Some of the only pleasant memories he had of his childhood had been engaging in those activities, with his dad, no less.

"Karla says you run a nightclub now."

He glanced over at Karla who looked as if she was biting the inside of her trembling lip to keep herself from smiling. Little minx. Now, how was he supposed to navigate these waters?

"Something like that, sir. A couple buddies and I who served together in Iraq started a private club a few years ago. Keeps me busy and out of trouble." *More or less.*

Karla's grandmother, sitting on his left, reached out to touch his hand. "I was in Aspen last winter and hope to get back there again. Do you ever get up that way, Adam?" *Thank God for Grandma and her many travels.*

"No, ma'am. I pretty much stick to Denver and environs."

"I stayed at a wonderful resort there, modeled after a chalet in the Italian Alps. I met a wonderful former Marine there."

"Just a Marine, ma'am. Once a Marine, always a Marine." He hoped the rote correction didn't sound disrespectful. He grinned.

"You know, he said the same thing." She giggled. Hearing a seventy-something woman giggling sure sounded odd. Didn't have the effect her granddaughter's giggle had on him—thank God. "His daughter and her family run the place. Top-notch accommodations."

Shit. What were the chances she'd stayed at Marc's family resort and was talking about his Gramps? This was hitting just a little too close to home.

"He served in World War II. I was just a schoolgirl then, but I still remember all the sacrifices we made. A feast like this would have been hard to come by. So much was rationed."

"Yes, ma'am. Those were tough times." He admired the generation that had gone through that era in American history. Adam wasn't quite sure what else to say, so he turned his attention to the mountain of food on the plate in front of him, then noticed Karla had hardly touched her turkey dinner. At the moment, her fork was pulverizing the broccoli casserole that he was pretty sure she'd made. If he didn't know it would attract unwanted attention, he'd have picked up her fork and fed her himself. She was too fucking thin. Besides, she'd lost last night's dinner when she'd been sick this morning.

During a particularly noisy discussion at Carl's end of the table about who would win the football game later, Adam leaned over to Karla and whispered so only she could hear. "If you don't clean your plate, I'm going to haul you over to Lake Michigan and warm your backside in front of anyone who happens to walk or jog by."

Karla looked up at him and he heard a tiny hitch in her breathing. Shit, did she want a spanking? If so, would she go all bratty on him and disobey just to get him to discipline her? Interesting. Maybe...

Then Karla speared a piece of turkey and brought it to her mouth, followed quickly by a bite of her broccoli casserole. As if on automatic, she took bites at regular intervals until she'd finished everything on her plate. So, what was she saying—that she didn't want him to discipline her anymore?

No shit, jarhead.

What the fuck was it with his internal critic now using Joni's voice?

More important, why did Karla's latest rejection bother him so much? What if she went looking for a new Dom in one of the BDSM clubs in Chicago? The thought of her walking into one of those places dressed in one of her sexy outfits caused him to lose his appetite now. Of course, she'd left the sexiest of the outfits behind when she'd packed.

Karla leaned over to him and whispered low and directly into his ear, "Sir, if you don't clean your plate, I am going to come to your room tonight and force you to eat me instead."

Adam's cock came to a full salute in about three seconds flat and he adjusted himself in the chair. Memories of going down on Karla's sweet pussy nearly caused him to come undone. *Shit.* He'd like to see the day when a sub could force him to do anything he didn't want to do.

Oh, yeah, like she'd have to use force.

Jesus Christ, they were in her parents' house, at their Thanksgiving table. What was the matter with him? Besides, he had to straighten out some shit from his past before he could ever plan a future with Karla. He planned to leave for Denver tomorrow. But he still wanted to get a chance to talk things over with her.

He reached for his fork and knife and cut off a piece of the ham, still finding it hard to believe she'd remembered that throw-away comment he'd made in the taxi ride nine years ago. Maybe when Karla said she'd waited her whole adult life for him, she wasn't kidding. Still, she didn't seem to have shown up in Denver looking for a romantic relationship. That just happened later. Didn't it?

When had he first noticed Karla was an adult? That damned audition, before he realized it was Karla. But when had she first shown she was attracted to him? It had to have been in Marc's playroom and that Shibari demonstration, where he'd tied her arms behind her using the Teppou technique.

Or was that just the first time she'd let him know she was attracted to him sexually? Sure, when she was sixteen, she'd declared her love on the porch of this very house. But the first time he'd felt she was speaking to him on a sexual level as an adult was when she sang *Song to the Siren* on the stage at the club. She'd been his siren ever since.

So, when had he fallen in love with her?

Yeah, there was no longer a doubt in his mind that he loved this sassy young woman seated next to him. She loved him back, too, even though she'd given up on him at the moment. So, what did he plan to do about it? He wasn't getting any younger. He needed to propose.

But not until after he took care of business in Minnesota. He wouldn't ask her if he couldn't be around to take care of her for a reasonably long time.

He glanced at Jenny who now stared at Karla with concern on her face. Had she noticed that her daughter was losing weight and not eating much, too? At least she'd eaten today. But, hell, she'd eaten last night, too. Did Jenny know about this morning? If he wasn't going to be taking Karla home with him, he needed to make sure Jenny and Carl kept an eye on her until he could take over that job again.

He cast his gaze in Karla's direction and saw the way she clamped her mouth tight and held her stomach. Aw, hell. Not again. Would she keep this meal down? Did she have the flu? He wanted to check her forehead, but didn't want to attract attention. Maybe after dinner.

He needed to take care of her. Even if he failed at meeting her emotional needs, he could meet her physical and financial ones. If there ever was any long-term relationship with Karla, he'd need to be more up front with her than he had been with Joni. Memories of Joni's words on those tapes still haunted him. She'd sworn he'd been all she'd ever wanted in a husband, in a man. But he'd short-changed her in the emotional department, even though she hadn't indicated this to be the case in the tapes she'd recorded in her final months. While he didn't want to repeat that mistake with Karla, he had to concede he just didn't have a fucking clue how to change.

He wished this meal would come to an end so he could get Karla alone to talk with her. To speed things along on his end, he dug in and finished everything on his plate before he remembered Karla's threat. Damn. Maybe he should fill his plate again so he could leave something and see if she'd follow through, because the thought of devouring Karla's pussy made his mouth water more than this meal did.

God, he had it bad.

* * *

After the dishes had been cleared and a game of Apples to Apples played—won by Adam who had an uncanny way of playing just the card that would play to the judge's emotions—Karla felt so drained, she'd bowed out of taking a walk with him. He'd felt her forehead and declared in his annoying mama-bear mode that she didn't have a fever. Well, at least she hadn't before he'd touched her.

How she'd missed his touch.

The emotional roller coaster and the queasiness in her stomach lately had her body screaming to regroup. As she watched him walk out the front door, she climbed the stairs to her room to lie down. She'd barely stretched out and closed her eyes when she heard the "She's a Maneater" ring tone on her phone.

Mistress Grant.

Her heart thudded and then stopped. Did the Marine have some info? Or was it too late, even if she could figure out what was eating at Adam from his childhood? Karla accepted the call and placed the phone to her ear.

"Hello?"

"Yes or no—are you alone?"

Karla sat up. "Yes."

"Good. I've found something that I'm not sure we'll want Adam to know about until it's been checked out."

Karla reached over to the nightstand to pick up her song-writing notebook and a pencil. "I'm ready." *For whatever it takes.*

"It was nearly impossible to trace him before he joined the Marines, as if he just appeared out of nowhere. Then my source found out he'd changed his last name. Montague is his mother's maiden name."

Well, he really detested his father, so Karla could understand that.

"His mother's alive. Remarried. Doing quite well, it seems. Adam's father was killed in a home invasion and she moved to Chicago soon after."

"Was Adam hurt in the home invasion?"

"From what I can tell in newspaper reports, he wasn't there. Only his parents. Maybe he'd already run away by then. Anyway, his mother remarried a few years later and started a new family. Adam has a half-brother and a half-sister."

"Oh, my God. Are they still here in Chicago?" Adam would so much want to have a family. He'd been putting together his own replacement family for years at the club—and his surrogate family always would be the closest he'd let anyone. But for him to have blood relatives would be so good for him, provided they loved him unconditionally.

"His mother's there. The brother has a business in Albuquerque and his sister is in graduate school at USC in LA."

"I need to call his mother before I tell him about her. Even better, meet her face to face. I don't want her to hurt him." *Again.*

"Yeah, I'd feel better if you checked her out. He doesn't need any bat-shit crazy woman messing with his head."

Karla smiled. Grant cared about Adam as much as she did. Well, maybe not *that* much, but she did care, as a friend and a fellow Marine. Good thing, because Karla wouldn't want to mess up Grant's pretty face in a knock-down, drag-out for Adam's affections. Yeah. Karla grinned. She was not ready to give up on her man.

Grant gave her the phone number and address. *My God.* She was so close; only ten minutes away, up on Lake Shore Drive. Apparently, the woman had done all right for herself—financially, at least—if she lived in that Gold Coast neighborhood.

After thanking Grant and hanging up, Karla just stared at the phone a moment. It was Thanksgiving night, but Adam would be leaving Chicago soon. There wasn't much time. She punched in the phone number and waited, not sure what she was going to say. *"Oh, hi. I'm Karla and in love with your son and just want to know what the fuck you did to him when he was growing up to make him so afraid to love me back."*

Okay. Maybe that was too much information for a phone call. She might need to save some of that for the face-to-face. Her heart pounded as she waited for someone to answer.

When a woman answered the phone, Karla gripped the phone. "Mrs. Gallagher?"

"Who's calling please?"

Cold. Aloof. Careful.

"Karla Paxton. You don't know me, but we have a mutual acquaintance that I need to talk with you about."

"And who might that be?"

"Your son—Adam."

The audible gasp told Karla she'd definitely hit a nerve. Good. She'd like to hit a few more.

"How is he?" The pain-filled whisper threw Karla for a loop.

"Fine. Well, mostly fine. But I need to know some things about his past. I need to meet you somewhere to talk about Adam so I can…well, just because I need to know. But there isn't much time. Can we meet tonight? I'm in Lincoln Park."

"I can't go out. Why don't you come to my apartment?"

She certainly was more trusting than her son. After arranging a time to meet, Karla ended the call and swung her legs over the side of the bed, then stood in one motion. The room swayed and she plopped back onto the mattress until the dizzy spell had passed. The queasiness she'd been feeling for the past few mornings was now becoming an all-day occurrence. Maybe she *was* getting the flu, but just didn't have the fever or chills yet.

Well, she didn't have time to give in to sickness. She had a mission to accomplish tonight. This might be her last hope to help Adam. Standing more slowly this time, she picked up the notebook with the address and headed downstairs.

Adam wasn't back yet. Good. She didn't want to have to lie to him. After explaining to her mom that she needed to run an errand, she grabbed the keys to the car and headed out the front door.

She met Adam on his way up the steps. *Fucking damn.* He gave her a smoldering look that turned her knees to jelly. "Karla, we need to talk."

Oh, great. Now he wants to talk. Okay, he'd wanted her to walk with him earlier, so maybe he'd wanted to talk then. "I totally agree, Adam, but not now. I need to run…to the store. I'll be back soon."

"I'll ride along."

"No!" His stunned expression forced her to slow down. "I lied. I don't have to go to the store. I just need to take a drive. Alone. I'll be back in a couple hours."

"How the hell far are you driving? It's dark."

"I've driven in the dark before, Adam."

"Yeah, and you had an accident recently. I don't want you driving around alone."

"Adam, there aren't any deer in Chicago. I'll be fine." Hoping to ditch him, she started down the steps toward the sidewalk. He followed her. *Double fucking damn.* How was she going to get rid of him? She needed to be at Mrs. Gallagher's in ten minutes. No way did she want to piss the woman off and lose the opportunity. But she wasn't about to let Adam tag along either. What if the woman *was* bat-shit crazy, like Grant said? Karla wouldn't expose Adam to any more emotional torture from the woman.

Adam grabbed her elbow and halted her. "What's going on, Karla?"

She couldn't meet his gaze, but he gripped her chin, his fingers biting her jaw, and forced her to look at him. How could she lie to him when looking into his eyes?

Please, Adam. Don't mess this up. I'm just trying to help you.

"I'm meeting someone. And I'm late."

Adam let go of her as if burned, but quickly masked the hurt expression. *Good God, Adam. Do you think I'm off to meet a lover? Don't you trust me even a little bit?*

"I see."

No, you don't. But she needed to go, and if this is what it took to get him to let her go alone, then she'd let him stew on it a while.

"I'll be back later. Don't wait up."

Now why had she added that snarky comment? Well, if he didn't trust her anyway, it wouldn't matter what she said. Karla turned and went to the family's sedan and got in. Her eyes blurred with tears. Why was she crying when what she really felt was blood-boiling anger at that impossible man she'd had the misfortune of falling in love with?

Dashing the tears from her eyes, she started the ignition and drove away. A glance in the rear-view mirror told her Adam was gone already. Figured.

Trust me, Adam. For once, just fucking trust someone to love you.

Chapter Twenty-One

Why wouldn't she just tell him who the fuck she was meeting? Adam pulled the keys out of his pocket, got into his vehicle, and followed her. He hoped he hadn't already lost her, but she could get into a lot of trouble in a city this big.

Maybe she was just getting together with some girlfriends who also were home for the holiday weekend. Then why didn't she just say that, rather than make him think it was another man? *Come on. She hadn't said anything to indicate it was a man.* Yeah, she'd just said someone.

What if it was one of those boys from high school she said only liked to talk about sports? Hell, she still didn't like sports. What would she have in common with them now? He watched her make a turn about a block ahead and hurried to catch up.

Adam argued with himself that he should be encouraging her to pursue someone her own age. But the thought of her being with another man rotted his gut. Deep down, though, he knew Karla wasn't off meeting a lover. Still, she was keeping something from him. Not that she owed him anything. They weren't together anymore, not even in a Dom/sub relationship.

Maybe they never should have been together in the first place. But that horse had left the barn and there was no going back now.

He'd known having Karla in his life would never be easy. She always would be unpredictable. He had to admit he loved that about her most of all. He'd led a safe, predictable life since he'd retired from the Corps. She'd stirred him back to life. Maybe he couldn't love her as perfectly as she ought to be loved, but he'd do his damnedest not to ever hurt her again.

A gust of wind buffeted the car, making it hard to keep it on Lake Shore Drive. She decelerated, and then turned into the garage of a posh-looking high-rise apartment building. *Damn.* He'd never find her in there. What if there was a guard or doorman or something? He stepped on the accelerator and followed her into the garage. She parked and he continued up to the next level, running to the elevator to see which floor she stopped on.

Two. Hell, he could take the stairs and maybe even see which apartment she went into. Fuck, this was more recon than he'd done since his days in Fallujah. He took the stairs two at a time and opened the door to peek out. Karla stood waiting outside a door about halfway down the hall. The door opened, but he couldn't see who greeted her. A kid maybe, judging by where her gaze focused. He grinned, a lot less worried.

After she'd gone inside, he crept down the hallway and checked the name on the door. Gallagher. The voices coming from within both sounded female. He recognized Karla's, but the other sounded like an older woman. Did she have a relative who hadn't come to dinner today? Or perhaps a former teacher? She was close to her music teacher, who had helped her get into Columbia.

He could play this guessing game all night, but, instead, he'd just stake himself out down the hallway at the opposite end from the stairs and elevator to wait for Karla to leave. He no longer needed to know who was in apartment 2F. But he did want to be sure Karla got home safely.

* * *

When the apartment door finally opened, Karla found herself staring into thin air. She lowered her gaze. The woman of Adam's nightmares was a thin and frail-looking one seated in a scooter-type wheelchair in front of her. Her rheumy green eyes carried only a hint of the lively sparks in her son's eyes, but she could see him in them.

"Please, come in, Miss Paxton."

Karla walked into the spacious living room, decorated in the clean lines of Scandinavian furniture. The hardwood floors gleamed. No area rugs to warm the room, but she supposed they would have obstructed the woman's limited mobility. The pieces of furniture that caught her eye, and didn't seem to fit the room, were the antique secretary desk in a mahogany or other dark wood, and the upright grand piano that had to be from the turn of the last century.

"Have a seat, Ms. Paxton." Karla took a seat on the beige bench-like sofa.

"Please call me Karla. And thanks for agreeing to see me on such short notice, Mrs. Gallagher." Karla waited for Adam's mother to roll herself into place a couple of yards in front of her.

"Can I get you something to drink? Tea or coffee? Pop? I've given my personal assistant the weekend off to be with her family, so I'm afraid you'll have to suffer from my lack of skills in the kitchen."

Karla almost smiled. *Like mother, like son?* "No, thank you. I can't stay long and don't want to bother you."

"No bother at all. I can tell you care about my son." She smiled.

Karla tried to give the woman the once-over without being too obvious. Her hair was soft-permed and silver-gray, a lighter shade than the grays on Adam's head. She wore wire-rimmed glasses with a designer brand name. When she smiled, little crinkle lines appeared at the corners of her eyes, just like Adam's. Her lips were a pinkish hue, matching her perfectly manicured fingernails. She wore a two-piece suit, conservative, stylish, but a little out of date.

"Are you Adam's wife?"

"No." *Not yet.* "We're good friends." *With kinky benefits.* "I work in a club he owns in Denver."

"What has Adam told you about me?"

Karla's gaze went back to the woman's eyes. "Not much." *Only that you locked him in something when he was bad.*

"My Adam didn't have it easy growing up."

No fuck. And he's mine now. You lost the chance to claim him a long time ago. Okay, she needed to cut the woman some slack, until she got the whole story. "Tell me more. I want to understand." *Understand him—not the insanity you and your husband put him through that gives him nightmares to this day.*

Mrs. Gallagher looked down at her hands, which she twisted in her lap. The knuckles were swollen with arthritis and she thought how painful that must be. Still, not as painful as what they'd done to Adam.

"His father was an alcoholic. Very abusive. He wasn't like that before the war. Vietnam changed him." A tear rolled down her wrinkled cheek and plopped onto her hand. She wiped it away as though pushing away a fly. Apparently, she wasn't any more fond of showing emotions than her son was. "I tried to protect him."

Like hell you did. Karla's breaths came in short, shallow bursts as the blood finally boiled to the surface. "By locking him up?" *Okay, so much for tact, Kitty.*

Adam's mother lifted her head and scrutinized Karla. "I didn't know what else to do," she whispered.

"Locking him up was the only option? Come on. He has nightmares about it to this day."

Mrs. Gallagher winced.

Karla took a deep breath. She was letting her rage get out of control. If she wanted to get the info she needed, she couldn't afford to piss the woman off.

The woman drew herself up straighter and sighed. "He was safe in the closet. His father couldn't beat him in there."

Wait a minute. She'd locked him up to *protect* him? "I don't understand. Maybe you'd better start at the beginning."

What unfolded was a tale of abuse at the hands of a monster who had some serious psychological problems. When she described the injuries both she and Adam had suffered at the man's hands, Karla wanted nothing more than to beat the ever-loving shit out of the asshole. If he weren't already dead, Karla would have tracked him down and done just that.

For Adam. For the little boy who had been so horribly abused and tortured. Then abandoned.

"Tell me what happened the night Adam ran away."

Mrs. Gallagher rested her head in her hand, her elbow resting on the arm of the wheelchair. "The worst night of my life. I lost my husband *and* my son; Adam because of my own stupidity."

"This was during the home invasion? I thought Adam wasn't there."

Adam's mother raised her gaze to meet Karla's. She studied Karla's face a moment, before her features softened and her frail hand went to the back of her neck to knead her nape, much like Adam did every so often. Seeing her do it sent a chill up her spine. Did Adam even know that was where he had picked up that nervous tic from?

"There was no home invasion. That was the night Adam's father was killed. The night I became paralyzed; the night I told Adam to run as far and as fast as he could and to not look back."

Karla didn't realize she'd ceased breathing until her chest began to burn. "What are you saying? Did Adam kill his...?"

The woman's watery eyes opened wider. "Good Lord, no! Not Adam. Me! I killed my husband." Tears streamed down her face, unheeded now. Her hands shook uncontrollably and she clasped them together. She lowered her voice to a whisper. "I couldn't take it anymore. I snapped."

Karla didn't know what to say. Adam's mother had just admitted to murdering her husband. What was Karla supposed to do with that? *Nothing*. She might have done the same if she were in that situation. That wasn't what she'd come here to find out. She needed to know what Adam saw. What he remembered.

"Where was Adam?"

"He was too big to lock into a closet anymore. I'd told him to stay in his room. It was Thanksgiving night."

Oh, God. No wonder he didn't enjoy the holiday. It didn't have to do with missing Joni. He'd lived through hell one Thanksgiving.

Mrs. Gallagher looked at the nearby coffee table where a fresh-flower arrangement including golden and burgundy mums and cream-colored alstroemeria was displayed. "He and his father had fought at the dinner table that day. He'd stood up to his father. They'd struggled, fell to the floor. He'd told his father to get the…to get off of him."

"Get the fuck off me, you son of a bitch!"

Karla remembered the time Adam had screamed those words and thrown her off his chest where she'd fallen asleep after her accident.

"Adam left the house to cool off, but this was much later. I guess he heard the intensity of the argument and my screams when his father took a baseball bat and struck me in the middle of the back. I crumpled to the floor and knew my spine had been damaged. I just didn't know how badly."

Karla's gaze went to the chair. A crocheted pink and maroon lap robe covered her thin legs.

"I dragged myself over to the nightstand and pulled out a pistol I kept there for protection. When he came at me again with the bat, ready to bash my head in, I guess, I just pulled the trigger."

Dear Lord. "What did Adam see?" Her voice came out in a whisper.

"He came into the room after I shot his father. He was already dead. I was lying in the pool of his blood on the floor, unable to get up. At first, I went on automatic and asked Adam to help me clean up the blood, as he'd done so many times before. Only before, it had always been Adam's or my blood. But then I just didn't care anymore. I didn't care if I went to prison for life. I could never be in a worse prison than I'd been in the past eighteen years. But I didn't want Adam to be taken down with me. He'd…made threats at the table that my family had overheard. He might have been accused of killing his father. So I told him to take the money we had in the house and to run."

Adam had seen his dead father lying in a pool of blood. He'd probably seen his mother battered and stitched up a million times, too, but to see her lying wounded and helpless… Karla glanced at the wheelchair again. Adam had run that night. He'd been running away from the horrific scene his whole adult life.

Oh, Adam. Tears spilled down Karla's cheeks. She needed to get back to him. To hold him. To take all the hurt away from the lost little boy inside him.

"I used to watch over him when he slept."

Karla's attention returned to the woman in front of her. "What?"

"I'd go into his room and just find a corner and sit and watch him sleep. So innocent. So brave. I wish his childhood could have been as normal and nurturing as my other two children's."

His mother had watched over him, much like Adam had watched over Karla. Another trait from his mother that he probably didn't even associate with her. Did those actions provide him with comfort when things were out of control? Remind him of his mother?

"He was such a beautiful boy. I had such hopes for him. He wanted to be a Marine."

His mother glanced over at a series of mostly old portraits on the upright grand piano showing six men in military uniforms, four of them recognizable to her as Marine uniforms. Adam said there had been Montagues in the Marines as far back as the Civil War. He must have been inspired by those photos while growing up.

"He'd have made a fine Marine. He was always trying to protect me. Adam had a penchant for doing the right thing, even when it wasn't the easy thing to do."

Karla wasn't sure if she wanted Adam to meet this woman again, but Karla needed to tell him about her and let him make that decision. But, if he chose not to see her, she should at least let her know how he'd turned out.

"Adam took the name Montague after he ran away."

"Oh, my goodness! No wonder we could never find him."

She'd looked for him? How sad they hadn't been able to reconnect sooner. Maybe things would have been different for both of them.

"Mrs. Gallagher, Adam *is* a Marine. He served almost twenty-five years and reached the rank of master sergeant. You can be very proud of him. He carried on the family tradition and served with great honor and distinction."

Fresh tears glistened in her eyes and spilled down her cheeks. "Do you think he'd ever want to see me again?"

"I don't know. I'll tell him about you, but we'll have to let him decide."

Mrs. Gallagher nodded, looking much older than she'd looked when Karla had entered her apartment less than an hour ago. Karla felt sorry for her, but still harbored some anger that no one had tried to do more to protect Adam while he was growing up. They hadn't lived in the dark ages. There were programs to help battered women and children. Locking him in a closet was not the way he should have been protected, because it only made him think he was the one who had the problem. The little boy in Adam hadn't understood. He'd thought he was the one being punished. Karla blinked the tears away that burned her eyelids.

"Thank you, Mrs. Gallagher."

Karla made to stand up and Adam's mother raised her hand to stop her. "Even if he won't meet me, I'd like him to get to know his siblings. He has a younger brother and sister from my second marriage."

"If you can give me their contact info, I'd be happy to share it." Karla wondered that neither of her children was with her this Thanksgiving night. Were they estranged, or just busy with their own lives? They didn't live nearby, according to Grant.

"I'm sorry you missed them, but when they get to Chicago to see me, they like to hang out with their old friends."

Well, she must have raised her second family well enough that they hadn't abandoned her. Karla waited while the woman went to the secretary desk along the wall near the opening to the dining room and pulled out a pad of paper and an address book. As she wrote with a shaky, but careful hand, Karla wandered over to the grand piano, a Steinway, and glanced at the framed photos, beginning with the oldest, a dashing young man in his Civil War-era uniform. He was the spitting image of Johnny Depp. *My God, it was as if Depp had posed for the photo or worn the uniform in a movie or something.*

"That's Johnny Montague, my great-grandfather. Quite handsome, wasn't he?"

"Um, yes." *Not as handsome as Karla's Montague Marine, of course.*

His mother grinned. "Yes, I know who he looks like. Maybe we're related somewhere back in history."

Karla grinned. Wouldn't that be a kick—Adam and Johnny Depp as long-lost cousins? But the lightheartedness of the moment disappeared when his mother handed her the piece of paper that would introduce Adam to the two newest members of his family, only these were blood relatives.

"Would you prepare them first, Mrs. Gallagher, so that, if Adam calls, it won't be out of the blue?"

"Of course. But they know they have a big brother. They know the whole story."

Karla looked down at the paper and saw that Adam's siblings were named Patrick and Megan. Fine Irish names. Well, time to get back to her house and figure out how she was going to share all of this with Adam.

She reached out and offered her hand. "Thank you again for letting me visit, Mrs. Gallagher."

The woman shook her hand, her upper lip trembling. "Please tell him I never meant to hurt him. That I…I love him. I could never tell him that, I guess because everything I'd ever loved, I lost. But I lost him anyway."

Feeling sorry for her, Karla bent down and brushed her lips against her cold cheek.

"I promise, I will."

She let herself out of the apartment and walked to the elevator then decided to just take the stairs. Driving back to the house, she tried to formulate her thoughts about how she planned to tell Adam. "Oh, guess what? I just met your long-lost mother and she wants you to know she loves you."

Oh, Adam. I hope you'll meet her. Maybe she can put some of your ghosts to rest.

As she turned onto her tree-lined street, her heart began hammering the blood through her veins, making her aware of the tension in her temples. What *was* she going to tell him? How was he going to take it? Oh, God, she hoped she'd done the right thing digging into his past.

She parked the car and ran up the steps, then had to grab onto the porch post to steady herself when another dizzy spell hit her. Maybe she'd better ask mom if she had anything for the flu, other than bed rest, which she didn't have time for.

Inside the house, she went straight to the stairway, knowing Adam wouldn't be downstairs with her parents. She knocked on his bedroom door. No answer. She spoke softly through the crack in the door. "Adam? Are you still up?" Silence.

"He's gone, Karla."

Karla's heart pounded against her chest like a bass drum as she looked back down the hallway to find her mother standing at the top of the stairs.

"What?" *Gone?* Karla reached for the doorjamb to steady herself. He'd left her? Why? Obviously because he thought she was seeing someone else. *Oh, Adam. Why do you have to expect the worst of people all the time?*

Well, tonight she'd certainly gotten an inkling as to why he expected people to abandon him.

"He never came back from his walk. I hope he found some place to get inside where it's warm or he'll be a Popsicle by now."

Relief flooded Karla's body and she sagged against the wall. Not *gone* gone, just out.

"Do you want to tell me what's going on between you two?"

Not really. "Maybe later, Mom. Right now, I just need to lie down. I think I might be coming down with the flu." She walked back down the hall, feeling her mother's scrutiny on her, but just walked into her room and closed the door. Her stomach churned, but she wouldn't give in to puking again. Feeling flushed, she went to the window and pressed her face against the cool glass.

Adam needs you.

The voice Karla now knew was Joni Montague's spoke as clearly as if she were standing beside her. Karla opened her eyes and looked to her side. No one was there, of course. Then she turned to the window and noticed that Adam's car was gone.

Maybe he hadn't just taken a walk. Maybe…

Panic set in and she ran to the bathroom and opened the door to Ian's room. His duffel bag lay open on the floor by the closet, and she nearly cried tears of joy. Instead, the now-familiar churning in her stomach began, and she ran to the bathroom in time to hurl into the toilet.

* * *

Adam waited a few minutes before hurrying down the hallway to follow her home. Standing at the end of the hallway for the past hour, he felt like a damned fool. Thank God no one had found him there, or they may have called the police on him.

If he wanted a relationship with Karla, there was no room for jealousy. He'd seen how that could affect a relationship with his parents. His father was always accusing his mother of having other men she was seeing.

Not that there was much hope for him having a relationship with Karla anyway. His coming to Chicago had been a mistake. He might as well head back to the Paxtons, get a good night's sleep, and head back to Denver first thing in the morning.

As he walked toward the stairway, he heard voices seconds before the stairway door opened and two young people came out, smiling. He made eye contact with the young man and felt as if he'd been gut-punched. It was like looking into the mirror—twenty years earlier.

Out of the corner of his eye, he watched as the young woman beside him stopped and stood stock-still, her jaw dropping open. "Oh, my God! Adam?"

How did she know his name? He turned toward her and saw his mother's face, the way she'd looked when he was a little boy.

"Wait in here, Adam. I'll let you out when he goes to sleep."

"I'll be good. Don't lock me in there, Mommy!"

Sweat broke out on his upper lip as his heart began to pound harder. What was going on here? Who had Karla been visiting—and why?

She looked like she wanted to run up and hug him, but restrained herself. *Thank God.* "Momma must have had a fit when she saw you."

Adam's hand rose to the nape of his neck and he rubbed the scar. He anticipated what was incoming and still couldn't help but ask. "Momma?" What the fuck? Was she saying his mother was in apartment 2F? Karla had been digging into his past? Had she discovered what he'd done to his father?

Jesus fucking Christ.

The young man cocked his head and squared himself as if to prepare for combat. "You didn't even see her, did you? What the fuck's your problem, man? She's been waiting for you forever. The least you can do is let her know you're alive before you disappear on her again."

If these two people were his half-siblings—and who else could they be—then obviously their mutual mother hadn't told them the story of that bloody night. Adam sure as hell didn't plan to fill them in. But what about coming face-to-face with the mother who had told him to leave all those years ago?

The woman extended her hand. "I'm Megan Gallagher. Excuse my brother. Patrick has just a little too much testosterone." The comment drew a glare from her brother that she either ignored or didn't see. She leaned to Adam, and said in a stage whisper, "Must be his stint in the Marines." Adam looked the younger man over with renewed respect.

Megan hooked her arm in Adam's. "Please, come inside. Momma isn't getting any younger. She needs to know you're okay."

"But don't go in there if you have an ax to grind," Patrick said. "She's been through enough." Protective of his mother. *Their* mother. Good for him.

"I've ground all my axes already." That may not be completely true, but he wasn't going to take out his frustrations on an old woman. She had to be in her mid-seventies by now. But was he ready to face her again after all this time?

Megan tried to steer him back in the direction of their mother's apartment before Adam had a chance to run again. He let her. Yes, the time had come to stop running. If his mother turned him in for killing her husband, his father, then he'd stand trial for the crime and suffer the consequences. Maybe he'd get some leniency for not having killed anyone else since then. Well, except in combat zones.

Thank God he hadn't admitted to Karla that he loved her. She didn't need to be saddled with a convict.

"God, you must work out more than Patrick does. You're built like a tank." Megan took her fist and playfully punched his bicep. She probably wasn't much younger than Karla, but his sister seemed so immature compared to Karla.

He halted just a few yards away from the door. If he was going to do this, he wouldn't be dragged into it. Megan let him go and looked up at him, expectantly. The playfulness was gone, replaced by worry. He thought he saw a glint of tears in her eyes.

"Please, Adam. She needs to see you, to explain what happened to your father. It's been eating her alive all these years."

What was there to explain? His flashbacks made it pretty clear what had happened.

Patrick walked around him and inserted a key into the lock, opening the door. He turned to glare back at Adam, waiting.

"You're home early. You'll never guess who visited me to…"

Momma. Her voice was softer, happier, than the last time he'd heard it. As if drawn by a magnet, he walked toward the doorway.

"Momma, there's someone else here to see you."

Adam reached the opening of the door, his heartbeat thudding in his ears, then walked inside, bracing himself for…a wheelchair? A much older version of his mother was sitting frail and tiny in a wheelchair?

Adam remembered how Karla's gaze had lowered when someone had answered the door earlier. It wasn't a child who had answered, but his mother. What had happened to her? Stroke maybe?

"Adam? Is it really you?" Her whispered words were spoken with such emotion; he couldn't help but think she was sincere. If the woman hadn't been in the chair, she surely would have hit the floor. Patrick and Adam both reached out at the same time to steady her upper body. Well, Patrick also held himself ready to deck Adam if he tried anything. *Good kid.*

Adam knelt on one knee and took his mother's shaking hand in his. With her free hand, she reached up and placed it against his cheek. Cold. Her hand was like ice and he took it between his hands, hoping to infuse some warmth into her. Tears streamed down her cheeks.

"Yeah, it's me…Mom." He couldn't really call her Momma again. Too old. Too much time passed.

She pulled her hand free of his and held both arms out to him. He went into her embrace, and the backs of his eyes burned as she wrapped her shaking arms around his shoulders.

Her voice wavered as she spoke. "I didn't think I'd ever get to hold you again, sweetheart."

He put his arms around her, but was afraid he'd crush the frail woman so he used great restraint. A brace covered her back, and he wondered if she'd been in some kind of accident. She laid her head against his shoulder and began to sob.

Adam didn't know how much time had passed when she loosened her hold and he was able to release her and put some space between them again.

"Your young lady friend told me you're a Marine, son. I'm so proud of you for reaching your goal, despite all that happened."

Adam wasn't sure what to say, but nodded to acknowledge her words. Now he needed to come clean. "I'm sorry, Mom. About Dad."

"What do you have to be sorry about?"

"What I did that night. I don't remember much, but…"

"Oh, Adam! You didn't do anything wrong. You never gave me any trouble at all. You were always such a good boy."

Joni's words came back to him. *"Adam, listen to me. You were a good boy. And you're a good man."* No, wait. That wasn't Joni. That was Karla's voice. What had made him think it was Joni? His thoughts were such a jumble right now. He wished Karla was here with him now, for some reason. Probably because she was so much stronger than he was at dealing with emotional stuff like this.

"Sit down. We need to talk. All of us." She motioned for the three of them to sit. He sat on the sofa, Megan taking the place beside Adam, and Patrick sitting in a chair nearby, not taking his vigilant gaze off Adam for a second.

Adam guessed his half-brother was about twenty-six or twenty-seven. Megan probably twenty-four or twenty-five. His mother must have remarried soon after he kil…his father was killed.

"Patrick and Megan know the story already, but I may need them for moral support."

Megan reached out to squeeze her mother's hand. "Momma, you didn't do anything wrong. You were put in a horrific situation where you did what you had to just to survive."

"Well, the grand jury did rule self-defense and didn't choose to take it to trial."

Adam wasn't sure what was going on, but was pretty sure they were talking about that night that had sent him running. But what they were saying didn't mesh with the flashbacks he'd had. "Mom, are you saying that you took a baseball bat to Dad that night?"

She crinkled her forehead. "Bat? No, he used the bat on me. That's what put me in a chair."

Something wasn't right. "But I remember standing over him with a bloody baseball bat in my hand. He was lying in a pool of blood. His head was bashed in."

"No, Adam. After he paralyzed me, I shot him. That's where all the blood came from, the head wound."

The memory Adam had seen last month flashed across his mind again. Of course. A bat wouldn't have caused that kind of head wound. The bullet had entered his father's forehead and blown out the back side of his skull.

"You picked up the bat that had been lying in his blood when you came into the room. Dear Lord, surely you haven't thought all this time that you'd..."

Adam shook his head. "Actually, I'd blocked it out until recently." But the images he'd seen had made him so sure that he'd done it. How could he have gotten it so wrong in his head?

"Oh, Adam, I'm so sorry you thought that, even for a second. You never could have hurt a fly. You always tried to protect me, but you don't have a malicious bone in your body. No matter what he would do, you usually just tried to put distance between the two of you, rather than fight back. Even earlier that day, when he started a fight at the Thanksgiving table, you just left the house to cool off."

Emotional avoidance. Adam still avoided emotional confrontations; hell, emotions period. Until Karla. And yet he continued to try to avoid admitting he loved her, or anyone else he cared about. Avoidance and lack of commitment made it easier when the time came to run. No sticky attachments.

Shit. He needed to get back to Karla, to tell her he loved her, to ask her to forgive him for hurting her. But he couldn't run from dealing with his mother and her needs at the moment either. At least she had two good kids to look after her.

"Tell me about your life, Adam. Not a day went by that I didn't wonder what you were doing, where you were, if you were okay."

He heard the catch in her voice and wished he'd tried harder to find her. Hell, if not for Karla, he might never have found her until it was too late.

Adam described his first year on the run, eventually being taken in by some people who ran a shelter and helped him with GED classes. If not for them, he might never have been accepted into the Marine Corps.

"I came back to Minneapolis to check on you once, soon after I finished boot camp at Parris Island. Some other family lived in our house. You'd moved on."

"I had to get away; too many nightmares. I moved to Chicago, where I met Ryan, my second husband. He rescued me." Adam learned she'd been married to Gallagher almost twenty-eight years, but he'd died of a heart attack two years ago. He offered his condolences and couldn't help that his thoughts turned to Joni.

"I met my wife Joni during that visit. She died nine years ago this month."

"Oh, Adam, I'm so sorry." She reached toward him.

"We had twenty years together, including all my deployments."

"Tell me about Karla. She seemed like someone you'd want to have on your side rather than against you."

Adam grinned. Truer words had never been spoken. "Well, ma'am, I met her right after Joni died. She'd run away from home and I helped get her back home to her parents. She sort of latched onto me and we struck up a correspondence afterward that lasted until this past summer when she showed up at my cl...my house in Denver." He didn't need to go into what he did for a living now. Better to stick to the more "vanilla" version of his last thirty-four years.

"I could tell she cares a lot about you." There was a twinkle in his mother's eyes.

"Yes, she does. I care about her, too."

His mother smiled, but didn't say anything more. Then his newfound siblings shared a bit about their lives. It sounded like his mother had been well-loved and cherished by Ryan Gallagher, her second husband, which made Adam feel better about not being around to take care of her.

His mother stifled a yawn and he glanced at his watch to see that it was nearly midnight. "Look, I think I'd better shove off, but I'd like to come back again, talk some more, if that's okay."

"Of course, Adam, anytime. Consider this your home, too."

A home. He'd had a home with Joni, albeit in base housing, and the club had been his home since 2006. With Karla, he'd like to have a place they could call their own, without worrying about Marc, Damián, or anyone else dropping by unexpectedly all the time. He loved them like a brother and a son, but he had plans for Karla that didn't need an audience. They needed a real home, one without a sex club on the lower level; maybe just a private playroom or dungeon tucked away in some out of the way room for their private enjoyment.

Don't be thinking about dungeons in front of your mother, jarhead.

Ignoring the incessant internal voice, he stood and closed the gap to his mother reaching down to hug her.

"I love you, Adam. I never stopped. Not for a single moment."

Adam closed his eyes and held on tighter, morphing back to the little boy who'd never quite been able to protect his mother as well as he should have. "Love you, too…Momma."

After his mother loosened her hold on him, he stood and hugged Megan, then shook Patrick's hand, his brother having relaxed his guard a little bit. As he turned toward the door, Adam's gaze fell on the portraits on the piano and he was drawn to them like steel to a magnet. He remembered how the five men in their Marine uniforms had enthralled him as a boy. Four generations of Montagues—plus his father. He'd wanted nothing more than to be one of them.

But there were six photos now. He recognized Patrick as the young Marine in the first one. The next was of Adam's father, Staff Sergeant Virgil Griffin; odd that his mother kept the photo here. Maybe it was a reminder of some sort. After serving in the Corps himself, Adam had come to understand the man better, although he'd never forgiven him. He'd been a casualty of Vietnam, raging at life and everyone around him. Not an excuse, but Adam remembered how Damián had been during those first months after he'd come to live with him.

Right after he'd lost his foot, Damián tended to turn his rage inward, wanting nothing more than to end his nightmare, his torment, his life. Between the therapists at the VA center in Denver and Adam's forcing him to deal with it by talking about it, they'd managed to get to where Damián had regained some control over his life again.

Sadomasochistic scenes at the club seemed to push him into gaining better and better control. He'd never harmed a masochist; never scened when he was angry or in the belly of the beast. But Damián sure had given Adam a scare in San Diego when he'd come very close to killing Julio in cold blood, not that the shithead didn't deserve killing.

Adam hadn't wanted Damián's war trauma to lead to drinking or uncontrolled violence, a fate like his father's. While PTSD would always be there for the man he called his son, the young man was managing and coping with it as best he could. Maybe that's all Adam could hope for.

He glanced back at the proud young Marine in his father's portrait. Sure beat the alternative. How different the boy in this photo was from the man Adam had come to hate. He wished he could replace those violent images with this one. He wondered how things might have been different if there had been better treatments for his father's PTSD.

Adam's gaze continued down the line of photos until he reached the one of Captain Johnny Montague, a Marine who had spent the later Civil War years enforcing the blockade of the South. Adam had been riveted by the stories of how, long after the war, he'd rescued Adam's great-great-grandmother, an innocent immigrant from Ireland, from some horrible fate his mother only hinted at. Adam thought it must have had something to do with sex, given the face his mother had made when she told the story. Intriguing now, but he hadn't wanted to know more when he was a kid or a teen.

Adam turned to her. "Do you still own the Montague cabin?"

She smiled up at him. "Yes. Patrick's been refurbishing it, but trying to keep its old-fashioned charm."

"One of my best memories ever was the summer you, Dad, and I spent there."

"For the love of God, Adam, I don't guess I remember it as fondly. Your dad had lost another job. We couldn't pay the rent and that remote cabin near Deadwood was the only thing between us and homelessness."

"All I remember was fishing and hunting with Dad, cooking out…"

"There wasn't any electricity in the cabin. Cooking out was the only option if we wanted to eat a hot meal. You guys provided the main courses for our table, while I tended a small garden." She shook her head. "It was so hard living there."

Funny how their perceptions of that summer were so different; for eleven-year-old Adam, it had been a grand adventure—and one last chance to get closer to his Dad before all hell broke loose. With money scarce and liquor stores not within easy reach, his father had actually been pretty decent to him and his mother. Then his dad had gotten another job and they'd moved back to Minneapolis—beginning of the end.

Patrick came to stand next to him, having lost his defensive stance. "I've been working on the place as I can and hiring help as needed for the past year. There's electricity, hot and cold running water, indoor facilities, and the whole nine yards now."

Adam smiled. "I'd like to see it sometime. Let me know if there's anything I can do to help."

He still couldn't believe he had a younger brother and a younger sister. Looking at Megan, standing next to their mom with a protective hand on her shoulder, he didn't know how he could be much more blessed.

Well, there was still one thing missing from his life.

Adam said his good-byes, promising to stop by again before he headed out of town. He made his way back down to the parking garage and his car. The drive back to Karla's parents' house had him so deep in thought, he nearly missed her street. He had so much to tell her, he didn't know where to start.

Maybe he'd just needed to start with "I'm sorry."

When he let himself back into the darkened house using the key the Paxtons had told him was in the flower pot on the porch, he tiptoed upstairs. Dark and silent. He'd have to wait until the morning to talk with Karla. He got undressed and put on his USMC sweatshirt and sweatpants, and stretched out on the rack. But sleep wouldn't come. The events of the evening played over and over in his head. He needed to talk with Karla, but she needed her sleep.

Seeing how she'd looked when he'd arrived Wednesday and her being so sick yesterday morning renewed his worry about her health. *Fuck.* Why hadn't it occurred to him sooner? A sense of dread came over him that sent his heart racing and his gut into a tailspin. While he was on leave recovering from the shrapnel wounds in Afghanistan, Joni had exhibited many of the same symptoms—loss of appetite, weight loss. He didn't remember her vomiting, but he was out of it most of the time on painkillers. Obviously, she wouldn't tell him if she had been sick. But at some point he'd noticed and asked her. She'd told him she'd just been worried about him. Months later he learned her cancer had metastasized to the liver.

Sweat broke out on his forehead, cooling rapidly in the room's chilly air. He needed to get Karla to a doctor. Why hadn't he thought to do that sooner? What if Karla had something serious, too? Oh, God. He'd only just come to realize how important she was to him. Surely to God, the universe wouldn't fuck the two of them up the way it had him and Joni. No way. But Karla was young and, until recently, seemed healthy. It had to be something simple, like the flu.

It just had to be.

But his heart continued to beat rapidly. Images of Karla going through what Joni had endured put him on edge for the next few hours. Finally, unable to stay away from her any longer, he tossed the sheet back and crossed the room into the bathroom. The door to her bedroom was ajar and he opened it further, thankful the hinges were oiled, and slipped into her room.

Moonlight came in through the window and his eyes, already adjusted to the dark, made out her facial features—calm, peaceful, sleeping. He expelled the breath he'd been holding and his body relaxed. She was okay; for now, at least. He glanced around and saw a chair in the corner and decided he'd take up watch over her tonight. No sense going back to his rack, because he wasn't going to get any sleep this night. He needed to be near her.

God, how he'd missed her.

Adam missed when she challenged him. He missed when she surrendered to him sexually. He missed when she loved him in so many ways. Most of all, he missed that he hadn't loved her back.

Well, fuck that shit. He did love her.

No need to hide it or run from it. He loved Karla. He'd loved Joni, too, even if he hadn't been able to tell her. But he wouldn't leave Karla wondering. He'd tell her, just as soon as she woke up, and every day together for the rest of their lives. Again and again—and often.

He just hoped she was okay and they would have many, many years to wake up beside each other.

Chapter Twenty-Two

Karla's stomach churned with the now familiar queasiness she'd woken up to for the last week. She dreaded sitting up, because she'd have to make that mad morning dash to the toilet. She just wanted to stay burrowed under the blankets, but the sound of someone breathing brought her eyes wide open. She found herself staring across the room into Adam's intense gaze.

"We need to talk, Kitten."

Ka-thunk!

Oh, she so didn't need that submissive stomach-drop reaction right now. Tossing back the covers, she held one hand over her mouth as she gathered her hair in the other and ran for the bathroom. She'd barely lifted the seat before Adam's strong arm came around her waist, holding her as his hand grabbed her hair, fisting it to keep it from getting in the way.

"I've got you, Kitten."

The contents of her stomach emptied to her great embarrassment, but she didn't care. She always felt better afterward, for a little while, at least. She just wanted some relief, even if she'd have to face Adam in a few moments.

When it seemed the worst of it was over, she patted the hand he held over her abdomen to signal she didn't need him anymore, but he didn't let go. He helped her stand up straight and, when she started to move toward the sink, didn't relinquish his hold.

"Sit."

He lowered the toilet lid and started to guide her there, but she resisted. "I'm better now. Thanks."

"I. Said. Sit."

She looked up at him. "Please don't make my stomach go ka-thunk again."

"What?"

"Never mind." He cast a look at her that told her she'd better explain herself.

Ka-thunk!

"It's just that, when you go all Dom like that—or in Master mode, for that matter—with a look or a command, my stomach does this weird thing. It just sort of drops into my pelvis." When he quirked an eyebrow, she continued. "Okay, metaphorically drops, not literally. But I wish you'd stop doing it because my stomach's already off kilter."

He chuckled and went to the sink to wet a washcloth.

"What's so funny?"

Adam didn't answer right away, but returned to stand in front of her. "Tilt your head back."

Ka-thunk!

Damn him.

Like a puppet, she did as he instructed. He gently washed the sweat, tears, and grime off her face and mouth and rinsed the washcloth again, handing it to her. She held it over her eyes, hoping to avoid broken blood vessels and swelling.

"Kitten, I don't know how I could have been so blind."

After a few moments, she removed the cloth and focused on him, frowning. Just which of the many totally obvious things had he finally begun to see? He smiled enigmatically.

She missed that smile when his face grew stern again. "Now, brush your teeth, take a shower, get dressed, and be ready to leave in thirty minutes."

"I'm not leaving Chicago with you, Adam."

"I didn't say anything about leaving Chicago."

"Then where are we going?"

"Instant care, emergency room, clinic, your family physician—I don't care where, but I'm not going to watch you waste away another day without finding out what's wrong."

Karla saw the intense worry in his eyes. Hell, he was scaring her now, too. It wasn't like her to be sick. She hadn't had the flu since she was fifteen. What did he think it might be? Knowing he cared helped. *Well, duh, Kitty.* Yeah, he'd always cared about her. He just didn't care as deeply as she needed him to in a romantic way.

"Adam, I need to talk with you about where I went last night."

His body tensed; he made a fist before unclenching it. Adam wasn't going to be happy to hear what she and Grant had done, even if it was for his own good.

"We'll talk later. I'll see you downstairs in twenty-eight minutes." He turned and walked into Ian's room and she scrambled up to go to the sink and complete the first of the tasks he'd given her. He certainly was acting like her Master again. Or was it her Dom? It was hard to tell the difference sometimes; but damned if she wasn't right there at his beck-and-call again, falling for Master Adam all over again.

In his car, he asked her where to take her and she pointed toward downtown. Their best hope would be instant care, but the thought of spending hours there didn't really appeal to her. Maybe her mom could pull some strings, but she worked for a pediatrician. Karla hardly qualified for that kind of medical care. A few blocks from home, Adam pulled into a fast-food restaurant drive-through.

"Oh, please don't tell me you intend for me to eat."

"That's exactly what I intend, Kitten. What do you want for breakfast to tide you over until we get back to your mom's and tackle some of those leftovers?"

Her mom had made Adam and Karla promise they'd finish up some of the food in the fridge. Both of her parents were working long shifts today.

What could she possibly order that would stay down this morning? Nothing fried or spicy, which would be half the breakfast items on the menu at this place. "How about a yogurt?" The glare he shot her across the seat told her that wasn't going to cut it. "And a short stack of pancakes?"

"Better. But we'd better go inside for that."

At the counter, he ordered about three times that much food. She hoped he planned to eat more than his fair share. At a table in the corner, with the food-laden tray beside them, he slapped butter on her pancakes and poured two containers of syrup on it before placing the Styrofoam plate in front her.

"I'm not a child. I can take care of myself."

"Then prove it. Eat."

She narrowed her eyes at him, but he just looked pointedly down at the three large pancakes and she picked up the plastic fork and knife to dig in. Surprisingly, they tasted great and did ease the queasiness in her stomach. After she began eating, he seemed to relax and dug into his sausage and pancakes himself. Suddenly, she had an urge to add the yogurt to the pancakes and scooped it over the top.

"What the fuck are you doing? You're still going to eat them, even if you do crap them up like that."

She grinned up at him. "What's it to you how I eat my pancakes?"

"Just saying you *will* finish them."

"No problem. I just suddenly had a craving to have the two of them together. So, sue me." To prove to him she intended to follow through, she picked up the fork and crammed her mouth too full with the combo she'd created. Hmmm. Not bad, she thought, as she chewed.

He rolled his eyes and dug back into his own breakfast. Maybe now was the time to tell him about last night. She swallowed, took a sip of OJ, and leaned forward. "Adam, about last night."

His jaw stopped mid-chew, and he stared at her, his fork poised mid-air. No easy way to do this, so she might as well just say it. "I found your mother. She wants to see you."

"How'd you find her?"

That was it? He wasn't surprised, even curious—or furious, as she'd expected?

"I had some...assistance."

"Whose?"

She hoped Grant would understand why Karla ratted her out, but figured the Marine could hold her own with Adam, well, unless he restrained her. The thought of him restraining anyone but Karla made her stomach churn again.

"Grant."

* * *

Grant had invaded his privacy? Adam would never have believed the former lance corporal—and friend with benefits for a few months, before Karla had come back into his life this summer—would do something like that. The woman had always been so damned loyal. What was her motive?

Karla held up her hand. "Don't blame her. She was just doing me a favor." She laid down her fork and reached out to touch his hand. "When you were in the hospital after the cougar attack, you said some things about your childhood..."

God fucking damn. "What did I say?" He shook off her hand and leaned back against the molded plastic seat he barely fit in. Karla looked hurt, before she reached out again to brush her hand gently over his forearm. The girl was like a pit bull with raw meat. He searched Karla's intense blue eyes, trying to discern what she'd learned from his mother about his past. Thank God he hadn't done to his father what he'd feared for the last month or so, because he wouldn't have been able to offer her any kind of future if he had his father's murder hanging over his head.

"Enough for me to know you didn't have a very pleasant childhood. I thought maybe that had something to do with why…well, anyway, I wanted to track down the people who had…tormented my Dom and kick their asses until they apologized."

Her Dom?

He fought to conceal a grin. "Is that so? Did you succeed?"

"Well, no. I soon realized she was just another victim of your father's abuse."

He sobered. She was, indeed. Adam held his breath as the fleeting images of the bloody scene flitted across his mind. They would never make sense to him, but at least he understood his non-aggressive part in the scene now.

But the past was the past. He couldn't change what had happened then, but after talking with his mother, he wouldn't let it continue to have power over him. Somehow, though, hearing Karla claim him as her Dom eased tension in places he'd kept closed off to emotions for a long time. He had no doubt she would be a fierce mama bear, protective of those she loved. Marc said she'd even tried to wrestle the cougar off him.

Karla had shown him nothing but love, even when he'd been a total douche bag to her. She loved him, without a doubt, making him the luckiest man who ever lived.

He wouldn't be able to live another day without her. But he'd be damned if he'd tell her he loved her in a fucking fast-food restaurant. Still, he had a confession to make.

"Keep eating. There's something I need to tell you."

She took another bite of that disgusting concoction and chewed. When she swallowed and he still hadn't spoken, she reached out to stroke his hand again. "What is it, Adam?"

He hated the thought of upsetting her when things were going better between them, but a Dom and his sub should have no secrets. She'd just said he was still her Dom, hadn't she?

"I followed you last night."

She pulled her hand back. "You what?" The pain in her eyes tore at his gut.

"I'll admit, at first it was jealousy, pure and simple. But worrying about you trumped that. After what happened on your way back from Cassie's, the thought of you driving around alone…"

"You didn't trust me. I told you…"

"Don't interrupt."

She glanced down a moment before meeting his gaze once more, a steely resolve in her fiery blue eyes.

Hurry up and fix this, jarhead.

Don't you interrupt either, Joni.

God, he was losing his fucking mind.

He ran his hand through his hair, staring at his unfinished breakfast. After a moment, he gazed up at her again. "I watched you go into the apartment, no idea who you were seeing, and then waited at the end of the hallway for you to leave. I did a lot of thinking out there. You were in there for quite a while."

"We had a lot to talk about."

"Don't think I won't turn you over my knee right here in this restaurant, if you don't hear me out before you interrupt again."

She leaned forward. "I'd like to see you try it." Adam growled. But the flush that crept up her cheeks and the dilated pupils made his balls tighten. Maybe he still had a chance with her.

"By the time you left, I was feeling like a total ass. Long before you even came out, I'd made up my mind not to go to the apartment to see who you'd been visiting. I knew you'd tell me when you were ready, if I needed to know. I did trust you, Kitten."

She smiled and he had an urge to take her out to the backseat of the rental and take her fast and hard. *Damn it, man, get your fucking head under control.* He reminded himself how sick she'd been this morning and where they were headed. But the pretty flush on her cheeks and the flaring of her nostrils didn't indicate anything but a horny woman at the moment.

God, she might as well surrender to him now—and he didn't mean sexually. Damned if he'd fuck up with her again. He may have driven to Chicago alone, but she'd be beside him for the return trip.

"There's more. I ran into my brother and sister and they dragged me in to meet my mother."

"You mean you've already met them all?"

"Yeah, and it went pretty well. I even promised I'd stop by to say goodbye before we head back to Denver. We can talk more about this later." He looked down at her near empty plate. "You finished?" He rose as he asked the question and she nodded quickly and started putting the garbage on the tray. They quickly disposed of the trash and headed out to the car.

After holding the passenger door for her and making sure she was settled in her seat, he bent down, grabbed a fist full of hair, and tilted her head back. "You fucking turned me on in there, woman." His head bent down to hers and he brushed his lips across hers for a fraction of a second before his tongue plunged into her sweet mouth. She tasted of syrup and Karla and he devoured her like a starving man. His hand reached down and into the opening of her coat to pinch her nipple. She groaned in pain, and he felt as if he'd had ice water tossed in his face.

So sensitive. What if it wasn't liver cancer? What if she had breast can...

Aw, Jesus Christ. What kind of fucking moron was he?

"Karla, when was your last period?"

With heavy-lidded eyes, she tried to focus on his face, panting for air. "Period?"

Why hadn't he put it all together before? Hell, they'd had unprotected sex twice—exactly twice as many times as it would take to get her pregnant. Vomiting in the mornings, tender nipples, wild-ass combo cravings like yogurt and pancakes. With Joni, it had been oatmeal and peanut butter. Adam grinned when he remembered some of the interesting places he'd found for her to lick the peanut butter off him. But he'd drawn the line at the oatmeal. And he wasn't too sure about yogurt and pancakes. Maybe he'd work with the syrup.

As realization dawned on her, Karla's eyes widened. "I hadn't even noticed, what with everything that's happened in the last few weeks."

Fuck. Sounded like a distinct possibility he would soon become a father—only to a tiny baby, not a grown man like the father he'd become of Damián after the war.

"How many periods have you missed?"

"Just one."

She sure did have the symptoms awfully early, but he'd still lay odds that's what was going on. How did Karla feel about having his baby? Hell, Adam would be almost seventy by the time the kid went to college. She may have sole responsibility for the child for many years without him. How could he have been so fucking irresponsible as to put her into a life-altering situation like this?

He reached out and cupped her cheek.

"I'm sorry, Karla."

* * *

Tears stung the backs of her eyes. Well, at least now she understood the frequent waterworks. Haywire hormones. "Don't say another word, Adam. Just take me home."

Obviously, he regretted they'd made a baby together—and Karla didn't need a pregnancy test to know that's what was happening to her body. She'd never missed a period, not even with the stress of Ian's funeral and those subsequent grief-stricken months.

She remembered how she'd felt after Adam had taken her virginity, hoping they'd made a baby, but just hadn't given it another thought. For him to express regret now was too much to bear. She wanted to get back to the house and just lock herself away in her room to have a good cry. Oh, God, she was going to have a baby.

Adam's baby. Her hand pressed against her abdomen. She was growing his baby inside her body. A tear splashed onto her wool coat and soaked in. And he didn't want it.

"I love you, Karla."

She shook her head. The words she'd wanted to hear forever didn't mean anything now. He was just saying them out of his sense of duty; what he thought he was supposed to say to the future mother of his child, even his unwanted and unplanned child.

"Take me home, Adam, before I get out and walk."

He sighed. How much more could she be expected to take from this man? Adam reached across her and she braced herself for his touch, but he just took the seatbelt and pulled it across her, buckling her in like a child.

Adam closed her door, walked around the back of the car, and took his seat behind the wheel. He looked over at her, huffed, and started the engine. What did he have to be angry about? They drove a few minutes until he pulled into a strip mall and parked near the drug store.

"Stay here. I'll be right back."

He closed the door and locked her in, then walked into the store. Within minutes, he'd returned to the car with a small package in his hand. She resisted the urge to peek inside. None of her business. He placed it on the floor at her feet.

Thank God her parents were working today. She needed time to regroup before she could face them. What were they going to say about her getting pregnant and not being married—or attached even—to the father? She'd never wanted to disappoint them for anything.

He double parked in front of her house, but didn't cut the engine. "I'll be back as soon as I can. Get packed, then pack my gear. We're leaving when I get back."

"Adam, I'm not…"

"Don't make me punish you, Karla. Just do as I said."

Ka-thunk!

Stop it! Stop it! Stop it!

"Isn't this called kidnapping?"

Grrrrr. Her heart pounded against her chest. Had he just growled at her, like some kind of animal? She nearly grinned, but fought the urge.

"I have to say good-bye to my parents."

"Leave them a note or call them from the road. You'll see them again soon enough."

He wasn't making any sense. Maybe he was in shock, just like she was. "But—"

Adam handed her the bag from the drug store. "Here. I want to see the results when I get back."

The familiar initials for the popular home-pregnancy test kit stared up at her from inside the bag. Was her being pregnant contingent on him wanting her? What if she wasn't? What if she faked it and told him she wasn't?

His fingers clamped around her chin and drew her in his direction. "Don't. Even. Think it."

Ka-thunk!

Well, it wasn't like she'd lied to him. She was just playing the "What If" game. Still, she wished she could go back to his thinking she was really sick or something. He'd taken such good care of her then. Now he just bossed her around as if he were her…Master or something.

Time she got one thing straight.

"Adam, I'm never going to be your slave again, except maybe in the Arabian Nights room. That role might have worked for Joni, but I'm not Joni." Her throat and chest constricted. She'd said the words she'd been dreading since she'd left Denver Sunday. She wasn't the right woman for him, baby on the way or not. "I won't keep you from your baby, though. I want him or her to know you."

You'll make such a great father.

"You're damned right about that."

Right about which "that"? That she wasn't Joni or that he would get to know his baby? The ferocity of his tone caused her to look over at him and into his piercing green eyes. She didn't want to do battle with this man over what he thought was his. He'd crush any opponent without batting an eye. "Now, hurry up. I want to get on the road as early as possible. We have a long drive ahead of us."

Karla reached for the door handle, opened her mouth to argue before shutting it again. No way was she leaving Chicago today, especially not now. She really needed to talk with her mom. But there was no point in arguing with him out here. She opened the door, got out, and walked up the steps. As she let herself inside the house, she thought how flimsy the front door would be if he decided to break it down.

Oh, who was she kidding? He wasn't going to have to break anything down. She wanted to go with him, even under these circumstances. Maybe he'd come to admit he loved her someday, as well as the baby.

No! Karla paused in front of the stairs with one foot on the first step. She'd tried to settle for less than Adam's love before. She wouldn't go there again. If he didn't love her, she wanted nothing more to do with him.

Then why did she climb the stairs, go to her room, pull out her suitcase, and begin packing? When finished, she went to Ian's room and packed Adam's duffel bag. He'd been living out of it mostly, so there wasn't a lot to pack.

Last, she returned to her room, picked up the pregnancy kit, and headed to the bathroom. She was looking down over the stick, waiting for the results, when Adam's body heat enveloped her and he wrapped his arms around her from behind. She jumped and nearly dropped the stick into the toilet. Her hand shook so badly, he placed his steady hand over hers and pulled her tight against him. Tears pricked her eyes as his other hand came to rest on her lower abdomen.

"Mine," he growled.

She didn't know if he meant her, or the baby, or both, but at that moment, the test strip revealed what they'd both already known. A sob tore from her chest, even though she'd fully expected that result. A baby. She and Adam were going to have a baby. No, she was going to have Adam's baby. She didn't have Adam. He dropped the stick into the wastebasket and wrapped his arms around her midriff, holding her against him as she cried.

"I have you, Kitten."

"But I don't have you, do I?" she whispered. Adam grew tense. She remembered the last time she'd asked and wished she hadn't spoken those needy, pathetic words again.

"I want this baby, Kitten."

She waited, but no further declaration was forthcoming. "You want the baby."

"You're fucking right I do."

"But what about me?" She shook her head and another sob wrenched from deep within.

"I've wanted this baby's mama a lot longer than I even knew about the baby. You're both mine."

What was he saying? Her head hurt too much to process so much information. She wriggled free and turned around to look up at him, but his facial features swam before her eyes. His hands trembled as he cupped her cheeks and bent down to brush his lips over hers, sending a delicious tingling throughout her body.

"I love you, Kitten. Forever."

He'd finally said the words she'd been waiting to hear her whole adult life, standing here in the bathroom of her childhood home. She couldn't think of anything more ironic. Or perfect.

Her arms reached up and wrapped around his neck, holding him closer before she'd even realized what she was doing. His tongue teased at her lips. Rather than roughly invading her mouth as he normally did, he pressed lightly with his tongue and she opened up, welcoming him.

He held her as if he were afraid she'd break. Karla pressed him against the wall and fumbled with the buttons on the fly of his jeans. She'd missed him so much. She needed him. Right here. Right now.

He stilled her hands. "No. Not here. Not now." She groaned and he chuckled. "Hang on, baby tiger, but you're going to make an honest man of me before I touch you again."

Karla pulled away and met his gaze. "What?"

He knelt to one knee and took her left hand in his. "I'm not going to risk having anything else happen before I say these words. Karla Paxton, will you marry me?"

The room began to swim and she was afraid she was going to faint, but it was only swimming because she had more tears in her eyes. From the thousands of fantasies of having Adam propose to her that had flitted through her mind since she was sixteen, never in a million years would she have scripted it like this.

She just needed to make sure of one more thing. "Adam, I have to know. Would you love me, even if I wasn't pregnant?"

He stood and his big hands gripped her shoulders to the point of pain. "Kitten, I know it's taken me a while to figure things out, but I came to Chicago to bring you home—to our home. Things just haven't gone quite the way I'd planned. It's taken me a lot longer to realize that I've been falling in love with you inch by inch since I saw you standing on the stage at the club auditioning. But haven't I been showing how much I love you for more than a month now? Do you really have to ask?"

True up to a point, now that he'd finally opened his eyes and admitted it. "You've been showing me how much you love me since I was sixteen."

The sheepish grin on his face won her heart even more. "Hold on, Kitten. I want to be perfectly clear that I didn't see you as anything more than a pesky runaway and a kid back then. I'm not a perv. You just needed someone to rescue you."

"Yes, Sir. I know—and it drove me insane. I so wanted you to notice me as a woman." She narrowed her eyes. "You don't still see me as a kid, do you?"

He gently cupped her breast. "Fucking right, I don't."

Her breath hitched as his thumb brushed lightly over her sensitive nipple. *Squeeze it, Adam.* But he didn't get rough or show any indication this would go anywhere sexual, even if they did have the house to themselves. He really intended to make her wait? For how long? *Damn him.*

She reached up to stroke his whiskered cheek. "Maybe it wasn't romantic love, but I've felt your love, all the same, since I was sixteen. You protected me from harm. You took care of my needs. You even let me down gently when I declared my love for you on our front porch and scared the shit out of you."

"That's putting it mildly."

"Don't interrupt."

He lowered his head and cast a glare at her that sent her stomach tilting and whirling again, but she continued. "You wrote to me faithfully for more than eight years, always expressing your concern for my welfare, your interest in my life, your hopes for my future."

"Karla, just like I said in the airport all those years ago, you were the one who rescued me. You became a lifeline for me when life had become so empty. But I still was in guardian mode with you then. You need a caretaker more than anyone I've ever known, hon." She glared at him and he smiled, but didn't say more.

"Then, when I came to you in July all broken and so alone," her voice cracked as she remembered how low she'd been only four months ago, "you took me in, watched over me as I slept, chased away my demons, and introduced me to grown-up love. You encouraged me to fulfill my dreams. You showed me things about myself I never would have known without you. You let me love you, Adam. And you most definitely loved me back."

"I've been falling in love ever since I came out of my nice, safe little office to find this bewitching siren auditioning at my club. I'm not sure it qualified as romantic love at that point, though, because I got a raging hard-on as I imagined having rough sex with her—pulling her hair, holding her down…"

She leaned closer to him. "Oh, it counts for me. Please, Sir. I need that now."

He chuckled and held her by her upper arms to keep her from getting too close. *Now he'd better not start that again.*

"No, Kitten. I'm not finished." He grew serious and a knot formed in her stomach. "I just had some things to work out about Joni and my past."

"And have you…worked them out, I mean?"

"Yeah. I have. I think Joni wants us to be together."

"I more than think so." He cocked his head and she continued. "Nine years ago, when I followed you to Lake Michigan on that freezing cold Thanksgiving Day, I heard this unfamiliar and very disembodied woman's voice telling me to watch over you." His eyelids narrowed, but he didn't interrupt. "Then when everything had fallen apart for me after Ian died, I heard her again saying, 'Go to Adam. He can help.' Adam, I've heard the voice more times than I can say since you came into my life."

"What makes you think it's Joni?"

She paused. "I heard it again last Saturday when you were listening to those tapes in your office, and I realized who'd been talking to me all these years."

"You heard the tapes." He closed his eyes, sighed, and opened them again. His anguished whisper brought her hand up to stroke his cheek. "What did you hear?"

Adam's face blurred in front of her. "Just enough to send me running home to my parents. She said how happy you made her as her Master." Karla's heart pounded against her chest, but they needed to clear this up before they could go any further. "You said she was the perfect slave. I thought I could try one more time to be the slave you wanted, so I devised the harem-girl scene.

But that night I realized I never could be a dutiful slave for you, the way she'd been. I couldn't compete with a…"

"Wait. You thought…?" Adam pulled her into his arms and held her tight. "Oh, Kitten, you terrified me that night. Not at first. God, I loved watching you dance for me in that harem-girl outfit. So fucking sexy. But when you told me you wanted me to be your Master in that way, I freaked out. I was so miserable in the Master role with Joni, especially at first. Luckily, we managed to modify it enough to make it at least tolerable for me. But I can never do the twenty-four/seven TPE with anyone again."

Karla pulled away, dashed the moisture from her eyes, and glared up at him. "Then why did you propose a Master/slave arrangement for us?"

He grinned. "You, baby tiger, were supposed to run kicking and screaming from the room, not kneel beside me so gracefully and submit yourself to being my slave."

She melted inside. "Oh, Adam, I wanted you to love me so badly. At that point, I think I'd have done anything to please you."

"What changed?"

"I could no longer live with myself if I lost who I was just to please a man. Even if that man was you. While I still loved you heart and soul, I needed you to accept and love me on my terms."

"God, Karla, I…"

"Hush. I'm not finished."

"Did you just tell your Dom to hush?"

"Y—" Her eyes opened wider. "My Dom?"

"You'd better believe it, Kitten. I have no desire to make you my slave, but you can't deny your submissive nature any more than I can deny I'm a dominant."

"I wasn't trying to deny it. You were the one who kept telling me I wasn't submissive. I knew from the moment you restrained me in those ropes at Marc's house the freedom of letting go of control; the excitement of letting the man I love control my body and mind like that. I knew I wanted you to do it again and again."

"The ka-thunk factor, huh?" He smiled and she grinned back.

"I can't believe I told you that. Now it's gone straight to your power-loving head."

He chuckled and brushed a thumb over her cheek. "What else do you enjoy about being a sub?"

"Well, I can't really compare the sex we had to what non-dominant sex would be like..."

"Nor will you ever. Kitten, I'm afraid you are not destined to experience vanilla sex."

"No, Sir. Nor do I want to. Everything about sex with you, submitting to you, is so intense. So perfect for me. When you go all Dom on me..."

He grinned before his eyelids narrowed and he became serious. "Dominance isn't a club-and-bedroom-only thing for me, either. I'm used to being in charge of other people. Giving orders. I don't demand total body and mind control, but with your strong, independent streak, I'm going to piss you off more often than not."

She smiled, but figured she could work on that. She'd dealt with it this long, hadn't she?

He grew even more serious. "What about discipline? That's part of the Dom/sub package. When you disobey or get too bratty for me in a scene, you'll be punished. That's how you'll learn to do what's right the next time."

A shiver went down her back. "I understand, Sir." Oh, she loved calling him Sir again. "I don't like being punished, though. It makes me feel like a child and I don't like giving you any reason to think of me in that way ever again."

The corners of his eyes crinkled as he smiled.

"But I will accept your sexual dominance over me and, if I willfully disobey in a scene, I'll accept your punishment. I didn't tell you this before, and I know it was play and not really a punishment scene, but when you paddled me in your office, I had such a cathartic release. Better even than the ritualistic ceremonies Cassie and I have been doing."

His hands brushed down her sides and around to the back to cup her ass. He pulled her lower body against his.

But she wasn't finished. "Just don't expect total obedience all the time. We'll discuss and negotiate things we disagree on, Sir, like two adults. And, while I may sometimes play the little girl for my Dom in a role-play, I'm completely grown up. Just don't confuse the two, Sir."

He grinned again and reached up to cup her breasts and gently squeezed them, avoiding the sensitive nipples. "Oh, I assure you, I don't look at you as a little girl anymore. Nothing turns me on more than when the woman in you submits to me, whether for pleasure, discipline, or punishment. Lucky for you, the school-girl fantasy never did anything for me. I'm not into Daddy Dom scening, either." His eyes became steely blue. "But seeing you as my very own seductive harem-girl, having you play Nurse Karla for me, or just having this beautiful and seductive Goth singer luring me into her mighty net with her siren's song are all the fantasies I hope to fulfill every day for the rest of our lives."

Oh that sounded so good. The rest of our lives.

"You're mine, Kitten. Now, how long do you need to plan a wedding?"

She pulled away from his arms. "An hour. We can be at the county courthouse in an hour."

Adam laughed aloud. "No, Karla. I don't want you to have any regrets. I'll give you two weeks from tomorrow. But that means we need to start home soon. I'm going to leave a letter for your parents explaining what I intended to say to them when I asked for your hand."

He said when, not if. She smiled. He was so old-fashioned. She so wasn't. Oh, she hoped he wasn't looking for a satin-and-lace kind of wedding day, although she did intend to see him in his dress blues, at long last. Well, maybe she could wear satin for him—and a scrap of lace.

"I hope we'll have your parents' blessing, but nothing they could say or do would ever keep me from marrying you. They're just going to have to get on board the USS *Montague*, because we're setting sail and heading into the sunset and there will be nothing but fair winds and smooth seas wherever we go."

Okay, up to a point, but smooth seas sounded a little too dull. "But I like it rough, Sir." She reached down to cup his crotch and felt his erection, smiling at his pained expression.

He grabbed her hand. "I said, not now, Kitten."

Ka-thunk! Her nipples hardened and she found it hard to expand her lungs. She reached up and began unbuttoning his jacket and then his shirt.

Adam grabbed her hands and halted her movements. "What do you think you're doing?"

"I'm going to take these clothes off you, Sir, and have my way with you."

He didn't release her hands. "We're not having sex, Karla. I don't want to hurt the baby."

She stepped back and pointed her index finger at him. "Adam Montague, if you think for one minute I'm going to go seven months or more without sex, then I...I may have to resort to tying you to our bed to have my needs met."

His pupils dilated and she wondered if perhaps he would enjoy that. Hmmm.

"Don't even think it, Kitten. Now, get dressed. We need to get going. You have a wedding to plan. I don't want you waddling down the aisle to me about ready to drop a baby in my lap."

Karla giggled at the image he conjured up and wondered what she'd look like nine months along. He swatted her bottom, which only made her more determined they weren't leaving this house without having sex.

"Wait for me in your room, Sir. I'll be there in two shakes."

* * *

Adam sat on Ian's rack and took the ring from his pocket. He'd run over to his mother's not to get a ring, but to ask for the keys to Johnny and Kate Montague's 1880s Deadwood cabin. There was no other place he wanted to honeymoon with Karla than the cabin that had been such a happy place for him growing up.

When he'd told his mother he was intending to get hitched, and had gotten her assurance she'd be in Denver for the ceremony, she'd gone to her jewelry box and pulled out the ring that his great-great-grandfather had given to his Irish bride all those years ago. Johnny had been much older than Kate, too—and they'd lived a long, happy life. He wanted the omen of longevity on his side. The ring might be pretty plain by today's bigger-is-better standards, but it was steeped in love.

Tradition had it that Johnny had mined the pink-tinted gold himself right there in the Black Hills and had the ring made for Kate by a local craftsman. Adam needed all the omens and luck he could get for as many years as possible together with Karla—and this baby and any other children they might be blessed with. But he'd learned with Joni there were no guarantees in life. They'd just have to grab life by the balls and…

When he heard the bathroom door open, he pocketed the wedding ring again and turned toward the door, expecting to see her standing there, but she didn't appear. Thinking she wanted him to carry her luggage downstairs, he picked up his seabag and walked into the bathroom. He tapped on the door to her room.

"Open sesame."

He did as she bid him and there, lying on the bed on her side, dressed in the red harem-girl outfit she'd worn for him the other night was Karla, her face half covered in a veil and her left knee tented, revealing her long shapely legs and thighs and just a glimpse of her bare pussy. His dick rose to a full salute faster than he'd ever known it to before.

What the...?

"Karla, we have a long drive ahead of us." His voice sounded as if she had him in a chokehold.

"We have some unfinished business first."

"I told you I wasn't..."

Karla rose from the bed in one fluid motion, amazingly agile. Playing to music heard only in her head, she began to undulate her hips and belly as she made her way across the room toward him. She lifted the veil up over her head, holding it by both ends, then flung it behind his neck and drew his face down to hers, thrusting her tits toward him.

"Karla..."

Her lips brushed against his. She smiled. *Damn her.* How was he supposed to keep his head when she teased him like that? He managed to pull away, but his gaze lowered to her tits, barely covered in her beaded bra. She grabbed his forearm, whether to pull him toward her or keep him from running, he wasn't sure. Fiddling with the end of the veil, she wrapped it around his right wrist. His gaze went even lower, across her still-flattened abdomen to where her hips flared. The bumping of her bangled hips lured him into her net better than any sailor's snare ever could. The red scarves that made up her skirt hid her charms again, thank God. He wasn't going to indulge in his baser needs today.

She pulled him by the wrist toward her twin bed. *No, Kitten. This isn't going to happen.* Karla was pregnant and he wasn't going to do anything to jeopardize the safety of this pregnancy. Joni said their stillborn son's umbilical cord had formed a knot, probably when he'd done a somersault months before, the doctor had said, which had cut off the oxygen during delivery.

Adam had always blamed himself for getting too rough with her during her seventh month, right before he'd left for Kuwait. No, sex in the later months would be strictly off limits. Even now, he didn't want to risk it.

So, why didn't his feet get the message and stop following her? Karla continued to hold onto the veil he now realized had been secured onto his wrist. She danced around him, twirling him around until the backs of his knees pressed against the mattress on her rack. When she pushed against his chest to try to get him to lie down, he stood his ground. Next thing he knew, she'd hooked his calf with her heel and ankle, much like she'd downed Julio, and he went tumbling backwards. The rack creaked and he was afraid they'd broken it.

Damn. Why did the image of sparring playfully with Karla—after the baby was born, of course—turn him on so much? They'd enjoyed that at the martial-arts center last month, for sure.

Before he could recover from the loss of his equilibrium—and maybe his mind—she tugged his arm toward the headboard, continuing to shake her hips in a delightful way before his eyes. Everything dimmed to the background and all he could focus on were her hips moving that way, her tits, her sexy body. But when he reached for her breasts, he found that only one of his arms obeyed.

What the f...?

Looking up at the headboard, he discovered his right wrist had been skillfully restrained to a knob on the post by her veil. Hell, he'd been outflanked.

"Karla, what the fuck do you think you're doing?"

"Pleasing my Master."

She smiled her seductive, all-woman smile and shimmied her tits toward him. His dick grew harder. She reached out to unbuckle his belt and undo the buttons at the fly of his jeans.

"Karla..."

"Yes, Master?"

"Remember what happened the last time you disobeyed? You will be punished for this—just as soon as you let me go."

"Is that a promise, Master?"

His dick sprang from the opening of his fly and into her hot little hands. Oh, she'd better believe it was a promise. But if she enjoyed orgasm torture so much, maybe he needed to use something a little less desired. He may only have his hands and his belt on him, but either would deliver what she needed in the form of punishment for daring to restrain him like this.

Her hands cupped his balls and she lowered her mouth to his dick, which bobbed in greeting as her tongue encircled the head. *Sweet Jesus, Mary, and Joseph.* He wasn't going to be able to stand much of this before he embarrassed himself.

"Release my arm, Karla. Now."

She didn't remove her lips from his throbbing dick right away, but met his gaze and smiled in the most seductive way before she hand-fisted him as her mouth let go of him with a plop. "Yes, Master. I'll be happy to help you find release."

"You're not going to be able to sit for the drive to Denver when my belt gets finished with your ass."

She sobered at the mention of his belt. Good. If she'd release him now, he'd go easy on her.

"No buckles, Sir."

Damn you, woman! "You won't be in a position to determine which end I use on you, Kitten." Of course, he'd never use the buckle on her delicate skin. And would only use enough force to make her bottom pink—maybe add a few temporary stripes. But she didn't need to know that. Maybe fear of the buckle would finally get her to obey him.

Hardly. She tilted her chin up in a delightful show of defiance. "I'll take that chance. I've missed you too much, Sir." Her hand tightened around his shaft as she stroked the length of him.

Oh, hell. Who was he kidding? How could he deny her what they both wanted? Maybe if he didn't go in for the rough stuff, he wouldn't hurt the baby. It was still so tiny at this point and he had months to go before he'd have to swear off sex with his baby tiger. But, restrained or not, he was still her Dom.

"Straddle me, Kitten."

She grinned. "I thought you'd never ask, Sir."

With his free hand, he reached up to help her mount him.

Karla parted her skirt, giving him a tantalizing glimpse of her creamy-white mound, and lowered herself onto his rod. As her tight, wet warmth enveloped him, inch by slippery inch, he realized with Karla he'd never know what to expect. Life would no longer be dull and predictable, as it had been until she'd shown up on the stage at his club. Thank God. She'd brought him back to life.

He may not know up from down—or Top from bottom, he thought, as he gripped the veil tying his wrist to her rack—but with Karla at his side loving him, as long as he lived, he'd know he loved her, and would make sure she knew it, too.

Now and forever.

* * *

Karla looked down at Adam, smiling up at her. For the first time since she'd stood in her apartment in New York and made up her mind to find Adam, she was at peace. Her world without Ian in it had righted itself. If they had a boy, she was certain Adam would agree to name him Ian.

Adam's hips bucked up and she smiled, realizing she'd lost her focus for a minute, but he commanded her attention once more. She seated herself on him fully, the bangles on her bra shimmying as she pumped up and down on his penis. So full. But something was missing. She needed...

"Remove the bra."

Her clit zinged. Oh, yes, she needed Adam to control her again. Succeeding at tying him to the bed was exhilarating and she loved the sense of power, but the sex wouldn't be nearly as powerful as when he was in charge. She reached both hands behind her and released the hooks and slid the beaded garment off. Her breasts felt swollen, bigger than they'd been just a month ago. She enjoyed the size, but they were so damned tender now. The thought of his putting nipple clamps on her would probably send her howling like a cat in heat.

With his free hand, he reached up and pinched her nipple. The exquisite pain sent another zing to her clit. Or maybe not. Karla reached up and pulled on the loose knot in the veil until she'd released his wrist. Adam wasted no time reversing their positions, although she could tell he was holding back as he thrust his penis inside her, even as he pulled back and entered her again.

More. Why didn't he take her the way he had before? "Harder, Master." She reached up and pulled his hair, hoping he'd know she needed that, too.

He stopped and looked conflicted for a moment, but when she thrust her hips up at him, he took her hair in his fist and pulled her head back, then plunged his tongue into her open mouth. *Yes!* This was what she needed. Her Adam.

He pulled his mouth and penis from her at the same time and cupped her breast as he slid down her body to suckle on her ultra-sensitive nipple and nip at her swollen areola. "Oh, God, yes! Don't stop!" Her hands gripped the sides of his head, holding him in place.

He growled and removed his mouth. "Hands above your head."

She obeyed and he trailed tiny bites and kisses along her abdomen, where he stopped for a moment and placed a reverent kiss over her lower abdomen, before he continued his carnal exploration. She opened for him as he reached her mons, no longer worried he might not like kissing her pussy. She needed his lips and tongue on her. She needed release.

His thumbs spread open her cleft and his tongue teased the sides and top of her hood, carefully avoiding her clit.

"I want you shaved all the time, Kitten. So fucking sexy."

"Yes, Sir." She thrust her hips upward, trying to make contact with his mouth, his lips, his tongue.

"Lie still."

His command elicited a groan from her, but she grabbed onto the pillow above her and held on, willing her hips to remain still, too. Easier said than done. She needed to move. She needed him moving inside her.

"Take me, Master! Now!"

He stopped and she looked down to find him scowling at her. "I'm on top now, Kitten. Don't forget your place again."

Ka-thunk!

"No, Sir. I'm sorry. I didn't mean to be a bad li'l kitten." She stuck her lower lip out.

He groaned and abandoned her pussy to stretch out over her again. "Brace yourself, Kitten."

She held onto the pillow in an iron grip and he rammed himself into her to the hilt. "Oh, God! Thank you, Sir!" Again and again, he battered against her pubic bone. She'd have bruises tomorrow, but didn't care. She wanted him to take her and take her roughly. The way they both loved it.

His finger slid between their bodies and stroked her erect clit. "Come with me, baby tiger."

"Yes, Master…oh, yes, Adam!"

Always.

Chapter Twenty-Three

Karla leaned over the banister and saw several Marines in dress blues, their hats—no, they called them *covers*—and gloves tucked under their arms, chatting with Rosa, Teresa, and José. The entire downstairs of Marc's house was filled to capacity with all those who loved her and Adam.

Her parents stood nearby talking with Mrs. Gallagher, Adam's mother, and his sister Megan and brother Patrick. Patrick wore his Marine uniform, having carried on the family tradition, as well. She was so happy everyone had hit it off when they'd gone out to dinner last night. Karla really liked the Gallaghers and hoped Adam would get a chance to get to know them better. Daddy looked up and winked at her and she smiled back. She hadn't really prepared anyone for what to expect today, least of all Adam.

Adam had contacted his buddies from his twenty-five years of service, including some who had served under him in Afghanistan and Iraq. She'd been pleased that the Richardsons, the couple they'd stayed with at Camp Pendleton last month, were able to attend. She had no idea how word had spread so quickly among them but, judging by all the men and women in uniform milling about downstairs, Adam must have been surprised and pleased that so many Marines had made the trip. Some had only arrived home from duty in recent days, she'd learned from Marc last night. Such a fitting tribute to show the love and respect they had for the man who gave so much of his life to the Corps and to serving his country. Her chest swelled with pride at the thought of becoming this hero's wife.

She heard the guitar intro of "Your Guardian Angel" playing, knowing it wouldn't be long now. She and Adam had been guardians for each other and would continue to do so for the rest of their lives. Only now they'd have a baby to guard over together, too. Her hand rested on the beaded satin fabric covering her lower abdomen. Unbelievable.

She stepped away from the railing, knowing that was the second-to-last song on her playlist before she would go down the stairway and become a part of Adam's life forever. The last two weeks had been like a dream and a nightmare combined as she'd made the whirlwind arrangements for this monumental day.

Don't puke, Kitty.

Her mom said the nausea had only lasted until about the third month for both of her pregnancies. Karla hoped that meant she only had another month to go. She couldn't wait until she could start enjoying the "glow" and natural high pregnant women were supposed to experience. Her mom also said she'd noticed that glow at the Thanksgiving table, but Karla couldn't imagine what she'd been looking at. Glowing didn't describe what she'd been feeling that day.

So far, so good today, though. She'd thrown up first thing this morning, as usual, but had kept her yogurt-slathered pancakes down and was now looking forward to enjoying all the great-smelling food Angie had prepared for the reception. *And the cake! Oh, my God!* While Angie wasn't a pastry chef, she had a friend from school who was and he'd made the most beautiful three-tiered wedding cake for them.

Everything had come together so perfectly, considering the short notice they'd given everyone. She turned to Cassie, dressed in a white Peruvian lacy blouse and peasant skirt, red ribbons streaming from her beautiful dark brown hair. "You're sure about this, Kitty?"

Cassie had arrived last night, too, and they'd stayed up half the night talking, most of the time spent with Karla trying to convince Cassie that Adam was right for her.

"Oh, Cassie, I hope you'll get to know him better. I've never known anyone better suited for me than Adam. I love him with all my heart." Karla stroked her friend's soft cheek. "I hope you'll find your Adam someday, too."

"I'm not looking for a man. I'm happiest when I'm alone, up at my cabin."

Oh, Cassie, I miss all the fun we had in those early years back in college. But that Cassie was dead. She loved her friend, no matter what, and was so happy she'd be here as her maid of honor today.

Cassie adjusted Karla's red rhinestone necklace. "Wait 'til he sees you, Kitty. He won't be able to keep his eyes off you. You're sure he'll be okay with this?" Cassie pointed behind them.

Karla grinned. "He might as well get used to it, Cass. He isn't getting a traditional wife."

Angie laughed as she came up beside them. "Keep them on their toes, ladies. It's what they want secretly." She also wore a white peasant skirt and blouse. Karla hadn't wanted either of them to go to the expense of buying outfits they may not wear again. When both told her they had almost matching outfits, Karla thought that would look just fine.

Angie's long tresses were bound in a hair corset Marc had fashioned for her this morning. He'd used a red ribbon that matched the ones in Cassie's hair. Of course, Cassie wouldn't let him near her, so she'd left hers down. But they both were beautiful just as they were.

Angie laughed again. "He'll never be the same—thank God—but he doesn't seem to mind a bit that you've turned his world upside down in such a short time. Marc said you're what's been missing from his life for a very long time." She gave Karla a quick peck on the cheek. "So, do you want me to call your escorts upstairs now?"

"I'm ready." Karla had never been more ready for anything in her life.

"But first, thanks again Angie, for the incredible food you prepared. If I live to be a hundred, I'll never be able to cook like you do."

Angie smiled and hugged her again. "Tell you what. I'll leave the singing to you and you can leave the cooking to me. Now, I'd better get them before Adam wears a hole in Marc's hard-wood floors."

Minutes later, Angie led Karla's four uniformed escorts up the stairs. Each was dressed in formal military attire—Marc, Damián, Grant, and Patrick. She'd learned a lot about military weddings lately and had tried to incorporate as many of those traditions into their day as possible. Not that she'd conformed and gone completely traditional.

Damián looked so handsome in his uniform with his swarthy good looks. She was so happy he'd been able to fly his entire family out here, with some help from her father booking the flight for Rosa and the kids. Of course, he'd ridden his Harley back from California. Karla wouldn't have gone through with the wedding without Adam's adopted son by his side. She'd have just postponed it, not that Adam would have been very happy about that.

He'd refused to give in again on their biggest disagreement since they'd returned from Chicago. No sex until after they were married. He'd become an old-fashioned spoilsport all of a sudden, but she knew he was as ready as she was for tonight.

Next up, Marc, who had served on the ground in Iraq with Adam's unit as its Corpsman. Dressed in his Navy blues, he marched over to her and bent to kiss her on both cheeks in his old-world Italian style. When he stood and looked down at her, he grinned. "That man isn't going to know what hit him. But I, for one, sure am happy you finally knocked some sense into him, Karla."

She smiled up at him. "You've been my champion ever since he was in the hospital, Marc. Thank you—for everything."

"You deserve all the thanks. I love that man like a brother." His voice choked and tears formed in her eyes as she remembered the tattoo on Adam's back memorializing Marc's brother, Gino. "I know you'll take good care of him."

Marc stepped back and Damián stepped up to give her a peck on the cheek. "Dad's pacing like a caged panther down there, you know. I'm just glad it was you who captured his heart, *querida*."

Karla gave him a hug and kissed him on the cheek. "I'm so glad he has you, too, Damián. You'll always be his special son. And I know you'll be an awesome big brother to our baby."

Karla and Adam hadn't kept the baby a secret from their closest family members. Of course, everyone would know soon enough, and if anyone thought that was the only reason they were marrying, well, who cared? Adam loved her for herself. That's all that mattered.

Karla noticed Grant standing awkwardly to the side. She'd never seen the woman appear nervous before. Karla walked over to her on silent feet. "Mistress Grant, thank you for taking such good care of Adam until I could take over." The woman visibly relaxed, accepting a reassuring squeeze from Karla's hand. "And thanks for bringing his mother back into his life." Reuniting Adam with his mother had helped him put to rest so many of the torments of the past, and went a long way toward making him able to move on, unsaddling so much of the grief from the past. Now he had siblings, too.

The female Marine smiled and executed a salaam and a bow before Karla. "Thank you for making my master sergeant so happy." She sobered. "There was never anything serious between us, you know. We clash in too many ways. I was just safe. No emotional strings. That's the way we both wanted it. As soon as you came back into his life, I can state unequivocally he's only had eyes for you. As it should be. You're so perfect for him."

Karla smiled, hugged the woman, and then turned to Patrick, who walked over to her. He stood nearly as tall as Adam and bent to kiss her cheek. "I'm looking forward to getting to know my brother and his wife better in the years to come."

They shared a laugh and Karla turned to let Cassie adjust Karla's veil over her face; Angie pulled back the curtains for Karla to crawl onto the litter just as the Middle Eastern strains of "Bird of Paradise" began to play from below.

She nodded. "I'm ready." *Dear Lord, was she ever ready. Watch out, Master, here I come.*

She adjusted her silver satin harem skirt over her bare legs, tucked her feet under her bottom, feeling the beads on her silver slippers biting into her ass. At least she hadn't incurred any more punishments since they'd returned from Chicago. His belt had been brutally painful, even though she knew he could have made it much worse if he'd had his heart in it. He'd enjoyed every minute of her restraining him, though, despite his feeble protests. That's probably why he hadn't used the buckle on her. She shuddered, in a bad way, to think what that would be like.

But playtime had been nonexistent since Chicago, too, what with all the wedding plans. Tonight that would change. She couldn't wait.

The bodice she and her mother had decorated had cap sleeves and covered her midriff. She didn't want any of their guests to have a heart attack if she'd shown up in nothing but a beaded bra and harem skirt. She and her mother had beaded the thing until their fingers were raw, but it was beautiful, gold beading and trim against the silver satin. Her mother had nixed the idea of red and black fabric and beads, and even cringed at Karla's insistence on mixing silver and gold, but hadn't said another word knowing it could be much worse.

Karla made sure she had the veil adjusted to cover only her nose and the lower half of her face. She wanted nothing obscuring her view of Adam once she alighted from this contraption. The four uniformed escorts each took a post, one at each handle of the gilt-edged harem litter she'd rented from a specialty shop in Denver, and at Marc's command lifted in unison.

Karla hoped Damián's prosthesis would support him on the stairs, but he'd insisted on being among those who carried her to Adam, and she wouldn't deny him anything after all he meant to Adam. He'd taken up a position in the rear, so that the bulk of her weight would be on Marc and Patrick.

Angie walked down the stairs first, then Cassie. Karla's heart pounded as the litter bearers began to march slowly down the stairs. The view of the city's skyline spread out before her as they approached the first landing. She hoped they could find a house as comfortable as this one. Adam had told her they'd be house hunting just as soon as they returned from their honeymoon. He still hadn't told her where they were headed on their wedding trip, only that it would take them about a day to drive there, if the weather held up. She really didn't care where they went, as long as she was with him.

The litter bearers made the turn on the landing, and then proceeded down the next set of stairs. She looked up and saw Adam as a bit of a blur through the litter's curtains and perhaps a few tears. He stood straight and tall, magnificent and dashing in his dress blues—cover and gloves tucked under his arm, sword in its scabbard, and his jaw hanging open. She smiled, loving his reaction. Quickly, he regained his composure and grinned back at her, then his body relaxed and he shook his head. Clearly, he wanted her to shake up his life as much as she wanted to do it.

Titters of laughter and murmurs reached her ears, and she heard her mother whisper, "That's my girl." Karla couldn't take her eyes off Adam. A sudden and unfamiliar shyness enveloped her, and she smiled. She'd never seen him in his uniform, except in his portrait—so handsome, proud, and honorable. Her Adam. At last. Tears blurred her vision.

Damn. No tears. Not today. This was the happiest day of her life.

As the litter was lowered to the floor, Cassie and Angie lifted the curtains and each held out a hand to help her exit its confines and stand. Her parents came to stand in front of her and she looked up at her father, who also had tears in his eyes. *Oh, dear.* Now she stood no chance of maintaining her composure. Daddy never cried. She stood on her slippered toes to kiss him.

"I love you, Daddy," she whispered through her constricted throat.

"I love you, too, sweetheart. I can't believe my little girl is all grown up. Just assure me this is what you want and that you're happy."

She took his hand and squeezed it. "Oh, Daddy, Adam completes me. I've never been happier in my life."

He hugged her and kissed her cheek through the veil. Then she hugged her mother, who also had tears in her eyes. If they didn't stop with all the crying, Karla would be a blubbering mess by the time she joined Adam. But she didn't care anymore if she cried. She couldn't wait a minute longer to be united forever with the man she loved. She turned toward Adam as he handed his cover and gloves to Damián who stood on his left.

Captain Reed, the Navy chaplain, waited on Adam's right. In addition to his many ribbons, she noticed the golden cross on his collar. He smiled and asked, "Who gives this woman to be united in holy matrimony?"

Her father's voice quavered as he answered, "Her mother and I do."

Then Adam stepped forward to meet her, his elbow crooked for her, and the waterworks began in earnest. She would have stumbled if he hadn't reached out to steady her, then he tucked her hand in his elbow and placed his warm hand over her cold one.

Home.

Her chin quivered as they stepped closer to the chaplain. The next part of the ceremony was a complete blur. All that registered was that she promised to love, honor, and obey Adam and he promised to love, honor, and cherish her. Nothing else mattered.

"The rings, please," Captain Reed asked. Damián and Cassie handed them to Adam and Karla and they held them in their cupped and open hands as the chaplain made the sign of the cross over them and said a blessing. Her ring for Adam was a bright shiny platinum. She hadn't wanted yellow gold like the one he wore for Joni. But her attention was riveted on his large hand holding the burnished ring of pink-tinted gold. How unusual. She'd never seen anything like it.

Adam's hand trembled as he placed the beautiful ring over her first knuckle, and said, "Karla, this ring is a token of my love and faithfulness to you, always and forever." His fingers shook even more as he pressed it over her wider knuckle. A perfect fit. How had he known? "This ring brought my great-great-grandmother many years of happiness and I hope it does the same for us, love."

Adam loved his mother's family heritage, especially these ancestors she'd come to learn more about on the long drive from Chicago. They mirrored her and Adam in so many ways, including their age difference. She blinked rapidly, not wanting to miss a moment of this for anything, but so overwhelmed by the emotions she was feeling, the greatest of which was Adam's love.

Taking a deep breath, she reached for Adam's hand, warm and comforting, and took his hand in hers, placing the ring over the first knuckle of his finger, much as he had done hers.

"Adam, this ring is a symbol of my love and faithfulness to you and I promise to be your wife, your partner, your lover—always and forever." She held onto Adam's hand like a lifeline, never wanting to let go, and smiled up into his moss-green eyes.

The chaplain addressed their friends and family next. "Will you who are present here today surround this couple in love, offering them the joys of your friendship?"

"We will."

"Will you support this couple in their relationship? At times of conflict, will you offer them the strength of your wisest counsel and the comfort of your thoughtful concern? At times of joy, will you celebrate with them, nourishing their love for one another?"

"We will."

Hearing the love and support filling the room, and with Adam standing at her side, Karla couldn't help but know she was the luckiest woman alive.

"By the power vested in me by the State of Colorado, I now pronounce you husband and wife."

* * *

Adam had told the padre earlier he didn't need anyone telling him when it was time to kiss his bride. He'd know. So he reached out and unhooked the left side of the silver veil to reveal the luscious lips of his beautiful, sexy harem girl and bent down to brush his mouth against hers, then took her hair corset and pulled gently, but firmly, to open her mouth to him.

He heard the titters of their friends and family, but most of them knew which way he swung. Damn it, he hadn't kissed her or even touched her since they'd returned to Denver. She'd been staying here at Marc's, tied up in preparations for the wedding. Obviously, she'd been busy. When he'd seen them carrying the harem litter down the stairs, he'd nearly lost it.

Only Karla.

Mine.

He deepened the kiss and heard the chaplain clear his throat, but didn't care. He wasn't finished. She wrapped her arms around his neck and pulled him closer. *That's my girl.*

He broke off the kiss with great reluctance and whispered in her ear, "Tonight, you will surrender to your sheikh totally and completely, baby tiger." When Karla's knees buckled, he steadied her and pulled away to gauge her reaction, seeing the smoldering desire and dilated pupils. No doubt, they mirrored his own eyes.

The sound of the guests tore his focus away from his gorgeous bride. A flurry of activity ensued, from going through the buffet line and getting the guests eating to spending the next hour or so greeting those who had joined them for their special day. To say he was surprised at the number of active and retired Corps members on hand was an understatement. When he'd put the word out to his Facebook group, he'd never expected so many of them to drop everything to be here. *Semper Fi.*

Angelina approached them and, in a stage whisper, asked Karla, "Are you ready to cut the cake?"

Karla nodded and hooked her hand into the crook of Adam's elbow. They followed the chef who had pulled off an amazing feast for their friends on extremely short notice. The woman would be a catch for any restaurant or catering business in town. Maybe she'd land a job as a result of today's event. He knew it was bothering her that she didn't have a job yet, although she still had some events in her hometown of Aspen Corners that she was obligated to do as part of her catering business there.

Adam had been too nervous to look around the room much, so this was the first chance he'd gotten to see the cake. It stood three tiers tall, columns lifting the top tier above the others, and what looked like fresh red roses decorated the base. The cake topper caught his eye and he chuckled. It showed a groom in Marine dress blues carrying a harem girl dressed in red. How she'd managed to get that done on such short notice, he had no idea, but had learned to never doubt the resourcefulness of his wife. He laid his cover and gloves on the table nearby.

When Angelina picked up a knife, Adam drew his sword and smiled as Karla waved away the knife. Ah, so his bride had done her homework on military wedding ceremonies, which pleased him greatly.

He presented the sword to her and she nibbled her lower lip as she looked at the cake, seeming to determine how best to tackle the task at hand. Then she grinned and leaned toward him to whisper, "Fear not, Your Excellency. I watched a YouTube video on how to do this."

"Well, I know how much you've learned from online videos in the past, so I have no doubt you'll be a pro at this, as well, in no time."

Karla blushed the prettiest shade of pink and he grinned, knowing she remembered exactly which video he was talking about. She smiled up at him.

"Excellency, if you would be so kind as to guide my hand."

He placed his hand over hers and they cut a piece from the top tier. Taking the slice into his hand, he broke off a piece and fed it to his wife. He looked forward to feeding her many, many times in their years to come.

Karla took a piece and threatened playfully to smear it across his face, but at his growl, she held it patiently to his lips, waiting for him to open. He nipped her fingers in the process of taking a bite. He couldn't wait to get her to the honeymoon suite he'd reserved downtown. They wouldn't hit the road until the morning, probably late morning, if he left her as exhausted tonight as he intended. God, he'd missed her.

Afterward, as he and Karla continued to make the rounds greeting their guests, he caught sight of Staff Sergeant Anderson. Adam scanned the room looking for Marc. Luke and Grant were tending bar, as Angelina and Cassie served the cake. Finally, he found Marc pouring champagne at a table in the corner of the dining room. Damned if he wasn't serving bubbly to Marc's Gramps and Karla's grandma, the two of them with their heads bent toward each other as they shared a toast and a laugh. Love was in the air for more than the bride and groom today. Age didn't matter. It was never too late to love. He squeezed Karla's hands, so blessed that he had her.

But he needed to do something right now without her. "Excuse me for a minute, Kitten, but I need to make some long overdue introductions." He bent down to kiss her lips—big mistake. After a few moments, he broke it off while he still could and sent Karla off to talk with her parents. When Marc looked in his direction, Adam motioned for him to come over.

Marc grabbed a couple of champagne flutes and came over to them. "Yes, Top." Adam stared at him for going all formal. "Sorry, it's the uniform. Old habits and all." Marc grinned. "Where's your wife? Surely you haven't ticked her off already."

"No, she's not tired of me yet." He glanced over at her and saw her looking at him with longing. Her come-hither smile just about did him in, but he forced himself to turn back to Marc. "There's someone I want you to meet. From Kandahar." Marc's sobering expression told him he knew who that would be.

"I'd like that very much."

They walked over to Anderson who stood with his petite Filipino wife and a little girl who must be ten now. Anderson introduced his wife and daughter, and then Adam indicated Marc.

"Anderson, there's someone who's been wanting to meet you for a long time, but the opportunity just never arose. This is a Navy Corpsman who served in my unit in Fallujah."

Marc extended his hand to the man. "Marc D'Alessio. Adam tells me you were with my brother, Gino, when he was killed."

Mrs. Anderson gasped and tears came to her eyes. She placed a protective arm around her daughter and her arm behind Anderson's back. He shook

Marc's hand. "Your brother saved my life. I can't tell you how sorry I am he was killed. I think of him every day and the sacrifice he made."

"When Adam told me what happened and about you having a wife and baby back home..." Marc smiled at the little girl and her mom, "...I know my brother would have made the same decision ten times over."

Karla slipped up beside him. He didn't really want her to have to hear this conversation, but couldn't very well tell her to shove off. He introduced her to the Andersons.

"Mrs. Montague, your husband was a hero to the men in my unit who were caught in a bloody ambush in Kandahar. Knowing him, he probably never told you anything about that."

Fuck. He *really* didn't need her to hear this. "Anderson, it was good to see you and your family and thanks for coming, but I think Karla and I need to..."

"Tell me more, Staff Sergeant Anderson. I always want to know more about my husband's military service."

Adam grew more and more uncomfortable as Anderson recounted his actions that day, losing two of the men in the unit that had been ambushed, taking shrapnel to the back.

"So, you're confirming what I've known all along." Karla turned to Adam and smiled, pride shining in her eyes. "My husband is truly a hero—and I'm not the only one who thinks so."

Adam shook his head. Apparently she hadn't heard the part about the men he'd lost. No convincing her otherwise, he could at least distract her. He took her by the arm, "If you'll excuse us, I think my wife and I need to be thinking about shoving off soon." Marc quickly excused himself, as well, and hurried off in the direction of the foyer.

"Kitten, if I hear one more thing about heroes, I'll take my belt—buckle and all—to your soft ass." She giggled. *Damn her.* His balls tightened. "Run upstairs and change. But bring the harem costume with you. You'll need it tonight."

She practically ran up the stairs—well he had told her to, hadn't he?—and he enjoyed watching her ass mold against the satin harem shirt.

"I thought I told you not to let her get away."

Adam didn't have to turn to know Richardson had approached. The two had served together in the first Gulf War and had remained friends. When he'd taken Karla on base last month to meet him, Adam had wanted to have his friend ask him what the fuck he was thinking being with a woman half his age.

Instead, his buddy had practically told him to propose to her before he left the base.

"Don't worry, you old devil dog, I'm only letting her out of my sight for short periods at a time."

Richardson grew serious. "I just want you to know I'm glad you got your head out of your ass before you lost her. I knew from the minute I met her she'd make sure your life would never be the same—thank God. Now, if you'll excuse me, duty calls."

Fifteen minutes later, after Adam had quickly made the rounds thanking everyone who had played some part in making this wedding day special, especially for Karla, he noticed a number of his buddies had disappeared, including Richardson. He grinned. Of course.

He sought out his mother and made sure she didn't go out in the cold for the final ceremony and found her talking with Marge.

"Well, son," Marge looked over at his mother and said, "I'm sorry. Old habits."

His mother waved away her concern. "Nonsense. I'm glad Adam had someone to mother him all those years we were separated." The two women smiled at each other and he thought he saw the beginnings of a friendship forming.

Marge turned to him once more. "Anyway, Adam, I just wanted you to know I'm so happy for you. Karla's everything you deserve." He saw a twinkle in his former mother-in-law's eye, and he smiled.

"That she is."

After telling them it would be best if they stayed inside where it was warm, he guided them to a window at the front of the house where they could observe the formal farewell. As he turned toward the foyer, he heard them continuing their conversation where they'd left off at his interruption.

Minutes later, in the foyer, he looked up to see Karla coming down the stairs wearing a black cocktail dress and carrying a small suitcase. He ran up the stairs to take the luggage from her. "You shouldn't be lifting that."

She rolled her eyes. "Adam, there's hardly anything in it. Besides, I'm not an invalid, you know."

"You just promised to obey me, so starting now, new rule: No heavy lifting."

She sighed. "Yes, Sir. But that wasn't heavy."

He rolled his eyes. Keeping this woman under his thumb was going to be next to impossible, but he had a lifetime to work on training her. "Let's go."

"But I haven't had a chance to say goodbye to my parents or your mother or..."

"You'll see them soon enough. We'll stop by tomorrow to say goodbye before we head off on our honeymoon."

She quirked an eyebrow, but turned to allow him to wrap her cape around her shoulders, pulling her hair corset out and letting it drop with a thud against her back. Memories of the floggers he'd used on her came to mind and she couldn't wait to get him alone. He wrapped his arm around her, picked up her suitcase, and they headed toward the front door. Adam put his cover on his head and managed to get his gloves on before the command was given.

"Center face!" The officers and NCOs who had been gathering at the front of the house formed two facing lines. "Draw swords!"

"Oh, my!" He looked down at his bride, whose eyes were open wide. She looked up at him. "Did you know about this?"

"I had my suspicions."

"I read about it online, but didn't have the first clue how to figure out who was eligible to be in the arch, so I just didn't think about it any further."

"My guess is, this is Marc's doing."

Their friends and family were gathered on the lawn, with snow flurrying around them.

Chaplain Reed, who had been giving the commands, announced, "Ladies and gentlemen, may I present Master Sergeant and Mrs. Montague."

"Ready, Baby Tiger?"

"Ready and willing, Sir."

The two of them walked side-by-side, arm-in-arm under the saber arch. As they approached the end of the arch, the fourth and final pair of swords lowered, blocking their path.

"Price to pass—a kiss!" Richardson announced.

Adam stopped and turned Karla toward him. She giggled until he lowered his face to hers. As his lips pressed against hers, she locked her arms around his neck, opening to allow him to claim her warm, soft mouth. He should cut this short. Hell, they had the rest of their lives together and people were freezing out here. But he enjoyed kissing his wife too much.

His wife. Damn, but he liked the sound of that.

When he pulled away, he heard her moan in frustration and she gave him a smoldering look. As the swords were lifted, forming an arch once more, they walked underneath.

Richardson tapped Karla on the ass with the broad edge of his sword. She squealed in surprise. "On behalf of the United States Marine Corps, welcome to the family, ma'am."

Everyone laughed. Karla surprised Adam by turning around and walking over to Richardson. "Don't worry. I'll take good care of him, Master Gunnery Sergeant Richardson."

He grinned at her. "It's Kevin, ma'am, and I never had any doubt you would."

Adam took her elbow and turned her toward the driveway, anxious to show Karla what he'd bought her as a wedding present. Of course, he'd had to go with a used 2010 H3 model...

Karla stopped short again. "What the f...heck is that?"

Adam looked down at her and smiled. "My wedding present to you."

The shiny white vehicle in the driveway, decorated with red balloons and streamers, sported what he hoped was washable paint proclaiming the couple soon-to-be inside was "Just Hitched." He turned to Marc and Damián and glared. They just smiled back, proud of their work.

"Adam Montague, if you think I'm going to drive around in that...that...tank, you need to have your head examined."

He turned his attention to his bride again. His very ungrateful bride. What was the problem? He'd thought she'd be pleased to have her own vehicle—and to see how far he'd go to protect her and the baby. Might not be armored, but it sure as hell would be bigger than most things she could hit. Besides, did she know how hard it was to find one of the discontinued vehicles available on such short notice? Hell, he'd had to have it shipped halfway across the country. What ailed the woman?

"You're not going to be driving around in anything that's not safe. I'm thinking of the kids, too."

She looked up at him. "Kids?"

"Well, one at a time, of course, but I thought we'd have maybe half a dozen or so."

Karla's jaw dropped and he fought the urge to take her mouth with his. Instead, they broke apart and her gaze returned to the vehicle, then back at him. She smiled sweetly, but the smile didn't reach her eyes.

"Adam, dear, it was very nice of you to get this for me." Her gaze grew steely. "But there's no fu...freaking way I'm driving around in a Hummer."

"You'll drive whatever I tell you to drive."

"I'm not your slave. We're not TPE. And I am not driving that…that tank."

Adam was speechless. They'd been married a couple of hours and already she was defying him. True, they weren't TPE, but… "What happened to the part about you obeying your husband?"

"Well, if my husband makes unreasonable demands, I reserve the right to disobey—respectfully, of course." Again with the saccharine smile.

He took her hand and placed it tightly in the crook of his elbow before he gave in to the sudden desire to give her a wedding-day spanking over the hood of the Hummer in front of her family and friends. He led her to the passenger side of the vehicle and opened the door. "I'm driving tonight. Tomorrow, we'll share the drive to our destination, or you won't have your honeymoon anywhere but in our bedroom at the club and you won't be able to sit down for at least three weeks."

He could almost see the wheels turning in her head. After a few moments, she pulled the cape to herself and got into the Hummer, making sure the cape wouldn't get caught in the door. He shook his head and, as he walked around the hood of the "tank," as she called it, he heard Marc's laughter. Adam refused to look at him and give him any satisfaction.

Clearly, his wife needed to learn more about obedience and respect for her husband—and her Dom. Starting tonight.

Epilogue

Damián climbed the external stairs to his apartment in the renovated motel building and unlocked the door. He'd left Rosa, Teresa, and José at Marc's house after Dad's and Karla's wedding reception. Lots more room there than in Damián's one-bedroom apartment. Besides, Marc had promised to outfit them at his shop and take them up on the slopes for ski lessons tomorrow morning. None of them had ever been skiing. Neither had Damián, for that matter, and he didn't think he ever would be. The kids were especially stoked about it.

His family planned to stay a couple more days, and then fly back to Solana Beach. Without him. Rosa insisted she was okay now, although he wasn't so sure. But Savi had gotten his sister started in therapy sessions with a colleague and, with her ex in custody for rape, assault, and breaking and entering, Rosa wasn't as scared.

Time for Damián to start job hunting Monday. He'd managed to save up some money, hoping to start his own shop someday, so it wasn't as bad as when he lost his job at the hotel after he got fired for rescuing Savannah. As an amputee, he sure didn't have the Marines to fall back on this time.

Maybe he'd go by the bike shop where he'd worked until Teresa was raped and see if they'd take him back. If not, he could put in his application at some other shops in town. Maybe someday he'd have his own shop.

Yeah, right after pigs start flying.

The money he'd been saving had gone to help Rosa and the kids, so he was back at square one. He went to the fridge and pulled out a Dos Equis bottle. With the remote in his other hand, he sat down on the couch and flipped through the channels until he found the cable show on Harley Davidsons and leaned back. Mid swig, the doorbell rang.

Who the hell would be coming over here tonight? He never had company. Maybe something was wrong with Rosa or the kids. With a sigh, he laid his bottle on the coffee table and hauled himself up out of the couch.

He looked out the peephole, but only saw the back of someone's head. A redheaded female, someone he didn't recognize. Sliding the deadbolt, he opened the door. As if in slow motion, Savi Baker turned around to face him. She wore sunglasses, which was odd, considering it was nighttime. But he recognized her slender, perfect nose and those sexy full lips.

His heart had jumped into his throat. "Did something happen to Teresa?" Savi had been his niece's therapist since she was raped early last month.

"Teresa? No." She held out her hand with the palm facing him to allay his fears. "No! I'm sure she's fine."

Then what the hell was Savannah—Savi—doing in Denver? A blast of cold air made him aware she wasn't wearing a very substantial coat. "Come in." He stood out of the way and motioned her inside.

"No, I can't. I..." She turned and looked down at the parking lot, then back at him, a crease in her forehead. What was wrong? His protective instincts went on red alert, but first he needed answers.

"Why are you here? How did you find me?" *What's wrong?*

She lowered her head a moment. "I looked at the next of kin info in Teresa's file."

Wasn't that against some code of ethics or something? Not that he'd complain. He'd dreamed of her finding him like this many times. Well, maybe not in this exact scenario, but...

"We need your help."

"We?" *Marisol? Where was Marisol?*

She turned away again and he glanced down over the railing to see what or who she was looking at, but didn't see anyone. When he looked back up at Savi, she'd removed the glasses. Her right eye was swollen and puffy. Someone's fist had slammed into it.

Damián felt the beast stirring to life. "Who hit you?"

"I can't say, but we need a place to hide out for a while, until I can figure out what to do."

Shit. "Marisol? Is she okay?"

Savi nodded. "She's asleep in the car. We drove day and night. I was afraid to fly or stay in motels. I didn't want to leave a trail."

What the hell was going on with her? Who was chasing her? And why?

"Look, that car's going to get cold PDQ. Why don't you get Marisol and come inside to warm up?"

She held her arm to her side and admitted in a husky voice, "I can't lift her." Did she have other injuries? Maybe he needed to get Doc over here to check her out.

"Give me your keys. I'll get her."

She seemed reluctant to turn her keys over to him at first, but when another blast of cold air hit her in the face, she looked down at the parking lot and pulled the keys out of her jacket pocket. "Follow me."

"No. You don't need to be going up and down those stairs. You look like you're about to keel over. Just tell me which car."

"The light blue Nissan." She pointed at a sedan parked under the light.

"Go sit down. I'll be right back."

Good thing he hadn't removed his prosthesis yet. He didn't want her to see his gimpy leg. He went back down the stairs, holding onto the rail so that he wouldn't have a misstep, and walked across the lot to the car. Using the remote, he unlocked it and found Marisol lying across the back seat, even though she was still strapped in. He unbuckled her and pulled her toward him.

She moaned in her sleep.

"Shhh. It's okay, *bebé*." He remembered all the times he'd carried Teresa to bed when she'd fallen asleep watching TV and wished his niece was that small and innocent again. Marisol's dead weight lay against his shoulder and he closed and locked the door again. He'd come down for the luggage, if any, after he got this little bundle into bed.

The stairs were a little trickier to ascend this time, but he managed to hold onto her with one arm while he used his other to help pull them up the stairs and remain steady. At the top of the stairs stood Savi; apparently, she hadn't trusted him to carry her daughter without supervision.

Yet she'd driven halfway across the country to come to him for help of some kind. What was up with that?

Savi fell into step beside him and opened the door, then locked it again after they'd entered the apartment. He turned to whisper to her, "Help me get her into bed. Then we'll talk." Damián led the way across the living room and stood beside the bedroom door, which Savi opened for him. A blast of cold air hit him. He'd need to turn the heat on in here to warm it up. He'd give Savi and Marisol the bed and he'd sleep on the sofa. Good thing the bed had clean linens and was made up.

Savi pulled down the red, green, and white mosaic comforter and he laid the little girl's head on the pillow and guided her legs onto the bed. When he reached to remove her shoes, Savi grabbed his hands.

"No! I'll do that."

Holding up his hands, he backed off to let the girl's overprotective mother take care of her, while he went to the wall near the doorway to turn up the thermostat. He whispered, "It'll warm up in here in no time." Savi left Marisol's clothes on and pulled the comforter and sheet over her, bending down to kiss her. Damián couldn't help but notice Savi's curvy ass in her tight jeans. He tried not to remember their day in the beach cave, making love and connecting in such a way he'd never thought they'd be able to leave each other.

But they had.

Savi stood and turned and he noticed she winced and held her hand to her side again. Had someone hit her in the ribs? What the fuck had happened? Did a perp connected with one of her clients come after her? Shit. Doesn't the clinic offer any kind of protection for its counselors? That was a dangerous line of work, given the violence and abuse associated with her clients.

Madre de Dios. What if it was her husband? That made more sense even. Domestic violence was rampant these days. He planned to get some answers and soon.

He motioned for her to precede him back into the living room. When he started to close the door, she stayed his hand. "No!" She looked apologetic for getting so excited. "Mari might wake up and be frightened to find herself in a strange bed."

Sure. Why hadn't he thought of that?

"Can I get you a Coke, beer, tea, or something?"

"No Kool-Aid?" She smiled and her teasing took him by surprise.

"Sorry. When the munchkins aren't around, I prefer beer." He smiled.

"A Coke sounds good. I need to keep my wits about me."

Damián wasn't sure if it was because of him or whatever threat she was running from. He hoped it wasn't him. Surely she knew by now he'd never hurt her. Hadn't he proven that in her hotel room and at the beach all those years ago?

Considering how she hadn't wanted to have anything to do with him since then, maybe not. He went to the fridge and pulled out a can of Coke. "Glass and ice?"

"No. The can's fine."

He handed it to her. "Let me take your jacket."

"No, I'm fine. I'll just keep it on."

Fine. Only she wasn't fine and he needed to find out what was going on. He motioned for her to have a seat on the couch and picked up the beer bottle he'd been drinking from when she'd arrived. *Jesús*, he needed to get buzzed. He needed to dull every sense he could, especially the throbbing in his dick. Having Savi so close again, without anyone around...

Well, her daughter was sleeping in the next room. That would definitely curb his baser needs.

"Who hit you?"

Savi slowly lifted the can to her lips and tipped it back, drinking long and slow. Stalling, no doubt. Finally, she lowered the can and stared at it, tracing a worse-for-wear, pink-polished fingernail around the rim. He let the silence swell until he couldn't stand it any longer.

"Was it your husband?"

She looked up, her brows furrowed, then shook her head. "I'm not married."

Divorced or never married? He didn't want to get too personal, but there was the matter of getting her injuries checked out.

"I have a friend who was a corpsman—a medic—in Iraq. Will you let him check your injuries?"

She squared her shoulders, ready to do battle. "What injuries?"

"Well, there's the black eye, swelling, bruising on your face. You've also been favoring your left side. Did he hit you there, too?"

She sagged into the couch a bit. "It's nothing."

"Let my friend be the judge of that."

"I'm not leaving Mari."

"Who said anything about leaving? He'll come over here if I ask him."

"No. The fewer people who know I'm here, the better."

"Who are you running from, Savannah?" Maybe if he used the name she didn't want to connect with anymore, he could get her to show some emotion other than fear.

Savi's blue eyes flashed. "I told you not to call me that."

Bingo. Now she was angry. He liked seeing that emotion better. "I liked your hair better blonde. Why did you change it?"

"None of your business."

He leaned toward her and saw fear flash in her eyes. "Hey, *chica*, you just showed up on my doorstep out of nowhere, beaten up and on the run. You're the one who asked me for help, so don't go getting all defensive. I'm just trying to figure out what the hell's going on."

He took a long draw on his beer, draining the bottle, then lowered the bottle to his lap—hopefully obscuring his hard-on—and stared at her. After a moment, she reached up and twirled the end of a curl. *Dios*, her hair looked so soft.

"I felt safer changing my appearance."

Well, he'd expected her to respond that she'd just felt like it or got tired of dumb-blonde jokes or something. Her response indicated she'd been on the run or trying to hide from someone for a while, because she'd been a brunette a month ago when he'd first seen her again. Now a redhead.

"Marisol's father?"

Her hand froze and she looked up at him again, studying his face for some time. "What about him?"

"Is he the one who roughed you up and sent you running?"

Her body relaxed into the couch and she took another swig of the soda. "No. He's been out of my…out of the picture from day one."

Damn. She'd had to raise her daughter on her own. That was rough. What kind of bastard would get her pregnant and leave her like that?

He was dying to ask if her Sugar Daddy, the man who'd told him never to put his hands on her again, had been the one to beat her, but playing twenty questions wasn't going to get him anywhere. She wasn't going to answer even direct questions.

"Let me see where you're hurt."

She grew tense again, but didn't make eye contact. "No. I'm fine."

"Bullshit, *chica*." When she looked up at him again, he held her gaze. "Your choice—me or my friend? Which will it be?"

She shot daggers at him for a moment, but he didn't back down. Leaning forward, wincing at the pain, she laid the can on top of an automotive magazine on the coffee table and sat back against the couch.

"It's nothing. Really. Just a bruise."

"I'll be the judge of that. I have some…expertise with bruising. Remove your jacket."

After a few seconds, she raised a shaking hand and unhooked the belt of her hip-length jacket. Her hands continued to shake as she reached up to undo the first button.

"I haven't ever hurt you, Savannah. Have I?"

He couldn't read her expression. Hell, that was supposed to be an easy question. Why was he no longer certain of her response? What had he ever done to hurt her? She was the one who refused to have anything to do with him after their perfect fucking day at the beach.

Cool it, man. Give her time.

When she finished unbuttoning the coat, she peeled it off, revealing a cobalt blue blouse. More buttons. He wanted to reach out and unbutton them himself, letting his fingers graze against the tops of her breasts, but instead she leaned against the back of the couch and lifted the tail of her shirt. He caught a glimpse of black and blue marks along her ribcage. All carnal thoughts left his head.

"Lie down."

"No!" She took a deep breath and stood, wincing. "I'd rather stand."

He stood, as well, and leaned closer, reaching out his hand. While he didn't touch the bruising at first, she gasped when his fingers made contact with her for the first time in more than eight years.

Get a grip, man. And not on Savannah.

The bruising appeared to be two or three days old, tops, given the still-dark coloring. Her skin was so white, though, that it was hard to tell. There didn't seem to be much swelling, but how was he to know if there was some kind of internal injury or a broken rib? This wasn't an impact area he played with, either, so he didn't really know what the danger signs were.

"I need to ask Doc what to do."

With Savan—Savi, he'd learned not to ask, just do it. He pulled out his phone and hit Marc's speed-dial. His friend answered after three rings, sounding sleepy. "Sorry to wake you, man, but I need your help."

"Shoot."

"A friend of mine has been in…some kind of fight and she has some bruising over her ribs."

"Getting a little rough with the subs, Damián?"

"Man, this is serious. It's not from impact play. She's been punched by a fist, it looks like. Under her breast. Where the ribs are. The bruises are still dark in color. Happened at least two days ago." He looked up at Savi, who nodded in agreement and held up two fingers in a vee.

Marc went into Corpsman mode. "Could be some internal bleeding, fractured rib, or other problems. You should have her checked out at the ER."

"Can't do that. What's plan B? What can I do?"

"Starting tomorrow, you could apply some heat to the bruises. That'll speed up the healing. Ice wouldn't be much help this long after the injury. That should have been done right away. Ask her to take a couple deep breaths and see how much pain it causes. If she can't fill her lungs, then get her to the ER whether she wants to go or not, because it could be something serious."

"Hold on." Damián lowered the phone. "Take some deep breaths. Really fill your lungs."

She tried to do as he told her, but he heard the catch in her breath as she winced slightly. He put the phone to his ear again. "Might be a problem with her breathing, Doc."

Savi stood taller. "No, there isn't. I'm fine"

Damián stared at her. Why wouldn't she admit she was in pain?

"You still there, Damián?"

"Shoot."

"Now, I want you to press on her sternum."

"I didn't take anatomy, Doc."

Marc laughed. "Her breastbone—the bone right between her breasts."

Damián looked at her chest. *Oh, yeah, like she's going to let me do this.*

"If you press there and she experiences a sharp pain, it could mean a fractured rib. Just take the heel of your hand and press there—not too hard. Support her back. You'll know right away if there's a problem."

Oh, there was a problem, all right.

"Be right back." Damián laid the phone on the coffee table and moved closer to Savi. "I need to check for a broken rib. Just try and relax."

She took a step back. *Yeah, that's what I figured.* "Hold still, *querida*." He maintained eye contact with her. She was afraid, but did a good job keeping that emotion out of her eyes. She almost went into some kind of emotional shut-down, her gaze becoming empty. Dead.

Damián placed his left hand in the middle of her back and his right one between her breasts and felt the bone. He'd never really thought much before about there being a bone there. He pressed firmly. No response, well, except for his dick which probably was as hard as her breastbone right now. At least nothing seemed to be broken. With reluctance, he let her go, but she continued to stare into space.

"Savi? Look at me." She blinked and turned toward him. "Where'd you go?"

"Go? I didn't go anywhere. Just check for the broken rib and get it over with."

What the fuck? He'd known women to go into subspace and block out parts of a really intense scene, but how the hell had she shut her mind down so completely like that in the space of seconds? When he touched a woman, she usually remembered. Hell, maybe he'd just see if he could get a response from her this time.

He placed his hand at the small of her back again. She jumped.

"Wait. I'm not ready yet."

"You don't have to get ready for anything. Just look at me, *querida.*"

Her eyes scrunched up in distress. "Take a deep breath and let it out slowly." She did as he instructed and relaxed by small degrees. "Good g...good." Better not freak her out with words like *good girl*.

He laid his hand on her chest again and this time felt her heart beating wildly. She drew another breath, sharper this time. "Just relax. I'm going to press here, but tell me if it starts to hurt."

He applied even less pressure than he had before and she cried out in pain. *Fuck.* He let her go. Why hadn't she acknowledged the pain before? Shit. Did that mean she had a broken rib? Suddenly, he remembered the phone and picked it up.

"Doc? You still there?"

"Yeah. I was about to disconnect, figuring one thing was about to lead to another until I heard that scream. I think you'd better get her to the ER, Damián. They need to check for internal injuries and they can probably give her something for pain."

"We have a couple problems with that. One is that we need a babysitter."

Savi held up her hand. "No! I'm not going anywhere and even if I did, I'm not leaving Mari with strangers."

"Doc, do you have any friends who can provide a medical assessment without leaving a paper trail?"

"What the hell is going on there?"

"I haven't a fucking clue, but it's the only way I'm going to get her to cooperate."

"Let me call a friend and see if he'll open up his clinic tonight for you to take her there. But as soon as you find out what's going on, I want a full report. This had better not be anything illegal, either."

"No, nothing like that. Just call me back ASAP."

He disconnected the phone and just stared at Savi. "He's going to try and find someone to take a look at that rib. Do you want to lie down with Mari and rest a little?"

"No. I can't breathe when I lie down. I'm fine."

"You're *not* fucking fine, Savi."

She cringed at his tone. He needed to cool it, but if she said everything was fine one more time, he'd…drive his fist through a wall or something. Damn it. What was going on here?

"Who are you running from? Who did this to you?"

No hesitation this time.

"My father." She held her hand over her stomach as if the words had made her nauseous.

"What?" What kind of father would…aw, hell. After Teresa, he didn't have to ask what fathers could do to daughters.

"He tried to take Mari from me. I guess he saw me on the news footage from Julio's arrest and tracked me down after all these years."

News footage? Damián hadn't even known there were media there. But Savi and Teresa had been outside while he'd given his police report.

"I can't let him anywhere near her. That's why I came to you."

Damián was still reeling from the shocker that her father had beaten her like this, but had no clue what had made her trust him.

"The way you took care of Teresa. The way you were ready to kill Julio. We need that kind of protection right now. Will you help us?"

* * *

Adam placed the box under the tree. Thank God the jeweler also did gift wrapping, because the job Adam had done on the other box was piss poor. He'd let Karla sleep in, since he'd had her up half the night, chained to the bed. He hadn't gotten rough with her, even though she'd goaded him to a few times. So far he'd managed to retain the upper hand on her brattiness.

His dick got hard just thinking about her bright pink ass.

He looked out the picture window at the snow falling softly. A deer wandered up to the feeder Karla had placed out there last weekend, saying she was worried that the poor babies weren't finding enough to eat. She had such a soft heart and probably wanted to make amends for killing one of them, he supposed.

Soft arms wrapped around his waist. "Merry Christmas, Master Santa."

He chuckled and turned around to greet her sleep-riddled face. The lines of her pillow still creased her cheek. He reached up to trace the lines before grabbing her hair and pulling her head back. He lowered his mouth to hers, open and waiting for him.

His tongue delved inside and did a tango with hers as his hand skimmed over her shoulder and down to her breast. When he squeezed her swollen nipple, she gasped and pulled away. So sensitive. He smiled.

"How's your stomach this morning?"

Her smile told him all he needed to know. "First time since last month that I haven't said good morning to John first thing."

His hand covered her abdomen, still relatively flat, but he thought about the baby growing inside her and his heart filled to the point of aching. His baby. What better present could she give him? Well, becoming his wife had been even better. Now he hoped to make her his in another way. He hoped he wasn't rushing things. Once she was ready to commit firmly, they would have a public ceremony. But for now, this was between the two of them, and he wanted to keep it that way.

"I'll start the fire. Why don't you get dressed, harem girl, and meet me here in a few?"

Her eyes sparkled and she giggled, causing him to throb. *God love her.*

He'd barely gotten the fire roaring before she was back, wearing the red harem costume, her feet bare and her Christmas-red painted toenails gleaming after the spa treatment he'd insisted she take while he went back to the jeweler's two days ago to pick up the gift he'd ordered special made. They'd worked on it night and day, the artisan said, to finish in time. It was a work of art. He couldn't wait for her to open the box. Well, both of them.

Adam trailed a finger over her collar bone. "Why don't we have our Christmas first?"

"Wait! There's something I need to add to the tree."

She went back into the bedroom and soon came out carrying the angel tree topper Joni had tucked away in the box of treasures for him. Adam's gaze searched Karla's eyes, seeing only love.

"I found this in your office."

He nodded, too choked up to say anything.

Karla touched the wings of the angel. "We would never have gotten together if not for Joni, so I owe her a special debt of gratitude for entrusting her Master to me. I don't ever want to replace her—as if I ever could! But I do think she's ready to move on now."

Adam nodded again, still unable to speak, but he'd gotten the same vibe since before the wedding, as if she'd accomplished her mission and needed to get on with more important things.

The tree was only six feet tall. Because they hadn't brought any decorations with them—except for Joni's angel—they'd simply decorated it with strings of popcorn and cranberries, some paper snowflake ornaments Karla made, and an old bird's nest she'd found during one of their hikes week before last. They'd bought some LED lights at the drug store when they were in town, but must have gotten an old batch.

He steadied her as she stood on tiptoes to place the angel carefully on top, arranging the champagne-colored skirt over the top boughs of the tree.

"Sorry the lights didn't work."

"No worries, Adam. She's perfect just the way she is."

Connect the angel light to the tree, jarhead.

"What did you say?"

"I said she's perfect the way she is."

"No. After that."

"Oh, you mean about connecting the angel to the tree, jarhead?"

"Yeah. You could have asked with more respect."

"I didn't ask, Adam."

"Then who…?"

Adam looked up at the angel. The voice *had* sounded like Joni's—but that would be ridiculous. If it were her… Wait a minute. Karla had heard her, too. She'd said Joni had spoke to her a few times over the last nine years. "Just how often do you hear her?"

She giggled and his erection pressed against her butt. "Other than the times I already told you?"

"Yeah. Is it daily, monthly, annually?"

"Usually when she wants to help me, or you. She told me to kneel before our Shibari session."

Adam remembered seeing her kneeling so beautifully for him, taken aback that she'd know to do that while she waited. Joni, of course, would know.

"She sent me to you in the shower when I was in subdrop and didn't know it."

"I always told her to come to me when she was in subdrop. I guess she hasn't forgotten."

"She said she talks to you, too, you know."

"Yeah, well, maybe. She usually calls me jarhead when she thinks I'm fucking clueless."

She laughed. "I guess she knows you can't discipline her for being a brat where she is now."

Adam chuckled and released her to reach up to find the light socket on the angel. When he brought the cords together, the clear lights burst forth shiny and bright from the lower boughs to the angel's wings.

"Well, I'll be damned." He came back to stand behind Karla and wrapped his arms around her. "This ghost stuff is just between you and me. Anyone else would say we're friggin' nuts."

"She's more a spirit on a mission than a ghost. Not to worry, though. She's leaving soon. Said three's a crowd. Joni told me to bring the angel, by the way. She said it would help her to go toward the light and to seek another land."

"The poem."

"Poem?"

"Yeah, she left me a poem called 'If You Forget Me' and that was one of the lines—'to seek another land.'"

"Well, she knows you won't forget her, but said she's glad you're finally ready to set her roots free so she can fly."

Adam hadn't been able to let Joni go because of his guilt and remorse for not loving her well enough. Now he understood that he'd loved Joni as well as he could at the time. But Karla had waged war on his heart and finally shown him he'd known all along how to love fully and honestly. For the rest of his life, he intended to make sure she never doubted his love.

He hugged Karla closer, splaying his hands across her midriff and resting his cheek against hers as together they stared up at the angel, both apparently lost in the magic. He hadn't seen the angel on a Christmas tree in more than a decade. He would never be able to place it on a tree without thinking of Joni, but was glad his first wife didn't plan to haunt them forever. As always, Joni was right. Three's a crowd.

For the first time in years, he was caught up in the Christmas spirit, too. He couldn't wait to see Karla's face when she opened her gifts. He hoped she'd accept them.

She had turned his rudder in a totally new direction. He and Karla wouldn't always see eye to eye on everything. Hell, maybe not even on most things. But they'd always be there for each other.

"Thank you for…everything, Karla. I love you so much."

Her hands covered his and he felt her smile against his cheek.

"Hearing those words...that's the best Christmas present ever."

He broke away and turned her around to face him. "Oh, you're not getting off that easy."

Her eyes gleamed in anticipation. "I can't wait for you to open my gift."

"You didn't have to get me anything. Just having you..."

"Nonsense. Um, Sir." She looked contrite. He just grinned back at her. "It's just a start, but I hope you like it." Curious now, he watched her go back to the tree and pull out a flat square package with holly-leaf wrapping paper and a tiny red bow.

Adam picked up the two gifts for Karla. "Let's go sit by the fire, Kitten."

He carried the boxes over to the sheepskin rug and pillows he'd positioned in front of the native-stone fireplace. He couldn't help but admire the phenomenal job Patrick had done restoring the cabin, while keeping all of the original features important to Adam, like this fireplace. He could picture Johnny Montague, and maybe even Kate, hauling the stones to create it as they built their home together.

Adam glanced up over the mantel to the portrait-sized photograph of Johnny and Kate in their later years, sitting astride a beautiful bay stallion. The picture had hung in the living room of his home in Minneapolis as a boy. His great-great-grandparents also had more than two decades separating their ages, but the love they shared was evident in their eyes, and in the way he wrapped his arms around her waist as she sat on his lap across the saddle. Her shoulders were straight and strong and he had no doubt the woman had done her share of hard work on their homestead.

Adam's attention strayed to the coiled rope held in Johnny's hand, resting on Kate's lap. The rope had fascinated Adam since he was a boy, and he wondered now if that was why he'd become so interested in Shibari. He smiled wondering what Karla would think if he ever used rope that scratchy on her skin.

Karla knelt down beside him. "Open it!"

Adam turned his attention back to Karla. "Are you giving your Dom orders?"

"Certainly sounded that way, didn't it?" His bratty bride grinned. Incorrigible.

"Anticipation is good for Doms, too, you know."

"I know, but it's hell for us subbies. I can't wait to see what you think of what I made for you."

She made him something? Adam ripped the paper where it had been taped down and revealed a CD with a cover showing the Shibari suspension scene they'd done in October, while she was his slave. He'd snapped some photos before bringing her out of subspace. On the CD cover, the words "Touch Me" and "by Master Adam's kitten" were emblazoned in bright red letters. His throat grew tight, and he looked up at her.

"You wrote a song for me?"

She nodded, tears shimmering in her blue eyes. She cleared her throat. "For you. Here," she said, taking the CD from him, "let me put it on the laptop so you can hear it."

She cranked up the speakers and he heard a Goth-rock beat softer than some of what she sang at the club, likely a concession to his not being into the hardcore stuff. Her beautiful voice began singing about all the places she wanted him to touch her. Not just places on her body, but places like the floor, the table, the shower—conjuring up memories of some of the places he'd already touched her. He smiled, and his dick responded to the visceral images in the lyrics.

I see you wet your lips
You know I can't resist
Just want a little taste
So, there's no time to waste
You know I like it rough
I just can't get enough
Not feelin' no shame
When I'm screaming out your name!

As the music continued to play, he pulled her on top of him, gripped her hair in his fists and pulled her mouth to his. When the song ended, he released his grip and she sat up, straddling him and staring down. She waited for his response. Hadn't he already shown her? He grinned.

"Don't ever sing that song on stage or on any of your future CDs."

She drew her brows together. "You didn't like it, Sir?"

"Oh, I liked it—too much." He slid her body down to his crotch where his hard dick pressed against her pussy.

She grinned, her eyes sparkling. "I see, Sir. Well, that one will be just for us."

He brushed a strand of hair from her eye. "Kitten, I am so proud of you for writing and recording a song for me. I never told you before, but the MP3 player and songs you sent me in Iraq helped keep me sane those nights when I laid awake in my rack and would have dwelled on all my past transgressions. You were something beautiful and innocent in a world gone mad. I know you're going to be a huge success when you start selling your music online—your other music."

Her smile grew wider. "Thanks for having faith in me, Sir." She bent down to brush her lips against his.

"I think it was you who had the endless well of faithfulness, Kitten, especially when it came to me. *Semper Fi*."

"Well, since I'm now a member of the Marine Corps family, I'll always strive to live up to the motto."

Gently turning, he lowered her onto her back on the rug and kissed her as he slid his hand under the cup of her bra and pinched her nipple. He took advantage of her soft gasp and invaded her lips. So sweet, so warm. His hand lowered to her mons and he spread the folds of her scarf skirt, touching her bare pussy. Wet for him. Only him.

"You asked to be taken on the floor, Kitten."

"Yes, Sir." Her breathy whisper nearly undid him.

"Turn over. On your knees and elbows. Then brace yourself, because I'm going to ram my dick so deep inside you, you are going to taste me. Is that clear?"

Her pupils dilated. "Sir, yes, Sir!"

He chuckled and leaned back, smacking her on the ass for her insolence as she scrambled to get into position. He knelt behind her, unhooking her bra and sliding it down her arms. When she moved to rise up and remove it completely, he pushed against her back. "Stay. I didn't give you permission to move."

He lay over her back, supporting himself with one hand on the floor as his other pulled and teased her nipples.

"Take me, Sir. I need you."

He removed his hand from her tit. "Kitten, we've talked about this before. You do not tell me what you need. I already know what you need."

"But, Sir, you don't seem to know that I need it now! Ow!"

He'd squeezed her tit harder than he had lately, but one way or another, he needed to exert his control over the situation before she ran all over him.

"I'm sorry, Sir. I'll be patient. Take as long as you need to."

Was she insinuating he was old and slow? "Why, you little brat…" He rose up onto his knees and undid his button-fly jeans, allowing his rigid cock to spring out and thump against her ass. He pressed his middle finger into her wet pussy to make sure she was ready, pulled his finger out, and then grabbed her hips and rammed himself inside, entering her fully.

"Oh, yes! Harder, Sir. Take me harder!"

He growled. Later, he'd enjoy punishing her for continuing to try to top him. Right now, all he wanted to do was bury himself inside her to the hilt, over and over again, for the rest of his life.

* * *

When Karla could form a coherent thought again, she felt Adam pull out of her. Too languid to move, she remained with her butt up in the air, resting her head on her hands. He pulled away, patting her butt, and she missed him immediately. He cleaned them up. Karla laid down again on the sheepskin rug.

"Now, I need to get up off the floor and get your presents."

"Presents?" What could he possibly have gotten for her? She already had everything she wanted. She rolled over onto her back and looked up at him.

"Yes, presents—but with some strings attached."

He retrieved the two small boxes he'd placed near the fireplace earlier. "You'll have to excuse the wrapping on the first one. I'm all thumbs when it comes to this kind of thing."

"Never judge a book by its cover, Sir."

"Truer words were never spoken. I still remember seeing you standing there on my stage in a Maid Marian costume."

"Hey, it was popular in the club in Soho."

"Well, I prefer the way you're dressed now." Well, she certainly wouldn't have shown up in Soho wearing this, but she'd already worn it to the club once, the night she'd thought she could submit to being Adam's slave. What a nightmare that had been.

He knelt down beside her and handed her the one he'd wrapped first. Her throat tightened. When she moved to sit up, he held out his hand to her, bringing her into the cradle between his thighs and wrapping his arms around her.

Safe.

Karla had the wrapping off and was about to open the long box when he stayed her hand. She heard him take a deep breath.

"Kitten, what's in the box is something you will choose to wear the first time. This is something I can't order you to do. But once you accept it, you will wear it whenever and wherever I tell you to wear it. Do you understand?"

Her hand began to shake in his. "I think so, Sir." Her chest tightened with emotion and her eyes burned. She knew before she opened the box what was inside. Adam released her hand and she opened the lid. There, nestled in tissue paper, was a black leather collar with red spikes. She touched the leather. So soft, like baby's skin. But the spikes were made of cold, hard metal.

"The leather is soft, like you." He stroked her cheek. "The spikes signify your love of rough sex."

She giggled. "I always wondered about all the different types of collars and what they meant." She pulled it out of the box and heard something jangle. Turning it over, she saw a dog tag attached to one of the D-rings. "Montague, Adam M." was imprinted in the first two rows of metal, as well as his service number, rank, even religion. Lutheran.

"I didn't know you were Lutheran."

"What? Oh, the tag. Yeah, well. We went some when I was a kid." He pulled a chain from around his neck that had an identical dog tag. "I'll always wear the other dog tag, indicating we're one body, not two, forever joined."

The tag swam before her eyes and her hand shook so badly, it jangled again. She reached up and wiped the tears from her eyes and looked again to find a padlock and an anchor attached to the same ring, etched with the words *"Semper Fidelis."*

Always faithful.

"You know what the motto means. You're mine, Kitten. Only mine. We'll be faithful to each other until death parts us."

"Maybe even longer, Sir. I am yours and yours alone."

He wrapped his arm around her upper body and pulled her against his hard chest.

Home.

"Are you saying you'll agree to wear my collar, Kitten? You don't have to agree today. If you do decide to wear my collar, though, we'll want to have more formal ceremony at the club with our friends, when you're ready to make the commitment publicly."

Karla broke away from him and scooted around to face him, dashing more tears from her eyes, but no longer caring if she acted overly emotional. Next to her wedding, this was the most important commitment she'd ever made. She knelt as gracefully as she could and held the collar out to him. At first he looked puzzled, as if he thought she was giving it back. Then she took her free hand and lifted her hair, exposing her neck.

"Please, Sir. I would be honored to wear your collar. To have you teach me to be the best sub I can be, one you can be proud of. To be obedient to you always—well, as much as I can." She grinned.

He chuckled. "Don't worry, Kitten. I'll continue to try and keep you under my thumb. But I enjoy disciplining and punishing you when you get out of line, so I'm sure we'll be fine."

Karla nibbled her lower lip. He'd paddled her really hard last night for her brattiness. She really did need to try harder not to disobey. Adam dug into his pocket and retrieved a key and unlocked the one-inch padlock at the back of the collar. *Oh, my.* The lock was for real.

Adam paused and looked up at her. "You're sure you're ready for this, Kitten? Do you have any questions you want to ask?"

"Will we continue to negotiate, until we know what each of us needs and wants?"

"Yes, always."

"And, just to be clear, I'll be your sub, not your slave."

He chuckled. "You'd better believe it. I think I've had enough slavery to last a lifetime."

"Then I can't think of anyone I'd rather be padlocked to, Sir." She grinned.

Adam crawled on his knees behind her and opened the collar, placing it against the slim column of her neck and adjusting the size to fit her. He slipped two warm fingers between her neck and the leather to test the tightness.

"How does that feel?"

"Wonderful, Sir."

She felt a little tug as he buckled the latch and then heard the click of the padlock as it was snapped in place. His. She was his sub. He was her Dom. Her nipples bunched in anticipation of their time together. Soon.

His lips pressed against the curve of her neck and her breath hitched in her throat. Her head lolled to the side, giving him better access. But he pulled away.

"You're not finished yet, Kitten."

She turned toward him again and furrowed her brows, wondering what she was supposed to do, when he held the other box in front of her. This one was very professionally wrapped. She liked Master Adam's wrapping job better, because it was more…Adam. Rough and unrefined. Perfect.

Karla took the box and carefully tore off the paper, then opened the lid. Inside, there was a slim black-velvet box. Pulling it out, she lifted the hinged lid.

Gleaming against a black velvet backdrop lay an exquisite filigreed collar in silver or platinum studded with diamonds and encircled with ribbons of pink and green gold. The pink was much like her wedding band.

"Those ribbons are made of Black Hills gold and the filigree is platinum, like the ring you gave me on our wedding day. I commissioned it soon after we arrived here, when you were at the grocery store gathering up supplies. This is the collar you will wear in public. Read the inscriptions."

She held the collar closer. On the pink ribbon, she read, "To the woman who brings me to my knees." And on the green ribbon, "Always and forever." She remembered the first time she'd brought him to his knees, in a dirty ladies room in the Chicago bus terminal. She looked up to see a gleam in his eyes, as if he too remembered that time. And here he was, once again, on his knees before her.

"Yes, Kitten—always and forever."

Glossary of Terms
for *Nobody's Hero*

Above My Pay Grade—expression denying responsibility or authority (indicating that the issue should be brought to higher-ranking officials). Alternatively, **Above Your Pay Grade** is a semi-sarcastic way of telling someone that they're not authorized to receive certain information.

Aftercare—period of time after intense BDSM activity in which the dominant partner or a designee cares for the submissive partner. Some BDSM activities are physically challenging, psychologically intense, or both. After engaging in such activities, the submissive partner may need a safe psychological space to unwind and recover. Aftercare is the process of providing this safe space. (Source: xeromag.com)

APO/FPO—Army Post Office or Fleet Post Office. Which one is used to deliver a mail to deployed military personnel depends on the theater command authority (the senior commander in charge of operations for that deployment) and what support staff they are using. If the theater command authority rests with an Army or Air Force Theater Commander, then you get mail in theater from an APO; if the theater commander is a Navy or Marine CO, you get your mail through an FPO. (Thanks to Top Griz for explaining this, after the fact, for me. He said when he was in Iraq in 2004, he had an APO. I used APO in MASTERS, as well.)

ASAP—as soon as possible

"A" School—Not all Navy enlisted careers require skill training, but for those that do, advanced training begins at "A" School. Through extensive classes and on-the-job training, Navy personnel learn the fundamentals of their chosen technical field. In the Rescue Me series, Marc attended A-School at a time when Navy hospital corpsmen training was condensed to about 3-4 months because the nation was fighting two active wars. Nowadays, training to become a corpsman takes about a year.

Bebé—baby, in Spanish

Bottom—in a BDSM scene, the person to whom the action is being delivered by a "Top." (Also see **Top**.)

Cara—dear, in Italian (*Cara mia* means my dear)

Chicano—a North American term for a person, especially a male, of Mexican origin or descent

Chica—girl, in Spanish

Chico—boy, in Spanish (a term Damián also uses for his penis)

Chiquita—little girl, in Spanish

Clusterfuck—a messy situation (also Clusterfucking-A)

Corpsman—Navy personnel trained to administer medical aid in the field (similar to a medic in the Army); Navy hospital corpsmen served with both the Navy and the Marines. Often referred to as "Doc," when assigned to a Marine ground unit, the corpsman must train with the Marines and will be treated like a Marine by the unit.

Cover (noun)—hat

CSH—Combat Support Hospital (like MASH units in past combat arenas)

Devil Dog—term for Marine, supposedly originating in World War I by the Germans using the term *Teufelhunden* (or more correctly, *Teufelshunde*). The child of a Marine can be referred to as a Devil Pup.

Digitals—digital camouflage uniform, also referred to as MARPAT (Marine Pattern), Desert Digitals, cammies, or digis/diggis

Dio—God, in Italian. (*Mio Dio* is my God)

Dios—God, in Spanish

Doc—nickname for the Navy hospital corpsman attached to the Marines (also see **Corpsman**)

Dom/sub or D/s Dynamic in BDSM—a relationship in which the Dominant(s) is given control by consent of the submissive(s) or bottom(s) to make most, if not all, of the decisions in a play scene or in relationships with the submissive(s) or bottom(s).

F-Bomb—saying the word "fuck" (most likely at a time or in company it is inappropriate)

Glissando—a rapid sliding up or down the musical scale

Got your back, I've—Someone is saying they are going to watch out for and be a second set of eyes for someone else. To protect them, look out for their best interests, stick up for them, and let them know if they have missed something. Also "I've got your six," which means the same thing.

(Six refers to six o'clock on the face of a clock, assuming the person's front is the 12 o'clock station with the left side being 9 o'clock and the right 3 o'clock.)

Goth—a person who wears mostly black clothing, uses dark dramatic makeup, and often has dyed black hair

Grunt—term for an infantryman in the U.S. Marine Corps (once derogatory, now more neutral)

Head—Navy term for bathroom or latrine. Also used as a term for the penis or the act of oral sex.

Helo—helicopter

High and Tight—nickname for a common variant of the buzz cut, where the hair is clipped very close. Led to the nickname **Jarhead**.

IED—Improvised Explosive Device, a bomb constructed, set, and detonated in unconventional warfare

In-Country—phrase referring to being within a war zone

Instant Care—a healthcare facility that takes walk-ins on an urgent or emergency basis but charges less than an emergency-room visit

Jarhead—pejorative term for a Marine, probably originating from a description of the **High and Tight** haircut, which resembles the shape of a Mason canning jar.

Ka-thunk!™—the way Karla describes the feeling of her stomach dropping when a Dominant gives her a "Dom" stare, command, or praise; the word has been trademarked by Kallypso Masters LLC

Keyboard Jockey—Marine term for a person whose job causes him or her use a computer for a length of time

Lance Corporal (LCpl)—the third enlisted rank in order of seniority in the U.S. Marine Corps, just above private first class and below corporal. It is not a non-commissioned officer rank.

LED—Light Emitting Diode that emits light when a voltage is applied to it and that is used especially in electronic devices, Christmas lights, etc.

Little Head—reference to when a man is thinking with his penis instead of his head

Machismo—an attitude, quality, or way of behaving that agrees with traditional ideas about men being very strong and aggressive

Madre de Dios—Mother of God, in Spanish

Maman—mama, in French (keep in mind Savannah's mother was born in France this was the term she wanted her daughter to call her)

Marine Mattress—a female Marine who is thought to be sexually promiscuous with other Marines

Mariposa—butterfly, in Spanish

Master Sergeant (MSgt)—The eighth enlisted rank in the U.S. Marine Corps, just above gunnery sergeant, below master gunnery sergeant, sergeant major, and Sergeant Major of the Marine Corps. It is equal in grade to first sergeant. It is abbreviated as MSgt. In the U.S. Marine Corps, master sergeants provide technical leadership as occupational specialists at the E-8 level. Also see "Top."

Master/slave Dynamic in BDSM—A BDSM relationship, usually a 24/7 TPE one, in which the Top is referred to as the Master and the bottom the slave. People in a "Master/slave" dynamic often see dominance or submission as a cornerstone of their identity and an essential part of who they are as people. This dynamic may affect and inform almost every aspect of their lives, but there is no one-size fits all and each member in such a relationship consents to enter into such an arrangement.

Merda—shit, in Italian

Mierda—shit, in Spanish

Mikes (example, 3 to 4 mikes)—military term for minutes

Mio angelo—my angel, in Italian (*il mio angelo* in third person)

Mio Dio—My God, in Italian

MP—military police

MRE—Meal, Ready to Eat, the standard US food ration for personnel in the field where cooking facilities aren't available. (Sometimes referred to as Meal, Rejected by the Enemy or Meals Rarely Eaten.)

Munchkins—another word for small children

NCO—Non-Commissioned Officer (SNCO is Staff Non-Commissioned Officer for those in ranks E-6 and higher, including Master Sergeant)

Nipple nooses—a non-piercing form of tit torture in which the nipples are "lassoed" with string or wire which is then tightened to cut off sensation to the nipple; usually results in pain when the nooses are removed and circulation returns

OFP—Own Fucking Plan, term for when a Marine does what he wants to, when he wants to, and gets away with it. Someone who is OFP might also use DGAF (Doesn't/Don't Give a Fuck).

Orgasm torture—The BDSM practice whereby a bottom or submissive is forced to orgasm multiple times in quick succession, usually under the control and command of a Dominant; a form of orgasm control

PCH—Pacific Coast Highway, which runs along the coastline of California, Oregon, and Washington. Roughly follows US 101, with some variations due to changes in these routes.

PDQ—pretty damned/darn quick

Pequeña mariposa—little butterfly, in Spanish

Petit mort—literally means little death, in French; a term for orgasm

Pop Smoke—to leave quickly or hastily; from the method of throwing a smoke grenade to mark a landing zone or conceal a retreat.

Predicament bondage—A type of bondage in which the intent is to place the bound person in an awkward, difficult, inconvenient, or uncomfortable situation, or to set out a challenge for the bound person to overcome. For example, a person might be bound in such a way that his or her hands and feet are largely but not completely immobilized, then asked to perform a task (such as to serve the dominant partner a drink) which is made difficult by the bondage; or, a person might be bound and told to hold a weight in his or her teeth attached to a line connected to nipple clamps in such a way that if he or she drops the weight, it will suddenly yank off the nipple clamps, then be spanked or tickled in an attempt to get him or her to drop the weight. (Source: Xeromag.com)

Princesa—princess, in Spanish

PT—physical therapy. **PTs** (mentioned in later books in the series) refers to the uniform worn for doing workouts while in the Marine Corps

PTSD—Post Traumatic Stress Disorder, is a mental health condition that's triggered by a terrifying, often life-threatening, event (combat, attack, rape, abuse, incest)

Puta—whore or prostitute, in Spanish

Querida—darling, in Spanish

Rack—bunk or bed

Recon—reconnaissance. In the Marine Corps, trainees in the recon unit are referred to as "ropers" because of the ropes attached to the backs of their uniforms during training.

Rehab—rehabilitation. In this saga, refers to the period of time Damián spends in recovery from his combat injuries.

RPG—Rocket-Propelled Grenade, is a shoulder-fired, anti-tank weapon system that fires rockets equipped with an explosive warhead. These warheads are affixed to a rocket motor and stabilized in flight with fins. The RPG became a favorite weapon of the insurgent forces fighting U.S. troops in Iraq and was sometimes used in place of mortar, as happened on the rooftop attack.

Safephrase—a phrase agreed upon prior to a BDSM scene that can be used to end (temporarily or completely) a play scene

Safeword—a word agreed upon prior to a BDSM scene that can be used to end (temporarily or completely) a play scene

SAPI Plate—body army consisting of a ceramic-covered steel plate, which is worn over the chest and back. The original SAPI Plates didn't have much protection on the sides, but the Super SAPI Plates corrected that flaw in 2005 (too late for Marc, though). Incidentally, Kally's son works for a factory that makes the ceramic portion of these.

SAR—Search and Rescue

Salaam—an obeisance performed by bowing very low and placing the right palm on the forehead; a salutation or ceremonial greeting in the East

Screw the pooch—to make a catastrophic error or failure; to fuck things up royally

Seabag—term used by sailors and Marines to describe their duffel bag for storing their gear

Sears Tower—once the tallest building in the world, located in Chicago. Now known as the Willis Tower (except by Chicago residents and those old enough to remember the Sears Tower)

Semper Fidelis (or Semper Fi)—Marine Corps motto; Latin for "always faithful"

Shibari—A type of bondage originating in Japan and characterized by extremely elaborate and intricate patterns of rope, often used both to restrain the subject and to stimulate the subject by binding or compressing the breasts and/or genitals. Shibari is an art form; the aesthetics of the bound person and the bondage itself are considered very important. Also sometimes called kinbaku. Most technically, shibari is the act of tying, and kinbaku is artistic bondage. In general use, however, shibari and kinbaku are often used as synonyms. (Source: Xeromag.com)

Skivvies—men's underwear

SOB—Son of a Bitch (a derogatory term that seems to be insulting the mother more than the subject). Also appears in the series as "sonuva bitch."

Soldier—Term to describe a member of the U.S. Army. Also considered a derogatory term to a U.S. Marine (Although Adam lets it slide when Karla calls him one because her brother is a U.S. Army soldier and she wouldn't know about this being an insult, he isn't too pleased that the pimp in the bus station uses the term to refer to Adam.)

SSC—Safe, Sane, and Consensual kink scenes with a safeword that doesn't carry the level of risk some edgeplay does

Subdrop—The temporary depression experienced by submissives/masochists hours or days after intense BDSM play. To learn more about subdrop (and the related Domdrop or Topdrop), I encourage you to read the blog written by one of my editors, Ekatarina Sayanova, explaining this phenomenon at http://rosesandchains.blogspot.com/2014/02/subdrop-and-domdrop-very-real-phenomena.html.

Subspace—A state of mind that a submissive may enter, particularly after intense activities and/or (depending on the person) intense pain play, characterized by euphoria, bliss, a strong feeling of well-being, or even a state similar to intoxication. Thought to be related to the release of endorphins in the brain. The euphoria associated with subspace may last for hours or sometimes even days after the activity ceases. (Source: Xeromag.com)

Teppou—the "rifle" tie in Shibari

Tesoro mio—my treasure, in Italian

Top—1) In the U.S. Marine Corps, master sergeants may be referred to by the nickname of "Top." This usage is an informal one, however, and would not be used in an official or formal setting. Use of this nickname by Marines of subordinate rank is at the rank holder's discretion. 2) In a BDSM scene, the person delivering the action to a submissive or "bottom." (Also see **Bottom** and **Master Sergeant**)

TPE or Total Power Exchange—a relationship in which one person surrenders control to another person for an indefinite duration, and in which the relationship is defined by the fact that one person is always dominant and the other is always submissive. One of the more extreme forms of power exchange. Sometimes referred to as lifestyle D/s. (Source: Xeromag.com) Also see **Master/slave Dynamic in BDSM**.

USMC—United States Marine Corps

Woody—an erection; hard-on

About the Author

Kallypso Masters writes emotional, realistic Romance novels with dominant males (for the most part) and the strong women who can bring them to their knees. She also has brought many readers to their knees—having them experience the stories right along with her characters in the Rescue Me Saga. Kally knows that Happily Ever After takes maintenance, so her couples don't solve all their problems and disappear at "the end" of their Romance, but will continue to work on real problems in their relationships in later books in the saga.

Kally has been writing full-time since May 2011, having quit her "day job" the month before. She lives in rural Kentucky and has been married for 30 years to the man who provided her own Happily Ever After. They have two adult children, one adorable grandson, and a rescued dog.

Kally enjoys meeting readers at national romance-novel conventions, book signings, and informal gatherings (restaurants, airports, bookstores, wherever!), as well as in online groups (including Facebook's "The Rescue Me Saga Discussion Group"—send a friend request to Karla Montague on Facebook to join if you are 18 or older and don't mind spoilers. Kally also visits the Fetlife "Rescue Me! discussion group" regularly). She hopes to meet you in her future travels whether virtually or in-person! If you meet her face to face, be sure to ask for a Kally's friend button!

To contact or interact with Kally,

go to Facebook (http://www.facebook.com/kallypsomasters),
her Facebook Author page
(https://www.facebook.com/KallypsoMastersAuthorPage),
or Twitter (@kallypsomasters).

To join the secret Facebook group Rescue Me Saga Discussion Group, please send a friend request to Karla Montague and she will open the door for you. Must be 18 to join.

Keep up with news on her **Ahh, Kallypso…the stories you tell** blog at
KallypsoMasters.blogspot.com
Or on her Web site (KallypsoMasters.com).

You can sign up for her newsletter (e-mailed monthly) at her Web site or blog, e-mail her at kallypsomasters@gmail.com, or write to her at

Kallypso Masters
PO Box 206122
Louisville, KY 40250

Get your Kally Swag!

Want merchandise from the Rescue Me Saga? T-shirts and aprons inspired by a scene in *Nobody's Angel* that read: "Master Marc can put me in culinary bondage anytime." A beaded evil stick similar to the one used in *Nobody's Perfect*. Items from other books in the series will be added in coming months. You can even order paperbacks of the books themselves, personally signed by Kally. With each order, you will receive a bag filled with other swag items, as well, including a 3-inch pin-back button that reads "I'm a Masters Brat," two purple pens, bookmarks, and trading cards. Kally ships internationally. To shop, go to http://kallypsomasters.com/kally_swag.

Excerpt from
Club Shadowlands
(Book One in the Masters of the Shadowlands Series)

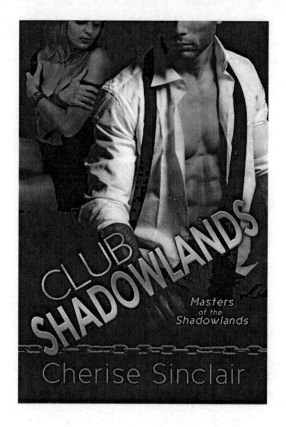

Club Shadowlands (excerpt)

Copyright 2009, 2013, Cherise Sinclair

Her car disabled during a tropical storm, Jessica Randall discovers the isolated house where she's sheltering is a private bondage club. At first shocked, she soon becomes aroused watching the interactions between the Doms and their subs. But she's a professional woman—an accountant—and surely isn't a submissive…is she?

Master Z hasn't been so attracted to a woman in years. But the little sub who has wandered into his club intrigues him. She's intelligent. Reserved. Conservative. After he discovers her interest in BDSM, he can't resist tying her up and unleashing the passion she hides within.

And now a special excerpt from Cherise Sinclair's *Club Shadowlands*, the first BDSM Romance Kallypso Masters ever read (way back in April 2009). Being Kally's first Dom, Master Z holds a special place in her heart—and fantasies. Just reading this excerpt makes her want to revisit Master Z in this re-edited version from the original.

* * * *

An eternity later, she spotted a glimmer of light. Relief rushed through her when she reached a driveway studded with hanging lights. Surely whoever lived here would let her wait out the storm. She walked through the ornate iron gates, up the palm-lined drive past landscaped lawns, until finally she reached a three-story stone mansion. Black wrought iron lanterns illumined the entry.

"Nice place," she muttered. And a little intimidating. She glanced down at herself to check the damage. Mud and rain streaked her tailored slacks and white button-down shirt, hardly a suitable image for a conservative accountant. She looked more like something even a cat would refuse to drag in.

Shivering hard, she brushed at the dirt and grimaced as it only streaked worse. She stared up at the huge oak doors guarding the entrance. A small doorbell in the shape of a dragon glowed on the side panel, and she pushed it.

Seconds later, the doors opened. A man, oversized and ugly as a battle-scarred Rottweiler, looked down at her. "I'm sorry, miss, you're too late. The doors are locked."

What the heck did that mean?

"P-please," she said, stuttering with the cold. "My car's in a ditch, and I'm soaked, and I need a place to dry out and call for help." But did she really want to go inside with this scary-looking guy? Then she shivered so hard her teeth clattered together, and her mind was made up. "Can I come in? Please?"

He scowled at her, his big-boned face brutish in the yellow entry light. "I'll have to ask Master Z. Wait here." And the bastard shut the door, leaving her in the cold and dark.

Jessica wrapped her arms around herself, standing miserably, and finally the door opened again. Again the brute. "Okay, come on in."

Relief brought tears to her eyes. "Thank you, oh, thank you." Stepping around him before he could change his mind, she barreled into a small entry room and slammed into a solid body. "Oomph," she huffed.

Firm hands gripped her shoulders. She shook her wet hair out of her eyes and looked up. And up. The guy was big, a good six feet, his shoulders wide enough to block the room beyond.

He chuckled, his hands gentling their grasp on her arms. "She's freezing, Ben. Molly left some clothing in the blue room; send one of the subs."

"Okay, boss." The brute—Ben—disappeared.

"What is your name?" Her new host's voice was deep, dark as the night outside.

"Jessica." She stepped back from his grip to get a better look at her savior. Smooth black hair, silvering at the temples, just touching his collar. Dark gray eyes with laugh lines at the corners. A lean, hard face with the shadow of a beard adding a hint of roughness. He wore tailored black slacks and a black silk shirt that outlined hard muscles underneath. If Ben was a Rottweiler, this guy was a jaguar, sleek and deadly.

"I'm sorry to have bothered—" she started.

Ben reappeared with a handful of golden clothing that he thrust at her. "Here you go."

She took the garments, holding them out to keep from getting the fabric wet. "Thank you."

A faint smile creased the manager's cheek. "Your gratitude is premature, I fear. This is a private club."

"Oh. I'm sorry." Now what was she going to do?

"You have two choices. You may sit out here in the entryway with Ben until the storm passes. The forecast stated the winds and rain would die down around six or so in the morning, and you won't get a tow truck out on these country roads until then. Or you may sign papers and join the party for the night."

She looked around. The entry was a tiny room with a desk and one chair. Not heated. Ben gave her a dour look.

Sign something? She frowned. Then again, in this lawsuit-happy world, every place made a person sign releases, even to visit a fitness center. So she could sit here all night. Or…be with happy people and be warm. *No-brainer.* "I'd love to join the party."

"So impetuous," the manager murmured. "Ben, give her the paperwork. Once she signs—or not—she may use the dressing room to dry off and change."

"Yes, sir." Ben rummaged in a file box on the desk, pulled out some papers.

The manager tilted his head at Jessica. "I will see you later then."

Ben shoved three pages of papers at her and a pen. "Read the rules. Sign at the bottom." He scowled at her. "I'll get you a towel and clothes."

She started reading. *Rules of the Shadowlands.*

"Shadowlands. That's an unusual na—" she said, looking up. Both men had disappeared. Huh. She returned to reading, trying to focus her eyes. Such tiny print. Still, she never signed anything without reading it.

Doors will open at…

Water pooled around her feet, and her teeth chattered so hard she had to clench her jaw. There was a dress code. Something about cleaning the equipment after use. Halfway down the second page, her eyes blurred. Her brain felt like icy slush. *Too cold—I can't do this.* This was just a club, after all; it wasn't like she was signing mortgage papers.

Turning to the last page, she scrawled her name and wrapped her arms around herself. *Can't get warm.*

Ben returned with some clothing and towels, then showed her into an opulent restroom off the entry. Glass-doored stalls along one side faced a mirrored wall with sinks and counters.

After dropping the borrowed clothing on the marble counter, she kicked her shoes off and tried to unbutton her shirt. Something moved on the wall. Startled, Jessica looked up and saw a short, pudgy woman with straggly blonde hair and a pale complexion blue with cold. After a second, she recognized herself. *Ew.* Surprising they'd even let her in the door.

In a horrible contrast with Jessica's appearance, a tall, slender, absolutely gorgeous woman walked into the restroom and gave her a scowl. "I'm supposed to help you with a shower."

Get naked in front of Miss Perfection? Not going to happen. "Thanks, b-b-b-but I'm all right." She forced the words past her chattering teeth. "I don't need help."

"Well!" With an annoyed huff, the woman left.

I was rude. Shouldn't have been rude. If only her brain would kick back into gear, she'd do better. She'd have to apologize. Later. If she ever got dried off and warm. She needed dry clothes. But, her hands were numb, shaking uncontrollably, and time after time, the buttons slipped from her stiff fingers. She couldn't even get her slacks off, and she was shuddering so hard her bones hurt.

"Dammit," she muttered and tried again.

The door opened. "Jessica, are you all right? Vanessa said—" The manager. "No, you are obviously not all right." He stepped inside, a dark figure wavering in her blurry vision.

"Go away."

"And find you dead on the floor in an hour? I think not." Without waiting for her answer, he stripped her out of her clothes as one would a two-year-old, even peeling off her sodden bra and panties. His hands were hot, almost burning, against her chilled skin.

She was naked. As the thought percolated through her numb brain, she jerked away and grabbed at the dry clothing. His hand intercepted hers.

"No, pet." He plucked something from her hair, opening his hand to show muddy leaves. "You need to warm up and clean up. Shower."

He wrapped a hard arm around her waist and moved her into one of the glass-fronted stalls behind where she'd been standing. With his free hand, he turned on the water, and heavenly warm steam billowed up. He adjusted the temperature.

"In you go," he ordered. A hand on her bottom, he nudged her into the shower.

The water felt scalding hot against her frigid skin, and she gasped, then shivered, over and over, until her bones hurt. Finally, the heat began to penetrate, and the relief was so intense, she almost cried.

Some time after the last shuddering spasm, she realized the door of the stall was open. Arms crossed, the man leaned against the door frame, watching her with a slight smile on his lean face.

"I'm fine," she muttered, turning so her back was to him. "I can manage by myself."

"No, you obviously cannot," he said evenly. "Wash the mud out of your hair. The left dispenser has shampoo."

Mud in her hair. She'd totally forgotten; maybe she *did* need a keeper. After using the vanilla-scented shampoo, she let the water sluice through her hair. Brown water and twigs swirled down the drain. The water finally ran clear.

"Very good." The water shut off. Blocking the door, he rolled up his sleeves, displaying corded, muscular arms. She had the unhappy feeling he was going to keep helping her, and any protest would be ignored. He'd taken charge as easily as if she'd been one of the puppies at the shelter where she volunteered.

"Out with you now." When her legs wobbled, he tucked a hand around her upper arm, holding her up with disconcerting ease. The cooler air hit her body, and her shivering started again.

After blotting her hair, he grasped her chin and tipped her face up to the light. She gazed up at his darkly tanned face, trying to summon up enough energy to pull her face away.

"No bruises. I think you were lucky." Taking the towel, he dried off her arms and hands, rubbing briskly until he appeared satisfied with the pink color. Then he did her back and shoulders. When he reached her breasts, she pushed at his hand. "I can do that." She stepped back so quickly that the room spun for a second.

"Jessica, be still." Then he ignored her sputters like she would a buzzing fly, his attentions gentle but thorough, even to lifting each breast and drying underneath.

When he toweled off her butt, she wanted to hide. If there was any part of her that should be covered, it was her hips. Overweight. *Jiggly.* He didn't seem to notice.

Then he knelt and ordered, "Spread your legs."

* * * *

Club Shadowlands is the first book in the popular Masters of the Shadowlands series by USA Today Bestselling author, Cherise Sinclair. For more information, visit her at www.CheriseSinclair.com.

The *Rescue Me* Saga

Masters at Arms & Nobody's Angel (Combined Volume)
(First in the *Rescue Me* Saga)

Masters at Arms is an introduction to the *Rescue Me* Saga, which needs to be read first. The book begins the journey of three men, each on a quest for honor, acceptance, and to ease his unspoken pain. Their paths cross at one of the darkest points in their lives. As they try to come to terms with the aftermath of Iraq—forging an unbreakable bond—they band together to start their own BDSM club. But will they ever truly become masters of their own fates? Or would fate become master of them?

Nobody's Angel: Marc d'Alessio might own a BDSM club with his fellow military veterans, Adam and Damián, but he keeps all women at a distance. However, when Marc rescues beautiful Angelina Giardano from a disastrous first BDSM experience at the club, an uncharacteristic attraction leaves him torn between his safe, but lonely world, and a possible future with his angel.

Angelina leaves BDSM behind, only to have her dreams plagued by the Italian angel who rescued her at the club. When she meets Marc at a bar in her hometown, she can't shake the feeling she knows him—but has no idea why he reminds her of her angel.

Nobody's Hero
(Second in the *Rescue Me* Saga)

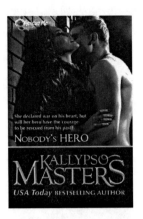

The continuing romantic journey of Adam and Karla from *Masters at Arms & Nobody's Angel*, which ended in a dramatic cliffhanger that sets up the opening scene of *Nobody's Hero*.

Retired Marine Master Sergeant Adam Montague has battled through four combat zones, but now finds himself running from Karla Paxton, who has declared war on his heart. With a twenty-five year age difference, he feels he should be her guardian and protector, not her lover. But Karla's knack for turning up in his bed at inopportune times is killing his resolve to do the right thing. Karla isn't a little girl anymore—something his body reminds him of every chance it gets.

Karla Paxton fell in love with Adam nine years ago, when she was a 16-year-old runaway and he rescued her. Now 25, she's determined to make Adam see her as a woman. But their age difference is only part of the problem. Fifty-year-old Adam has been a guardian and protector for lost and vulnerable souls most of his life, but a secret he has run from for more than three decades has kept him emotionally unable to admit he can love anyone. Will she be able to lower his guard long enough to break down the defenses around his heart and help him put the ghosts from his past to rest? In her all-out war to get Adam to surrender his heart, can the strong-willed Goth singer offer herself as his submissive—and at what cost to herself?

Damián Orlando and Savannah (Savi) Baker also will reunite in this book and begin their journey to a happy ending in *Nobody's Perfect*.

Nobody's Perfect
(Third in the *Rescue Me* Saga)

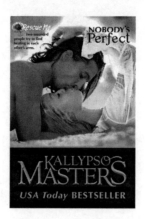

The continuing story of Savannah Gentry (now Savi Baker) and Damián Orlando from *Masters at Arms & Nobody's Angel* and *Nobody's Hero*.

Savannah/Savi escaped eleven years of abuse at the hands of her father and finally made a safe life for herself and her daughter. But when her father once again threatens her peace of mind—and her daughter's safety—Savi runs to Damián Orlando for protection. Eight years earlier, Savannah shared one perfect day with Damián that changed both their young lives and resulted in a secret she no longer can hide. But being with Damián reawakens repressed memories and feelings she wants to keep hidden—buried. After witnessing a scene with Damián on Savi's first night at his private club, she begins to wonder if he could help her regain control of her life and reclaim her sexuality and identity.

Damián, a wounded warrior, has had his own dragons to fight in life, but has never forgotten Savannah. He will lay down his life to protect her and her daughter, but doesn't believe he can offer more than that. She deserves a whole man, something he can never be after a firefight in Iraq. Damián has turned to SM to regain control of his life and emotions and fulfills the role of Service Top to "bottoms" at the club. However, he could never deliver those services to Savi, who needs someone gentle and loving, not the man he has become.

Will two wounded people find love and healing in each other's arms?

Somebody's Angel
(Fourth in the *Rescue Me* Saga)

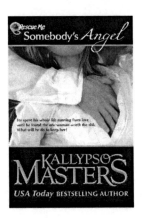

The continuing story of Marc D'Alessio and Angelina Giardano.

When Marc d'Alessio first rescued the curvaceous and spirited Italian Angelina Giardano at the Masters at Arms Club, he never expected her to turn his safe, controlled life upside down and pull at his long-broken heartstrings. Months later, the intense fire of their attraction still rages, but something holds him back from committing to her completely. Worse, secrets and memories from his past join forces to further complicate his relationships with family, friends, and his beautiful angel.

Angelina cannot give all of herself to someone who hides himself from her. She loves Marc, the BDSM world he brought her into, and the way their bodies respond to one another, but she needs more. Though she destroyed the wolf mask he once wore, only he can remove the mask he dons daily to hide his emotions. In a desperate attempt to break through his defenses and reclaim her connection to the man she loves, she attempts a full frontal assault that sends him into a fast retreat, leaving her nobody's angel once again.

Marc finds that running to the mountains no longer gives him solace but instead leaves him empty and alone. Angelina is the one woman worth the risk of opening his heart. Will he risk everything to become the man she deserves and the man he wants to be?

CPSIA information can be obtained at www.ICGtesting.com
Printed in the USA
LVOW07s2210200814

400102LV00028B/1212/P